# CLOCKWORK
# PHOENIX

# Edited by Mike Allen

Mythic Delirium
BOOKS

mythicdelirium.com

**CLOCKWORK PHOENIX 4**
*Edited by Mike Allen*

Cover: solar images courtesy of the Solar & Heliospheric Observatory (SOHO), a collaboration between ESA and NASA.

Cover Design Copyright © 2013 by Mike Allen

Additional copyright notices can be found on page 275.

ISBN-10: 0988912406
ISBN-13: 978-0-9889124-0-3

FIRST EDITION
Trade Paperback Edition
July 1, 2013

Published by Mythic Delirium Books
3514 Signal Hill Ave. NW
Roanoke VA 24017
www.mythicdelirium.com

Printed in the United States of America

*For Anita,*
*and for Mom, Greg, and Eddie,*
*in Dad's memory.*

# CONTENTS

# INTRODUCTION

## *Mike Allen*

Welcome to the book Kickstarter built, the fourth volume of *Clockwork Phoenix*.

In the introductions to the first three books, I played a little game. Rather than attempting to explain exactly what my goals were in assembling each individual volume, I'd compose a prose poem addressing the reader that featured a phoenix made of clockwork, a creature somewhere between a character and a motif. The beings this phoenix encountered and the settings it moved through would all be cobbled from the imagery of the tales that followed, and the poem would end with an event that segued right into the beginning of the first story. My intent was to teach the reader to watch for recurring themes and patterns as she moved through the book.

There. Now I've stepped out from behind the curtain and given the game away.

I had another reason for crafting such elliptical introductions. When I first began batting about the idea that became *Clockwork Phoenix*, a number of anthologies were in the pipeline that served as manifestos for the latest iterations of the weird tale, such as Delia Sherman and Theodora Goss's *Interfictions*, Ann and Jeff VanderMeer's *The New Weird* and Ekaterina Sedia's subversive *Paper Cities: An Anthology of Urban Fantasy*. While my concept for what sort of story would appear in *Clockwork Phoenix* was nebulous at best, I knew that I wanted to create an anthology that partook fully of the trends variously described as interstitial, new weird, slipstream, as well as other types of strangeness, without laying claim to an agenda. Rather than sporting the term for a new movement like a name badge, it would simply *be*. My title, *Clockwork Phoenix*, wasn't intended to conjure a new mythological beast; rather, it was meant to signify a jarring, surreal juxtaposition.

By the time I started editing the second volume, I could articulate my approach—I wanted stories that were bold in the style of their telling and also emotionally satisfying; experimental yet coherent and engaging.

But those who followed this series closely know that I always buried that little tidbit in the backs of the books, somewhere within my editor's bio. My actual introductions were always meant to tease without enlightening; to make no assertions at all about what you were about to read.

I believe this *rebirth* requires a different approach.

When I put the finishing touches on *Clockwork Phoenix 3*, I expected it to be the end of the series. I'll always be grateful to Vera Nazarian of Norilana Books for bankrolling and publishing the first three volumes, but by the time the third one appeared, Norilana, alas, had clearly struck a financial atoll and would no longer be able to fund a project on that scale. And realistically speaking, the *Clockwork Phoenix* books are works of art and labors of love, and about as uncommercial as anthologies can get, which meant that despite the starred reviews and award nominations, the chances of another publisher taking up the cause were slim to none—and proved to be none.

Yet I couldn't escape the feeling that *Clockwork Phoenix* had burned to ash with its business still unfinished.

This notion became reinforced as I continued to hear the same question even after a year had passed, asked online or in person at conventions: When are you going to edit the next one?

Credit must go where it's due. My buddy Michael M. Jones first brought up Kickstarter.com as an option. His own anthology project, *Scheherazade's Facade: Fantastical Tales of Gender Bending, Cross-Dressing, and Transformation*, had been orphaned by Norilana's financial troubles. He found a new publisher, Circlet Press, who would take on the book if he could find the funds to pay the authors. In March 2012, he set up his Kickstarter page, made his pitch, and the very generous online sf and fantasy community came through for him. Once I saw that happen, I knew I had to give it a try.

I discussed it with colleagues and friends and became the beneficiary of some wonderful behind-the-scenes brainstorming, especially from Elizabeth Campbell, Rose Lemberg, and Ken Schneyer. Anita pledged to lend her crafter's talents to creating rewards for pledges, and in July 2012 we launched, just a couple of days before formally announcing the campaign at Readercon in Boston, where all three of the previous volumes had their debut. It felt like leaping off a ledge into the dark, with no way to know where or how we'd land.

You know how it ended. Whether an object of printed pages or words shimmering on the screen of your e-reader, you're holding the result in your hands.

More than 270 donors—some contributing through means other than Kickstarter—pledged to bring this book into reality. In the Acknowledgments section you'll see a long list of names, people we want to thank, people to whom this book owes its existence. It's not complete—not everybody chose to be publicly acknowledged. I'm grateful to all our backers, all those who critiqued and brainstormed, all those who spread the word, all those who offered help with prizes. This is your book as much as it is mine.

Now, what about this book?

I couldn't be happier with these carefully arranged gardens full of dangerously sharp leaves.

We have eight alumni from the previous volumes of the series, and ten newcomers. We have science fiction, because I'm of the belief that sf is a facet of fantasy and deserves as much stylistic and poetic exploration as any other facet of the genre. You'll find the light-hearted and the bleak, the surreal become familiar and the familiar turned strange. You'll see innocence shattered and trickles of hope discovered in the midst of horror. We'll take you swimming in otherworldly waters and show you many, many ways to enlarge the definition of *family*.

If you're still with me, if you haven't done what you should have done in the first place and gone wandering among the wonders ahead, then it's about time you did. I'll take my leave.

The path through the gardens begins on the next page. Your first guide awaits.

# OUR LADY OF THE THYLACINES

## *Yves Meynard*

She was meant to be diurnal, yet the girl most often woke in late afternoon, to a sun already declining in the sky. The worst heat of the day was fading by then, though no part of the Garden was ever unbearably hot, even under the midday sun. The girl thought there must be a roof of sorts, one she could not see, but which shielded the Garden from the excesses of the sun. Or perhaps part of the heat was bled into other dimensions, there to harmlessly dissipate; she understood very little about such things, and the Lady vouchsafed few explanations.

It was because so many of the Lady's friends preferred dusk or darkness that the girl found herself usually waking so late. There was nothing she liked so much as to sit at the feet of the Lady and play with Her friends. There were birds who could not fly; big shaggy animals that walked very slowly, as if always asleep; tiny spiky beings with short snouts and faces that remained always hidden; fat and cuddly animals that dug into the ground; and many, many other kinds. But her favorites were the stripeys: not just because they were the prettiest of all the Lady's friends, but because they were the ones that responded best to her love. When they appeared, they would approach the girl boldly, sniff at her hands and feet, sometimes her crotch. They suffered her to pet their thick, soft, yellow-brown fur; the

**12**

smallest of them, which had a black tuft at the tip of its tail, even let her hold it in her arms and kiss it for a few minutes at a time. When the Lady spoke to them, the stripeys looked at Her with attention, though like all the other friends it was hard to tell if they understood anything or just responded to Her voice. Sometimes as She spoke the stripeys rose up on their hind legs, their stiff tails held behind them keeping them in balance. The girl had given them names based on the number of dark stripes running across their back and rear haunches: Thirteen, Sixteen, Twenty . . . The littlest one was Seventeen or Eighteen, depending on how you counted one bifurcate stripe.

The girl did not see the stripeys all that often. The Lady had many friends, and the girl could never tell which kind she would see. And sometimes when she went to spend time with the Lady there were no friends at all there, only the Lady herself, and that meant there would be a lesson: some new words to learn, the names of the stars, calisthenics routines, baton twirling.

On that afternoon when the girl woke, the number of days since she had not seen the stripeys had risen to fifty. That was a big number, if you counted days and things of that sort. The Lady would have told her it was a tiny number for seconds, stars, and atoms, because She always made a point of correcting the girl when She could, of forcing her to think about things from another side. But the girl had been growing wiser, and sometimes now she was able to argue the point. She wasn't sure—she could never be sure—but she thought the Lady was pleased when that happened. And so she held on to her initial thought, that fifty days without seeing the stripeys was a long time, and it made her feel disappointed, and she really hoped that tonight they would be there when she went to see the Lady.

And in fact, if they were not, then she would take a great dare and ask the Lady to call them. It had been a long, long time, far longer than fifty days, since the girl had dared to ask the Lady for anything. She was too old now, the Lady said. Long past infancy, when she could wail and beg for the nipple, and incur no blame. She was growing up, and she had to fulfill her promise, said the Lady, but She never would clarify what that meant. The girl had had to learn not to wish for things, to take the world as it was, in all its mystery. She wondered, more and more, if that was true to her nature or not.

The girl swung her legs down from the ledge where she slept on a pile of sere grass. On the flat rock at the far end of the cave where she lived, she found the Lady had made food appear, which She did at odd intervals, supplementing the berries and nuts and roots the girl normally ate. The Lady's food was as juicy as fruit but the juice was salty, not sweet. It filled the girl's stomach wonderfully and made her feel very good; after eating that food, her ordinary diet always paled, but she could not depend on the Lady's generosity to eat. That was definitely one thing she had learned not to ask for.

This time, next to the pieces of food, there was also a dress. The girl usually went about naked, and whatever clothing the Lady gave her felt more like an impediment than anything else. Still, if the Lady had seen fit to give her a dress, the girl would wear it today. It might well please the Lady.

She struggled with the garment for several minutes until she'd figured out how to put it on: this was more complicated than the other dresses she'd worn. Once she had wrapped her mind around its shape, it made sense. There was a bit of rope as part of the dress, just under her collarbone. Once she had put the dress on, the girl pulled on the rope and felt the garment tighten snugly around her. This was a good dress, she decided. Unlike the others, which flapped around her knees and made it hard for her to run, this one allowed her full freedom of movement; it almost felt as if she was naked. The color was exciting, too: her old dresses had always been white or pale yellow, while the new one was a confusion of colors, greens, browns, and grays, in irregular splotches.

The girl stepped out of the cave that was her home and wandered down the grassy slope. The flowers and bushes and trees of the Garden filled her senses. There was no animal life about; there never was, unless you chose to count insects. Only in the presence of the Lady did any friends ever manifest themselves. From her point of view, the girl lived all alone in the Garden.

She came to a path and reluctantly stepped onto it. The tiny rounded pebbles, scorched by the sun, dug into the soles of her feet uncomfortably. Still, to show that she was growing up, she strode down the center of the path all the way to the heart of the Garden, the inner enclosure where the Lady dwelled.

The enclosure was defined by a wall, narrow and perpendicular to the ground, that curved smoothly all around. There was but one break in its continuity, barely as wide as the girl was tall. The height of the wall made the aperture look as narrow as a finger. Whenever the girl passed through, she hunched her shoulders and had to resist the temptation to turn herself sideways and hug one side of the opening.

The enclosure was open to the sky—at least it seemed to be, though when it rained, not a drop of water ever fell within the wall, no doubt because it was torqued into additional dimensions. So it was a different kind of place, inside the Garden but perhaps not really part of it. It had its own light, too. When night fell and the Garden grew dark, it would still be light here, because of the lamps: clusters of glowing spheres, a few large ones and many much smaller spheres, like the bubbles in soap froth. They glowed with a bluish light, the tinier ones so small that they never properly resolved in the girl's sight, unfocused blue dots she might have doubted had any tangible existence. The bigger spheres were physical enough: taut membranes, uncomfortably warm though not burning. She avoided their contact at the same time as she craved their light, her poor diurnal eyes inadequate to the task of properly seeing the world once the sun had gone from the sky.

On the inner curve of the wall pictures were hung: flat images surrounded by sticks of wood that made elongated squares much wider than they were tall. The girl loved to spend time looking at them. The Lady's friends were all there. It was strange how much she loved to look at the pictures since she could just as easily go to the Lady's side and gaze upon Her friends in the flesh. The Lady had said many times that this was one of the characteristics of being human: that humans loved the representation of a thing more than the thing itself. The girl did not really understand this, but she pretended she did, to please the Lady. Neither had the girl ever been able to grasp how the images were created. She could grab a stick and make lines in the sand, and dimly intuited a similar process was involved; beyond that, things remained a mystery.

This time the girl did not let herself be distracted by the images, no matter that she could have stepped only a short way around the great curve of the wall and seen a picture of stripeys. She wanted the thing itself, and she had decided she would be bold enough to ask for it.

So she approached the dais and the great throne atop the highest step. She kept her eyes away from the throne, where the Lady sat cloaked in a radiance that could hurt her eyes. She dropped to her knees at the foot of the lowest step and bowed her head. The Lady had taught her in calisthenics how to bow and curtsy; how to kneel properly, keeping her legs coiled tightly, ready to spring when least expected.

After a time she felt the touch of fingers in her hair and upon her neck; the next instant she jumped up, thrusting her right fist in the air, putting all her energy into the leap.

It felt like long seconds before the girl fell back to earth, to land on the balls of her feet. Her knees flexed to absorb the shock; she stood erect, straight and still, for more long seconds, until she sensed the painful radiance had lessened. Then she raised her head to look up. She saw the Lady upon her throne, ten feet above her head; She looked back at the girl and beckoned with a finger.

The girl climbed the first step of the dais. Now, all about her large-boled trees rose. Three birds were busily feeding on the leaves of small shrubs that grew among the trees. They carried their heads forward at the end of long necks, yet even so they stood taller than she was. Their plumage was flecked brown and white, with purple at the throat. One spotted her, stopped its feeding and opened wide its beak to give a call: a deep wail that resonated in her bones. The girl stayed motionless for a long while, until the bird quieted down and returned to its feeding. Still the girl waited, then she edged silently around the three animals, avoiding their notice. These birds were among those of the Lady's friends that scared her, even though she would eagerly spend time with them when possible. Theirs was a terrible beauty—not unlike the Lady's.

The girl walked away from the three birds, going downhill and into denser clumps of trees, until she came across a wide block of stone in the middle of a clearing. Then she lifted her gaze again, and saw the Lady atop Her dais, beckoning her. The girl curtsied with one hand hidden behind her back before stepping forward and up, into a vast expanse of sand. She strode along the crest of a dune; some sand crumbled under her feet and slid downslope. She saw no friends; between this crest and another one some grass and spindly trees grew, and she guessed the friends might live there. They were probably very small.

At the end of the sand crest she came across the next step of the dais, and saw the Lady still beckoning to her. She stepped up again, onto the shore of a lake. She saw movement in the water and instantly jumped to the side and away, racing at full speed away from the jaws of the friend who dwelled in the billabong. She saw its eyes surveying her even from a long distance, the rest of it almost completely submerged. It had made no attempt to jump out of the water; always the Lady had told the girl she was safe in Her presence. But She had never said the girl should not be frightened of scalies; and so she remained.

At the far side of the lake she saw the last step to the top of the dais, though the Lady was not visible. Once she had reached the step, the girl waited a long moment for a sign. When none came, she steeled herself and stepped up. Sometimes one had to take risks.

She found herself back within the great inner enclosure, next to the Lady's throne, high in the air. Still the curved wall rose higher about them, and the girl saw pictures ringing the inside curve, pictures too small for her sight to resolve clearly at this distance. She thought that they showed even stranger animals than she had ever seen in the flesh: great armored monsters with a curved tail ending in a knurl of bone; beasts with four pillarlike legs and heads covered with horns; shaggy, green-furred things taller than trees. Up and up the wall rose, and the pictures spiralled upwards. If she fastened her gaze to them, she could go on and on along the spiral to infinity, torquing into three extra dimensions; yet if she focused her sight on the wall itself, then she could see its top, not so high as the top of the trees all around.

"Come close, girl," said the Lady with her smooth, slick voice. The girl's own voice she always saw in her mind as many lines in parallel. There was a screeching that was part of it, especially when she was excited. The Lady's voice was a single line, or not even a line at all, it was like a ribbon, thick and dark, without asperity.

The girl came close to the Lady's knee and halted. The Lady's unshod, pale green feet rested on a cushion; her legs were wrapped from ankles upwards in a gold robe. Her knees were at the level of the girl's head. She was, as ever, unsure what was expected of her; she risked putting her hand on the Lady's knee and when this brought no rebuke, she leaned her upper body against the Lady's legs and wrapped her arms around Her knee. The Lady's flesh was pliant and cool; there was no sense of the bones beneath, only of a firm, elastic flesh, cool as a piece of metal left in the shade on a summer's day.

The girl felt the Lady's fingers in her hair again; she sighed in contentment and closed her eyes.

"Girl," said the Lady, "it's good that you came early tonight. I have to show you something, and talk to you, before the sun goes down. Climb upon my lap."

The girl grabbed a handful of the Lady's golden robes and with a twist of her body, launched herself upward into Her lap. The Lady looked down upon her, Her green face unreadable as always, Her black eyes gleaming in the light from the orange sky. The Lady's crown, which rose so high above Her hair, caught the rays of the sun and flashed burning gold.

The girl, drunk on pleasure, filled with a sudden wild joy, dared to make her request.

"Oh, Lady," she said, her voice still making screechy jagged lines in her mind's eye, "Lady, it's been so long since I've seen the stripeys. Could You please, if You want, let me see them—"

She had hoped to hear *yes* and she was prepared for *no*, but when the Lady said "I can't" the girl was taken completely aback. Throughout her life the Lady had told her *you can't* and she had learned never to argue this. For the Lady to state that She Herself could not do something . . . it was unprecedented, astonishing.

The girl wanted to ask why, and dared not. As she let her mouth gape open, the Lady answered her unspoken question.

"I can't, because they are all dead. You won't see them anymore; no one ever will."

"Dead?" The girl's voice was a strangled whisper. "All of them? But they were young; all except for Fifteen. It's all right for Fifteen to die, not the others."

The Lady was silent a long moment; the girl felt Her cool fingers at her side, more prison than cradle.

"That isn't how it works," said the Lady at last. "It is possible to die even when you're young. It's called 'being killed.' It has happened before, many times; but you didn't notice it. There have been other friends gone, who will never be seen again."

"But why did you do it? Why?"

The Lady's expressionless face bent down toward her a fraction more.

"I did not do it. I have never killed. All of my flock are precious to me, because they are the last. You most of all, because you alone can understand your state. None of the others have a care. They live as their ancestors always did, and die still in ignorance. You know that you are the last, you have always known. Which makes you still more precious."

The girl was weeping with grief and incomprehension. "I don't know that word," she sobbed, "precious."

"It means 'of great worth' or 'very important.'"

"So I'm of great worth because I'm the last . . . "

"And because you know it. But you don't really understand it. It is too soon."

"Too soon for what?" the girl asked.

"I am forbidden from explaining things to you. I think that . . . that they fear you too much; they fear what you might become, given just a little bit more time. After all, you come from a long, proud line. Even as your forebears killed themselves they died with pride, believing they left nothing behind them but ashes."

The girl buried her face in the Lady's dress, pawing at Her breast as she used to do when she was younger. The golden dress melted away and the Lady's viridian breast was revealed, her dark nipple as wide as the girl's face, already oozing milk. But then the Lady covered Her nipple with Her hand, before the girl could even think to suckle; after a second the opening in the dress sealed itself up. Gently but firmly the Lady pushed at the girl's head and made her look up.

"No," said the Lady. "No, not that. It's too late now. I can no longer offer you comfort. You time here is done. When the sun has gone down, then you must leave."

"You want me to go back to my house? Why?!"

"No. I mean leave here. Leave the Garden. Forever."

The girl said nothing for a long moment, stunned by the enormity of this latest betrayal. The grief that filled her was too loud for reasoning and too deep for screams. She could only say, softly, "I just wanted to see the stripeys again."

"They are dead," repeated the Lady, and then she used other words the girl could harldy parse. "They were taken out, and hunted, and killed. Like all the others before them and all the others yet to come. They were precious because they were the last, and so I was paid a small fortune for their death."

"Why?" protested the girl. "Why? Why? Why?"

"I have no choice in the matter. That is my function; that is who I am. Do you understand, girl? Don't mistake my purpose. I do not preserve; I procure. I was shaped for that only. I am paid in energy to continue my own existence; it is a joke, of sorts. You are a wild animal who thinks she is a person; I am a slave who deludes herself she has some freedom."

The girl was weeping again; the tears that filled her eyes blurred her vision and the Lady's form swam in the reddening sky like a fish in a pool of blood.

"It is not even justice," said the Lady. "They are not punishing you; they are not exacting vengeance. They do what they do because they wish to . . . ."

With one cool, gigantic thumb the Lady wiped the girl's eyes clear; they burned now, devoid of moisture. She wished to sob and cry, but no tears came, and her breathing was suddenly not her own: smooth and regular, as if someone else were breathing for her.

"Listen," said the Lady, bending Her expressionless face above the girl's. "Look."

She held up Her left hand, the crystalline one, transparent except for a few metallic flecks in the depths of Her flesh. Above Her cupped palm appeared images that drew the girl's sight painfully.

"See this. Remember it." Something black, long as the girl's forearm, slimmer than her wrist. She thought she understood it.

"Is it a gun?" asked the girl.

"In many ways, it is more like a glove," said the Lady. The girl saw Her fingers wave, transparent shapes only perceptible because she knew they were there. She wanted to say the thing would never fit a hand, but she stayed silent; another image had bloomed above the Lady's palm, a pair of flattened spheres the color of the sun and of oranges, a wide gash in the middle of each.

"They have six eyes," said the Lady, "in three dyads. If you destroy a single eye, it is not a severe injury, as the other will take over its function. But if you destroy both, then there is a significant loss of coordination and balance. A sharp stick can break the cornea; you need to jab as deep as your hand is wide to destroy the nerve."

With great effort the girl tore her gaze away from the eyes in the Lady's palm, brought it up to look at Her face. It was as void as it had ever been, even with its mouth half-open; Her eyes were twin pits of darkness. It was impossible to tell if She was heartbroken or gloating.

"You have spent your whole life here," said the Lady. "You know that within the Garden some of the ten dimensions are unfurled and torqued outward. Outside, this is not the rule, and almost always and everywhere there are only height, width, and depth. But they have access to the same technology that made the Garden possible. Individual . . . " She paused for a long moment, immobile. The girl felt herself stop breathing. Her heart began to pound louder and louder—then suddenly she was drawing a huge breath, and the Lady continued: "Individual generators are not as powerful as those in operation within the Garden; their range is limited and they may unfold only two other dimensions. But this is still enough to take you by surprise. A hand may come for you from inside a rock, even if you cannot see the arm it belongs to."

The light was fading; the girl felt that she could hear the sun sliding down the bowl of the sky. The Lady's nocturnal friends would be coming out soon. Not the stripeys; never the stripeys anymore, never again.

She had come down from the Lady's lap; she was standing next to Her throne. The air about her felt thick and brittle; both of the Lady's hands, green flesh and invisible crystal, cradled her like a doll. The Lady was so close to her yet far away at the same time: the door to the Garden was opening and all distances were being shattered.

"They killed all your friends," the Lady was saying. "They seized upon the desolation that Man left behind him and merely completed his work. You are the very last; after you there can be no others. Make it count."

The sun had set completely. The sky still held a ghost of light, red as an apple, as coals, as blood. The girl stood at the top of a small hill that emerged from a forest. In the far distance she saw crests of rock; from her left came the purl and mutter of a stream. Stars were beginning to appear within the vault of heaven: Achernar, Rigel, Toliman. The girl wrapped her arms around herself; for a long moment she wanted to do nothing more than collapse into a ball on the ground and wail. But the words of the Lady had sunk into her, and she could no longer cry. She was of great worth; she was very important. She was the last.

The girl crouched and felt around her feet; rose up with a straight branch in her hand, the size of the batons she used to play with. Its tip was a broken-off shard of wood, pared and wickedly sharp, a little longer than the width of her palm. She turned her back on the dying sky; eyes alert for boulders, her bare feet shrinking from contact with the treacherous rocky ground, she picked her way downslope. Once she had reached the forest, she began to run.

# THE CANAL BARGE MAGICIAN'S NUMBER NINE DAUGHTER

## *Ian McHugh*

Something thumped onto the deck. Behra peered out into the rain from the shelter of her little hut at the front of the canal barge. The only light nearby was from the barge's running lanterns and the open door of the coal furnace at the far end of the deck. The glow of the town's street lamps was too weak to reach across the canal.

Her half-brother, Geneic, was by the furnace, his heavy Saltukkuri features lit orange while he bent his back against the downpour, shovelling coal. In the shadows of his brows, his eyes glowed a deeper red than the fire. In the wheelhouse beyond him, Behra could make out Chiufi's smaller silhouette. Their father and Sorgui, Geneic's twin, were asleep belowdecks.

A small shape skittered across the deck, nearer to Behra than to Geneic. She bit back a cry. Whatever it was, it wasn't the right shape for a rat or a water dragon or a cat. She waited, watching and listening. The only movement on deck was Geneic, the only sounds aside from the patter of rain were the rasp of his shovel in the coal and the thud-thud of the barge's steam engine.

She sat back, dissatisfied, and pulled her blankets back around her. Her ankle chain scraped across the boards.

"Don't be afraid," said a tinkling voice, right beside her in the hut.

23

Behra yelped.

"Shh!" said the voice, urgently.

Her heart rattled inside her ribs. Slowly, her eyes began to make out the speaker. It was man-shaped, slender, but it stood only about the height of her knee, the top of its head well clear of the hut's low roof.

"Are you a fairy?" she breathed.

The visitor laughed, a sound like the chimes Behra had sometimes heard on the sedans of Ornomagnen ladies, and stepped from the shadows into the faint light of the deck.

Behra's eyes widened. The visitor was a porcelain doll, its sculpted features those of a young Ornomagnen gentleman. It was dressed in a gentleman's frock coat and hose, damp from the rain, its outfit completed by tiny brass-buckled shoes and a tricorn hat.

"You're a doll," Behra said.

"A golem," it corrected. "I am in disguise. Do you speak Ornomagnen? My Rhuinish is limited."

Behra blinked. It hadn't occurred to her what language they were speaking. "Only a little." She could understand better than she could speak.

"No matter," said the doll, briskly. "I am Palinday." He swept off his hat and executed a courtly bow, revealing a head of real yellow hair, tied with ribbon at the back of his neck. His eyes glittered blue, catching the lamplight.

"Behra."

"Little Nine?" he said in Ornomagnen, translating her name. His face moved so little as the doll spoke that Behra wondered if she imagined his amusement.

She pulled away, tucking her knees up in front of her. Her chain clanked. Palinday's eyes followed it from her foot to the ring bolted to the frame of her hut. Now she was certain that his expression changed, painted brows drawing together in a frown.

She glanced towards the back of the barge. Geneic was looking towards the bank, sniffing the air. Chiufi, too, had turned his head that way.

Palinday said, "Hide me!"

Behra looked at him in confusion, but the doll was already burrowing under her blankets.

"Hide me," he repeated, muffled by the covers.

An approaching commotion reached her ears. Disregarding the rain, Behra crawled half out of the hut to see.

Soldiers flooded onto the bank, bursting from several streets at once. Their shouts identified them as Rhuinishmen. They milled about, musket barrels and halberd blades catching the light of the lamps many of them held, while their dogs cast this way and that along the canal wall.

One raised his voice above the rest. "You there! Bargeman! Did you see a fugitive come this way?"

There was quiet for several heartbeats. The soldier crabbed sideways as the barge continued to chug along. Geneic stared mutely back at him. Then Chiufi called back from the wheelhouse, "Beg pardon, sir, but my brother don't speak."

"Then speak for him, boy!" said the soldier. "Or fetch up your captain if you have not the wit to answer for yourself! And bring your vessel in to the bank."

Behra eased back into the shadows of her hut. She couldn't help a guilty start as she bumped against the doll's hard little limbs. Chiufi slowed the barge but made no move to steer it to the bank. Geneic's sloping brow beetled as Chiufi called for him to take the wheel. Chiufi hurried for the hatch at the rear of the barge and disappeared below. Geneic's silhouette all but filled the wheelhouse, his eyes glowing sullenly.

All the soldiers were keeping pace with the barge now. A squad hurried ahead. There was a bridge at the end of the town, Behra remembered.

An angry bellow announced their father's emergence. Aghor stamped up onto the deck, followed by Sorgui. Chiufi slunk up the ladder behind them and along beside the barge's rail to join Behra in her hut. He squeezed her fingers, his gaunt features tight with worry. Behra felt her face heat, acutely conscious of the fugitive hidden in her blankets.

Aghor planted his feet wide to face the soldiers, ignoring the rain, his sleeveless vest exposing the black bramble tattoos coiled around his arms, fists on hips to pull back the vest and reveal the belt around his thick waist, made from the mummified foetuses and umbilicals of Behra's sisters.

She saw many of the soldiers draw back, making signs in front of their hearts to ward off black magic. Behra's lip curled. The soldier who had called out to Chiufi raised his voice again, but there was a tremor in it now. "Bargeman, bring your vessel to the bank. We are hunting a fugitive and have reason to believe it may be on your barge."

Her father lifted his chin. "In whose name do you order this?"

"In the name of Lord Tibuir," said the soldier, some of his confidence returning with the invocation of his master's name.

Aghor grunted and spat into the canal. The soldier's posture was rigid, full of offence and fear. "And what manner of fugitive is it," said Aghor, "that you refer to as 'it'?"

"A golem," said the soldier, "in the form of a child's doll."

Aghor guffawed. "A doll, is it?" He started to turn his back. "I have no truck with Ornomagnen trickery. Go back to your kennels, dogs. Tell Tibuir's Hound that if she wishes for Aghor's vessel to be searched, then she should come and see to it herself."

Behra wondered if the soldier would argue, or perhaps even order his fellows to shoot, but her father's name had power among Rhuinishmen. Hearing it deflated the last of his bluster.

A shadow passed across the barge. The bridge. Behra looked upwards as they cleared it. A row of pale faces peered back from under the brows of their helmets.

"I wonder what that was all about," said Chiufi.

"It's here," Behra said.

"What?"

She felt Palinday shift behind her. "It's here. The doll, under the . . . "

She froze. Their father was striding towards them. Behra didn't look up as he squatted in front of her, the shrivelled corpses of her aborted sisters dangling between his thighs. Chiufi gripped her fingers hard. She squeezed back, afraid for him, too, and wishing her hate could give him strength.

If their father found the doll, it would be Chiufi who would be punished for her misdemeanour, not Behra. She tried not to look at her brother's fingers, clenched in her own, at the small, misshapen nails that had grown back after Aghor had pulled them.

Her heart beat painfully hard. *I'm sorry, Chiufi.*

"Hand," Aghor said.

It took all Behra's will not to slump with relief. Her arm trembled with it as she held it out. From the corner of her eye, she saw her father drop his scrying bowl onto the deck. His rough fingers caught her hand, bending it back. She gritted her teeth as the point of his knife dug into her wrist, opening a vein.

He squeezed, dripping her blood into the bowl. A sharp porcelain elbow or knee dug into the side of her leg like an accusation. She tried to keep her breathing steady. Surely her father must sense the doll's presence.

Sorgui crouched by the boat's rail, eyes closed, his brutish face lifted to the rain. He must have felt Behra's scrutiny, because he twisted his neck to look back, his red eyes locking with hers.

After what seemed an eternity, her father released her.

"Boy," he said to Chiufi, "get back to the wheel."

With a grunt of exertion, he rose and walked away, not waiting to see if Chiufi complied. Behra sucked her bleeding wrist. Chiufi released her and pulled out the grimy rag he kept in his pocket to quickly tear off a strip. Behra watched her father squat in front of the coal furnace and open the hatch. He reached in, bare-handed, to take out a burning coal which he dropped into the scrying dish.

Behra felt heat spread up her arm and through her chest.

"It *is* here," said Chiufi, in surprise.

Palinday had sat up.

"You have to get off this boat," Chiufi hissed, catching Behra's wrist to bind her cut, his movements hurried. "If father finds out about you, we'll get hell for it."

Behra only half-heard him. Her head was full of her father's murmured incantation. The words blazed across her mind. "*Sarhgu torosch abh. Sarghu feic abh . . .* " she mouthed. She didn't know what the words meant, but she knew what they did—a scrying spell.

Palinday watched her. "He uses your blood to power his magic."

"She's the ninth daughter," said Chiufi. He finished tying his knot and released her.

"Ah," said Palinday. "That is a foul thing."

"Foul or not, it'll go even worse if you're found," Chiufi snapped. His fear grew like a cloud in Behra's altered perception.

"He's looking for me now," said Palinday.

"Then go!" Chiufi sounded almost in tears.

Behra could feel her father's probing thoughts pressing up against her own. She pushed back, Chiufi's fear making her react without thinking. Aghor's attention slid easily aside. He didn't react, unaware of what she had done. Her pulse thumped, surprise and relief combined.

"I must get to Ardonailles," Palinday announced. He stood up, set his hat onto his head, and stepped out into the rain.

Chiufi let out a whine of terror.

By the furnace, Aghor looked up. The spell blinked out and Behra snapped abruptly back to her proper senses. Sorgui rose, looking to their father for instruction.

"Aghor the Bargeman," Palinday said, in Ornomagnen. "I am here."

"So you are," replied Behra's father, after a moment, in the same language. "And what have you done, little golem, to pull Lord Tibuir's beard?"

"I have information for Lord Emieldraeu," said Palinday. "The reward for aiding me would be substantial."

"The King's Spymaster," said Aghor. Then, sharply: "You would have me betray a fellow Rhuinishman to our Ornomagnen oppressors?"

"I think you have little fondness for Lord Tibuir," said Palinday, giving Sorgui a glance as he strolled past him. "And the slogans of the oppressed do not sit well on your tongue, magician."

Behra's father chuckled. The sound made her shiver. He stood, towering over the little doll.

Palinday stood his ground. "I am well warded against harm."

Aghor gave a snort. "I have cargo for Verdecastre. We can take you on to Nouvebourg from there."

"Ardonailles," said Palinday. "I need to get to Ardonailles."

Aghor's eyebrows rose. "Not to the King's city?"

"My journey needs to be direct," said Palinday. "You will be amply compensated for any loss on your cargo."

Behra's father regarded the doll for a moment, then harrumphed. "Very well, little golem. It pleases me to irk Tibuir. Too often business interferes with such pleasures. I will have that reward and compensation."

"And you will not punish the girl for hiding me," said Palinday.

Behra recognised the danger in her father's sudden stillness. Sorgui dropped halfway into a fighting crouch, broad hands flexing. It was several heartbeats before Aghor spoke, and when he did, there was an edge to his tone that belied his words, "Indeed. It would seem that she has brought me fortune."

His gaze fell on Chiufi. "Boy! Get back to the wheel!"

* * *

The skies had cleared at last. Behra sat out on the deck with Chiufi, enjoying the sun while they shared a pot of salted gruel. Palinday remained in the hut, sheltered from prying eyes.

Geneic and Sorgui squatted together by the wheelhouse, gazing incuriously at the traffic passing on the water and the canal-side road. Aghor was at the wheel.

Behra looked up at the pale walls of the fortress city as they slipped by. The flat tops of the walls bristled with cannon. Banners fluttered in the breeze, bright against the sooty background of smoke from the city's manufactories. She recognised the red and gold of Ornomagne hung above the green and white of Rhuin.

Palinday spoke up, "Those . . . " He paused. "Your father's belt, those are your sisters?"

Behra hunched her shoulders against the question. Chiufi answered, gruffly, "They are."

There was another silence from the doll. Behra concentrated on the castle flags.

"And your brothers?"

"Father made them birth early," said Chiufi, "same as our sisters, and tossed them over the side. At least one, after me. Probably others, before. All but them two."

Behra's eyes were drawn to Geneic and Sorgui, crouched side by side like a pair of gargoyles. Their half-human, half-demiman faces always looked sad to her when their expressions were relaxed.

"And them?" asked Palinday.

"Father bought himself a Saltukkuri bitch, and got them on her," said Chiufi. Noticing that Behra had stopped eating, he pulled the gruel pot onto his lap to scrape out the last of it.

"How many women?"

"Our mother, theirs. Others, maybe."

Behra's hands hurt. Her fists were clenched, nails digging into her palms.

"Bloody Sword and Chalice," the doll muttered.

The canal broadened, docks lining the bank, bustling with barges and carts. Behra gazed up at the black iron girders of the steam powered dock cranes, like a row of giants' gallows. Immense iron gates stood open, the way between them a gaping black mouth in the wall with portcullis teeth, swallowing and regurgitating endless streams of carts and coaches, riders and walkers. A train of coal wagons rattled along narrow tracks into the darkness, towed behind a huffing steam engine.

"Boy!"

Chiufi flinched at Aghor's shout. Behra touched his arm before he went. "Be strong."

"To the bow, boy!"

Soon now, Behra thought, doubting even as she told herself. Could she really be strong enough?

Her chain tugged against her ankle. She looked to see Palinday running his tiny, perfect fingers over the links, porcelain clicking on metal. His eyes met hers. "This chain is not thick," he said. "It would be easily broken."

Behra cast a glance over her shoulder at her father in the wheelhouse. He was looking past them at the waterway ahead. She glared at Palinday. "Be silent!"

He stared back with his gemstone eyes. "He always knows where you are."

"The thread that joins us gets thinner as we get further apart," Behra said. "I think it would break, if I got far enough away."

"You've tried," said Palinday.

Behra looked away, feeling hot moisture in her eyes.

"It was Chiufi your father beat when he caught you," he guessed.

She shook her head. Not a beating. Her hands twitched, about to lift and cover her ears, filled again with her brother's awful, wrenching cries as his fingernails were pulled out.

She covered her grief and guilt with a snarl. "One day . . . "

Palinday's eyes glittered. "My master, Lord Emieldraeu, would give you sanctuary."

For a moment, Behra could hardly breath.

The thud of the steam engine was slowing. She looked around.

Ahead, the land dropped away abruptly on either side of the canal. In the far distance beyond the edge, she could see low hills and chequered farmland. A gantry spanned the canal. Chimneys poured out thick smoke from the roof of a brick engine house on the bank. The canal ended in a wall inset with a row of gated, iron-sided bays. The gates of one bay opened, releasing a brief rush of water and a laden barge.

Aghor's barge slid smoothly into an open bay, Chiufi fending it off the walls with his barge pole. High on the gantry, gears and chains clanked. The gates were lowered, one behind the other. Lock workers guided the inner gate into grooves in the walls of the bay, turning it into a tub that held the barge and the water on which it floated.

Aghor emerged from the wheelhouse. Behra saw the eyes of the Rhuinish tax collector widen. She heard him stammer as he hastily stamped her father's manifest and took no money before he turned to wave urgently to his fellows on the gantry.

Ponderously, with tortured screams of metal on metal, the lift tub began to descend the steep face of the Rhuin Wall. Palinday risked peeping around the edge of the hut. Behra had a sudden urge to reach out and touch his fine clothes, stroke his golden hair. She kept her hands in her lap.

"Now there's a thing," the doll said.

Beyond the girders of the lift tower, the city extended out onto an outcrop of rock, prow-shaped, walled tiers descending the height of the cliff.

"Rhuincastre," said Palinday.

"Neic ap Nagh," replied Behra, giving the great city the Rhuinish name she'd always heard her father use.

"The anvil of kings," said Palinday, in Ornomagnen.

Beyond the city, a broad waterfall tumbled over the edge of the cliff. The sheer face of the Rhuin Wall extended into the distance in both directions, unbroken as far as the eye could see.

Palinday ducked back inside as the counterweight tub passed, going the opposite way. A row of children of different ages, boys and girls, sat on the other barge's deck. One little boy waved.

"Father!" called Chiufi. He was on his tiptoes on the barge's rail, leaning out against the tub wall to look down.

Aghor stamped over to see. A quick glance and he swore and swung back around. "Golem! How well can you hide yourself?"

The doll got to his feet, his tiny tricorn hat in his hand. "I cannot be scryed out."

"That is fortunate," said Aghor, striding to the back of the barge, "because Tibuir's Hound is waiting for you below."

Behra's chest tightened.

Palinday trotted after Aghor. "You have a hiding place for me?"

Behra's father opened the hatch to the coalbunker. Palinday peered inside, then stepped back. "I am not going in there," he declared.

"It's in there or over the side," said Aghor.

Behra caught her father's subtle hand gesture to Sorgui. While the doll still hesitated, she watched her half-brother slowly extend a long-fingered hand towards Palinday's back. She squeezed her lips together, desperate to call out a warning.

Sorgui struck. With a squawk, Palinday toppled into the bunker.

"Bury yourself deep, little golem," said Aghor, and slammed the hatch shut.

Geneic and Sorgui chuckled their slow, barking laughs.

Chiufi slunk across to join Behra by her hut. Their father pulled his shirt off and dropped it to the deck, planting himself where he would be most visible to the lock workers. After a moment he reconsidered and hurried over to Behra, drawing his little knife and gesturing impatiently for her hand.

This time he only pricked her finger, squeezing painfully to smear her blood along his forearms. He marched back to his post near the rail, wiping the blood over his tattoos and muttering a hasty incantation.

"*Guigen negui rei,*" Behra mouthed. "*Guigen negui rei.*"

The bramble tattoos on Aghor's arms began to writhe like nests of spiked snakes. The skin on Behra's arms crawled in sympathy. With an effort, she pushed the words to the back of her mind.

She leaned close to Chiufi, her lips almost touching his ear. "We'll run at Ardonailles. Palinday says his master will protect us."

Chiufi gasped and stared at her. Terror made him shake his head.

Behra gripped his hand, bigger and stronger than hers. "We *must.*"

The lift reached the bottom of the cliff. She saw soldiers among the lock workers, dressed in the same uniforms as those they'd seen the night before. Lord Tibuir's men. She saw lock workers and soldiers alike blanch at the sight of her father.

A pair of workers hurried to open the lift gates, ignoring the angry shouts of a soldier with a gold-trimmed jacket. Behra caught the brief, satisfied twitch at the corner of her father's mouth as the gates cranked up and the barge bumped out of the lift tub on a rush of water.

There were Rhuinish soldiers lining the low parapet on the near bank, more soldiers crowding a barge anchored cross-wise to the canal, partly blocking it. Some of the soldiers held the leashes of dogs. There were others with the soldiers, too, shorter and stockier, stooping with flat heads thrust forward, red eyes gleaming. Saltukkuri—true demimen, not half-castes like Geneic and Sorgui. Behra looked between her half-brothers and those on the shores, noting the differences, the flatter foreheads and heavier jaws of the full-bloods. Geneic and Sorgui stood up tall, lifting their heads and puffing out their chests, making themselves as large as possible.

The Saltukkuri with the soldiers had chips of red jewel in the centres of their brows, seemingly embedded there. Among them stood a Rhuinishwoman in red robes and cloaks, a similar, larger jewel upon her own forehead.

Her expression was thunderous. Up on top of the lift gate, there was scuffling between the workers and soldiers, the soldiers beating at the workers with the butts of their weapons.

Chiufi sprang up as their father barked orders. Aghor wore a lopsided smirk as he set his sons to work bringing the barge in to shore. Glancing up at the fracas on the lift gate, he called out to the woman magician, "It seems that folk still fear the old ways more than your new tricks, Hound."

"Simple folk are most easily fooled by simple tricks," the magician woman replied. "We will search your boat, Aghor."

Soldiers reached out with hooked poles to catch the barge's rails.

"Ah yes, your master's lost doll," said Aghor. "If Lord Tibuir plays with his dolls as he plays with his page boys then I can understand why the thing ran away. But you will not find it on my barge."

Tibuir's Hound stepped aboard.

"Where are you headed, Bargeman?"

"Verdencastre," said Aghor. "Then Nouvebourg."

The Hound arched an eyebrow. "Indeed?"

Soldiers and Saltukkuri swarmed after her, surrounding Aghor, Geneic and Sorgui. There was a deal of grunting and growling between the Saltukkuri and Behra's half-brothers. She shuffled back into her hut. The movement caught the red-robed magician's eye. Behra stared up at her. The Hound's skin was very pale and smooth, her hair and eyes very dark. Her face was handsome and unyielding, like the statues of warrior queens that Behra had seen once, in the southern provinces.

Disgust curled the Hound's lip. "The old ways, is it? What you practice is an abomination, Aghor. Yours was never the true path of our people." She raised her voice, "Search everywhere!"

Dogs were brought aboard. Soldiers clattered belowdecks, the hatches of the cargo holds and coalbunker were flung open. Behra's fingers knotted in her blankets as she watched the soldiers poke their halberd blades into the bunker.

"There, too," snapped Tibuir's Hound.

Rough fingers caught Behra's arm. A soldier dragged her out of her hut and pulled her blankets out after for the dogs to sniff. The animals were in a frenzy of excitement.

"Father!" Chiufi cried.

He was by the far rail of the barge, pointing urgently over the side.

"Father, I saw it! It jumped over!"

Aghor stared at him, the first time in her life Behra had ever seen him dumbfounded.

The soldier holding her joined the rush to that side of the barge, dragging her with him. Her chain yanked at her ankle as she reached its farthest extent. On the water, ripples spread in an expanding circle.

"Get some men to the far bank!" the Hound shouted. Standing close to Behra, she said, "It seems you had a stowaway, Bargeman."

"So it would appear." Aghor's face was purple, set in a furious scowl. "Where was it, boy? Where did it spring from?"

Chiufi cowered. "I didn't see, father."

Aghor cuffed him across the top of the head.

The Hound sneered. "Perhaps your old ways are not so puissant as you think."

Aghor's face darkened further, filling with shadow. The tiny bodies of Behra's sisters danced on his belt. Behra could feel the power suck into him from all around. He would need to bleed her deeply to regain his strength after this. *Learn*, she told herself, and tried what she felt him doing. She found that she could, and suddenly was, siphoning energy from the air, the water lapping around the barge, even the planks beneath her feet.

She turned her thoughts on the man holding her.

Invisible flame seared up the bones of her arm. The soldier grunted and let go. He stared down at Behra in surprise.

Aghor spoke, magic making his words slam like clashing stones. "You no longer have reason to hold us, Hound."

The Hound regarded him coolly, but her face had become even paler. Her men drew back. There were muffled yelps from among the Saltukkuri. A pulse ticked in the Hound's throat.

"As you say," she grated. She turned on her heel, shouting, "Clear the barge! Search the canal!"

Behra looked at the red welt on her forearm in the shape of the soldier's fingers. She felt the rough energies dissipate from her father's body, back into the air and water. They still throbbed in her, filling her with feverish heat. Aghor snapped a curt order to Geneic and Sorgui, who flinched in unison. They left off posturing at the departing Saltukkuri and picked up bargepoles to clumsily push the boat away from shore.

Aghor looked down at his youngest son. Chiufi tensed visibly as his father raised his hand again. But Aghor stroked the place where he had struck before.

"Did well, boy."

Behra noticed the tremor in his fingers as he lowered his arm.

The next morning she lay in her blankets, still weak and exhausted, while Chiufi fed her gruel with vegetables and salted meat, a worried frown on his face the whole time. Palinday watched in silence, his coal-smeared face solemn. Behra's father had taken a lot of blood, all the strength she had gained from copying his spell and more, but she didn't care.

He hadn't known. She had worked magic and he hadn't known.

The river was heavy with traffic, ocean-going ships sharing the water with steam barges and the pleasure yachts of the idle rich. Behra gazed up at sailors climbing about the rigging of a sailing ship, high above, its sails lit gold by the lowering sun.

Aghor had left Palinday in the coalbunker most of the night. Behra had heard the doll's tapping and his frustrated shouts in the dark. Finally released, Palinday had emerged black from head to foot, spitting angry. "There was no justification for holding me in there so long!"

Aghor had looked down at him mildly. "Tibuir's Hound will not be fooled for long. You cannot be scryed you say, little golem, but it is harder to hide an entire barge. She will have eyes on us." He turned away. "Be thankful I did not hold you in there all the way to your Lord Emieldraeu."

Palinday had washed his face and hands as best he could, but his fine clothes were spoiled.

Behra heard her father shout. The bowl clattered down beside her as Chiufi sprang to obey. She felt the barge tilt as Aghor turned hard on the wheel. Buildings loomed on either side, casting the barge in sudden shadow. She felt the thump of the engine drop away, twisted her neck to see Chiufi jump ashore, rope in hand. They had pulled in to a narrow warehouse canal.

Palinday was on his feet. "Why are we stopped? This is not Ardonailles."

Aghor glanced his way, shrugging a long coat over his shoulders. "I have business here. You will not be delayed for long, little golem."

He hopped lightly over the rail and they watched him stride away between the warehouses. Chiufi came back aboard and slunk over to sit with Behra and Palinday.

"Would your lord really protect us?" he said, softly.

Palinday looked at him. "Yes."

"Then we will run with you when we reach Ardonailles," said Behra. Chiufi's face was drawn, tense.

Palinday shook his head. "My mission must not be endangered."

"But you said . . . "

"I will return for you," Palinday said.

Behra blinked rapidly, her eyes suddenly hot. "We will be gone."

"Then I will find you," said the doll.

"Swear it," said Behra, between clenched teeth.

Palinday looked from her to Chiufi. "By my maker's honour, I swear it."

Chiufi nodded, but Behra saw from his face that the courage he had screwed together had crumbled once more.

Behra reached out and gave his hand a squeeze.

\* \* \*

A crowd gathered as the night deepened. Rhuinish folk, although they were in Ornomagne proper now. They waited quietly, squatting on the wharf or leaning against the warehouse walls. Most of them had brought gifts, ranging from baskets of vegetables to bolts of cloth. Sorgui and Geneic squatted side by side at the rail, their red-eyed gazes alert.

Palinday observed the assemblage nervously. "Who are they?"

"Folk seeking spells or charms from father," said Chiufi stiffly, after a moment. "They always gather, wherever we dock."

The doll's porcelain brow creased a fraction. "How do they know?"

Chiufi shrugged.

"They always do," said Behra.

"I dislike this," Palinday grumbled. "Where *is* he?"

It was a while before Aghor returned. He marched through the crowd without acknowledgement, yelling for Chiufi to fire up the engine and cast off. The supplicants watched in silence as the barge was pushed away from the wharf and backed slowly out of the canal.

"Ardonailles," Palinday announced.

Behra looked around the side of her hut. The lights of the great port city, trading hub of the Ornomagnen Empire, sprawled along either side of the river and across the many islands of its delta. Staircases of canal locks ascended the long slope of the north bank between the close-packed streets. The river itself had broadened and slowed as it neared the sea, more than a mile wide now, its surface rippling with reflected light and shadow.

Geneic squatted close by, near the starboard running lantern with an anvil between his knees, hammering a twisted grapple hook back into its proper shape. Chiufi was at the wheel, angling the barge across the flow of traffic towards the south shore. Sorgui crouched idly near the coal bunker, his shovel across his knees, watching the river traffic.

They passed a brightly lit fortress island, iron-sided Ornomagnen warships drawn up alongside, powered by steam and sails and bristling with double and triple decks of guns.

"There!" Palinday called out, pointing to a canal mouth in the southern bank.

Chiufi steered the barge into a district of run-down terraces and tenement blocks. There were no locks here, the city's southern suburbs sprawling across a flat plain. There was little traffic about on the dimly lit streets, although it was still early. Geneic stopped hammering.

"Girl, hand." She hadn't noticed her father's reappearance on deck. He stood over her, holding his scrying bowl.

Behra held out her arm.

Palinday watched Aghor pull out his knife. "What scrying is there to do," he said, "when we are at our destination?"

Behra winced as the point of the blade penetrated. The mummified, half-formed faces of her sisters gaped up at her with sightless eyes.

"You think the Hound would dare pursue me into the heart of Ornomagne?" Palinday persisted.

Aghor spared him a glance as he stood. "Don't you?"

Palinday flicked the brim of his hat with his fingers and stuck it on his head. He noticed Behra's gaze on him. "Tibuir's Hound does not know for sure that I am aboard," he said. "And we are far afield of where she thinks us to be headed. There are many waterways to hunt." He drummed his fingers, tinkling hollowly, against his knees. "She would be reckless to try anything so far from her lord's domain. And she fears your father, besides."

Behra was drifting as he spoke, her body heating as the burning coal landed in the bowl of her blood. She murmured along with her father's incantation. The words had an unfamiliar texture in her mind. It was no spell she had ever heard before. "*Addrakkur naskkur sakkul urukh thoth nakkur thoth . . .*"

Palinday looked at her, his jewelled eyes glinting. "That isn't Old Rhuinish." His mouth moved with Behra's. "And it isn't a scrying spell." He started to stand, then suddenly clutched at his head. "My wards . . ."

Geneic's hammer smashed into his chest. Behra screamed. Shattered bits of the doll bounced across the deck, flying free of his clothes, some skittering under the rail to splash into the water.

"The head! Find the head!" bellowed Aghor.

Geneic lifted Behra and dumped her out of her hut, so he could rummage in her blankets. She looked down into her lap. Palinday blinked up at her, his neck sheered off cleanly just below his jaw.

"Hide me."

Behra clapped her hands over the doll's face an instant before her father barged past. She looked around for Chiufi, found his shocked gaze already on her as he hurried up from the wheelhouse. He grabbed a running lantern off its hook and made a show of joining the hunt. Behra saw him pick up something, not breaking stride, and keep moving over to the rail to stoop again.

"Father," Chiufi straightened, holding up his prize to the light. Palinday's hat. "It was under the rail."

A range of expressions crossed Aghor's face as he stared at the hat. Slowly, he pushed himself upright. "You wouldn't lie to your father, would you, boy?"

Chiufi's jaw trembled.

He had closed the engine throttle, Behra realised, before he left the wheelhouse. Undirected and barely making headway, the barge was slowly turning across the canal.

Aghor began to swear, his fists clenched so tight they shook. Behra's aborted sisters silently cursed along with him. The shadows deepened in the hollows of his face and spread. Sickly light leaked between his curled fingers. Beside him, Sorgui and Geneic cringed, their red eyes slitted almost shut.

"Having some difficulty, Bargeman?" a woman's voice called out.

Tibuir's Hound sat on horseback at the edge of the canal.

"None that's any business of yours, Hound," Behra's father grated, his voice heavy with magic.

Hooves and boots clattered on stone, riders and foot soldiers appearing on both banks. Red Saltukkuri eyes glowed, the squat, hunched figures of demimen scattered among the Rhuinish troops. Crossbows were levelled.

*Crossbows*, thought Behra. Not muskets. *Silent.*

A horse whickered, a crossbow string creaked in the descending quiet. Behra heard a low growl from Sorgui by the wheelhouse.

The red stone on the Hound's brow caught the light of a streetlamp. "You seem to have gone astray from your destination," she drawled. "It is a curious coincidence that your failure of navigation has brought you here." She leaned forward in her saddle, her eyes wide. "Did you know, Aghor the Bargeman, that the King's Spymaster maintains a house in this part of Ardonailles?"

Behra's hands shook on top of Palinday's sculpted face. She heard him gasp, felt his lips move against her palm as he mouthed curses. Her father and the Hound glared at each other.

The sound of more tramping boots cut through the standoff. "Stand down!" a new voice cried. "Stand down in the name of the King!"

Bright-liveried Ornomagnen troops marched along both sides of the canal. Behra gasped. Brass, four-legged battle golems marched with them, their mantis arms upraised.

"*Silbuim meneich!*" spat Behra's father, and all hell broke loose.

Along both banks, Rhuinish crossbows suddenly caught on fire. The archers dropped them with shouts of surprise. Bolts flew in all directions as the bows bounced on the ground. Some thunked into the wooden deck of the barge. Soldiers and horses screamed as they were struck. The Ornomagnen troops discharged their muskets. Ornomagnen and Rhuinishmen both charged. Saltukkuri leapt onto the barge.

Sorgui and Geneic surged to their feet, laying about with the tools to hand, bigger by far than their full-blood brethren and with all of a demiman's strength. Chiufi smashed his lamp into the face of a Saltukkuri warrior who landed beside him. Flaming oil sprayed over the shrieking demiman.

Tibuir's Hound gave a shout. Aghor grunted as if struck and fell to one knee. Behra felt a squeezing pressure in her chest.

"*Telais ac ulh,*" she mouthed her father's snarled counter spell. "*Telais maliel ap naghai.*"

The Hound cried out, scrambling clear as her horse collapsed under her. She landed awkwardly, both hands stretched out like claws. Behra could feel the spells clash in the air between them, probing for weaknesses in the other's defences. Her skin stung as if scalded.

A demiman's fallen axe lay within reach.

Now, Behra thought. Her fingers closed on the axe. "Chiufi!"

He ran over to her and she thrust the axe into his hands. His eyes were huge, the whites showing all around.

"What's happening?" demanded Palinday, as soon as his face was uncovered.

"We're going now," said Behra, holding her brother's gaze.

Chiufi swallowed and nodded, fumbled about for her ankle chain and smashed the axe down onto it.

Behra mouthed spells, drawing power into herself. Chiufi's breathed plumed in the suddenly cold air. He struck the chain again. This time the links parted.

Chiufi stood, hauling Behra up with him. She clutched Palinday's head to her chest and led Chiufi towards the back of the barge. Sorgui flung a broken demiman into a crowd of his fellows near the wheelhouse. The barge had continued to slew across the canal. Its stern bumped against the stone wall of the bank. Chiufi pushed Behra up ahead of him and leapt after.

She stood, marvelling at the feel of cold stone under her bare feet, so different from the smooth planking of the barge's deck. There was a roar from the boat. Their father had noticed her absence. His rage thrummed along the thread of power that bound them.

Behra lashed out, unthinking. *"Telais ac ulh."* In her terror, she forgot the rest of the spell. But Aghor gave a shout of surprise. It rose to an outraged bellow as the Hound took advantage of his distraction.

Chiufi grabbed Behra's wrist and they fled.

They raced down darkened streets, past frightened faces peeping from windows and doorways. Behra struggled to keep up with her brother. Her lungs and legs burned, unused to such exertion. Her feet were quickly bruised. She soon began to flag.

Chiufi slowed and stopped at a crossroads. He fumbled Palinday's head from Behra's grasp and held it up. The world spun around her. She felt faint.

"Why did he smash you?" Chiufi panted.

"To get the scroll out of my head and know the secrets it holds for himself," said Palinday. "To use them, or sell them to the highest bidder."

Chiufi looked around. "Which way?"

"I don't recognise the street," said Palinday. "But we left the river east and north of my master's house. Go south and then west."

Chiufi turned uncertainly.

"That way!" Palinday snapped.

Behra felt a familiar pressure against her thoughts. "He's coming," she gasped.

Chiufi caught her wrist again. "Run!"

She stumbled after.

On through the streets they ran, Chiufi dragging her along, sometimes holding her up, Palinday's head held up in his other hand. The doll barked directions, guiding them deeper into the city. A sharp pain started in Behra's side.

The sense of their father behind them grew stronger and stronger. "He's coming!"

"Not far!" cried Palinday. "My master will be there."

"I can't," Behra wept.

"Keep going," Chiufi said, his own voice almost a sob. "He's coming."

Closer. And closer. She could feel the killing fury in him. And power—more than she had ever felt him hold.

Chiufi would die if he caught them. She would be flogged, no doubt, and returned to her hut and chain. But Chiufi would die.

For his sake, Behra kept running.

"Here!" Palinday shrieked. "Here, on the left! The third house along!"

The townhouse was one of a row fronted by gated courtyards. Behra swayed, barely able to stay upright, staring up at the house in confusion. Surely the King's Magician must live in a palace?

Chiufi rattled the bars of the gate and shouted. "My Lord! Open up!"

Palinday gave a wail of dismay. "My master isn't here! He's supposed to be here!"

Their father's presence was overwhelming. *He's here*, she thought. Her tongue refused to cooperate. *He's here!*

"Hold me to the lock," said Palinday.

Chiufi did so. The doll whispered into the keyhole and, with a loud clang, the gate sprang open.

"Chiufi!" Behra gasped.

There was a bellow from the corner of the street.

"Inside!" cried Palinday. "He won't be able to pass the gate."

Chiufi flung Behra through and slammed the bars shut behind them.

She almost fell, but he lifted her and dragged her across the courtyard towards the door of the house.

"*Talais ac ulh,*" she mouthed, caught up in her father's spell. She felt it gather strength, wanted to shout a warning. "*Telais maliel ap naghai.*"

With a scream, she wrenched herself free.

The air detonated between her and Chiufi. He was hurled away from her by the impact of the spell. Behra sprawled, twisted to see her brother bounce off the stones. Palinday's head sailed through the air to smash against the wall of the house.

Chiufi's screams rose to a shriek. Blood bubbled from his eyes, ears and nose.

"Chiufi!" Behra cried. She lurched upright, thrust her hand into the arc of power between her father and brother, thinking madly to bat the killing magic back towards Aghor.

She felt her fingerbones snap, the skin on her hand blistering and bursting. The force of the spell spun her around and back to her knees. There was a cry of surprise from outside the gate.

Behra whimpered, cradling her shattered hand. Tremors ran through Chiufi, then he lay frighteningly still.

She felt her father building another spell. "No," she said. "*No.*" She drew in power, felt the air crackle against her skin. "*Silbuim meneich*," she said aloud—her spell, not his.

Aghor disappeared in a flash. Heat washed back over her. She heard the thin screams of her sisters, felt her father's shock, his pain, his rage quickly returning.

"No!" She got to her feet, lifting her hands, broken and whole, towards him. "*Silbuim meneich!*"

This spell had far more force, but this time he was ready, too. More of the blast bounced back through the gate, knocking Behra over. She thrashed about, beating at the flames on her smock and hair.

There was silence from her father, no sense of the chord that had joined her to him.

Shaking, she crawled over to Chiufi. He still wasn't moving. She reached out to him with her good hand, fingers fluttering over his face. His chest rose, suddenly, and fell. Then again. Her vision blurred.

A clatter of hooves outside the gate made her look up.

Her father lay prone on the road. A horseman loomed over him. Aghor raised a hand weakly. The rider held out a forked staff to touch his fingers. Behra felt the words of power pass between them. Aghor's back arched, and he slumped and fell still.

The rider dismounted. He pushed open the gate and strode across the yard. Behra shrank back. Pale eyes bored into her from under thick white brows. He went straight past her, stepping over Chiufi, to where Palinday's head had smashed against the wall.

The old man stooped, then straightened with a tiny paper scroll in his hand. "Ah, my friend," he murmured. "I sensed too late that it was you the Hound had cornered on that barge, and then you ran away from me."

His gaze fell once more on Behra.

"Please," she said, "help my brother."

A knock at the door woke Behra from her doze. She jerked her head away from the wall behind her chair. Chiufi lay unconscious in the bed, bandages swathing his eyes and ears. His mouth was open and slack, but his chest rose and fell.

The door opened and a man with polished black skin came in. No, not a man—a golem, though he was dressed like a man and moved as smoothly.

The ebony golem saw her awake. His sculpted face shifted fractionally, approximating a smile.

"Behra."

The voice was nearly the same—deeper, but tinkling with music. And he still had blue gemstone eyes.

Behra stared in wonder as Palinday came to perch on the edge of Chiufi's bed.

"I told you I was in disguise," he said. He reached across to brush his hand gently across her splinted fingers. He squeezed her good hand, his touch cold and unyielding. "You are safe."

"And my father?"

"My Lord Emieldraeu has laid a geas upon him. He cannot approach you or do you harm. You are safe." He patted her fingers. "You had already beaten him, you know, before my master intervened."

Behra shook her head. It was too much, too overwhelming. "Chiufi?"

Palinday's voice softened. "He will live. My master believes he will regain most of his hearing and his voice, in time. His heart and lungs, too, will mostly heal."

He raised his hand to wipe her cheek with his fingertip. "Do not blame yourself. You did what was needed—both of you," he said. "Lord Tibuir was plotting rebellion. Now the King can strike first, before Tibuir is ready. You and your brother may have saved Ornomagne from a terrible civil war." Behra thought that if he was a man, he would have sighed. "Or made it less terrible, at least. And you saved yourselves."

Behra was only half listening. "What of his eyes?"

"Ah."

She imagined him blinded for life, yet another terrible hurt, taken for her sake. It was too much to bear.

She saw Palinday's mouth stretch into another fractional smile, his fingers reach into the pocket of his vest. He turned Behra's hand over and dropped something into her palm. She looked down at a pair of glass orbs. Set into each was a faceted blue gemstone identical to Palinday's eyes.

"His eyes cannot be saved," the golem said, "but he will be well cared for."

# ON THE LEITMOTIF OF THE TRICKSTER CONSTELLATION IN NORTHERN HEMISPHERIC STAR CHARTS, POST-APOCALYPSE

## *Nicole Kornher-Stace*

THE ONE WHO GOT AWAY
AREA: 513.842 SQ. DEG. (APPX. 1.29%)
FROM THE PALISADE CHART: PINE PITCH, BIRCH BARK
WINTER

Seven stars: three major, four minor. Six represent the head, heart, hands and feet of an androgynous child; the seventh, an object gripped in the child's left fist. Regrettably, this object's identity remains a puzzle that has thwarted both the restoration efforts of our team and the scrutiny of every expert in the field: this sector of the chart, including roughly 1/3 of the lower-left quadrant of the One (to say nothing of its neighbor, the Flensed Bride, foxed down to her caption—see fig. 1), is obliterate. A further unhappy consequence of this damage: it is impossible to tell whether the child in question is hugging itself (as children will, against cold or loneliness or fear) or if its wrists are tied.

Any scholar of the charts will forgive me—posthumously, at least—for saying that the trickster constellations prove, time and time again, the *trickiest* to study: whereas the constellations out of history (e.g., the Payload, the Comet, the Exodus, the Pest), those shaped by daily circumstance (the Huntsman, the Pitfall, the Bear), and those obviously conjured by minds seeking to realize them with wish (the Wellspring, the Garden)

46

tend to leave us careful breadcrumb trails to follow, in the form of Songkeepers, journals, and old books, the trickster constellations set us a puzzle on the best of days, an ambush on the worst, and it is utterly in keeping with the trickster's own motif that, at times, even the most meticulous of combings comes up emptyhanded, yielding little but a tag-end or a fragment of a tale—or, in the case of this odd little constellation, nothing.

In default of contextual evidence, the imagination picks at clues, thumb-and-forefinger, as if at a spider in the stewpot, or undetonated ordnance in the path. From this figure's caption we can glean it "got away," but from what? When? And how? Is it a refugee? An escaped prisoner? A ghost?

Of a certainty this was the constellation mothers made offerings to, when their infants' fevers spiked, and the one whose name lost wanderers invoked on lonely roads—but why? Those who threw themselves upon this trickster's questionable mercies did not lead easy lives. Their very bones assure us of this: soft with radiation, pitted with disease. Their toothless skulls give tongue to songs of loss. Was the object of these prayers then to be returned unto oneself, one's place, one's family—or to be spirited away from all of these, propelled headlong into some gentler tale?

If so, this may explain occasional depictions of the One alongside a waterspout or cyclone, natural phenomena which folk belief endows with an almost mystic sense of *quid pro quo*; they were widely thought to serve as conduits or tunnels drawing souls from this plane into another, and those from others into this, thus counterpoising each potential world against the rest.

Similar formations in other charts: THE CHANGELING (Trench Chart, NQ3), DEATH (Sail Chart, NQ3)

When Archivist Wasp found the bottle on her doorstep, she knew at once the ghosts had left it there, because it smelled of salt. Most of what she found there in the dawn still wore a stink of dirt and ash, from where someone had exhumed it; or of dirt and sweat and cooking, the close smells of a little house, from where someone had sewn or pieced or woven it in the few hours of ashy light each day allotted. A heel of acorn-flour bread, a clutch of stunted onions and a seashell; a scarf knitted of nettle yarn and a pair of horseleather gloves, clumsily stitched and too short in the fingers, but warming as she tugged them on. A bright orange plastic pitcher, clouded with its ancientness and warped with some past heat, which sloshed with rainwater as she dethroned it from its place of honor in the cairn of offerings. The movement dislodged a sharpening-stone and a sort of torque someone had fashioned out of scavengings: empty cartridges and tarnished rings and bits of colored glass flanking a single tiny locket with a blue-and-white enamel windmill on the front. And someone had shored up her sagging doorframe with the same bits of salvage that the rest of the Archivist-hut had been pieced of for as long as Wasp had known. Underneath it all, at the time of the first Archivist, it could have been made of anything.

Fear-gifts, blood-gifts, bribes. Most days she left the lot of it to the snuffling shrine-dogs who prowled her hut to ensure her obedience—first subtracting maybe a few dried apples, maybe a bullet for a gun she may yet find, maybe some corpse's stolen shoes—only to have new cairns rebuilt by eager hands during the night. After all, there was no other sword between the living and the ghosts than her; no other intercessor, no other keeper of the door. She could purge a poltergeist, send the shades of cradle-deaths to quicken fallow wombs, tether a ghost in place with salt to ward a scraggled field against the tithing of the crows. And it was she who gleaned the shards of histories and pieced them, tipped voice like sips of water down the throat of a dead world.

And she'd gladly let the gifts rot down to mulch, and their givers along with them.

But the bottle smelled cold and clean and salt as seas she knew were salt because the ghosts had told her so. The smell on it, and the whitegreen of the glass, put her in mind of licking icicles. Though the icicles she knew were riddled with flaws and streaks of grit, she believed the ghost who'd said the icicles of the Well-Before had frozen clear as windowpanes.

("As what?" Wasp had asked. "Windowpanes," the ghost had repeated. Then, "Crystal," it had offered to her blank look. "Plastic sheeting?" At last she'd understood. In her head—for she possessed neither paper nor the letters to put on it—she'd written *windowpanes*. Written *crystal*. And tipped the ghost out of its jar to go its way.)

She turned the bottle back and forth in the light, watching how the glass warped the roll of paper within. Of course the ghosts had not brought it there, any more than the sea could bring her shells; only that their migrations had disinterred it from wherever it had been concealed and someone had found it, plucked it gingerly from the ground as though it might well bite, and brought it to the only person any of them knew who'd bite back harder.

Also odd: the sheet of paper inside the bottle was nothing like the ones she'd seen from time to time on traders' wagons or bound into books in the Songkeeper's hut, burned or drowned or gnawed or sweet with rot. She sat on the rock that was her front step—gingerly, still sore from her last escape attempt, a week ago now by the moon—and studied it, flattened against the tamped-earth path to her hut. The paper unrolled to the length of one of Wasp's long strides and was peppered with as many dots as there were windfalls in an orchard, skulls in a slagpit, or beans in a bowl.

*A map*, thought Wasp, who had seen such things before. *A map of stars.*

And then she grew very thoughtful, did Wasp with the ache still in her calves from the fleeing, with the rawness still in her lungs and a lattice of welts from the thornfield she had pushed through with the clamor of the hunt right on her heels, with the smell of the shrine-dogs still in her hair from the last time they'd run her down. With the scars on her ankles from the first time the Catchkeep-priest had had to drag her back, spitting and slashing, and smashed her feet between two stones. Sheer dumb luck, perhaps, or force of rage, she'd healed.

The next day, hunting, she packed the saltlick and the fruit and blade and bells as usual, but left her jars behind. She brought the map instead.

CATCHKEEP
AREA: **300.492** SQ. DEG. (APPX. **0.73%**)
FROM THE DOGWAGON CHART: LEATHER TOOLING, HORSEHIDE
AUTUMN

Sixteen stars: six major, ten minor, most of the latter representing teeth. This dog's jaw is like a beartrap, too huge for her head, dwarfing even the massive barrel of her chest and the bulging muscles of her thighs. Even today it proves no challenge to see her as the crafters of this chart must have done, the ones who venerated her deeply enough to hold her fellow dogs in such high regard—the pistons of her legs, the forges of her eyes, the fey flux of that awful guileful grin—and in truth it remains almost instinctive in the modern heart to cheer her on each night as she runs the moon to earth behind the hills. But she is Catchkeep, ghostherder and sentinel, constant as the stars that shape her nightly steeplechase; and when the lot of us is done to dust, she will not miss our rallying.

Of all this trickster's stories—"Catchkeep Chases the Comet's Tail," "Catchkeep's Biting Contest with Grandmother Shark," etc.—the one that comes to us the most well-preserved by far is "Catchkeep's Bequest," wherein a few short paragraphs (or, more pertinent to the experience of its original audience, a few minutes' telling) find that inimitable bitch whelping the First Litter, passing the Earth itself as afterbirth, then fashioning the world's first people out of dogs' skeletons rearranged to stand upright, inadvertently killing many when she tries to scruff those who dare disobey. It ends with Catchkeep commandeering the first makeshift vehicle of these people, who grew foolhardy or daft enough to try and tame her, and in so doing forming her sister constellation, the Empty Wagon (NQ3, fig. 2)—possibly a glorification of that people's own wagons, constructed of rusted-out automobile chassis welded to whatever scaffolding and stretched with whatever rotten fabric or brittle leather was to hand?

> *"The lot of you," said Catchkeep, "can go screw." And she took their wagon and drove it hard across the hills until all the dogs fell down dead in their traces, glowing bright as arc lights through the ash. Then she lifted each of them in her great jaws and tossed them up into the sky, gently as a bitch tumbling pups, and they dug in their footholds on the dark and paced their circles and curled up to sleep the sleep of stars.*

What she is perhaps best known as, however, is a herder of spirits: both those of the dead and the unborn. In this aspect she earns the fear of the diseased, the chased, and the condemned, whose souls it is her charge to bear away; also the veneration of the fallow-wombed, whose custom it was to set out the choicest bits of meat after their evening meal, in hopes of luring Catchkeep to the door.

Her former, baneful aspect is illustrated in a scrap of doggerel, perhaps a fraction of a larger piece of verse, found scrawled on a bit of scorch-edged paper rolled into a tube and tied off with a string, worn in a horsehide pouch as a crude little talisman against her inexorable teeth:

> *Catchkeep* [illegible], *running free,*
> *Herding the souls out over the trees:*
> *Cold ghosts you are. Till ghost I be,*
> *You have no power over me.*

Similar formations in other charts: THE LURCHER (Hothouse Chart, NQ4), THE HUNT (Pennon Chart, NQ4).

She turned the first four away with her blessing, for they were faceless, the height of her knees, and moved vaguely, as if underwater—but the fifth ghost Wasp saw up on the lightning-blasted ledge of Execution Hill was a tall one, easily a head higher than herself, and there was something about it that caught her eye. Not exactly awareness, never that; but a sort of daunted yearning that it broadcast, which she understood too well.

Before she put out the saltlick, she sat on her heels a moment to watch it. It fascinated her, the way the ghosts moved, pacing their confines like tethered dogs, sounding their boundaries, back and forth. She saw much of herself in them, so she never watched for long.

This particular ghost was walking down a corridor she could not see, turning invisible doorknobs. Its mouth moved, shaping the same word again and again, but no sound came out. A name, Wasp thought. It could have been anyone's. A lover's, a child's, a friend's. Wasp's mouth twisted: scorn or envy.

She wondered what had done it in, this restive ghost. If she waited long enough she would probably get her answer, but she'd lost her stomach for that long ago.

Hurriedly she laid the saltlick out and the ghost nosed forward, browsing at the air.

She never knew quite why the saltlick worked. Never quite cared. Another fragment of the ritual, she figured, another step in the dance of call-and-response that kept her here—not exactly like the ghosts, for no Archivist trapped *her* in jars for questioning, and not exactly unlike them, for her path was prescribed in lines as clearly drawn as any one of theirs. The saltlick worked, the Songkeepers said, because it put the ghosts in mind of the flesh they used to wear. The salt of sweat, of tears, of blood. It drew them. It made them remember. But there was no Archivist to lay a trail of salt for Wasp. Her rescue, or else her entrapment, was her own.

The ghost reached the saltlick and began to feed.

She gave it a moment.

"I am the Archivist," Wasp said, when the ghost had slowed. She gagged against the cloy of rote, but spat it anyway. "Catchkeep's emissary, ambassador, and avatar on earth. Her bones and stars my flesh; my flesh and bones her stars. I greet you."

The ghost looked up at her. This part used to frighten her a little: the sea change in the ghosts' eyes as the salt waylaid them, clogged their feet with the memory of clay. The look they'd wear, as though waking from a dream and seeing something wholly frightening which Wasp could not. It had not taken her long to learn that they were only seeing her.

She set the rolled map on the ground and toed it toward the ghost, who for its part was not cowering as most did but instead had drawn itself up to its full height and was peering down its nose at her as at a turd in the path it would have to step around.

Wasp hid her smile. She'd been lucky. She'd gone out to Execution Hill expecting to keep coming back a week, a month, before she'd found one quite like this. This was the sort of ghost that had retained or salvaged enough of itself to be searching for something, or someone, or somewhere, and the draw of it was stronger even than the salt. This one sought a *someone*, she was sure, and from the look of it, the days it'd lived out were long past. Then it was looking for a ghost. And it wouldn't find it on its own.

She hoped it was smart enough, or dumb enough, to bargain with.

"You're seeking," she said. The other ghosts walked or flew or fell through their last moments to all sides of her, oblivious, but this one, *this one* heard. It eyed that map the way a half-starved dog eyes carrion, and she held it up at armslength, keeping the salt between them; the ghost lunged and came up short, collared by the empty air. "Well. So am I."

\* \* \*

THE CINDER GIRL
AREA: 1119.303 SQ. DEG. (APPX. 2.71%)
FROM THE SINKHOLE CHART: RAZOR SCARRING, HUMAN SKIN
AUTUMN

Twenty-three stars: eight major, fifteen minor, including neither the visual binary blue supergiant representing her heart nor the nebula colloquially known as the Spool; while this latter's representation remains the subject of some debate, it is generally agreed to be *either* the Girl's navel or her womb. (If one can use *agreed* in fairness, conjuring as it does more a smiling accord over a glass of fine vintage than the panting stalemate reached by brawlers, each having succumbed less to his rival's blows than to his own growing lassitude.)

On some charts this constellation shares two major and one minor star with the Carrion Boy, whereas on others the Girl and Boy only border upon points (e.g., the Blood Quilt Chart, which depicts them handfast, or the Floodplain Chart, which shows them going at each other's throats with shivs).

The Lintel Chart (fig. 3) marks one striking departure: the two constellations are drawn together into one, torso to torso, while the stars designated elsewhere as the base of the Cinder Girl's childbed-pyre, her right knee, and the Carrion Boy's attendant crow are here shown to represent offerings—water, bullets, seed-fruit—heaped by persons unknown at their feet. The overall effect is that of a two-headed, four-armed monster god: arguably an attempt, in the spirit of the origin stories of the Well-Before, to explain away cases of severe mutation.

Apparently a light- or fire-bringer, the Cinder Girl was— and in some few rough backwaters of the Waste-that-was, still is—called upon, with that wayworn trinity of incantation, song, and sacrifice, to conjure out the sun from where it floundered in its yearlong skirts of ash. In fact, whatever demarcating line is sketched in between sun and Girl is vague; most indications hint there's no line there at all: she either *is* the sun, or else is swollen with it, as any mother is with any child.

Consider then this chart: carved into the flesh, from soles to brow, of a girl of childbearing age—more: one who has recently *borne* a child—but with interruptions in the chart over the girl's heart and abdomen, wherein are illustrated the binary blue supergiant called the Beartrap (see above) and the Spool Nebula, respectively. These breaks in the chart demonstrate a level of artistry ratcheted up several notches from that shown in the execution of its remainder, and the entirety of the scarring was performed very shortly before the death of its recipient via living interment in the ash.

The suggestion of apotheosis is not a subtle one. Pared down to its particulars, what we have in the Sinkhole Chart is a pair of extraordinarily well-preserved corpses—those of the abovementioned girl and her infant—the former being illustrated with both the hallmarks of the constellation whose avatar she likely is and the chart in which that constellation may be found, the latter (we are given to conjecture) as a stand-in for the sun the Cinder Girl gives birth to, and which is her death by immolation. (It remains also a matter of supposition that the ash burial edged out the conflagration in the affections of this girl's acolyte-executioners simply because they wished the chart to be preserved.)

The observant eye will glean hints toward this circuit of ritual human sacrifice—for crops, for rain, for the fertility of barren wombs—from the story cycles "Bones and Coins," "A Greener Grave," and "Cinder Girl Tricks the Honey Thief."

Similar formations in other charts: THE BONEWITCH (Palimpsest Chart, NQ2), THE CHOOSER (Fallows Chart, NQ2), THE QUEEN (White Chart, NQ2).

B y that evening, Wasp had learned her letters. The next day she could spell her name.

"Wasp," the ghost sneered, chafing at its leash of salt. "What sort of name is that supposed to be?"

"The one I was given," she answered placidly. Wasp could understand the ghost's frustration: it wasn't like it had come all this way up from the world Below just to teach a teenage girl to read. Still, a bargain was a bargain. And she was turning out to be a fast learner. "Because I was a fool and I let them make me fight for the privilege of being Archivist." She told it about the night that she was chosen out of all the novices and made to challenge the current Archivist for her place. All that training, all that bloodshed, just to be deemed strong enough, cutthroat and holy enough, to wring ghosts free of stories and with them piece the story of the world before.

As she spoke she rubbed the ridged scar on her neck, shades paler, pinker than her skin, where the then-Archivist had drawn first blood. Wasp hadn't been expected to get up from it. She smiled, remembering.

"After that they called me Wasp. Because I'd poisoned my blade and I stabbed her full of holes with it."

"How fierce," the ghost said, mocking. "How proud. All the thwarted dignity of a whipped dog. Have you ever seen a wasp? A live one?"

She had not.

"Nuisances," the ghost said. "You'd like them. They can do nothing else but sting."

(*You daft bitch*, the Catchkeep-priest said in Wasp's memory. *You malapert. Why do we keep you? You're no solace to anyone. You couldn't unpuzzle a snarl in your hair.*)

(*You keep me,* Wasp had replied, *because none of you can kill me.*)

Wasp gritted her teeth. Bent her head back to the map. Read *spool*. Read *blue*. Read *trap*. And dreamed of the constellation the Catchkeep-priest's blood would make upon his clammy robes.

THE CARRION BOY
AREA: 487.012 SQ. DEG. (APPX. 1.19%)
FROM THE BRAINPAN CHART: SCRIMSHAW, WHALEBONE
SUMMER

Ten stars: four major, six minor, and a further two to designate the eye and tail of the attendant crow toward which he is discovered making full-body placatory gestures. A random selection of charts lists the crow as either the Boy's sidekick (the Holly Chart), his anima (the Chalk Hills Chart), his nemesis (the Gatekeeper Chart), or virtually anything between (both the Riot Shield and Blast Charts—fig. 4—provide striking deviations). Even the Boy's posture of deference, which renders this constellation unmistakable in any sky—balanced on one foot, head down, arms up and out, hands open, palms heavy with offerings or bribes—is variously interpreted, beyond its face value, as either a game, a gambit, or a trap.

More curiously still, six of this constellation's stars belong to binary systems (two visual, one eclipsing), and as the stars shift back and forth by virtue of their mutual orbits, they completely change the shape this constellation describes upon the earthbound viewer's sky: slowly the crow's wings shift to become the boy's, and the crow vanishes altogether.

Setting aside the sheer technical achievement that this chart represents—albeit carved, one suspects, with a blade not much at ease in service to the arts, still it covers, in nearly microscopic detail, the entire frontal bone plate of the skull of a juvenile male *Orcinus orca*, incidentally providing an embarrassingly large component of the bone record of a splendid creature long-extinct—it appears to have served as, or been associated with, an object of some ritual significance. The skull itself was found interred in ash, alongside the corpse of a young man staked down, apparently alive, to a stretch of barren, heavily irradiated slag.

However, unlike what the host-canvas of the Sinkhole Chart (see above) experienced, this was no ash burial: what covered this chart and its—what? Ancillary? Chaperone?—was that which the winds had drifted in. One particularly intriguing aspect of this find was the presence of nine pairs of crows' wings, affixed between the stakes and their victim's flesh at wrists, elbows, knees, ankles, and neck, presumably to buoy up his manumitted soul to whatever fairer skies awaited it. Another was the assorted heap of limbs that lay atop the corpse: some crudely hacked, some removed with surgical precision, but all well-muscled and apparently quite healthy up until the very moment of subtraction.

No more colorful, perhaps, than the traditions upheld in the veneration of any of these tricksters, although quite probably more grotesque, and considerably more infamous, is the custom in the cult of the Carrion Boy toward ritual self-mutilation.

As always it is difficult to ascertain whether it was the custom that shaped the way of life of its practitioners, or the way of life that shaped the custom; puzzlingly, some few seem to spring up like daisies on a slag-spit, self-engendered and unreasoning. This is one of those.

Owing most probably to the striking lack of sheltering features in the landscape where these people chose to settle, a large fraction of their cultural experience was warfare: preparation, avoidance, aftermath, glorification. Upon reaching physical maturity, all young men and women (with the exception of those pregnant, nursing, or convalescent) entered into a combat training regimen that only the most charitable would term rigorous. At the culmination of the training, those whose lives it had not claimed were made to choose a part of their own bodies for dedication to the Carrion Boy in a ritual taking place under that constellation's ascendancy. The most common form this dedication took was amputation, but simple mangling of the flesh was also widely used. All these gentle ministrations were performed with the aid of song ("Carrion Boy Feeds the Crows" was a particular favorite) and vast quantities of scorchweed wine.

One would soon have little doubt whether one's offering was deemed acceptable to the Boy: accounts still survive of bodies found turned literally inside out, bodies found tied literally into knots, bodies hanged from points quite inaccessible to human agency (see fig. 5 for artist's interpretation).

Similar formations in other charts: THE SCAPEGOAT (Stairwell Chart, NQ2), THE JUGGLER (Flotsam Chart, NQ2).

The slow burn of autumn congealed into winter, the edges of the map grew sticky with apple juice and the dirt from underneath Wasp's bitten nails, and the ghost was getting restless. "This is not a map to walk by, idiot," it told her, standing by in silence as she lay out the saltlick and the apples and the little dish of blood. As she crammed ghosts into jars and took them back to the hut where she paced the tiny room of it nightlong, four paces by four, and questioned them. Each with its story of a long drop on a short rope, or a fall down the stairs, or a half-dozen bullets sinking themselves, wet as kisses, in its erstwhile flesh. Or of a strange deep sick-smelling sleep, stalked by the dreams of dreams. Or nothing. "Or can you fly now? It will lead you nowhere."

Wasp said nothing. Not when the ghost berated her, not when the snow caved her roof in, not when she neglected her duties at the shrine and the dogs caught her at it and went to fetch the Catchkeep-priest, and the Catchkeep-priest came to lash her raw and lick the blood away. Blasphemy, for she was Catchkeep's puppet, her blood the blood of stars. Even as the priest hissed his wet breath down her neck the dogs were tonguing up that holy blood from the floor where it had spattered. Half-dazed with pain and rage, she thought she saw one lift its head and smirk.

She could feel Catchkeep rising up in her, all teeth. Wasp steeled her mind and shoved her down. She'd free *herself*.

"I had to lie," she told the ghost. "I thought I needed you to teach me how to read the map. So I could. So I." Something tightened in her throat and she ground down on it hard. "But it's just junk. A relic for the idiot Songkeepers. A few seconds of heat." And she tossed it on the fire. "There's nothing past here," she said, eyes averted. "Only more."

One evening she caught the ghost scratching at her door like a cat. She recalled how she had first seen it, walking down a hall she could not see, turning doorknobs. Even as she watched, it began to pace that hall again, two steps from her own door to the wall of the hut, then straight out through the wall. Sticking her head outside, she could count out twelve more paces in the snow before the ghost slammed into empty air at the end of its tether like a bird into a window. When its circuit snapped it back, the snow where it had walked was left unmarked by any prints. Until she fell asleep she watched it pace out through the wall into the snow and be returned, one arm outstretched, one hand rattling at locks that were not there.

Where the last light hit the ghost, it shone straight through.

THE BONESETTER
AREA: 442.122 SQ. DEG. (APPX. 1.07%)
FROM THE RAILWAY STATION CHART: SPRAY PAINT, RED BRICK
SPRING

Thirteen stars: four major, nine minor, and barely visible through its pall of ash (best seen, in fact, in a wind too foul to allow for comfortable viewing: it scuds the cover sideways off the stars, like prying up a scab).

This constellation is a strange one. Crouched low on the horizon, hulking and spidery at once, it tiptoes hunchbacked through the fallen cities, downbent as though searching, by which it earns itself the alternate appellation Ragpicker (the best extant example being found in the Lighthouse Chart, fig. 6); sinister yet oddly delicate, its stars are among the last to prick the darkling sky, among the first to be annihilated by the coming of the sun.

As is also the case with the One Who Got Away (see above), few clues survive regarding the figure behind this constellation. Unique to it, however, is that whatever evidence might have remained seems to have undergone systematic eradication, for reasons only guessed at, by people of whom nothing is known save their creation of the chart via which this constellation reaches our notice.

As always, uncertainty is hypothesis's breeding-ground: here the theorists swarm like flies to carrion, all too eager to spawn fresh execrations upon the heretofore unsullied lap of scholarly intent. They hold that this evidence was destroyed out of pure fear of the Bonesetter's return to earth out of the sky, where up until that point he had been chained, like many a chastised fellow-trickster from the stories of the Well-Before, by the very stars that outline him to mortal eyes.

They also hold that it is from this trickster that we get the songs "Marryings and Buryings" and "Scavengers' Circus," as well as the expression "a bonesetter's gambit," still in use today to describe apparently anything from anodyne to idiocy. But as the vast majority of these theories share an irritating tendency to go out on a limb and then saw it off behind them, all we can rely upon with any certainty is the chart itself, and, tricksterish in its own way, its lips are sealed.

Similar formations in other charts: THE RAGPICKER (Mural Chart, NQ1).

When the salt had worn it to translucence and a faint smell of copper, the ghost finally began to talk, though it told her nothing she did not already know. She'd netted enough ghosts by that point, left enough of them huddled in their terror on her shelf and telling each other tales of elsewhere to keep their longing for escape alive, to know just what it was about the map that drew it. Listening to it now she could almost see the pale ghost-roads that linked the stars, could almost see it walking them, both feet freed, heart light, and not alone.

She wondered after the other ghost, the one it sought. Had Wasp salted that ghost, caught it, crammed it in a jar, reeled its memories out hand over hand, and dumped it out amid the scorchweed and windfalls to wend its way back to its wandering? Or had it gone on, the way the tales said that they could go on, and left Wasp's captive ghost behind? Even if she freed this ghost now, would it go on chasing the other as a dog chases its tail, or the sun the moon: reaching always, all unreached?

*At least it has something important to search for*, she thought. *All I can think of to look for is a way out.*

Wasp blinked. For a fraction of a second she had seen something like a dream. In it, a daisy-chain of Archivists went back and back and back, an ancient hut their jar, their holiness shackling them as sure as salt. She had forgotten what it was she sought before she only sought escape. If she'd sought anything at all.

The daisy-chain could knot her up into it and continue on. Or she could end it here.

Before she knew what she was doing, the knife was in her fist. She crossed the tiny room to where the ghost sat slumped. Kicked the salt clear from its feet. Held out her hand.

It trusted neither her grin nor the glint in her eyes, but got up all the same.

THE ARCHIVIST
AREA: 65.002 SQ. DEG. (APPX. 0.16%)
FROM THE RAGTREE CHART: PLANT-BASED PIGMENT, HUMAN SKIN
WINTER

Four stars, all minor: hardly enough to reasonably discern the image of what this tiny grouping is meant to represent; namely, a woman with a knife in one hand and a sort of scroll in the other, frozen in the act of stepping forward.

This trickster's status as culture-hero is provisional—her motives are dubious, her intentions suspect, the queues to her shrines no longer than the trails of corpses that rattle along in her wake through a half-dozen tales—but persistently widespread.

What makes it particularly strange is that she seems to have played culture-hero *to the very spirits of the deceased.*

If this woman truly was, as a fairly large body of conjecture suggests, one of the Archivists, the historian-priestesses of the bitch-god Catchkeep (see above), she would have been an extremely capable fighter, trained since early childhood to single combat and little else, and it is true her skybound avatar does hold her knife point-out, in brawling stance, against the vacuum of space.

But why the scroll? These priestesses are well known to us for their striking methodology, half clever half quaint: while the quantities of information they gleaned from their informant ghosts was massive, nothing was committed to paper, for paper had they none. It is a reasonable supposition that to a one they were in fact illiterate. So this constellation, gazing blankly out at us from a face it does not have, begs the question—why should the ghosts have borne this woman any loyalty at all? Had she gone turncoat? Shirked her bound and holy duty to enslave them? Flouted Catchkeep's law?

The only clue we have can be found in a strange fragmented text discovered with the Ragtree Chart, interred beneath that tree itself. (The tree in question is a crabapple, and a curious one. Thrice the size it ought to be, at one point it appears to have grown up through a sort of hut, its footprint approximately four paces by four, constructed of automobile parts and leather and stones: most of the leather is long gone, but the framework that once supported it, in minor part, remains.)

The text itself is in grievous disrepair, scrawled on a few palm-sized fragments of scorched paper crushed into a glass bottle of palest green. Interestingly, it appears to have been penned by two different hands: first in a dire penmanship, blocky and childish, which peters out as though in great exhaustion midway through; the writing that continues after, while legible and even flowing, gives the observer the unmistakable impression that its scribe was able to maintain only through great concentration only the most tenuous grasp on his writing implement (which appears to have been a pin or needle dipped in blood)—as though he, or it, were made mostly of air.

If we are reading the text in its proper order, it tells us how an Archivist of Catchkeep, name of Wasp, in a total upheaval of all of the ritual structures of Catchkeep's worship, challenged her keeper/overseer in single combat and bested him. Gravely wounded, she used the last of her strength to free all of the dead man's captive ghosts and destroy every last one of the Archivist tools (see fig. 7 for a replica of a typical field kit) by which those ghosts and others had been hunted and enslaved.

It is not known what became of her—whether she died in her blood on the dirt floor of the priest of Catchkeep's house or else somehow healed her wounds and went on to become the sort of patron saint for ghosts the evidence suggests.

In the end, every wildly disparate theory sinks its roots in the same pot: the proto-tale rather uninspiredly entitled "Archivist Wasp Frees the Ghosts." Wherein, after destroying Catchkeep's priest and all his tools, our mortally wounded heroine conjures Catchkeep herself down out of the sky and tricks the dog-god into suffering the newly-released ghosts to climb up upon Her back. From there they are borne, clinging on like barnacles, aloft into the night. Meantime, our retired Archivist and a single anonymous ghost (though some sources insist that there were two) remain to see that none are left behind, vowing to rejoin the others when their work on earth is done.

*And if they're not there yet,* as every version of the story always ends, *they are here still.*

# BEACH BUM AND THE DROWNED GIRL

## *Richard Parks*

The drowned girl was a corpse drifting to shore on the evening tide, her eyes wide and staring. The not breathing part of being a corpse was easy. She found that what really gave her trouble was not blinking. Unlike breathing, it was a habit she'd found very hard to break.

Her once-white dress was tattered enough so that it flowed and drifted with the current. Strands of seaweed tangled her pale arms and legs and a small crab nipped at her ear. She didn't bother to brush it away, even though its claws tickled. She could hear the surf rolling not more than twenty yards distant, from the sound of it, and she didn't want to give the game away.

A small shark circled her hopefully, but when it got too close something in its primitive brain fired a warning and it immediately flicked its tail and disappeared into deeper water. She almost smiled, but didn't think a smile was proper in a drowned girl. When the tide finally retreated, it left her washed up on the beach about ten paces from the surf, and there she waited with the patience of the dead to be found.

So patiently, in fact, that when someone finally did approach, she was dreaming of swimming alone through an ocean of stars and didn't hear him until he spoke.

"Excuse me, but were you going for horror or pity? I was just curious."

The drowned girl saw the young man leaning over her now, since she'd lost the trail of the comet she'd been chasing just a moment ago and her eyes now focused on where her body, at the moment, resided. The interloper looked young, about the age that the drowned girl appeared to be, and she knew in him it was just as big a lie. His hair was dark, his body tanned, his eyes older than the sands of Egypt.

"Excuse me?" she asked, pausing first to spit out a bit of sea water and a tiny periwinkle that had hitched a ride. She didn't stop to think how she could speak without breath, any more than she worried about why she didn't need to breathe in the first place. It was just the way things were.

"The effect of the tableau you've created," the young man continued, "What effect were you going for?"

"The effect is the thing," she said finally. "Not which one."

"I see. I just wondered because your eyes were open and staring. That's best for horror. For pity, the eyes work better closed. If it was me, I'd go for pity. Such a tragic fate for such a pretty young girl. You could work that."

"I'll keep that in mind."

Uninvited, he sat down a few feet away. The drowned girl turned her head to look at him looking at her. It was still dark there on the beach. There was a moon, but she didn't need it to see, though she thought the effect of the moonlight on the water was quite poignant.

She thought his presence somewhat rude, but admitted to a certain curiosity herself—it wasn't often she met one of her own kind . . . if by "not often" one meant "never." Since she existed, she did assume that others did, though this was the first proof of this assumption that she'd actually come across.

"My name's Damon. That is, I call myself that. I like the name. The people I meet call me the beach bum. Or rather, that's what they think when they think of me. Rather old-fashioned, but it suits me."

The drowned girl thought about it for a moment. "Lucia," she said finally, referring to herself. "Do you mind? It rather spoils the effect if someone comes across me and I'm not alone. I'm the drowned girl. I should be found alone."

"Don't worry, you will be. This is a stretch of protected shoreline. No one lives nearby and no one will come along until morning this time of year, and that's still an hour or so away. So. What happens then?" Damon asked.

"It varies," she said. "Sometimes they scream. More often they just stare, then run away to call more people over, and someone remembers to call the authorities, and police come and surround me and measure and take pictures, while a crowd comes to stare. Later I go in a plastic bag."

"Then what?"

"Usually to the morgue and to a cold place there. I stay for a while, and then I leave before the autopsy. I've never actually had one, but it sounds unpleasant."

"'Drowned girl's body disappears,' eh? Keep that up and you'll be a sort of urban legend . . . or I guess that's the point."

She frowned then. "What's that?"

"In your case, the pictures are there but no corpse, and it happens over and over. Sort of a Flying Dutchman of drowning victims. Essentially a story that almost everyone's heard and some believe, but isn't true."

"I'm true," she pointed out.

"Yes, but that doesn't matter. The legend is the important part."

The drowned girl shook her head. "I like it when they find me."

"Ah. So it's the attention you crave, yes?"

She thought about it and realized that entity calling himself Damon was probably right. She couldn't say why that annoyed her. "What's wrong with that?"

She wasn't looking at him just then, but she knew he was smiling. "Nothing," the beach bum said. "I'm the same way."

"What do you do?"

"I'm the boy they meet in the summer. The one who is at the beach every day. Where you're unexpected, I'm anticipated, often hoped for. Wanted, I think. I'm here when they want me to be. Someone usually does."

She frowned. "A beach bum. That's all?"

"I don't mind, because you'd be surprised how much that is. Consider—everyone remembers you, but in your case no one's glad to see you. When they recognize me for the first time, what I am or will be to them, they smile. I like it when they smile."

"Perhaps, but what about after?"

His smile turned a little sad. "The end is never as happy as the beginning, but one has to follow the other." He shrugged. "Some hate me. Some wish they'd never met me. And there are even some who remember me fondly. But, either way, and as with you, they all do remember."

"Otherwise . . . ." The drowned girl who called herself Lucia didn't finish the thought, but the beach bum would not let it go.

"What happens then?"

"I start to leave. There's a place where they are not. I swim through stars and chase comets there. It's beautiful, but it's lonely. I think I'm dreaming then."

He nodded. "Did they need us once, do you think? The way we need them now?"

"They need us still. Maybe not the way they once did; I'm not sure if I remember that part right. But they do need us. Otherwise, why are we here at all?"

"I hadn't thought of that," he said, wonderingly. "I think I need to."

"Suit yourself." She glanced toward the east. "The sun will be coming up soon."

He nodded. "Then I guess I should go now?"

"Goodbye," she said, and that was all, because it was time to be a corpse again. And, for a little while, dream of chasing comets. She remembered being lonely, but she did not remember feeling so much alone, the way she did now. That was new.

It was probably three years before the beach bum saw the drowned girl again. He looked down at her on the narrow beach, noting that she had closed her eyes. "Good choice. The pitiful look really works for you."

"Go away," said the corpse.

"Look around you," said the beach bum.

The drowned girl reluctantly opened her eyes. They were on the narrowest stretch of beach that could possibly hold a body. High, rocky cliffs loomed overhead, but trees grew at the top and there was greenery and vines wherever they could find a hold in the fissures of the rock.

"In a war not so long ago, people from the losing side used these cliffs to kill themselves by leaping into the ocean. People still use this place to kill themselves; it's become a tradition. No one except the authorities and the jumpers come here, and the ones in charge come along in a boat and pull you off the beach with a long hook and stuff you in a bag. I do not think they will remember you for long, so you might as well talk to me."

She stood up then, shedding seaweed, a marine snail, and one pathetic little puffer fish. She found a boulder half in and out of the surf and sat down. "Are you following me?"

The beach bum smiled. "I'm doing the same thing you're doing, in my fashion. I'm surprised we hadn't met before that last time."

Neither spoke for a little while. The beach bum leaned against the rock wall, the drown girl perched, mermaid-like, on her boulder. The longer she sat, the less corpse-like she became, and it occurred to the beach bum that she had never smelled especially corpse-like even that first time he'd found her washed up with the tide. He sniffed the air discreetly, but the only scent that came from the direction of the drowned girl was a strange combination of sea water and cinnamon.

"I can't do the full effect," she said. "If that's what you were wondering. I can't rot, even in the sun. I can't bloat or change colors. I'm always recently drowned, no matter how long it takes for them to find me. So. I wonder where I'll wash up next?"

Blushing slightly, the beach bum said, "The current here runs north. China, most likely."

She nodded. "I've probably been there, but I don't remember. How do you know about the current?"

"I'm a surfer, when I'm expected to be. We know weather and currents and where the waves are the best. What's it like?"

She frowned. "What's what like?"

"I'm by the ocean, but I'm seldom in it, except splashing around near shore. What's it like out there in the dark, far from land, drifting?"

"Peaceful, except when it storms," the drowned girl said. "Then I roll and spend a lot of time bobbing around under water. Mostly the ocean rocks me, and it's quiet, not like near land. That's when I sleep, and dream."

"Of comets?"

"And stars. That's where I am, then, until I wake up. But sometimes there are creatures beneath me making lights under the water. Blue lights and green lights, red lights . . . like I'm floating over the stars again."

"It sounds nice."

There was a brief silence, but it was the drowned girl who broke it. "So what's it like?" she asked then. "Being with someone, I mean."

"For a little while you're the focus of all their attention. At other times, they are the ones who are the focus of my attention, or at least I think that's how they perceive it, and it makes them happy. It's attention born of a deception either way. Sort of like what you do."

The drowned girl thought about it. "Deception. Yes, I suppose that's true. But you get to touch them. Or they touch you. Same difference. No one touches me if they can help it."

The beach bum got up and walked over to the drowned girl and he put his hand on her shoulder.

"I don't mind touching you," he said.

She almost smiled, like some great leviathan almost but not quite breaking the surface of the ocean. The beach bum thought he knew why. He didn't feel the same thing that she didn't feel.

"Something about us just isn't real, when we're away from them," he said finally, and took his hand away. "I'm sorry."

"Do you ever dream?" she asked, as if she hadn't heard a word he'd said.

"Huh? Oh, yeah. Sometimes, you know . . . between. Like when you're drifting on the ocean. When I'm least real."

"What about?"

He sighed. "The same thing you do. Sometimes I wonder what it means. I wonder why we dream of stars when we're less real."

"Are we really less real? I think it means that we are real, more real than we know, and the stars are waiting for us. Some day, when the reasons we're here don't make sense anymore."

The beach bum didn't say anything for a while. "It's a lovely thought. I guess one day we'll find out."

"One day," she said, but he knew her thoughts were far away from him, drifting on a nighted ocean, floating among the stars.

"My name's Damon," he said.

She shook herself. "What? Oh. You told me that already."

"I know, and thank you. But it may be a long time before we see each other again. I want you to remember my name until that happens. I want you to remember me. Can you do that?"

She took in a breath. She didn't mean to. She didn't even realize for a little while that this is what she had done. The drowned girl had forgotten to remember not to breathe. She let it go, feeling the warmth of it as the breath escaped her body. She wondered, just for a moment, what it would feel like for the beach bum to touch her then. She finally shook her head. "You said yourself that we didn't matter. Not to each other, anyway."

The beach bum hesitated. "And *you* said that we might be wrong. And if we *can* be wrong," he said after a while, "Why couldn't it be about something that matters?"

The drowned girl took another breath. On purpose, this time. "I'm Lucia."

"I'll remember."

"No you won't," she said.

He shook his head firmly. "I promise."

"You always say that."

"To *them*," said the beach bum, waving a hand to the rest of the world. "Not to you."

"I'm Lucia," she repeated, so softly that he wasn't even sure who she was talking to. Perhaps to him. Perhaps to herself.

The drowned girl closed her eyes, slipped into the water and drifted away. Later she dreamed of stars, and comets, and then of something else. She dreamed that some where, some when, some desolate stretch of sand, the beach bum waits. Damon waits for her. And he does remember.

# TRAP-WEED

## *Gemma Files*

*For their land-longing shall be sea-longing and their sea-longing shall be land-longing, forever.*
>    —An old legend of the Orkneys, concerning those seals who shed their skins to become women and men.

Any selkie can be Great, if he fights for it when challenged. We are by no means a democracy.

But for myself, I did not care to, and was driven forth, into deeper waters. So I swam until my fat and fur could no longer warm me, 'til the chill had almost breached my heart. I swam 'til my lungs gave out, then sank, deep into darkness.

When I woke, I found myself aboard-ship, peltless and doubly nude. A lean man stood looking down on me, his elegant face all angles, while others watched from behind, above . . . so many, for this creaking wooden shell to carry ocean-bound in safety. I had never seen such a number before, all in one place.

(For we stay as far from human men as possible on Sule Skerry, if we can, unless our instincts drive us otherwise. We know their works.)

I was gasping, painful all over, in strange places—burnt and scraped, as though I'd been dragged over rocks. Indeed, my arm had a chunk torn from it, neat and triangular—nipped straight

**70**

out at the point where it blended into shoulder, that same place I saw most mariners adorn with tattoo-work. I gaped at this a while, then tried to touch, and flinched from the sting of my own fingers' salt.

"I wouldn't do that," the man advised, without sympathy. "Call it the price of your salvation—a lesson either to keep to shallower waters or learn to hold your breath longer, when you choose not to."

Though it had been some time since I tried for human speech, I found it returned quick enough. "Where . . . am I, sir?"

And this he smiled at, grimly enough—no surprise there. Since in their hearts, most men like the pap they call courtesy, that sorry salve to their impossible pride.

"This scow of a brig's mine, by right of seizure," he replied, sweeping a contemptuous little bow. "*Bitch of Hell*, some call her, or *Salina Resurrecta*, since she's cobbled from shipwrecks. While I myself am Jerusalem Parry, captain: A pirate, as you suspect. You were *drowning*, meantime—a sorry sight, in one sea-bred. Yet Mister Dolomance here brang you up, before mortality could quite take hold entirely . . . and while I misdoubt he did you as little hurt in the performance of it as he might have, we must always recall how those he comes from are not known for their restraint, in general."

"Mister Dolomance?"

"Aye, that's he, hid over yonder, where he likes it best—you'd be dead if he hadn't found you, or if he was still able to do as he wished, instead of how I tell him to. For which you should, in either case, be suitably grateful." Fixing me with cold, pale eyes, then, like two silver pennies salt-blanched to the color of water-cured bone turned coral: "And what are we to call *you*?"

*You could not say it if you tried,* I thought. But since I seemed compelled to answer, I rummaged for the last human name I'd heard—the one that boy I'd pulled from his boat's kin had called after him, its syllables dissolving down through water into meaningless sound by the time they reached the cave where my sisters kept him tethered, forcing him to sire a fresh crop of younglings. What they did with him after I never witnessed, for I was already at the sparring by then, about to choose discretion over valor, exile over family. Indeed, it only now occurred to me, I might not see them again, in his company or otherwise.

In that moment I knew myself alone, entirely, lost amongst those who normally hate and prey on us—who either club us dead to steal our skins in error, thinking us only animals, or make away with them when we're foolish enough to leave them unguarded and detain us for *their* pleasure, breeding children who will never feel at home on either sea or shore. And so, seeing no other way out, for the time being—

"You may call me Ciaran, sir," I said, at last.

To my left, I heard the thing Captain Parry called Mister Dolomance give out with a disgusted little noise from his hidey-hole—half snort, half spit—and turned, abruptly far more angry than bereft, to confront whatever creature had dragged me up onto this rotting, lurching mass of timber held together mostly by barnacles and forward motion, at the still-sore price of its snatched mouthful of flesh.

I found him squatting on the weather deck in a strange nest made from two massy coils of rope with a tarpaulin slung overtop, keeping himself moist by angling into the splash from a nearby cannon-port's mouth. Standing, he would be half as tall as Captain Parry but a good two hands broader, squat yet sleek. With doll-eyes and an almost lipless mouth hiding a serrated bear-trap bite, he sported what some sailors called "a drowned man's pallor," close-wrapped to save himself from burning in direct sunlight. It was that sea-bed dweller's skin of his, I later found out, which had left me so raw, drawing blood from frictive angles on the very briefest of contacts.

*I know you now,* I thought, meeting that lidless black gaze, if only for a moment; he well might mock, since his own kind were known to scorn names entirely. So the fact that he answered at all to that mockingly polite and inexact one the Captain'd applied to him showed just how puissant this man's magic must be, when reflected in "Mister Dolomance"'s grudging obeyance, his infinitely resentful loyalty. Or, for that matter, the mere fact of Parry being yet alive, having not only bent this tadpole version of a Great White shark to his will, but forced it to assume a (mostly) human form, while doing so.

I have no doubt but that Mister Dolomance perceived both my terror and my pity, though his waverless glare rejected them both. And so we stood a while, locked in mutual regard: one cold-blooded, the other warm, doomed to meet for the first time in assumed shapes, confined to this creaking hulk. Me with my man-shape like a secret weakness revealed, as though I'd been forcibly shook inside-out; him with his man-shape imposed from the outside-in, never more than cruel illusion. For beneath it, he remained all rough muscle and horrid teeth, a terrible hunger, not even held together with bones.

Though we suffered the same privations, we could never be allies. I was prey to him, as much as any other thing without Captain Parry's power to protect it.

"Well, then, gentlemen," my captor told me, meanwhile, and Mister Dolomance as well—I could tell from the begrudging liquid grumble Mister Dolomance gave Parry back, by way of a reply. "Shall we retire to my cabin, and speak a bit further?"

And since there seemed no option *but* to go, I bowed my clumsy, fresh-made man-head, and went.

"I will trouble you for my skin, sir, if I may," I ventured, when the door was safely closed behind us.

By the look of his possessions and on closer examination, I gathered that Parry had once been of some quality, as humans reckon such things—regally slim, his fine hands sword-callused and ink-stained, not roughened with rope. If he went un-wigged, that seemed to be by choice; the hair thus revealed was still mostly brown, though shot through with hints of grey. There were also more books in his quarters than I had seen in my whole life, though grantedly, the sea does not treat such objects well.

But the Captain only shook his head. "No, I'll take care of that awhile yet, as I hold most of my crew's effects in trust for them. For we are none of us here entirely by choice, you see—not even me."

"Surely, though, it can matter little to you if I remain. I am no great hunter, like your . . . Mister Dolomance, there; my place is near the shore, not the open sea. And while some of my people have magic, of a sort, I am not one of them."

Parry sniffed again, prim as any cat. "I have all the magic I need already at my disposal, 'Ciaran,' and little liking for competition. You would provide me a very different service; less a tool to my hand than an object-lesson, for others."

"But what use can I possibly be of to you, bound *or* free, when you have one of the ocean's greatest nightmares sworn to your service already?"

"You undervalue your own impressiveness. My men fear me, and rightly, because I have a way with supernatural creatures, so adding a selkie to that roster cannot do me ill, even if it does me little comparative good."

Having no arguments left, I resorted to simply pointing out: "I . . . am no sailor, sir." To which Captain Parry gave merely a chilly smile, as though to say that was both of no matter and hardly a skill requiring great genius to master.

"Oh, you'll soon learn," was all he replied, and waved me away.

Thus I found myself press-ganged, after a fashion; I betook myself to the quartermaster and begged my share of the ship's labour, setting myself to it with energy, if not much effect. Yet the crew, on the whole, were kind—perhaps because they were sorry for me, a thing so far out of its place, if not its element.

And always I could just glimpse Mister Dolomance stalking attendance, following at the Captain's heels even while his gaze roamed after me. The farther we went from land, the happier he seemed, his sharp grin less a threat than a promise. While I wished myself increasingly back with my kin, fighting for supremacy I neither craved nor thought myself fit to hold, on that bloody rock; anywhere with land and sea alike, in close enough proximity to swim between.

As my despair mounted, I prayed outright to the eel-tailed Maid of the Sea (whose teeth are fishbones and whelk-shells, whose wet breath smells only of salt, and cold, and death), though She was far more likely to answer Mister Dolomance than the likes of me. But then again, my elders had taught me his kind do not trust in invocations to free them from mishap, if their own strength proves unequal to the task. For they are a harsh people, the sleepless ever-moving ones, even to themselves—unwilling to incur debts they do not wish to pay, even to the goddess who watches over all such wrack as we, the fertile ocean's muck and cast-offs. Its children, lost at sea, or out of it.

As time wore on, meanwhile, the quartermaster grew friendly with me, giving me leave to eat raw fish from the common net, and stroking my hair as I did. "Do not be sad," he would say; "the Captain will tire of ye soon enough, like any other toy he plucks from the deep. 'Sides which, were you bound for anywhere in particular? No? Then it'll serve you just as well to stay a while wi' us; just drift along, as if current-borne. See where *that* takes you."

"Do I have a choice?" I asked him, sullen, picking bones from my flat, blunt man-teeth. Only to have him laugh aloud at my bitterness, matching it with his own.

"Do any of us?" he asked me, in return.

The answer, of course, being no. We all existed entirely subject to the Captain's whim, just as he himself was inwardly consumed by a seemingly constant quest for novelty, sharp-panged as any mere bodily famishment. Those silver-penny eyes of his always scanning away at the horizon, seemingly incognizant of Mister Dolomance crouched like some lump of pure hatred made flesh at his side—though not so much *ignorant* of his closest companion's feelings, I eventually came to see, as simply content to ignore them.

Rumours followed Parry, as with any other fatal man, so I listened to them whenever they were offered, eager for any possibility of escape. "Captain's cursed, is what I 'eard," the second gunner said at mess, as the rum-cup was passed 'round one way, the water-cup the other. "'Twas laid on 'im 'ow 'e can't set foot on land . . . "

The first gunner, impatient: "No, fool, for I've seen him *do* so, to his cost—it's that he can't *stay* on land, or he starts to bleed."

"Aye," the quartermaster broke in here, nodding sagely. "I was there as well, that same occasion, and saw what come out—enough t'fill a slaughterhouse trough, and him so pale t'start with! Which is why he stays afloat, these days, and sends Mister Dolomance out scoutin' for prizes instead, settin' him t'bite through anchor-ropes or gnaw holes in some other ship's side. For it's wrecks the Captain wants, as we all know, and there's no earthly reason why he should be content t'wait for 'em to happen natural . . . not when he has so many other ways to make it so."

*But to what purpose?* I almost asked, before thinking better of it. Answering myself, as I did, with the sudden realization: *To cobble this ship of his ever-bigger with them, of course. To grow his kingdom—or increase his prison's capacity, at the very least.*

*Salina Resurrecta, Bitch of Hell; Parry's Doom* they called it, as well, whenever they thought him too deep-engaged in his arcane business to notice. A blot of a thing, literally engorged with flotsam from every prize it took and scuttled, hull gaping open maw-like at Captain Parry's gesture to suck in whatever items he—or it?—most took a fancy to. Thus it increased in size, steadily, over the months I spent as just one more item of that literally damnable vessel's cargo—sprouted fresh decks and hulling, masts and port-holes rabbit-breeding 'til the whole ship sat taller against the waves with a veritable totem-pole of figureheads to guide it, a corpse-fed trail of destruction left behind in its ever-widening wake.

I remember the Captain standing high in the fore-deck, shaking that hex-bag he used to raise fog and draw storms out into the wind, full to its brim with less-than-sacred objects. These I saw variously, at differing times, when he would reach in and withdraw them for specific tasks: A wealth of red-gold hair, braided and knotted nine times nine (this aided in illusions); some dead babe's finger, pickled in gin (he used it as a pointer, to navigate). An eyeball carved from ivory, set with the skull and crossed bones in fine black jet, was all that was left of the *Bitch*'s legendary former Captain Rusk, fashioned to replace one lost in battle and plucked from his barnacle-torn corpse after Parry had him keel-hauled, scraping him dead on his own ship's bottom-side—a trophy for luck, perhaps, though Parry sometimes raised it to his ear and gave that cat's-wince smile of his, as if it whispered advice to him.

But then there was an idol of dark wood, too, so gnarled one could barely ascertain its shape and studded all over with rusted nails, staining its weathered skin like blood—who had Parry stolen *that* from, and why? Bone fragments, sea-glass, scrimshaw, plus what I took to be a serrated tooth from Mister Dolomance's smile, knocked violently free at its root. And deep down, far beyond my reach, though I caught the occasional teasing glimpse of it, now and then . . .

. . . my skin, contradictory heart of all I was, reduced to one more fetish, one more weapon in Parry's arsenal. One more tool to bend the great Mother Mister Dolomance and I shared to his all-too-human will.

"*Who* was it cursed him, though?" I demanded, eventually, scrabbling for some sort of detail to use against Parry, some way out of this closing trap. To which the quartermaster replied, musingly—

"Now, that I can't say, young Ciaran. Only that it happened quick enough, without warning, some time after he first took the *Bitch* in mutiny, I think, and laid our old Captain down. So perhaps it was Solomon Rusk's work, not that I ever saw him do for any who rose against him with weapons other than sword and fist, previous. Still, keel-haulin' is an ill death, a singularly painful end . . . and it does give you time t'think on things, I can only s'pose, when you're down there under-hull . . . "

"How foolish he'd been to bring Parry on, in the first place?" I suggested.

A nod. "Maybe so. Rusk took him off a Navy prize, y'see—found him down in the brig like cargo, iron-collared, and knew him a magician bound for the next port of call, to face the King's Justice: be burned alive or hanged in chains, depending on the Admiralty's fancy. Those other blue-coats who swore the ship's Articles t'keep their lives were mightily afeared of him already, sayin' how he was accused of all manner of wizardous ill-doings—necromancy and doll-makin' and catchin' gales in a sieve, the way most sailors think only women do. But Captain Rusk, he wouldn't be warned away, not once his temper was up, or his interest piqued. He'd have a man-witch at his beck and call, or know the reason why."

"Most magicians die in the uncollaring, don't they?"

"Aye, for them rigs don't have locks, just seams—the witchfinders put 'em on hot and force 'em sealed, so's they'll waste all their effort one one last spell to keep from dyin'; Captain Parry keeps his cravat high for a reason, t'hide the scars all 'round his neck. But Rusk broke it open, with his hands; he was a strong man, and always knew the trick of twistin' where a thing was weakest."

"I 'eard this tale, too," the second gunner chimed in. "'Jerusha, I'll call ye,' he said, 'seein' you owe me all.' And Parry just snapped at 'im, like they was two gents in a drawing-room: 'Sir! I have not given you permission to use me thus, familiarly '"

"No, and he never did, did he? Though Solomon Rusk, bold bastard that he was, wasn't a one t'ever pay such niceties much mind . . . "

So Parry had begun in servitude himself, of the same sort he practiced on Mister Dolomance and me—a slave turned slave-master who, just like the shark-were, had no sympathy for his own past weakness, let alone the weaknesses of others. I *fought free,* he might say, if questioned; *do the same, if you can . . . and if not, stop your whining.*

(Yet for such a creature to base his power in the sea, where nothing is permanent, ever . . . not the shape of land, the ebb and

flow of tide, or even any clear distinction between what makes
one more itself than the other . . . )

*I think you court destruction, sir,* I thought, allowing myself
the very faintest beginnings of hope. And would almost have
risked a smile to myself, had I not been so afraid he might be
watching.

On those few brief occasions when we put ashore to trade,
restocking with food and weaponry, the Captain always
hung back, with only Mister Dolomance (who had an instinctual
distrust of anything under his feet which did not move according
to the ocean's in- and out-breath) for company in his watery exile.
And though other times women might come aboard, for the crew's
recreation, the Captain never indulged himself, though he might
have had his pick—being not only undeniably handsomer than
any other man on his ship, but having far better manners.

Instead, the two of them would retire early, and I would peep
in through the window's crack to discover them bent together
over parchment, Mister Dolomance squeak-gurgling away in
Parry's ear while his master scratched away furiously with
pencil and charcoal, checking and re-checking measurements
with various instrumentation. And slowly, I came to figure
they must be making a map together, hopelessly impenetrable
to any land-dweller's eyes: A grand survey of the ocean's most
uncharted areas, from the *bottom up.*

"He seeks for a place more land than sea, yet neither," was
the quartermaster's theory. "Only there might this bane of his
be lifted, and he find peace, if that's indeed what he's after."

"Do you doubt it?"

"With the Captain? Where he's concerned I doubt all things,
'til I'm told otherwise. 'Tis the best policy I've found, thus far."

I glanced away, just in time to catch my fellow captive—
listening too, as always—shoot me what passed for a smirk on that
mask-like parody of a human face of his, as if to say: *What fools!*

Indeed, it did often seem to me the crew barely knew whereof
they spoke, notwithstanding the fact they'd spent far more time
under Parry's rule than I had. And one way or another, for all my
researches, exactly nothing they—or I—had discovered about
him could in any way free me from my situation. I remained
trapped, his possession, his slave; yet still worse, for I was not
even of any great interest to him, of any particular *use.*

It galled me to realize this, almost as much as it galled me to realize I cared, either way. But perhaps Captain Parry was not altogether human either—partly dragon, maybe, for his twinned love of gold and fire, his magic, his damnable arrogance; partly wolf, for his love of blood.

Or he was just a man like any other, plundering this great sea-womb and stealing its children, using power he had no right to to bend our Mother herself to his selfish desires. Would that make things better, or worse?

I could not fight him, either way—not I, who had declined to fight even my own kind, against whom I might have stood some chance of success. So I must find some other, more subtle, way . . . think myself out of this trap, like the man he'd condemned me to pretend to be, instead of the seal I so heartily wished I still was.

So I thought, and thought again, and thought yet further. Until, at last—I found a way.

One night, while Mister Dolomance swam his own discomforts away in the sea below's black bosom, I threw a rope over the ship's side and shimmied far enough down to face my fears—plunged my face into the water and took a deep, drowning breath, opening my mouth wide enough to let words leak out, trusting the water to carry them to Mister Dolomance's ear-holes, translated thus into speech we might both understand.

*We must work together,* I told him, *to gain our freedoms.*

A gulp, and the reply came back, harsh even through silky fathoms: *Clumsy sea-cow in man-skin, born neither of one sort nor the other, you fat-greased, fleshy* thing! *What could you offer that* I *had any need of, save for enough of your meat to fill my craw, and your too-hot blood to wash it down with?*

I had expected nothing less, nothing more. Yet I spoke on, anyhow, and he . . .

. . . hard words aside, I could tell, even then: Mister Dolomance *listened.*

There was a long silence, after. So long I feared he might be swimming closer, too intent on an easy kill to truly mull my plan over.

But: *I accept,* he said, at last. Just that.

*Good,* I replied. And shimmied back up, before the crew might find me gone.

\* \* \*

We did not consult long, Mister Dolomance and I, in forming our plans; I knew from the start just how ill-suited by nature he was to be anything like the planning sort. Yet it is always in their desires that men make themselves most vulnerable, and though Mister Dolomance had surely never looked to, we both understood he had already gained far more insight into our captor's yearnings than I ever would.

So—having extracted such intelligences about the hungers which drove Captain Parry as my co-conspirator was capable of giving—it fell to me, instead, to find a way to turn their direction to our mutual benefit.

It was not so much that the Captain trusted Mister Dolomance (for in truth, he trusted no one, thinking no one equal enough to him to merit such a gift). Yet, as had already become rapidly clear, he placed a quite foolish amount of trust in his dominance *over* this awful creature, whose taming-by-force formed much of his own reputation.

"I think you are not entirely honest with me, sir," I heard him say, one evening, over those charts of theirs. "Yet so long as you do what I require, I find I care little what details you may think to withhold."

A mistake, on his part. And to not consider *me*, at all, in his equations . . . this was a mistake too, though he did not know it.

Not yet.

The *Bitch* made on, leading ever-westerly, with Mister Dolomance's grumbles our pilot's only guide for navigation. Islands grew scarce, and stores likewise; the crew grew unhappy, yet loath to express it. While Captain Parry kept his face carefully schooled, with only the dullish glint in those sea-burnt eyes to indicate a growing undercurrent of excitement—until the night when I saw him stride into the mess unexpectedly and swig lit rum from the communal store along with the rest, all of them too disconcerted by far to refuse him a part in their drunkenness.

Later, his back set against the fore-deck's supplemental mast while the crew reveled down below, I watched him stare out over the topmost figurehead's shoulders at the dark billows Mister Dolomance hid in, and mutter to himself: "Hell gape to take you, Solomon Rusk, if it didn't that day, the way it should have—you had no stink of the true practitioner about you, trained or un-, that I could discern. How was I to know it hid in your blood, any more than you did, waiting for that very last breath to bring your death's vow of ruin on me to fruition?"

Here he actually paused a half-moment; I swear I saw him listen, as to an invisible companion. Then grimace at nothing and reply, pale face suddenly touched with heat—

"'Nice as a divine' . . . yes, you *would* say that. But here is truth: You took liberties with me, though I warned you not to, and this is the result. Do not think to deny it! I swore you ship-loyalty, nothing more, but you were not the sort to stint yourself and you have reaped bitter fruit from that decision since, dead man. So you may complain all you wish when drink opens my ears, but I have suffered long enough for your sins, as well as my own. I *will have my place*, got for me with the sea's help, and you—you will have nothing. Now stop your mouth, before I prison your ghost in a bottle and sink you further still; from this instant forward you may watch but not touch, not ever again, and choke on the sight."

All at once, the humid breeze seemed to turn sharp-cold, blowing in one bitter gust from where the Captain sat to where I squatted, listening; I shivered to feel it pass by, as if touched by some strange hand. Behind us, meanwhile, the quartermaster took up with a chantey tune, fellow after fellow soon joining in as a bawling round. Quickly, I recognized in it a song usually attributed to Captain Kidd, here modified to fit a different, entirely predictable personage:

> . . . oh, 'Salem Parry is my name, as I sail, as I sail,
> The root of my infame, as I sail, as I sail,
> My faults I will display,
> Committed day by day—
> Damnation be my lot, as I sail . . .

For every legend, good or bad, warrants a song made from his exploits. But sailors are fatalists all, drowned men kept upright sheerly by luck's vagaries—and thus unlikely to stay long impressed by anything, or anyone, who claims to be able to cheat destiny forever.

> . . . So we'll taken be at last, and then die, and then die,
> Though we have reigned awhile, we will die—
> Though we have reigned awhile,

*While fortune seemed to smile,*
*We must have our due deserts, and still die . . .*

If Parry found the implication insulting, however, he gave no
sign of it; his fine-cut face stayed closed and stony, indifferent
as always. And his thoughts, now he was done discoursing with
Captain Rusk's ghost, remained his own.

The next day, we finally reached that place Mister Dolomance
had described to me—a great knot of weed flowering up from the
ocean's bottom, roots sunk two hundred feet or more, down to
the darkness where blue-clear water becomes mulch-black sand.
For even at its very deepest places, the sea too gives way to land,
eventually.

(And might this have been the worst part of old Captain
Rusk's curse, made all the more potent by his extremity—for if
there were truly no place without land, how could the ocean ever
be anything but a stop-gap, a salve between bleedings against
pain that never fully died? Which, in turn, perhaps explained
so much about Parry's manner, his stiff coldness, his constant
distraction; things become clearest in hindsight, always, after
the fact. *Long* after, most often.

(But since I am now coming near my own story's end, as
you can no doubt tell, I judge I too may well be falling into a
distraction. So I will take care to try and tell the rest of it through
without embellishment, from here on.)

We nosed in slowly, seeking not to entangle ourselves, 'til
the weed-forest's thickness made it impossible and we dropped
anchor as best we might, hooking it in the crook where three
branches grew together at the holdfast like ivy. Parry and a
small party took to the boats, following Mister Dolomance, who
merely gave that creaky laugh of his when Parry vented his
doubts as to where, exactly, he might be leading them. For once,
I felt I could tell exactly what he was saying:

*If you believe me capable of deception, wizard, even when*
*still so ensorcelled I keep this shape you've laid on me, then it is*
*yourself you make look bad, not I.*

At this, Captain Parry merely sniffed yet once more,
forbearing response—haughty as the Devil himself, if with far
less reason—and waved the oarsmen to their task, bidding them
into the weed's heart 'til all of them were eventually lost from
sight. The remaining crew stayed on deck, watching after with

weapons ready, lest their master send up some sort of signal for aid. But since I knew exactly what they would find if they only went far enough, I slipped down below and performed a few small tasks, while no one else was looking.

One boat came back, the quartermaster at its helm. "Captain wants ye, Ciaran-boy, and quick-smart," he called up to me. "To 'bear witness to his triumph', or some-such nonsense."

"Coming," I said, and was over the side a second after, not waiting on a ladder or rope; I hit the water with a splash and let the man haul me bodily aboard, all uncaring of how wet I got these ill-fitting clothes I soon expected to no longer have to wear.

The Captain's boat had moored, again by tethering itself to whatever was handy, right by a weed-clump so thoroughly knotted it had grown a sort of skin, fleshy-rough as any mushroom. A veritable floating island, such as crews tell tale tales of from one end of the sea to the other, never for a moment thinking to set foot upon its like in real life. And it was here that Jerusalem Parry already stood, boot-heels sunk just a bare quarter-inch into the spongey mass below; stood and swayed slightly, braced against pain, 'til he was sure no blood would come. Whereupon his bitter mouth finally stretched wide and he threw back his head to laugh, delighted as any child with the way his magic had brought him at last to that place he'd so long sought for.

"See?" he called to me, triumphant. "I stand victorious. Though Rusk stole the land from me, yet have I conquered; the sea itself delivers whatever I demand, no matter how impossible!"

"Mister Dolomance and myself, rather, to whom *you* now owe a debt of thanks."

Parry raised a brow. "Mister Dolomance has proved a treasured investment, undoubtedly," he admitted with surprising grace, "so much so I may even free him for it, one day. But you've given me little enough during your stay with my crew, aside from sullen looks and poor labour. Or am I mistaken?"

He thought to toy with me in his customary style, all aristocrat's drawl and fine vocabulary—as he'd done with Rusk, perhaps, who'd seemingly found it more attractive than I. But because I knew something the Captain did not, for once, I met his insults with a similar grin.

"As it ensues, yes," I replied. "For instead of giving, I have in fact *taken* something, without your notice."

"Explain yourself, sir."

I shrugged. "Wait, and see."

Out where weed gave way again to ocean, the *Bitch* floated low, lapped at by some gentle tidal gyre; we caught yet more music off its thronged deck, playing counterpoint to light laughter, scuffle and jesting. But all this changed a moment later, when—with a flash and muffled roar, like some cracked cannon's back-fire—its magazine, which I'd carefully set fire to before disembarking, went off, blowing her hull so far open her guts were laid bare. The mainmast went one way, the mizzenmast another, tearing wood like splintery paper; screams rose, as did smoke, and flames.

Had he been still on board, Captain Parry's magic might have turned the trick, but from here, there was no help for it: those careful bonds suturing wreck to wreck dissolved, leaving the ship itself to slide apart in chunks and sink, taking the bulk of his crew down as well.

Parry's smile became a snarl, his eyes two werewolf moons "You flotsam scum," he called me, words ground out between his teeth like bones. "God curse the day I ever let you on my vessel."

"Yes, and that was entirely at *your* pleasure, was it not? Well, I wish you full joy of that call, just as you once wished Rusk's ghost joy of his, when you thought no one was listening . . . and joy of this new home of yours, likewise, for however long your stay on it may last."

Caught gloating as only fools do, I was so puffed with my own cleverness that I barely registered Parry's hand slipping inside his coat, though I knew what it was he kept there. But when he withdrew the hex-bag, brandishing it like a pistol, I at least knew to shy away; the boat rocked sharply, salt spray slopping in over the side, prompting the quartermaster—shook from his shocked silence, and grabbing for his oars—to swear in three separate languages.

Still: "Not so much as I wish *this* joy on *you*," Parry told me, coldly. And upended the whole mess into the waves between us—bottle-finger, eyeball, hair-rope, fetish, tooth and all else, useless to him in his current cheated state, except as one last weapon. Since, at the very end, yet another thing more came slipping out to feed the churn . . . my skin.

*My skin.*

I must confess I almost went in after it, just on the off-chance, before I recalled what lurked in wait below. But then I caught sight of Mister Dolomance, still crouched in his captor's shadow, tearing away at his own parody-of-human disguise in a paroxysm of painful delight: mouth already ripped to either earhole with new teeth sprouting up along the bottom jaw in a bloody spray, muzzle punching out triangular, while his eyes—already far too widely spaced for comfort—migrated to either side of his head, losing their minimal ability to blink entirely. Shoulders hunched and splitting down mid-line, too, as his fin's long-buried crest at last came arching up between . . .

*All your bad works brought to ruin in the same instant,* I thought, staring Captain Parry down, straight in his silver-penny glare. *All you've sowed bloomed up full, sir, and ripe for reaping; well, I do hope you relish the taste of it, you sad fellow sport of unnaturalness. What little you can swallow, that is, before the end.*

Beneath the Captain's boots, the weed-island rocked and buckled, forcing him down on one knee. I watched it crack, pull apart at its weakest points, and remembered how Mister Dolomance had described the forest that supported it, where his kin (who do not of a custom flock, or even pair, at least for longer than it takes one to get a kit on another) glided so close they risked touching in order to graze the schools that fed on those mile-high weed-fronds. It was always twilight there, a purple half-night forever blood-tinged, the water itself heavy with rotting meat; a bed of infinite appetite upon which every prospective victim knew they would, at least, die full-stomached.

This was what Jerusalem Parry found himself momentarily balanced above—a chasm of open mouths, all waiting to take a bite, before what was left of him drifted to the ocean's mucky floor. Yet even as he summoned his last few shreds of power to stave that judgement off, if only for a breath, he opened himself to the surprise attack he should have *most* feared, all along: Mister Dolomance, leaping high in mid-spasm to bite deep into the Captain's unprotected nape, severing spine and the spell which kept him man-shaped alike. The shared arc of that jump threw them both sidelong, dragging Parry off-balance even as Mister Dolomance's legs shrank vestigial, once more fusing to form a tail; the weight of it put them down together with a great slap, waves gouting high, and slammed shut a blue-water door upon them both.

It was done, then—our revenge, complete—and Mister Dolomance surely got the lion's share of spoils, though *I* was the one self-condemned to live out a false man-life 'til laid in some land-bound grave. And since cowardice, at least, could never be counted amongst his sins, I somehow knew the Captain would go down fighting, to the very last . . . that image bringing me a variety of pleasure, at least, even as grief for my own losses cored my buried seal's heart.

The quartermaster pulled to with a will, meanwhile, and I took up oars as well, helping him put enough distance between us and the *Bitch*'s overthrow to make sure we were well out of range before the true frenzy began. After which we drifted, delirious with heat and fever, with hunger our only company; it occurred to me more than once, during this phase, that if I *had* managed to regain my true shape then the man I shared this boat with would have slit my throat long since, and be already picking his teeth with my bones. But thankfully, another ship picked us up before he could fully recall what lurked inside me, instead of thinking of me only as a boy—a tender thing, more his kin than not, to be protected rather than eaten.

"Ye're one of us now, son," was the last thing he spoke to me, which I know he meant kindly. Yet I just shook my head, waiting until he slept to steal what few coins he still possessed to pay my passage and roll him out through the sluices with a splash so quiet I reckon it was barely heard, either above-decks or under.

It was an impulse and no doubt an unworthy one, for I did feel bad after, if only a little while. But the feeling did not last long, confirming what I hoped was still true, even in my current skinless state: That we were *not* alike, he and I, no more than I and Mister Dolomance. That we never could be.

By ship after ship and voyage after voyage, sometimes spaced years apart, I made my long way back to the Skerry where I took up residence on the shore, gazing each day from cliffside across to the home I would never regain. I built myself a boat, and fished from it; I made myself a life, and lived it. At a midsummer dance, I told a girl my name was Ciaran, and married her. Our son became Young Ciaran, in his turn.

And then, one day, I pulled up my net to find a skin—*my* skin—inside it.

\* \* \*

Now it is late, and the fire is almost out. In the other room, Young Ciaran and his mother lie sleeping; my tale is told, in almost every particular. So I sit here and stroke the long-lost pelt spread out upon my knees, so soft, so durable . . . barely a mark on it, though my own hide has grown rough from ill-use, and not even a tear to show where the scar I once took from Mister Dolomance's teeth should be. Indeed, it reminds me of nothing so much as its polar opposite, my former co-conspirator's skin, which—like Captain Parry himself, as one man learned, to ill-profit—could hardly stand to be touched at all, at least from some angles, without danger of wounding. Never without cost, of one sort or another.

*Tonight,* I think, *I will go swimming.* And I smile, even knowing what probably awaits me, out there in the dark stretch of water between beach and Sule—something cold-blooded, grown huge as a bull in its far-roaming freedom, with little about it to indicate it was ever forced to walk upright, bowing and scraping at the whim of a man whose magic kept it prisoned in a shape it never would have chosen otherwise. For unlike my own kind, Mister Dolomance was only made to be what he is, not what he could be; his sort have no use for contradiction, let alone for metaphor.

Yet we are both equally treacherous, he and I—just as our Mother the sea is, in Her changeable yet unchanging heart. We cannot be overborne even by the subtlest magics, as Jerusalem Parry learned too late; we cannot be trusted, ever, even by those who love us. And as the sea is my home, so I will be proud to die there, if I must . . . more proud than I ever would have been to die on land, had I been forced to, as for so many years I was certain I would be.

Perhaps, though . . . perhaps I *will* fight, this time, the way I declined to, so long ago. Why not? What more do I have to lose?

Little enough, in the end.

The tide turns. The fire becomes ash. I rise. And here—in silence—is where I take my leave of all you who listen, closing the circle with these words: Just as any man may seize power if he consents to pay for it, by whatever method, any selkie *may* be Great, eventually . . .

. . . if he cares to.

# ICICLE

## *Yukimi Ogawa*

"You should stay," her mother said on the day of her departure. "You really shouldn't go. Things are only worse out there. Humans. Heat. Currents. And . . . Humans."

The daughter shrugged. "But I'm half human, an't I?"

"That," her mother heaved a sigh, which froze the moisture in the air into shimmering dust, "was the biggest mistake. . . . Not you. He was."

"I know what you mean. But. You know what I mean."

The mother gave another sigh, this time faint. "Yes."

The daughter hugged her mother tight, and then, iced tears rolled out of the mother's eyes, like mercury out of a broken thermometer.

"Go well, Tsurara, my dear," said the mother as she pulled back. "And be careful of the mountain crone."

The daughter nodded, and started to descend her way, through the forest, out of the mountain. Before and below her, the plain spread; beyond it, she imagined, the ocean that she had never seen.

Although she was half human and half snow-woman in blood, Tsurara turned out to be almost human. She couldn't freeze things to death like her mother, nor could she disassemble into a

snow storm and then freeze back into shape. All she could do as
a snow-woman was float high in the air and sleep in the clouds,
where the temperature was low enough so that every drop of
water remained as ice fragments; when she was conscious
enough Heat didn't bother her so much, but when she was off-
guard it could melt her for good (she had lost half her hair when
she was three).

Another peculiar thing about her was that she had an icicle
resting just beside her heart.

Her mother decided it was probably some mutant kind of
thing, and she blamed it on the girl's father, who was a human,
and who was a "pathetic, stupid thing" that wandered into
the mountain long ago. One day when Tsurara was less than
a year old, he left them without a word. "How could he?" her
mother would demand, usually of her fellow mountain spirits, or
sometimes even crows, who weren't really friendly to mountain
spirits but surely hated humans. "How could a father leave his
child with an icicle in her chest, constantly threatening to pierce
her heart?"

The heart itself was made of the year's first snow that fell
on the couple the day they met. It hurt easily when the tip of
the icicle touched it. When Tsurara was very small, all the
spirits who lived around her cave were always worried that her
icicle might stab her heart at any moment, and so they decided
to protect her. When she stumbled, one or two gusts of wind
always appeared from nowhere and supported her. When she
got lost, all the ghost fires in the mountain came to light her
way home, always keeping well away from her so that their heat
wouldn't irritate her skin. Even the mountain crone, whose best
recreation was to suck blood out of a human child and therefore
was despised by all other mountain spirits, left Tsurara alone.

They all loved Tsurara (except for the crone), for she was the
first child in a long time in the mountain. And they all (including
the crone) hated her human father. She grew up protected, and
was taught to hate her father.

One winter, when she was eleven or twelve, Tsurara found
a stray wind, crying behind a cedar tree. She instinctively went
over and hugged the little wind with her cold arms, and the wind
shivered but giggled, and thanked her for the coldness.

"I got astray from my family," the wind said, after rubbing its
already red eyes for a long time.

"Where are you from?" asked Tsurara.

"Ocean of the north." The wind shook happily at the memory. "We came up the mountain from the north side, and we were going down the south side all together, to the ocean of the south."

"What's . . . o . . . "

"Ocean? You don't know the ocean?" The wind's eyes were round. "Ocean is where all the winds and waters drift down to. Everything is blue there, but nothing's the same simple blue. Its surface is sometimes so flat that you could sleep on it for hours, and sometimes so rough that you could never bat an eye for days." It looked up at somewhere midair dreamily.

"Sounds like a very dangerous place."

"What's wrong with dangerous? That's how the world is, isn't it?"

Tsurara didn't know what to say to this. So she said, "Do you know how to get there? To find your family?"

"Yes. Down. Just down, and you'll always find the ocean. I got astray and I was feeling so lonely because I have to go down alone, but I'll find my family there for sure."

"Good for you." Tsurara nodded and smiled, still wondering why winds wanted to go to such a dangerous place.

"Thanks. And thanks again for the coldness."

The wind swirled around her once, and went as high as it could, then down the southern side of the mountain. As it went it gathered speed, and was soon out of sight.

That was when Tsurara started wondering about the ocean.

Years later, when she had learned not to let Heat bother her while she was awake without her mother's help, she decided to leave, to see the ocean for herself.

It took her months to persuade her mother. But in the end, her mother sighed her frost sigh and said, "I hate to say this, but sometimes you're so like your father. Your eyes are so much like his when you try to convince me."

"Are they?"

"That's the eyes that did it, I think, just before you were born . . . Anyway, there's no stopping you, is there?"

"No."

Her mother took the daughter's hands. Tsurara felt the comfortable coldness from the hands, and realized how much she would miss it.

\* \* \*

For the first time in her life, she was out of the mountain, was walking along a gravel road that cut through rice fields. The climate was too mild for her to feel comfortable; Tsurara had chosen a midwinter day for her departure, but without snow and with the Heat constantly looking down on her, her travel wasn't proving easy.

Before leaving, she had asked other spirits (like winds and foxes and racoons, who moved about rather freely) to tell her about humans and their lives. So she knew about cars and bicycles, but actually being almost run over by one was quite something. Tsurara panted, her chest aching and stinging, as a middle-aged man yelled at her from his van's window, something about kids these days not paying enough attention.

She wondered how long it was going to take. And if her heart would make it.

But once she decided to learn, she learned very fast, like a wind gathers speed as it glides down the mountain side. She soon learned to step aside as soon as she heard a car approaching, and then to walk on the edge of the road in the first place. And, by and by, she got used to surprises. Stray cats (who to Tsurara's surprise didn't talk) and plain spirits would dart out from here or there with no particular pattern or warning, and at first every time this happened she had to take a rest until her heart settled. She realized that surprises had always been there, they weren't there in the mountain only because her fellow spirits worked hard for her.

The next person she saw out of the mountain was an old woman who was carrying a huge supply of groceries, to whom Tsurara went over and helped on impulse, like she had embraced the young gust of wind. The woman smiled (humans smile!) and gave her a few rice crackers as a reward, and that was the first thing Tsurara obtained for herself.

She soon started helping people, carrying groceries with her cold hands that never made foods go sour, or showing people a safe way through a forest and across a river, with instructions from the local spirits. In exchange she would receive crackers and dried persimmons and bean curds, declining people's offer to let her share their pot of hot soup. At night she would float high in the sky and sleep among thin clouds, being carried away, from time to time, by Currents and getting lost. Her progress was slow, but everyday she was closer to the sea.

She came across a big town one day, and saw, as she floated that night to sleep, the ocean behind the high buildings of the town. At first she wondered what the strange plain was, because it wasn't blue at night and she didn't know that the ocean wasn't blue at night. But as she took a closer look, she could see that it was water rippling.

In a few days she was on the beach at last.

The sea spirits looked at her with curiosity. A white wave came to talk to her as she trotted into the cold water barefoot.

"Someone had been waiting for you," it said.

That moment, Tsurara noticed a boy walking down her way, along the line the waves were marking on the sand. She looked at him expectantly, but the wave hastily warned: "No, not him."

But before Tsurara could ask it who it meant then, the boy had reached her, had looked up, and then down, into her eyes.

"Snow is coming," the boy said, as if he had always known she would be there.

"Yes," replied Tsurara, looking up at the dear grey sky.

She demanded no explanation as she followed him to his small house, where he taught her how to clean fish, as if he were expecting her to stay with him for a long time. It seemed reasonable anyway, because her cold hands were perfect for handling raw fish. Only when he tried to touch her cheek, to rub the squid ink spattered there, she felt a sudden, sharp pain in the chest and crouched on the spot.

"What's wrong? What's wrong?" he repeated, utterly bewildered and panicked.

"My heart," she said, panting, "it's beating too fast. Let me have some rest, and I'll be okay."

The boy nodded, and watched as Tsurara knelt down on a cushion, as though he was worried that another touch might be fatal.

"My father died from heart attack a few years back," he said as he passed her a glass of water.

"I'm sorry," Tsurara said and sipped the water. It came straight out of tap and was reasonably cold, but not icy enough to make her feel better. "I don't have a father," she said at length.

"Everyone must have a father," the boy smiled weakly, and she realized she couldn't argue with that smile.

When her heart had settled and she was fit enough to eat, the boy asked her if she wanted her fish cooked, and she said no, she wanted them raw. But even fish were different from the ones from the river. She missed the slight scent of riverbed coming out of the meat and missed the icy water that came out of the rocks, instead of metal pipes.

The boy, on his part, tried his best to make her feel comfortable. When she said she had to sleep outside at night, he looked offended at first, but when she told him it was because of the heat from the stove, he cocked his head and frowned, but said no more.

"Tsurara, are you up?" In the morning he called out from the door to his hut, looking this way and that, not knowing where she had been during the night. She carefully descended to the back of the hut, and then approached him from behind.

"Morning," he greeted as he turned, "I have something for you." He indicated a huge linen bag on the floor beside the door.

In the bag Tsurara found ice cubes that smelt of fish.

"From the market," he nodded, when she looked up at him with delight. "I'll leave them here, in the cold, so you can come and fetch a few whenever you feel too much heat." Then he hugged himself, as a wind blew away all the warmth from him.

The boy smiled, trying best to not appear too eager to get back inside the hut, where the stove hissed. Tsurara wanted to hug him, but she knew her arms were too cold for him, and that her heart would beat too fast again.

For the first time in her life she hated the icicle, instead of her father.

The boy worked at the fish market nearby, where fish-stall owners and cooks bought fish from fishermen. While he worked, Tsurara wandered through the market's main building and found women repairing fishing nets and cleaning leftover fish to be dried or salted with guts. She introduced herself as the boy's cousin and joined them, learning more about the sea, and informing them, in exchange, when their husbands shouldn't go sailing even if the sea surface seemed flat, by translating the sea sprits' words. The women somehow took her seriously; the girl was too pale, too thin, not fit enough at all to tell that kind of lies, and one of them had lost her husband to the waves when the sea looked exactly the same.

After all, humans weren't that bad. And at the sea, humans and spirits were getting on fairly well with each other, though humans didn't know much about spirits.

As days turned into weeks, she thought of how she could make her heart stronger. She didn't expect there to be a way to remove the icicle, so she had to get along with it, but she didn't want to concede to it and give up other things in life. One day as she sat beside the boy, in a room that was too hot for her but was not warm enough for him, Tsurara reached out for his arm and pinched an end of his sleeve. He let her remain that way as he listened to the radio. A few days later Tsurara touched his hand, just the tips of the fingers, and another few days passed before she traced the lines on his palm. He never moved, to squeeze her hand or even to look at her to question; he simply waited, just as someone trying to feed sparrows with raw rice grains, without scaring the birds. It took them almost a week to entwine their fingers, and still she had to breathe harder and deeper as she looked down at the two hands.

At night she would put her hands on her chest in the middle of washing the dishes (it had become her job because she didn't mind cold water), and feel the slight lump there. Laying a cold hand on it soothed her, like her mother used to do to her when she was small. "Does it hurt again?" the boy asked from behind.

"No," Tsurara said, without turning around, "I'm only reminding myself that it's still there."

"Is it cancer?"

"No." She had learnt the word from one of the market women, and had thought, herself, that it was exactly like cancer, only she had to live with it forever, if she was to live.

"Are you scared?"

"No," she lied.

She heard him stand out of his flat cushion. She could feel his breath in her black, slightly wavy hair that was unlike her mother's very straight hair. She wanted to turn around and hold him, if she hadn't had an icicle in her chest. But now she couldn't blame her father; she was a creation of both of them, her father and mother, and without him, she wouldn't have been here in the first place.

The boy touched her hair a little, and turned away.

Her tears didn't freeze fast enough like her mother's. They formed icicles down her eyes, which scratched her cheeks and turned them pink.

One night she decided not to float in the sky. She slid into his futon and held to his arm tight, and the uncomfortable warmth kept her awake all night. The next night he held her; her harsh coldness kept him awake all night. Then the next night they kissed, warmth and coldness mingling on their lips, and she let him feel for the tiny, icy lump in her chest. He groaned as if it hurt him.

The next night, Tsurara no longer cared about her icicle.

Her heart flinched from the icicle's sharpness, but she concentrated more on the pain as he entered her, as his warmth warmed her icy body from inside. She felt her whole body becoming too hot, like even the Heat in the sky could never have done to her. She felt her icicle stab her heart and gasped, and clung to his neck and stopped breathing; he held her tighter and knocked all the breaths out of her, and let her believe for one second breathing was needless. She thought she was going to die, and she no longer cared. But then, something happened in her chest.

The icicle, which had always been there, which had always threatened to pierce her heart, melted and flowed into her veins. Her overheated body was now being cooled down.

The two of them felt her heart beating strong, so strong like it had never done, without the icicle that had always been suppressing its strength. She had thought her heart had been made of soft snow to the core, but now she learned the core was made of crystal, that had been materialized and nurtured by the mountain, and born to life by her mother and father. The soft snow, which had wrapped it all this time, dissolved and helped her body cool. The crystal heart no longer hurt—no, it did hurt, but for a different reason.

Later in the complete darkness, they held tight on each other, and she listened as he started to talk. "You remind me of an old tale that my father used to tell."

"Did he tell it to put you to sleep?"

"Right. Do you want to hear it?"

"Yes."

The boy shifted, and let her rest her head between his arm and his chest.

"Once upon a time," he started quietly, "there was a farmer deep in the mountain. He loved a woman and they had a kid. They were happy, only, for some reason, the wife wouldn't let him sleep in the same cave that she and the child slept in.

"One day as he worked, he came across a horrible-looking old woman, who had a huge cooking knife in her hand. His wife had warned about this crazy woman, told him not to go near her. But it was too late.

"'Are you going to eat me?' he said.

"'You are the one who eats,' the woman said. He asked what she meant. She said, 'your wife is a snow-woman. So is your child. Your heat is going to melt them down to death.'"

Tsurara flinched at the word "snow-woman." The boy didn't seem to notice—or if he did, he covered it by pulling her tighter against him.

"'That's why she wouldn't let you sleep in the same cave,' the woman went on. 'You are too warm. You must leave them, if you want them to live.'

"So the man left. He came down the mountain and to the sea. He became a fisherman, and worked very hard so that he would forget his wife and child."

"Did he?"

"No," he said, stroking Tsurara's hair, "he met a woman near the sea and they had a boy, but his family in the mountain always haunted him. He even wished the snow-woman would come see him out of the mountain, like in the old folk story."

"How does it end?" Tsurara asked.

"I never found out. If the man lived happily ever after, or if he was frozen to death by the snow-woman. Funny, but I don't even remember why I never did."

Tsurara slowly nodded in his arms.

"But this snow-woman," he hesitated here a little. "Don't you think it sounds a lot like you? I thought, when I first saw you," now his voice was shaking and the chest boomed uncomfortably, "the snow-woman finally came out to the sea."

Tsurara was silent for a long time, and he wondered if she had gone asleep. When she finally spoke, her voice was calm; so much so that the boy might have felt ashamed that his own voice had been so tingly. "Are you scared of the snow-woman?"

"No. I'm scared of what might be the truth."

Her tear-icicles formed and then dissolved onto the boy's warm skin. "Mountain crone."

"What was that?"

"Mountain crone," she repeated, looking up into his eyes. "She made him go."

The boy said nothing.

She had always known—both of them had probably known from the start. Him from his father's old tale, Tsurara from his name, Yukio, which had *yuki*—snow—in it; she knew, because there was a strange waviness in his hair at the back of the head, just like her; because they had the same obsidian eyes, which her mother often stared into and sighed, as if longing for something too far even to miss.

"Your father," she said.

"My father?"

"Is my father."

Tsurara could see many things creep into Yukio's eyes: confusion, sadness, and perhaps even conceding. "But it's impossible," he said anyway.

"It's not."

It was a statement, not an answer, nor a doubt voiced. Tsurara explained who she was, where she was from, and then, slowly and painfully, he understood.

So they wept. They feared, but waited, for the dawn to come.

"Will I never see you again?" In the morning he hesitantly asked, but he didn't sound like he wanted an answer.

"I don't know," Tsurara said, shaking a bit in the bright Heat, "I might leave the mountain again someday, now that I'm stronger. But first I have to go back, and tell the truth to Mother. Then Mother and I'll both have our revenge on the mountain crone."

"Right."

Then she departed without looking back. She knew where to go: Up. She would even run, as fast as she wanted, oblivious of all the warnings she had heard all her life. With a chest no longer inhabited by an icicle, with a heart that was stronger, she would embrace her mother and tell her that they had both been loved.

# LESSER CREEK: A LOVE STORY, A GHOST STORY

## A.C. Wise

Standing on the trestle bridge, a boy and girl stand side by side. They can just see the water through the trees. Directly below the bridge, abandoned rails curve gentle to their vanishing point. Weeds grow between the cracked ties, and two children walk, kicking stones along the track.

On the bridge, the girl looks at the water. Lesser Creek. It seems familiar somehow. The greenery does its best to swallow the sparkle and shine, keeping the light at bay. But all along the bank, running parallel to the tracks, muddy paths cut through the growth, and run down to the water's edge. Hoof-paths, paw-paths, and foot-paths, carve gaps in the green. They are made for stolen sips and stolen kisses, midnight swims, and midnight drownings.

She remembers fireflies.

Maybe it wasn't this bend of the creek, but some other. She wants to remember blue shadows between the trees, and the secret-wet smell of earth, bare feet trailed in cool water, and luminescent bugs flashing Morse-code transmissions from another world. And so she does. Who's to say her truth is wrong?

"It wasn't always like this, was it?" Memory nags, and she asks the question, wishing she didn't have to break the silence that has stretched between them for so long.

**98**

The boy beside her watches the children's dwindling figures, following the rails.

"Do you think we could catch them all?" he asks.

For a moment she thinks he must be talking about the fireflies she wants so badly to remember. But his past isn't her past; his memory is other-wise, and as inconsistent as hers. Who knows what meaning the creek and the rails hold for him?

Side by side on the bridge, the boy and girl are roughly the same age: fifteen, sliding backward to ten and upward to twenty, depending on who is looking. It is the age they've always been, for as long as they can remember. Which isn't very long.

She remembers fireflies, and sometimes, she remembers drowning.

She looks at the boy side-wise, wondering how he died. *If* he died. Have they had this conversation before? She picks up a stone, weighing it a moment in her palm before letting it fly. It pings the steel, reverberating like the memory of trains.

Maybe one of the children looks back at the sound, and maybe they don't. Everyone knows these woods, that bridge, these rails, that water, are haunted.

The girl picks up another stone, frowns, and closes it in her hand.

"Will we bet, then?" she says. This seems familiar, too.

"Yes, A bet," the boy agrees. "And a tally, on that big rock in the water."

He points through the trees; she knows the stone—a big boulder planted firm in the creek's middle, dividing the current.

"At the end of the summer, we'll count up the marks, and see who wins," the boy says.

A cicada drones. The sound means heat to her, summer-sweat and irritation so sharp she can taste it. She shivers all the same. It won't take much for the boy to win, between the airless nights and the far worse days, the sun beating down on everything and pushing people to the edge. She bites her lip, but she's already nodding.

The rails, stretching one way, lead to the horizon, and in the other, they lead to a town. It nestles around a vast crossroad, and maybe, for that alone, it's cursed.

Could it be the town that calls them, again and again, this boy, and this girl, in their myriad forms? Or does the town exist because they come here again and again to stand on this bridge, over these rails, beside that water, to bet on the town's souls?

The town has never borne her any love, the girl thinks. Not for the boy at her side, either. She should take joy in the reaping, but she never does. There is a hunger in her, a hole deep at her core; it is in her nature to wish that hole full.

She isn't greedy. One soul, just one soul, ripe and sweet as the last summer peach, might last her all winter long. She looks sidelong at the boy beside her, and breathes out slow.

"Deal," she says.

"Deal." The boy spits in his hand.

The devil's own twinkle shines in his eye. They shake on it, and go their separate ways.

And so the summer begins.

The first time you see her, you think: *She isn't real.* Because you've lived in Lesser Creek your whole life, and you've never seen her—never even seen a girl *like* her—before.

Your second thought is: *She's a ghost.* Because everyone knows these woods are haunted, and didn't a girl drown here years ago? All the stories say so.

She's sitting on a wooden bridge over the narrowest part of the creek. Her legs dangle over the water; one hand touches the topmost rail, fingers curled as if to haul up and flee at any moment. Her hair screens her face, but you know she's chewing her lip in concentration. Just like you know exactly what color her eyes are, even though you haven't seen them yet. They are every color you can imagine, and so is her hair. Because even looking at her full-on in the sunlight, you can't tell anything about her for sure.

She is definitely a ghost.

You sit next to her, legs dangling beside hers, close, but not touching. Your mismatched laces trail from scuffed shoes. She doesn't flee, and so you say, "Hey."

You say it carefully, not looking her way. You think of a deer, ready to be startled, though she's nothing like that at all. She could swallow you whole.

Where she sits, the air is cooler, like the deepest part of the creek, where the sunlight doesn't touch. Viewed side-wise, you can see right through her. Her skin is blue, her hair moonlight, and you just *know*, when she finally turns your way, her eyes will be stones, and her lips will be stitched closed. And you decide that's okay.

Then she *does* turn, dropping her hand from the top rail to the sun-warmed wood, almost touching yours. And she's as real and solid as you.

"Hey," she says, and smiles.

Nothing changes. She isn't real. She can't be. Because girls like her don't smile at you. They frown, and they're suddenly very busy, always with somewhere else to be when you're around.

*This* girl smiles at you. So she must be a ghost, even though the sunlight catches the fine down on her legs and turns it crystalline. You know it's a lie. The hair brushing her shoulders, the shadow in the hollow of her throat, the peach-fuzz lobes of her un-pierced ears, and the scab on her left knee—these are all a skin stretched over the truth of her. She is a hungry ghost, and she will devour your soul.

And you decide that's okay, too.

She tells you a name that isn't hers. You give her one in return. The water murmurs, and you talk about nothing. Time stretches to infinity.

Maybe, just maybe, her fingers brush yours when she finally stands up to leave.

"Will I see you again?" you say, hoping your voice isn't too full of need.

She doesn't answer, but her teeth flash bright in a nice, even row.

And so your summer begins.

The first murder occurred on a Tuesday. Or rather, it was discovered on a Tuesday, but the body had been cooling over two weeks, based on the flies buzzing over the sticky blood, and the discarded pupa cases nestled in the once-warm cavities.

Crime of passion. Scratches, bruises, evidence of a struggle, but none of a break-in. Spouses—one dead, one fled.

On a Thursday, the missing spouse turns up two counties over. A confession ensues.

Outside the county sheriff's office, the boy from the bridge leans against sun-warmed brick, and smiles. He chews bubblegum, shattering-hard, packaged flat in wax paper with trading cards. Collectors throw away the gum, keep cards. Not him. He savors the dusty-blandness, the unyielding material worked by teeth and tongue until it bends to his will. He throws the cards away, precisely because he knows they will be collectors' items one day.

He listens through an impossible thickness of brick, plaster, and glass to the blubbered admission of guilt. There are tears; he can smell them, even over the cooked-hot pavement crusted with shoe-flattened filth. It smells of summer.

Sweat and stress and a tipping point—all the ingredients he needs. A beery night, a whispered word, a suggestion of infidelity. A death born of rage. This is the way it's always been. His finger, the feather, the insubstantial straw snapping the camel's spine.

The boy pushes away from the wall. Struts, hands shoved deep in too-tight, acid-washed pockets. Hair, slicked back. He might have a comb tucked into one pocket, or a pack of cigarettes rolled in one white sleeve, depending on the slant of light that catches him.

He commands the sidewalk. Dogs, children, old men, fall into step behind him. Old women *tsk* from the safety of their porches. Young girls, well, it's best not to say what they do.

He heads west, strolling past scrub-weed and abandoned lots to the fullness of wild fields, cuts left to the creek.

He shucks shoes, wades in, and lays a hand against the massive boulder splitting the water. It is graffiti-strewn, perfect for sunbathing. Perfect for other things, too.

The boy chooses a sharp-edged stone from the current, and makes a single mark on the boulder's side—a white line on the grey.

His summer has just begun.

This is what the world tells us about girls: They are always hungry.

They are cruel.

They will suck out your soul, and leave a dead, dry husk behind.

They will laugh at your pain.

That's why we stitch up their mouths with black thread. We cut out their eyes, and replace them with stones to stay safe from their tears.

This is what the world tells us about boys: They are hungry, too.

They grab food with both hands, stuff it in their mouths, careless of what they eat, never bothering to chew.

They are too loud.

They break everything around them, without even noticing it is there.

That's why we catch them by the tail, so they won't turn around and bite. That's why we cut off their heads, fill their mouths with dirt, and bury them at the crossroads. That's why we burn their hearts, because unlike girls, we know they'll never feel a thing.

It is all true, and every word is a lie. Don't believe anything anyone tells you about ghosts or devils.

The second time you see her, you think: *This can't be real.* Because it's too perfect. It's the Fourth of July, and you're at yet another bend in the creek. (With her, it's always water.)

The grass is dry, but it remembers rain. The creek—angry here—smells of mud, death, and time. Things have drowned here. Things have been swept away and forgotten. Things sink, and sometimes they rise. But you take the water for granted; you always have.

A bonfire leaps high, smelling of meat and burnt sugar and wood. There are fireworks, fractured light captured and doubled, each boom-crack echoing your heartbeat and reverberating in your bones.

You are surrounded by people you see every day. They live behind counters in the local stores; they line porches, and spit tobacco; they drive the bus carrying you to school. Except tonight, they are strangers. Tonight they are demons. And in a world of strangers and demons, you latch onto the only girl you've never seen before. The only one you know for sure isn't real.

She is solid and warm. The fireworks stain her with cathedral window colors. She smiles, and her teeth turn crimson, emerald, and gold. She is fierce and wild, too hard to hold. But you take her hand.

She leans her head on your shoulder. Her hair tickles your skin, and you smell her above and beyond the campfire, which is black powder and pine needles. She smells of soap and smoke, but also of water, of deep and sunken things. It's a creek smell, and breathing it is drowning, but you do it just the same. You think: *This is love.*

It's the Fourth of July, but *this* is where summer begins.

There's a story they tell in Lesser Creek about a girl who drowned. She had just turned fifteen, or seventeen, or twenty-one.

Just shy of fifteen, she was sad all the time, without ever knowing why. There was nothing wrong with her, other than being fifteen—a world of tragedy in its own right.

The girl was hungry constantly, and never full. When she simply couldn't stand it anymore, she went down to the creek, filled her pockets with stones, and lay in the deepest part of the water with her eyes open until she drowned.

If you go to just the right spot, where the water is the coldest and your feet don't quite touch, you'll hear her. It's hard to be still, treading water, but if you hold your breath, make your limbs only a fish-belly flash in slow motion, never rippling the surface, she'll whisper your name.

These woods are full of ghosts.

Near twenty-one, she was a farmer's daughter. She got in the family way, and her parents locked her up, and forced her to carry the child to term. Maybe the baby was still-born, and maybe she delivered it screaming, bloody, and alive. Either way, she ran away the night it came.

She ran to the trestle bridge, and threw the baby off just as a train went howling past. Who can say which wailed louder, the baby or the train? Overcome by guilt, she threw herself after the child. Her body rolled down the slope, and the creek carried it away.

If you stand at the very center of the bridge and drop a penny, when it lands, you'll hear a baby cry. Except sometimes it's the lonely mourn of a train vanishing toward the horizon. And sometimes it's a girl, just shy of twenty-one, weeping for her sins.

At seventeen, she was murdered. Her killer cut out her eyes, and replaced them with smooth stones. He stitched up her lips with black thread, and left her in the shallowest part of the creek where the water barely covered her.

The stories say her killer was a drifter, or the devil himself. They say he confessed the same day the murder was done, screaming it all over the town square. When everyone came to see what all the fuss was about, he wept, inconsolable.

He cut her eyes out, because she wouldn't stop looking at him. He sewed her lips shut, because she wouldn't stop whispering his name. They hanged him just the same.

All of these stories are true. Every one of them is a lie.

The girls of Lesser Creek leave flowers for the hungry ghost at the water's edge, and burn candles in her nameless name. The boys bring pretty toys, and line them up all in a row. The old women bake oat cakes, sweetened with blood, and the old men mumble prayers. Each brings their hopes and fears, and such desperate love.

No matter what they bring, the ghost is hungry still.

The second murder comes late July. In-between, there are a string of assaults, a petty theft, one count of grand larceny, and a host of undocumented sins.

The boy follows the hoof-paw-shoe-hewn path through the branches to cross the shallow water near every day. He can do that, no matter what the stories say. The wavelets glitter bright, wash sweat and grime from his skin. His toes grip slick stones, and he never falls.

He makes another mark on the boulder's side. They multiply like rabbits, like flies. They turn the grey stone dense and arcane. There is power here not found in the other graffiti. And the stone itself is rife with meaning, too—stolen kisses, secrets trysts. Oaths are sworn here, fated for breaking. It is all his doing. Or so the oath-breakers and kiss-stealers say. He drove them to it; it's what devils are for.

He has a tally of at least a dozen-dozen, and it is only July. The girl's space is empty.

He watches her, sometimes, courting her soul slow, taking her time. She is hungry; the boy sees it in her eyes. But sometimes she smiles.

And when she does, he realizes his belly is empty, too.

The marks on the stone don't fill him like they should.

Once upon a time, he was a musician. Once upon a time, he was good at cards. He was driven out of town, beaten with a stick, hung at midnight. His heart has burned countless times. He has tricked and been tricked, loved the wrong man and the wrong woman. It is always the same in the end.

Once upon a time, he walked the rails. Once upon a time, a canvas strap bit his shoulder, soaking sweat, gaining dirt. Walking, he ran. He trusted wrong, sleeping in open boxcars, warming his hands by vagrant fires. He gave too much of himself away. He swapped stories, and accidentally told the truth.

He found himself dead, spit dirt from a shallow grave, and walked again.

He jumps on stumps and has a quick hand. Dice and cards always fall his way.

Even though the marks crowding the stone aren't as triumphant as they should be, the boy makes another one, and drops the sharp stone. The creek vanishes it, a card up a magician's sleeve.

This is what the boy and the girl both know, even when they made their deal: It isn't fair. They have been given roles to play—ghost and devil, hungry to the very end.

The summer ticks past, far too slow.

There's a story they tell about the time the devil came to Lesser Creek. The townspeople chased him all along the rails. They caught him, and killed him, cut off his head and buried it upside down. They drove a spike through the ground to make sure he couldn't pick it up again.

But will-o-wisps still drift under the trestle bridge in the dead-black of night, the devil's own lanterns, leading the damned to the water's edge. And if you walk along the ties at midnight and count thirteen from the moment you pass under the bridge, you'll hear the devil breathing behind you. If you take one step back, you'll find the twelfth tie missing and he will reach up and drag you down to hell.

The first time the devil came to Lesser Creek, he was just a boy, no more than seventeen. He committed a crime, or maybe folks just didn't like the way he looked at them. Maybe the summer was too hot, and tempers were too short.

Even though he looked just like an ordinary boy, they pulled up rail spikes, and nailed them right back down through his feet and his hands. When they came back after three days, the body was gone.

No one brings flowers or blood-sweetened cakes to the old rail line. When old women pass, they spit, and old men still drive an iron spike between the twelfth and thirteenth ties on moonless nights to this very day.

It is a lonely place.

When the devil came to Lesser Creek the second time, he made a deal with a drifter who dared to skim stones along the steel rails just to hear them sing. If the man brought the devil twenty souls by summer's end, his own would be spared, no matter how he sinned.

It was a mass-murder summer. A fire and brimstone summer. Preachers thundered through the churches of Lesser Creek, damnation heavy on their tongues. The air clotted thick; wasps drowned in sweat, humming between the pews and banging their heads against the stained glass. Birds fell from trees, hearts baked within the delicate cages of their bones.

All the fans stopped turning. Ice cream sizzled before it could touch the cone. Soda went flat in every fountain. Cold water forgot to flow, except in the creek where no one dared go. Wives beat their husbands; fathers cursed their daughters. Boys burst into tears for no reason and kicked their dogs.

And the drifter came, and the drifter went, and bodies piled like leaves in his wake. No one could ever say if he did the killing, or not. But every man, woman, and child in town swore up and down they heard laughter echoing along the train tracks, and it was the devil's very own.

The next time you see her, you *know* she is a ghost, because she kisses you. And girls like her don't kiss you.

You are sitting side by side, hand in hand, by the creek, always by the creek. Her feet are next to yours, relaxed where yours are tense. Your footprints sink into the mud. Hers are ephemeral, and disappear.

You grip her hand too tight, and sweat gathers between your palms. Planted in the dirt, feet in the current, you look toward the rock snagging the center of the stream. Graffiti scores it. It is a magical, mystical thing; a totem centering all the summer days in danger of flying off the edge of the world.

How un-solid these liminal years of your life are. At any moment, at every moment, you are in danger of losing cohesion. The rock in the center of the stream is eternal. It says *X was here*, and that is real—tribal and shamanistic. Written in stone it can't be denied. If you vanish, the rock will remain, a record of your being.

Here and now, she kisses you, and it grounds you, too. It is the culmination of a summer's worth of desire. It is the inevitable consequence of bridges and fireworks and the muddy banks of creeks. It is the only outcome of frog-song and bug-drone, and all the other milestones of the season.

And she says, or doesn't say, but you hear, "All I want is one little piece of your soul. It won't hurt, not yet. You won't even know it's gone until much later. One day, you'll wake up, not in love with me anymore, old, and looking back on your life, and wonder where that part of you went. It'll sting for a moment, and you'll move on. Is that so bad?"

Her fingers lace yours, and the whole time she looks at the water, not you.

She says, "I'll fill you up with me, so you'll never know anything is missing."

She pauses so you think she regrets what comes next. It's what you've always known was coming since you saw her on the bridge.

She is a hungry ghost.

Here and now, you love her for her pity. You pity her for her love. It isn't fair. And so you forgive her, because you've been hungry, too.

She says, "Before you agree, understand that if you give me that piece of your soul, it's mine forever. That's how love works. It consumes you. The moment it ends, you can't see past it to a day down the road when you won't be split open and bleeding for the whole world to see. In the wound, you can't see the scar, or even the scab. Memories and hindsight belong to the future. This is here, this is now."

You know how this will end. You have always known how this will end.

You hold her hand, tighter than you've held anyone's hand before, and you agree. You give her your soul.

The summer seems very short now. You have so little time.

A third murder rolls around mid August, but it holds no joy. The boy is winning by default. He longs for a reversal, a revolt, a turn of fortune. He longs for a trick to grab him by the tail.

He never asked for this, no more than she did. He is a ghost, and she is a devil. The woods have always been haunted, and so have they.

Vandalism. Arson. A near-murder that doesn't quite take. He whispers temptation. He pours jealousy, hate, venom, all into willing ears. In the end, he's powerless. So is she. They only take what the world gives them.

He makes another mark, drops the stone in the water. The creek chills him. He wades to shore, wishing the summer would end.

She tells you it is over.

She told you; she is telling you; she will always be telling you. And. It. Is.

Welts rise on your skin. Psychological, but so real.

Of course, it had to happen this way. Nobody loves you, ever loved you, ever will. And part of you knows, bitter, that you are being oh so dramatic, so you laugh. But you cry, too. She warned you, told you what she was doing as she did it, but you handed your soul over anyway, because you wanted it so goddamned bad.

Even though, deep down, you know, godfuckingdamnit, you will never be good enough to be loved. Someone else will always win, always be better than you. You will always be hungry, while everyone else is full.

So you walk the trestle bridge, where you can just see the water. You think about the summer, all the people who died, lied, cheated, and stole. The whole fucking town is going to shit, but what do you care? And what would they care if you jumped right now?

They probably wouldn't even notice you'd gone.

But you don't. You won't. And you turn away.

And maybe someone looks back at the sound of something heavy never hitting the rails. And maybe they don't. Because everyone knows these woods, that water, those trees, these rails, are haunted anyway.

She makes a mark on the stone, one shaky line. He stands on the shore, arms crossed, watching. He wants to smile, but it makes his cheeks hurt, as if the rock-hard bubblegum left splinters in his skin. His feet, planted in the mud, ache. He remembers running; she remembers drowning. In the end, it is the same.

In this moment, he loves her for her pity, and he pities her for her love. Could she, would she, ever pity him?

By the stone, she wants to weep, but she smiles, and it tastes of tears. She looks at him, standing in a slant of sunlight, watching her.

One soul, her tally.

He reaches for her, their fingers almost touching.

It is never enough.

His side of the stone is crowded; she has one single soul to her name. It is sweet, oh so sweet, but it won't sustain her to winter's end. His souls, crowded thick as they are, are candy-floss, melting on the tongue and never touching his belly.

They have played this game before, and no one ever wins.

She is sick to death of hunger and drowning. He is sick to death of treachery and spit-sealed deals. But they are what they have always been, and what they always will be.

These are the stories they tell you about hungry ghosts, and hungry devils. Every one of them is a lie, and all of them are true.

He reaches for her; she takes his hand. His fingers pass right through hers, leaving her hungrier still. His sigh is the echo of a lonely train running the rails out of town; hers, cold water running over stones.

The season ticks over to fall. A leaf drifts down, caught by the current and swept away, and they look to the bridge just visible through the thinning trees. They know, they both know, next summer they will stand there and start all over again.

And they ache, hoping next time they will remember, next time, they'll get it right.

# WHAT STILL ABIDES

## *Marie Brennan*

L et me tell a tale of my father's kin, for in me runs their blood, and so to me falls this burden: to keep the knowledge, the old-thought, the shape of how it began, as my father gave it to me.

H arvest-time it was, the time of reaping and of dying, when his breath stopped and his blood stilled, and they laid his body in the ground. He had a name then, that now is gone; my father knew it but told me not, saying it died with his life, and to speak it now would blight the speaker's tongue.

He died at harvest and they laid him in the ground, axe at his side and barrow built over his head. After that came winter, wolf-cold and sharp. It was a time of hunger, of bellies clenching hard and even kin looking upon one another with an unkind eye. Men tholed ill luck in those long nights: sickness and wound, horses lame and kine lost. Then came spring with storms, grimful rains to drown the fields, and the ground that was his grave became black with mud.

One night a man, Leofnoth by name, son of Leofmaer, hied to the eorl's hall to drink among the thanes, as was his wont, and a shame unto his wife. But when he came there, they saw he was white as bone with fear and his hands shook like leaves in the wind, though he had not yet taken ale. When they asked what had frighted him so, he said he had seen a man standing upon the grave.

For this they laughed at him, and gave him a cup to drink. But rest Leofnoth would not, holding that he told only truth, and furthermore that the man was no thing of this world. And so in the teeth of a storm, three men rode out to see what of what he spake.

Stood a dréag upon the brow of his barrow, feet mud-deep, neither shifting nor breathing.

Warriors they were, bold thanes of the eorl, who had seen that man buried and would swear their oath that he was dead. Yet there stood the lich: frost-shrunken his limbs and grey as old snow, like a curse upon the ground. Bold might they be, but near him none would go, for fear of this unearthly thing. Instead they settled that they would fetch a god-man, whose holy words would lay the wight once more.

But when came the god-man with them to the barrow at the mist-shrouded break of day, cast down he could not what had risen from that earth, for the thing was mightier than he. Whatever words said he, the bone-home neither shifted nor breathed, nor gave any show it saw the thanes and the god-man. Dead had he been, and so was he still, even upon the height of the barrow instead of in its heart.

The first of the thanes set himself to undertake what the god-man could not do, and bring low this weird thing. Fastened he his feet upon the ground, and put the heels of his hands upon the body, throwing against it all his weight. So might he have struggled against the mightiest tree, what little harvest had he for his work. Sought then the next of his fellows, and then the third, and then the three together, but all their strength could not shift the life-left flesh so much as the span of a hair.

Unrestful were their hearts at this, but hid they their fear with laughter, saying that the wight wanted only the freshness of the wind.

And so they left him there, for they could do naught. Came the children of the town to scorn at the thing, daring one another to feel the dréag's dead hand, and their mothers pulled them away.

Seven days after, came there a rider upon a horse, an errand-man for the eorl. As it went by the barrow his horse bolted in fear, dashing up the slope and hurling its burden to the ground. But struck the horse's hoof against the head of the man, and came thus his blood, soaking the loam at the lich's feet.

When came the thanes to gather up the errand-man's body, the dréag was not as he had been. Thick now were the arms withered by winter, ripe as the beginning of rot. But not like life was this; sick-swollen was he, full with the foulness of those who dwell with worms.

Among them were none with will enough to strike the wight. Frightened, left they the errand-man where he lay and rode back to their hall.

Then went out word from the eorl, that he would give rich gold to the man who rid him of this wicked thing. To this call came Aescwulf of the east, a warrior bold whose deeds men heard in tale and song, and said he that his sword would cut down what the god-man's words could not.

Therefore went Aescwulf to the top of the barrow with his sword in his hand, to meet the risen wight. Dry was his mouth and cold his blood at seeing dead flesh stand, but held he to his meaning and his end, lest he shame himself and his good name lose in the eyes of his fellow men.

With keen edge he cut, striking at the sticks of the wight, and meat and bone gave way before his blade. But fell too the sword from Aescwulf's hand: stopped had his heart at the start of his strike, and now he lay dead beside the dréag.

For Aescwulf was great mourning and great thanks, that he had freed the folk from their fear. To his kin gave the eorl the plighted gold and meed besides, for the loss of their fellow in so worthy a work. The wight his men graved in the ground once more, and gave yield to the gods that he should not leave another time.

But when waned the moon, stood the shape again on the height of the hill, the dréag as he had been.

Darker then were the days, grey the sky with clouds, and colder waxed the wind even as the summer grew. Came again the god-man, and four strong men with him, weaponed with whitethorn. For then was it the month of three milkings, and with the wood of that month might they steal the strength that fed his soul. At the god-man's rede bound they the bone-home and broke it from the earth, and once more laid it down where it should keep.

But in this doing, pricked the thorns of the wood into the men's hands, so that their blood fell onto the skin of the wight. Drank the grey flesh these drops and thereafter grew white, shining lich-sick as they steeked the barrow shut.

Still darker dimmed the sun, so that churl and thane and eorl alike dwelt in grave-gloom. Came then the rain almost without halt, drowning the home of seeds, killing the year before it lived. Empty were the keeps of corn after winter's end; hunger was man's dish, and want his drink, and the wolf of death came for many.

Thin grew the sky-sickle and withered into black, and when darkest came the night, rose again the dréag to stand upon the ground.

More gold gave the eorl, and clubs of the crabapple tree, for the boldest men to bear. Now this is the soul-strength of apple: that it is the tree of life, whose wood is bane to things of death. Hewn was this wood from a holy tree, and marked with runes by the god-man, to give it might against the dréag.

Rode forth six men who climbed the hill, and with reckless hearts put themselves against this threat. Scathed their clubs the skin, and with the first blow came the breath of the wolf, the wind of winter, from the wounds they made. Twice struck their arms, and crumbled the blossoms of the hedges into dust. At the last blow, fell the birds from the trees, their feathers breaking against the ground.

From the skin of the dréag wept tears of black blood, that froze the hands of the men. Numb-fingered, took they the raven's food and thrust it into the ground, stopping the way with stone. Then came the women and children, half-starved and scared, with shale from their houses and flint from their fields, to roof over the barrow so naught might grow upon it again. But beneath the blood, the hands of the men were white as midwinter snow.

Long then were the nights, though summer should have made sweet the sky. Brought the day little sun and no hope, and dwindled horse and kine for lack of grass. All kept watch for the waning of the moon, and what they knew it must bring.

When saw the watchers the wight again, it was the death of hope. No strength of sinew nor holiness of heart could drive the dréag down whither it should be, and its foulness drained the life from the land. Dim were the days and dead the fields, and the men with white hands walked about with empty eyes, stopping neither for food nor for sleep. Dread they woke in those who saw them, and in fear some sought to fight them; but when their foes their hands met, numb went their limbs, as if winter's cold bent their bones. And so left they such men to wander, and those who had not forsaken hope kept far from their path.

But unaware the eorl was not, and had readied himself for this rising.

On the ground before his hall stood a stone. Into this carved the god-man his strongest runes, and wrote over them with his blood, begging the gods, the great ones of the other worlds, to make the stone the stopping of this bane.

Sent the eorl the last of his thanes to the bone-home's bed, where the wight stood again. Dragged they the dréag thence, the white-handed ones walking after, as if they were the thanes of that thing. But stopped they at the stakes that marked the ground of the eorl's hall.

On that ground one woman came forth, having kissed her kin and bid them farewell; Saehild was her name, and well she knew this work would be her death or worse. But for the well-being of her folk, put she her hands to the lich's flesh, cutting it loose with an iron knife. Ulfcytel, best of the thanes, took the body-sticks she bared and laid them upon the stone, that the god-man had named the grinder of the grave. With other stones he broke them, stones carved also with the runes and blood of the god-man, while put Saehild the flesh into a churn of oak, whose staff then beat it soft. White grew their skin where it met bone and meat, but their word they had given, and break it they would not before they were done.

When ended their work, stood they with the empty-eyed ones; but their word they had kept, and so the eorl gave wergeld to their kin.

What abided still they put into a box, whose lid they nailed down with iron. At ene fell dead the god-man, and his body rotted where it lay. At this ill foretoken, more gave in to fear, but said the eorl that all his strength had gone into the spell, and his death was a mark of its might.

Few then yet stood at the eorl's side. Frost-bitten was the wind and dim the light, and held many to their homes; of those who did not, too many walked about bearing white skin and empty eyes. But yet lived hope in the eorl's heart. Took he the box and rode to the wealth-house of the dead, shifting aside the stone to bury his burden where first they had laid the lich, in harvest-time so long before. Then, having roofed the room anew, set he a watch, to see if things would now be well.

The end of this, all men know. Upon the dark of the moon, rose for the last time what men had thought to rid themselves of, fed full by the blood of the god-man, witlessly given. Came then those who yet lived, herded before the white-handed ones, to see the doom of the eorl, torn asunder for seeking to stop this thing. Fell his wound-flood upon the watching ones, waking hunger in their hearts. Crawled they up the barrow's side to beg the blessing from the dréag; cut he his arm, and from it drank they the wolf-wine, which gave to them knowledge of their wyrd, and new ravening.

A nd so has it been since that day. Never came the sun over this land after that; dwell we therefore in darkness, that men from without hold in fear. From our new god take we our gift, and do his will however he bids. All hail to the holy one, the bestower of blood, the gainsayer of the grave, whose life and might shall be everlasting.

# THE WANDERER KING

## *Alisa Alering*

It is Day 90 and most all are dead. Wanderers are dead, Fixers are dead, but me and Pansy are alive today, and we both want to be alive tomorrow. We want to find a way out of this deep dark bottom hole the world has fallen into.

We are in the potato man's house. He is dead on the floor and we look for something to eat. The potato bins stack top and top along the cold stone wall. It smells cool in my nose like dirt and mud, starch and flour. The potato man is not long dead, and smells sour coppery wet.

"Gone," Pansy says, her arm in the bins up to the elbow, fingers crawling on the bare boards.

"All?" I ask. There is one window, small. But we are in the forever days, and the light from outside shows the dark space of the potato man's life. The hard chair with the folded blanket. Pegs on the wall hang mattock, fork. I take down the mattock, swing and heft. Old dirt cracks off the head and crumbles on the floor.

Pansy gets down on her knees and leans under the bed. She drags out the trunk, goes through the clothes and blankets. "We're not first," she says, finding nothing worth having.

I tuck up my skirt and go up the ladder to the cramped loft under the musty eaves, where I find a dead bird, its feet in the

**117**

air, its beak so still I can see the holes of its nostrils. "Nothing here," I say, backing down.

As we leave Pansy spots the crown, hanging from a nail above the door. It looks to me like a pair of antlers, stuck on some skin, tied with string.

"The King," Pansy says. She comes from Wanderers, so she knows things differently. She says the King can lead us back to the top world, where things are right side up. She says we have to try it on, in case one of us is secretly the King.

I think we would already know, but she says you can't tell until the crown is on your head.

"You go first, Chool," she says. She rubs her palms across her eyes in that way that I have got used to.

"You," I say, because she wants me to say it. We have been together now since Day 45 when we hid from the Fixer men in the same storage shed among the grease drums and the fertilizer. I know how her wheels wind. I lean the mattock against the stone wall and take the crown. The antlers are sturdy, stubby prongs the color of a polished walnut, stitched with oiled thread onto a dark leather cap. Braided cord trails down over the earpieces, with a catch to fasten under the chin.

Pansy is taller than me. I reach high to hold the antlered cap over her head. She stands so still that I know she is listening all hairs on end. She is waiting for whatever form the magic takes. She is waiting to be King.

I push the cap down over her springy hair, holding out the earpieces. I balance the weight of the antlers between my open palms, then let go. I see the exact moment when she realizes nothing is going to happen. And maybe I see her think about pretending. But Pansy is honest. She puts her hands up beside her ears and pulls off the crown.

"Your turn," she says.

I know that I'm not the King, because I know what I have done. But that's not something I'm going to tell. So I stand still. I feel her breath on my neck, and then the lopsided weight of the crown settling along my head, the cap bending down my ear on one side. I give it a few beats, so she thinks I take it serious. I lift my shoulders, let them back down. "Now what?"

I give the crown back to Pansy. "What would a real King's crown be doing here?" I am looking at the rope bed and the tin teapot and the stack of turf beside the cold stove. Kings don't live like this.

"This King's not like that," she says. "Besides, maybe he—" meaning the dead potato man "—is come from the Kings' family line, maybe he's been keeping it. Maybe the King put it here for us to find." She holds the crown close to her face, letting the horns touch her cheek. Wanderers trundle the woods sniffing after invisible things. They know about finding. She looks into far distance, then back at me. "We have to try him," she says.

"But he's dead."

"Everyone's dead, Chool. We have to find the King." She takes the crown from me and goes over to the dead man. His wool vest is buttoned up straight to the chin. The slice starts there, halfway round his ear and into his hair. He looks up at the mud roof with his one eye left. Pansy picks his head up off the floor and rests it on her lap. She sets the cap on his head and holds it there, watching his ruined face.

Nothing happens, and Pansy closes her eyes. I hear the breath go out her nose. She eases the man's head down to the floor, where it rests with a little *thunk*. She stands and wipes her hands on the back of her skirt. Careful, she carries the crown.

We go out to look for the King.

We steer clear of the mines—that's Fixer territory. The Wanderers are dangerous, too, ever since they came fighting back around Day 30. But there's always been less of them—less in all, and less because they scatter through the woods on their business instead of fixing to the towns and mines.

We step along to the city, fitting the crown on all we come across. We sleep in the darkest part of the day when the sky dips to dark blue. At first, in the country, there aren't many heads to try. But we come up on the city, and we slow. We even try it on Fixers because Pansy says the King is the King and it doesn't matter whose body he's in. "The King is for all," Pansy says. "Anyone can carry the King."

We start down a back street at the edge of town, all trampled gardens and the backs of shops, bordered on the other side by the crumbled rocks of the old Wanderer's wall, tumbled down and the gaps slap-patched with crankling sheets of corrugated tin.

In the first ten days, the Fixers rounded up the Wanderers as they came into the bureaus with their gleanings to sell, and killed them all at once. These bodies are blown up big like water bags, gurgling and gassing and covered in flies, and we pass them by. We can't stand to get close enough to test them.

Up ahead, behind a garage, three women lie together in the road. Scarves flutter loose around their heads as if they had tried to hide their faces when they left home. Fixers or Wanderers or some other, I don't know. Two are huddled together, dying with their arms wrapped around as the knives bit into their backs. Glass glitters at the base of the wall, a broken bottle of soured milk. The third is farther away, stretched out flat. Slashes are on her legs and chest, and the flesh of her cheek split wide. A black-spotted pig has squeezed through a gap in the wall, and forages at her side, snuffling and grunting.

"Get away," Pansy shouts. She runs at the pig, waving her free hand.

The pig turns and charges her. Pansy leaps back. The crown tumbles out of her arms as she scrambles up the stone wall out of the reach of the pig.

I pick up the crown by the antlers, ready to leap up the wall next to Pansy. We can run down the length and find other bodies to test.

"No," Pansy says. "Try them first."

Keeping my eye on the pig, which has settled down to slurp clots of milk from the broken jar, I try the crown on the two women lying together. When I get to the separate one, I see where the pig has chewed two fingers from her hand. I crouch down beside her and pull back her scarf, peeling it loose from her scalp. Her hair is razored close to the skull, a soft fuzz. She has sharp black brows that wing together above her puffed eyes in a way that accuses.

I rock back on my heels. "This is stupid," I say. "No one's going to save us."

"Just do it," Pansy says. She wipes her hand across her eyes, digging at the invisible blood.

"There is no King," I say, mostly to myself. But I lower the antlers onto the woman's head, and as it skims her brow some force reaches out for the cap, sucking it down, gripping it against her skull. I try to snatch it back but it sticks fast. I drop the antlers like they're on fire and jump to my feet.

Red blood pumps out of the woman's pig-eaten fingers. The woman's eyes blink open, dark gold like the polished antlers on the crown.

\* \* \*

A hot wind blasts us in the face, carrying voices. Men talking and shouting on the other side of the garage.

Pansy stares at the dead woman wearing the crown of antlers and bleeding from the stumps of her fingers.

"We have to get gone from here," I say.

The woman sits up, gets to her feet. The antlers reach above her head, poking the sky. The cords dangle unfastened along her jaw. She wears a man's jacket, the rolled-up sleeves sliding down her scabbed arms. I can't tell if she sees us or not.

The men's voices come closer. They are in the street on the other side of the shops. The air carries the smell of their sweat and the dust they stir up from the road. I hear the stamp of their feet and the *zsh-zsh* swing of their knives. I look down the alley, then back at the woman. I am sure she was dead. Not just slightly dead, but very dead.

"Pansy," I say, "What is she doing standing?"

The woman takes a first step but her dead legs won't hold her and she stumbles. She reaches out a hand for the garage wall and gets herself right, leaving red finger smears on the yellow painted blocks.

Pansy leaps down from the Wanderer's wall, vaulting past the pig, which is rolling the bottle down the pavement with its nose, trying to get the last licks of sour milk trapped inside.

"Please, your Majesty" Pansy says to the woman, "show us the way out. Take us to the door."

At her words, the woman jumps like a rabbit and lurches into motion, walking fast. Her sandals crunch in the broken glass. She cuts into the alley that leads to the front side of the shops.

Pansy runs after her, and I grab her arm as she passes. "The Fixers are out there. We have to hide."

Pansy shakes free. "We have to follow her. The King knows the way out."

I want to scream at her stupidity, but with the men so near, I don't dare. I scuttle after her down the alley, my back against the block wall. I stick close to the building, crouch in the shadow.

The woman is on the other side of the open street, standing in front of the cracked glass of a restaurant window. She stares at her broken reflection. Pansy crosses towards her, and just then the line of Fixer men appear, marching together with tools in their hands, wearing their blood-stained overalls like uniforms. There are only six, but they bulge in the deserted street, filling it side to side.

The man in the lead, red-haired and broad, raises his fist, the blood-smeared blade held high. Beside him, two boys with first-haired lips lean into a sprint and streak towards Pansy.

My hand closes around the handle of the knife in my belt. Pansy and I have been together forty-five days, and we look out for each other. She is the only thing I have left in the world. But in my mind, I remember before. I see my own hand holding a knife, see the blade slice into flesh, part the seam of life and turn a living body into a nothing bag of skin.

Everyone said the Wanderers would kill us first. My head ran pictures of them slinking in from the forests with their dirty feet and animal noses, whispering their secret songs and carrying wet bags of gleanings, water dripping from the blades of their crook-armed diggers. On Day 3, I saw the crowd holding a girl down in my street. Her name was Bel. Grown men and women were spitting on her and kicking her and making her cry. My heart skittered, and I ran and joined them. The furnaceman's wife threw a stone. A boy next to me gave me a knife. Bel called me by name and begged me not to kill her. Snot ran from her dirty nose, and she jumbled up frightened stories, trying to remind me how we used to play frogstones together in the street when we were small.

My hand shakes. The Fixers are coming, and still I can't draw the knife.

I could step out into the road and tell the men I come from a Fixer family—that's one thing that Pansy already knows—but we are too late in the days for that to matter anymore.

Pansy tries to run, arms pumping, her skirt flying around her legs, looking too late for somewhere to hide. A mustache boy lunges, and brings her smash down in the dirt. I feel her hit in my own chest, bite to stop from crying out. The other five stomp forward, dust and stink and hungry blades.

In my eye's corner, I see the horns move. The woman turns her head from her reflection to Pansy, and the antlers swivel. She kicks through the restaurant window and heaves up a table as she leaps back into the street. With both hands overhead she smashes it down, breaks off the leg. She grips the end, double-fisted. She holds the sharp tip high, and walks into the crowd of men.

She swings into their stomachs, jabs into their ribs, cracks the table leg against their skulls. The men fall, toppling into the dirt.

Pansy runs to my side, unhurt. She holds onto me and I hold onto her. We watch the men destroyed, one after the other, until they lay scattered in the street.

The King drops the sword, and then she speaks.

"Where am I?" she says. This time I know she is seeing us.

I shove Pansy in the back. She made the King, so it's only right that she explain.

"You're the King," Pansy says. "You're going to take us to the right-side world."

"I was on my way somewhere," she says vaguely. She digs into her pockets, comes up with little belongings—a slip of paper, a coil of wire, a coin. Each one she holds up in confusion, lets drop from her hand. They fall on the dirt next to her sandaled toes.

A man on the ground groans, and his body shifts. His arm flails, and I stomp it.

"Can you take us?" Pansy asks.

"Yes."

The King leads us out of the city. We follow her along the Wanderer's wall into the country, where blackthorn tumbles over its fallen stones. Blood drips from the King's missing fingers. It bothers me that she is still bleeding. I tear the sleeve off my shirt and take the King's hand, wrapping the cloth over the stumps, tying it off across the palm.

As we travel, Pansy tells the King her story, the one she has already told me, about the man who lived next door.

"I used to call him Uncle," Pansy says. "He and his wife looked after me when my parents were out gleaning. When I heard about the killings in school, I ran to him and asked him to protect me. He dragged me down the stairwell, and pulled my hair and slapped me. He held a chisel to my face and told me I was a dirty Wanderer sow. He made me take off my clothes."

I go up behind and put my arm around her, but she shrugs it off. "When he was done," she says. "He sat over me with the knife, and I could see him wondering what to do. But then more men came up behind him, and beat him in the head. He fell on top of me. His blood—" she says, wiping her eyes with both hands.

The King walks ahead, her antlers against the blue sky.

"The Fixers," Pansy says. "I don't know why they started it."

"This time," I say. "But we all have something to answer for." The blackthorn reaches out from the side of the road, tears my legs.

Pansy looks at me sharp. "You told me your parents never hurt any Wanderers."

"They didn't," I say. "The fightermen herded the Wanderers into the hall. They handed out stones and knives to all of the Fixers and told them to kill the Wandering wood lice. My parents refused. The fightermen said if they wouldn't kill the Wanderers they were traitors and had to die. My parents still refused. So the other Fixers killed them."

The King turns her head, the golden antler eyes gleaming out at me from under the black wing brow.

I am telling the truth. I watched my father stand in front of my mother and take the first cuts. I saw him fall down, screaming, at her feet. I saw her cover her face and bend over him as the Fixers fell on her with their tools and fists.

When the sky dips dark, we lay down in the forest to sleep. The blackthorn is on the air, sweet with a scratch like hay, up my nose in the starlit air.

The King is stretched out, her neck propped on a stone to give her antlers clearance from the ground. Pansy sleeps, curled in front of the King.

I pull the knife from my belt and creep up beside them. The way the King looks at me with her antler eyes. She knows what I did, and I can't bear it. I raise the knife, hold it over the woman's head, ready to plunge into her eye.

Then, I see the bandage, the piece of my own shirt wrapped around the King's hand. She is already a bag of skin. She has crossed the line from living to dead, but here she is wrapped around Pansy, keeping her safe, taking her out of our upside down sunken world.

I put the knife away.

We follow the King all the way back to the potato man's house. The house has been set on fire, but the flame is out, smoldering. From the distance, we see dogs circling, running through the potato fields, but when the King passes in through the yard, they are gone.

The dark house smells of smoke, and the body of the potato man is gone. The dogs bark in the distance, and out the window I see their brush tails disappear over the hill.

Pansy hangs close by the King, who steps carefully over the place where the potato man lay. She picks up the loft ladder and leans it against the wall above the door. The empty nail hangs above the sill, where we lifted the crown.

Pansy holds the ladder, and the King climbs. At the top, she unwraps her bandaged hand. The blood runs new from her missing fingers. She dips the first finger of her other hand into the blood, and, starting at the nail, draws a square on the smoke-smudged wall above the door. She dips into the blood again and again until the line on the wall is clear and dark.

I stand by the small window, where in comes the blackthorn air, faint over the smoke and molded potato.

The King dips her head forward and taps the wall with her antlers, one-two. The wall splits along the blood-drawn line. *Click*, and a new door springs open. Inside the door she has drawn, instead of outside the potato man's house and a view of fields and forest, is a hollow space. Inside the space, steps lead up, a long staircase. Leaving the door open, the King backs down the ladder and stands in front of a wooden bench pushed against the wall.

Pansy watches, and wipes her hand across her eye, still trying to get the blood out. I wonder if she will still see it in the rightside world.

Pansy kneels down and kisses the King's undamaged hand.

"We're going up," Pansy says, looking at me.

I think about Pansy, how we found each other among the fertilizer, how we have traveled and survived for forty-five days, hiding and crying into each other's hair. I think about the knife in my hand, and the moment when the seams of life split and Bel's self fell out.

"You go first," I say. The King is patient, watching. The drip of blood from her fingers is drying up.

Pansy puts her foot on the ladder, and begins to climb. When she reaches the top, she lets go of the ladder and reaches one hand through the new door the King has drawn. She holds it there, watching, waiting. To see if she really can go. Then she brings her hand back, closes her eyes. Waits. Finally, she crawls up and over the ladder, and through the door. I see her legs, her calves and ankles below-skirt, and I watch each bit disappear up the stairs.

The King-drawn door bangs closed behind her. Its bloody edge-lines swallow back into the plaster wall.

I've always known I wasn't going. I am fixed here, stitched in place by what I have done. But that doesn't make no way out easier to bear.

The King drops down on the bench and slumps back, the tips of the antlers clacking against the stone wall.

My knees go, and I fall on the sooty stone floor in front of the King. I grab her hand, hold it to my chest, hanging on. Potato root is in my nose. "Oh, King," I say. "Don't leave me alone." I want the King to say something. That she understands. That she forgives me. That I had reasons.

She looks sympathetic, but she is dying. A last drop of blood falls from the stub of her middle finger. And then the King is just a bald-headed woman several days dead.

My throat closes up, my lids bang down on my eyes, shutting my mind, trying to stop me. The King is gone. Pansy is gone. The world where I have lived the first fourteen years of my life is over. If there is any world left for me to go, it is the one inside of me.

I let go of the woman's cold hand. I stand and face the empty room. It feels like the knife is back in my fist, only this time I am slicing into myself.

"I wanted to hurt Bel," I say. These words are the point of the knife, digging against resisting skin.

"It was a relief," I say. "It felt good." I work the truth harder, split the tough seams I have sewn. Something gushes out, warm and sour. "Once I hit her, I couldn't stop. It was the only way to be safe, the only way for the world to make sense again. I made Bel a bug, a germ. I struck and slashed with that knife, and my fear fell away."

I hold out my hand, staring at it. "Then she was dead, and her blood was wet on my skin. And I was even more afraid than I had been before."

Some last bit slumps out of me onto the floor of the potato man's house, and I am left standing in an empty bag of skin.

New things fill up my eyes. I had been looking slant through a bunched-up seam, and now the threads are cut and the fabric ripped away. Now I can see so much more. I can't see where

Pansy has gone, but I can see all of the potato man's life. I see the lines of him before they cut his throat. I see the bald-headed woman under the antlers. How she was just a woman on her way to the shop with a man who loved her and how she was cut down. I see the puddle of my frightened self on the dirty stone floor, wet and lumpen. The lines stretch and go in every direction.

Down my front, the potato air blows through the tattered edges of the self I have left. I am empty, open.

I go to the woman. Her face is blank and bloodless. I unfasten the antlered cap and take up the crown.

# A LITTLE OF THE NIGHT
## (EIN BISSCHEN NACHT)

### *Tanith Lee*

### Preface

Now he was an old man, but you could not entirely think of him in that way. He was lean and tall and hard as steel still, or he looked it. His face was lined, but his eyes had stayed jet black, and he had kept a full head of hair, even if the dark of it had changed to white silver. His teeth were good too—he could crack the shells of walnuts with them, they had seen that only this evening. And in his strong and well-made hands the sabre, when he lifted it, seemed quite as graceful and as dangerous as twenty, thirty years before.

Women had loved his voice, continued to do so. It was a beautiful voice even now, dark in tone, musical. He had persuaded troops into battle with those tones, given them the courage. He was a brave man, and intelligent as not so many were that were also brave. His name was Corlan Von Antal, and each of the sixteen men here tonight had served under his command. They called him, amongst themselves, Ursus (the Bear), and said it was for his famous cloak of black bearskin. But really it was for his valour and his power, his honour. And for the secret, forest-deep, whatever it was, that they had heard tell of, and that they sensed too about him. Besides, his hound was half wolf, and its pelt, like his, was silver. It would pad courteously from chair to chair when first they were seated, its massive ruffed head level with each man's heart; a colossal beast, but calm as a trained dove. It took a bear to govern a wolf.

The fire shone crystal red and amber, the tasty meal was over and the crimson wine was in the glass goblets, and all around the finely furnished old tower, in which he lived, went up through the eaves of the night, showing its yellow windows to the stars. Would he tell them the story, this year? He was sixty-five if he was a day. Surely he could trust them now, *now*, these officers of his. Surely now he *must* tell them, as they had always hoped he would when they visited him. But they had thought that last time, and the times before. He had been fifty, fifty-five, then sixty. He might live to be ninety, of course. And they— well they might even die, for they were still active soldiers, and though it was hard to recall sometimes, only these three miles from the town of Ruzngrad, the war was going on eighty miles in the other direction.

The young officer Nacek thought this particularly, as he sat watching Von Antal in the firelight. No man, Nacek reflected, old or young, ever knew how long God would give him. Every day ended in a night. The lights in the windows of the highest towers would go out. No one should keep silent forever.

But Ursus did not tell them anything tonight. Just as he never had. As, perhaps, he never would.

## One: Night

Forest-deep . . .
    The forests—
Corlan ran through them, his coat and shirt sticking to his back in a freeze of sweat, his thick sheaf of hair flattened into black water by icy rain. He was thirty-four. He was afraid.

He had killed a man. For a soldier currently employed in the chess manouevres of warfare, that would have been a superfluous statement, were it not that the man Corlan had killed belonged to his own regiment, an officer of equal rank. Gerner was a plague-pig, greedy, bloated, cras and vicious. His men suffered from him, which Corlan and his brother Knight-Captains had watched, and said, done, nothing, for Gerner was not the sort to listen. But days ago Gerner had gone into a small village in the forests' outskirt, taken every bit from it that was edible or portable, lined up the men and any male children and had them shot, then made his supper among the females. Some of his battalion had joined him with enthusiasm. Some always would. Others hung back. These village people had had little enough, and were not even counted among the enemy. A day after the "Feast", as Gerner had called it, three of his men deserted. Winter was beginning and the weather was strident; they were easily caught. Gerner had the trio hung up by their ankles from a tree and left in the sleeting rain till their brains should burst. He had also previously made a little supper on them, too.

They were young, not yet sixteen, and—as Gerner remarked— had the "beardless faces of girls".

One evening after that Corlan met Gerner unexpectedly, both of them alone and walking across a half-reaped, spoiled field, under the grey roar of the sky. And Gerner had smiled at Corlan. "You have some difficulty with me, brother Knight?" "Only one," said Corlan. "You still live." "Oh," and Gerner laughed, "so I do, so I do." In that moment Corlan, into whom the discipline of the military had been calcified nearly from birth, felt a cool high hand lift him upwards from his own body, until he stood some seven metres tall. From here, not dazed only a little surprised, he looked down on the ugly face of Captain Gerner. And then, almost gently, Corlan stepped forward and slammed his right fist into Gerner's jaw. Corlan felt nothing much, though he heard the crack of a tooth—or a bone. But when Gerner toppled over; Corlan stamped hard, once, on his guts. After which, as the creature writhed there, bulge-eyed, retching, and wheezing for air like a damaged street-organ, Corlan drew his army sword and decapitated him.

Only when he had wiped off the blade and re-sheathed it, with a certain military precision, did Corlan Von Antal drop back into his own skin. And at once, from a mad retributary angel he became a mad terrified boy. And the boy turned and sprinted from the field, straight through into the deepest avenues of the trees, nearly mindless, with everything lost and thrown away— Gerner, obviously, but also Corlan's prospects, career, family, friends, ideals—*life*—*heart*—lying in the rotted stalks like pieces of a broken plate.

\* \* \*

All told five nights had passed, five days, since the murder in the field.

That fifth night there was a bloody sunset, carmine and implacable. Cut off now from the army, he had found no shelter anywhere, and the few cold-withered roots he managed to grub did him no good. One afternoon he caught a rabbit, a skill from his youth. But then he could not kill it, not even efficiently and cleanly as he knew how to do. He could not kill it because he had, of all things, killed *Gerner*, and the curse of the outlaw was on him. So he let the animal go. Stunned, it kept like a stone long minutes in the frosty grass before bolting out of sight. There were streams where Corlan broke the morning ice and drank the water. He was used to that. By now the little pewter flask in his greatcoat pocket was empty of brandy.

When the blood soaked from the west, he sat on the ground and saw stars appear above, each one like the tip of a polished sabre driven through the uniform of the sky. Or they were shiny bullets.

Then the trees wept. Sleet striped through with a horrible, determined sound.

Well, why not just lie down here, just lie down and let the world that had cursed him finish him off? Or he could fire one of the shiny stars in his revolver through his head.

Eventually he got up, and ran—then only stumbled—on.

The stars were washed away.

And darkness fell like a curtain.

Maybe it was the days without food, or the peculiar roots, even the icy *chewiness* of the cold, cold water, that made Corlan think he met his grandfather about an hour later.

Corlan was walking by then, slowly. And the old man simply appeared between two of the pillar-like stems of the black pines. He was made of trees and winter, and his hair of the grey snowy rain. But he had *been* like that.

"Well, Cor, here you are," he said, thoughtfully, the way he had been used to, a couple of decades earlier.

Corlan's father was a bullying sot. The grandfather had often stepped between them. But whereas the father ruled through violence, the grandfather exerted command through his calm iron will. And where, perhaps, this had unhinged his own son, his *grandson* it saved. It was the grandsire, inevitably, who had weaned Corlan towards a military life. He had, too, taught him how to read and value books, to absorb music, to deal well with women, even those he loved. And to kill an animal for food swiftly and without redundant pain. "We are allowed to eat them, my boy," he had said, "which does not mean we should hold them in contempt. We must face the hard nutritional facts, perfect our methods, and cause as little suffering as possible. Respect your food, it was alive only yesterday. Hunting is a necessity, *never* a sport. We have the right to sustain our existence, but not to pretend those other things, upon which we prey, are unworthy of our concern and care."

Yet now, having spoken only his brief greeting, the grandfather merely stood there. And Corlan had the urge to go to him and kneel down and make a confession. The grandfather had nevertheless been dead for fifteen years. Corlan did not forget this. And next minute the old man's image faded in the rain, as the stars had.

And then, through the unfilled gap in the trees, which seemed damaged, Corlan saw the great pile of a building, reared up above the forest. Something in the rain outlined the building on the sky, although no lights showed in the bulk of it. A ruin, perhaps, some long-abandoned architectural hulk from the days of the Rupertian Conclave—centuries out of date.

Corlan stayed where he was, and looking upward at the masonry he felt a profound despair.

It was as if, he later decided, condemned to death, he had witnessed before him the proposed scaffold.

Yet he did not linger very long. He moved free of the dilapidated tree-line and started to climb the steep slope beyond. There was nowhere else to go. Or only one. And he was not ready, despite his previous thoughts, to go *there*.

By the time he reached a sort of fossilized drawbridge, and crossed by it over a type of pit, to a huge, arched, black door, Corlan had seemingly recalled every legend and eerie tale told of these forests. To see a ghostly grandsire was nothing. The vegetal labyrinth contained the strongholds of far worse phantoms, not to mention vampires, were-men, and ghouls.

He had always disdained such stuff. In childhood even he was seldom afraid of anything supposedly supernatural—the *natural* world being adversary enough.

When he struck the door he believed no one and nothing would respond. The door might even simply creak inward, unsecured in the building's abandonment. (It was a castle, towers here and there seemed to rise up from it, and it was far larger than any mansion.) But the door did not give. And all at once a greenish feeble light woke up overhead, in a shoulder of the stone, which was pierced he then saw by the thinnest slits of windows. This light began to crawl down towards him.

Corlan quietly considered taking to his heels. But that was an intellectual joke he was having with himself.

He did not truly expect some fiend to undo the locks and peer out at him. Alas, he was living in reality, not a book.

Something made grinding noises—bolts, keys, hinges, and a quarter of the black door opened.

A fiend looked out at Corlan Von Antal.

For a moment he gaped at it, and then he broke out laughing. "I've died and gone straight to Hell for my crime, yes?"

The poor fiend shook its head, from where narrow grey snakes of hair trickled, shaking in harmony. "Not so, sir. This is the House Veltenlak. What do you seek?" The voice was like rusty nails softly scratching together.

Corlan said, "I've lost my way," smiling still at the awful irony of his words. "I need somewhere to rest. To eat something, drink something not frozen mud, to sleep. Oh," he said unhappily, "if death's just sleep, I'll settle for that."

He was addled, of course, from events, and five days without food. He heard himself with censorious dismay.

But the poor fiend, he now realized, eyes adjusting to its waveringly hand-held lantern, was only a skinny, bent-over man, about a hundred years of age, which probably indicated seventy or so. He wore faded dusty eldritch black clothes, perfectly couth though worn out—as was he. His eyes were dull and watery, and his mouth, which now sadly smiled back at the visitor, contained, it seemed, only a third of the teeth God had originally planted there.

"We have not much now. But you are welcome. Come in, sir, come in. A little company will be pleasant for us."

\* \* \*

What did Corlan feel as he crossed that threshold? (Where the miniscule bones of a mouse lay like brown needles.) He was never certain, so weary, his head swimming. He always afterward had a vague notion he stumbled, and the old fellow did not reach out to steady him, only moved backward a step, and stood waiting a short way into what seemed to be a vast dark *cave*, whose high walls were of striated rock, and here and there on them something murkily gleamed or glinted, as the lantern-light trembled over it. Then, after Corlan had righted himself, if so he had to, the other man turned and limped off into the darkness.

Corlan looked about him with a sort of oddly uninterested curiosity. He began to see that they moved through and then out of some great hall, a place in the past for banquets and aristocratic councils. Up on the stone walls there were tattered banners fringed with ragged bullion, and antique swords and shields and other warlike implements, that shone and winked from their cobwebbing. A colossal hearth went by on his right, with two savage and enormous stone animals guarding it—he could not make out what they were. There was half an armorial motto, in Latin: *Non Omnis Moriar.* Now what did that mean? The grandfather would have known. *We do not die? We die? All things die . . . ?* No, not that . . .

Here they went round what seemed a very thick pillar, high as the inestimable roof, and possibly having the girth of three or four pines grown together. Now came a passageway, long and curving, like a static worm. The lantern splashed on running wet, puddles, on peculiar stainings and spidery cracks. The enclosure stank of rot and dampness worse than the hall. Something scrambled across the old man's feet and vanished—as it looked—into the blank wall. A rat, a lizard.

"Where are you taking me?" Corlan asked languidly. He was near to falling down.

"A kitchen below, sir. Teda keeps a fire there."

"Does she? Teda . . . And how do they call you?"

"Tils," the old man said.

"Whose house is this?"

"He is gone, sir." Oddly the old man's voice took on at this a weird harshness. He sounded younger, and more stern.

"*He,*" said Corlan. "But what is his name?"

The old man did not answer this. He said only, in an inexpressibly unnerving way, "He is dead, sir. Not spoken of. *Never* spoken of."

Corlan thought, Oh, then, one of the bloody story-book ghouls. Dead but still active and in residence. It *is* a story I've walked into. I don't care. Oh God I must lie down.

Just then they turned a corner and before them, along another paved stone walk—this without a roof—another door showed buttery light. Above, the rain, having successfully leaked its way into the house, had given over, and the weaponry stars were back in full force.

They got up a steep and pitted step, and Corlan saw now the roofed kitchen with a few lamps and a fire burning. A pot was slung over it. He smelled soup, and there was a loaf on a table, and coffee had been brewed, and there the white alcohol glittered in its decanter, schnapps or junever. This must be a dream then. He reached a bench and collapsed onto it.

There was also a woman, an old one to match the old man. Teda, presumably. Teda and Tils.

It was the ruined schloss of an undead vampire or werewolf, and these two old bundles of bones were doubtless mad as frogs, and ready to prepare any guest for the monster's delectation. Well, let them. So long as they fed him first.

He pulled some coins from his pocket, all he had—his pay was in arrears. It would save him from being robbed by them later. They were glancing at the money as he offered it, as if they had never seen coins before. Maybe they never had. The ghoul had taken care of them.

*We do not altogether die.*

That was what the Latin meant, surely?

Of course. How apt.

Corlan fell asleep.

*There is night. And there is the Night—the night-dark void that hides inside the often gilded covers of reality: The Abyss. A little of the latter goes a very long way.*

> Attributed to the philosopher Anton Woetzsner
> (1797-1889)

When he came to again Corlan believed he was in the open, out in the dark fracturing of the pine-pillared night. All was pitch-black, but for a row of savage scarlet eyes that seared at him, crouched low down, flickering with lust.

He did not think he would have time to grip the revolver.

One of the eyes blinked, and went out.

It was the kitchen fire. He was in the kitchen of the stone schloss, lying on the bench.

Corlan sat up. He drew out flint and tinder, struck a light. They had left a lamp on the table, which he lit. A bowl of the broth was there too, cold now but no matter, a chunk of the loaf. The coffee was gone, but not the junever-gin.

He ate in the half-light like a starving dog, knew it and cared nothing, his face almost in the dish, growling and grunting. When he was done, for a moment a fierce nausea gushed through him—too much after too little—then faded back, leaving only a dull digestive ache.

He sloshed the gin into a small chipped glass and swallowed two gulps.

Everything would improve now. They, the raddled old couple, had saved his life. Where had they gone to? Oh naturally, to alert, or to hide from, their master, the owner of House Veltenlak.

No, Corlan decided, he would stop that now. He was restored. There were no vampires, none of the other creatures either. This was only a ruinous heap, once grandiose, deserted as several of the ancient castles had been, since an era of war began.

Something hissed and whispered high up. A vaporous serpent came sliding towards him down the wall, and there another—another—

Corlan shook himself. Numbskull. It was only dust or powder escaping the ceiling. The entire habitat was crumbling. All about him, as he concentrated, his ears no longer dinning with fatigue and hunger, he could detect such sighs and grumblings, cracks and masonry groans. Subsiding, these doomed walls due to disintegrate and tumble, leaving only shattered stone blocks and part-standing shafts, through which the winds would blast their cannon-shot.

The fire was dying rapidly now, and the tepid kitchen growing ever colder.

But Corlan drank another glass of junever, and glanced about. He was refreshed. He wanted something to do until the morning came, when he would take himself off.

He wondered idly where Tils slept, and Teda. They had left the sparse column of coins on the table.

Standing up, he took the lamp, and went all round the kitchen, which was not itself very big, and gave on a second kitchen through a broken door. The second kitchen was itself broken, some of its roof down. Beyond, a yard, black with moonless night, and a well, but peering into this it seemed to have gone dry, only rain and muck inside. Three dead rats, coiled tight as rope, lay on the ground.

How long until sunrise? He took a reading from the patterns of the stars, where he could see them. Three, four hours, he thought.

Corlan went back through the kitchen and the corridors.

He reached again the vast hall-cave beyond the pillar with an odd suddenness. As if it had shifted and come to meet him. The unpleasant impression caused him to pull up and rigidly stand there. The flame in the lamp jerked and the stonework jumped with it.

This was when Corlan felt, he thought for the first, (but afterwards he was sure it was not for the first at all) a kind of seeping, leaching yet indescribable dread. Years after he would, to himself, compare all this to an abrupt loss of blood that for an instant made you lightheaded, and then sick, faint, leaden and ashen and barely conscious.

But his senses stayed intact, indeed quite keen.

He wondered had he been poisoned—venom in the food or alcohol. But it was not that. His guts had quieted. Yet—his hands shook, and it took all his will to steady them. He had been, in battle, reasonably cool. What was this? Nothing. Some childish fantasy lingering—

The horror, (for *horror* was in fact precisely what it was) did not let go.

Determined then Corlan went directly into the enormous hall. He reached the giant fireplace with its sentinel beasts. What were they? Wolves? Dragons? Some mismatch of both? He smashed the lamp straight down on the hearth so it shattered and the flame spilled out. He had seen immediately logs lay on the stone apron, laid ready if evidently for a great while unused. They were damp, too, the huge rainy chimney would have seen to that. But the lamp-oil anointed them, and spluttering, smoking blue and spiking out raw green sparks, they began to burn. Then the smoke went black, but already Corlan had seen ranks of filthy candles waiting all about, on the mantle, on tall candle-standards either side. The struck flint soon roused them. The smell was vile, animal fat in the wax, the rank unwilling wetness in the wood. Corlan's stomach heaved but he clamped his will upon it. Generally well-trained, his healthy body was used to obeying him.

He stepped back and looked everywhere around him, able to see it all finally, all the splendour of its dying hollowness.

And the horror increased.

It rose up through him as the sickness had done, but worse, much worse. Nor would it permit his steely will to order it down and away. It swelled through his belly and heart and throat and brain. It expanded in his mind and looked out through his fire-burning glaring eyes. It said to him, wordless, voiceless, in a language untranslatable but always known: Behold, Behold. Behold.

Corlan rushed across the hall; he did not know what he did, he was in retreat.

So he came to a staircase, the stone treads wide and shallow and rising upward between ranks of stone posts taller than a man, in the tops of some of which were older filthier candles, or only stubbs, whose melted greasy lace trailed downward.

Swiftly up the stair he ran.

The horror went with him.

It was thick as wax or stone, yet malleable, and it twisted inside him as a snake would.

It's real, he thought, blindly, madly, as he sprang from step to step. (Once, twice, tiny bones crunched under his feet.) *It exists—*

Then he had reached the top and ahead a great opening, like a mouth, toothed with bits of swords and shields hung there, gave on another corridor, very wide. The fluttering light below in the hall penetrated this passage.

Corlan, despite his confusion and fear, slammed to a halt, grabbing at the topmost stair-post.

One of the statuary beasts from the fireplace had got loose. It was here now, poised in the passageway, staring at him, its eyes not like fire at all, but a pearly, nearly opalescent colour, between emerald and blue Artic ice.

*This* fear was nearly welcome. It was so different from the *horror*.

Corlan found he had taken hold of the revolver, but his hand shook again; it was awkward—besides, how could he shoot a beast of stone? In those moments the thing gazed on at him, and all at once furrowing its brow, *frowning*, as a man would, puzzled and affronted by the idiotic antics of a stranger.

It had human eyes, the beast, regardless of their colours and luminosity. Then he knew what it was. Not a carving come alive but a physical animal, a huge, dark-ruffed wolf. He could kill it, then. Perhaps its splattered gore might appease the evil spirit that now pursued Corlan. But probably not. The wolf would be the monster's own familiar, would it not, beholden to its master. A vampire in legend was inclined to favour the wulven kind. Or again, a werewolf might change into just such an abomination.

I am going insane. Stop this. It's just an animal.

"Hey!" Corlan bawled suddenly at the motionless wolf, and waved his arms.

The wolf lowered its head, then turned from him. It padded off into the passage, not hurrying, neither startled nor enraged.

As it moved, its gait was slow and heavy. If it had been human its shoulders would have sagged. The ruffed head hung down. Halfway off into the dark, just before the darkness swallowed it, Corlan saw it pause. He heard it drinking, sluggishly and not for very long, then it slunk on, dragging its feet now, it seemed to him, as though exhausted.

In the end Corlan snapped off a piece of candle from the last of the posts, lit it, and went after the wolf. A short distance, and there was an old glazed clay bowl on the floor, which held the liquid the wolf had been drinking. Pink in colour—milk, Corlan thought, mixed with and curdled by blood.

Closed doors lined the passage. At the end the corridor branched both left and right, but either side was only a wreckage of smashed stone. There was another wide arched doorway in between, this slightly open. The wolf had gone in there; Corlan could smell it. Hesitating outside, he heard it jump up on something, and then settle. He heard it sigh, the same mournful sighing which the House Veltenlak constantly gave. The wolf must have copied it. Corlan did not enter the room.

All this while horror stayed fast inside him. As the wolf had, it seemed to be settling itself, lying down, making itself comfortable within his body, his soul.

He was so weary now. As if he had not eaten, not slept, was ill or wounded, or a slave worn thin with thankless, awful labour, and no hope anywhere, none. No chance at all.

## Two: Day in Night

*Non Omnis Moriar—*

*Behold* the voiceless wordless voice proclaimed.

It flung aside the curtains of unknowing and there, before him, lay an infinite vista. But it was a view without a single image in it.

*Behold* . . .

Non Omnis—the inscription, time-gnawed or hacked away.

*BEHOLD*—

Corlan woke, sitting bolt upright, like a puppet yanked into position on strings. His head rang and the room cartwheeled. He was back in the bloody kitchen. He could not recall returning here. Perhaps he had never left it, only got up and eaten the food—the bowl stood empty that had held the soup . . . or had it held curdled blood and milk? Crumbs on the table, the decanter of gin one quarter less. So, got up, eaten, drunk, lain down again and slept, dreamed of roaming the stenchful ruins, lighting fires, while some maleficent entity fastened upon him. Utter nonsense.

Deep in his sinews he felt the horror stir. He resisted instinctively, since it did not exist.

The old woman—Teda?—was creeping into the kitchen, sparing him a solitary glance fraught with misgiving, or—could it be compassion?

Corlan rose, nodded to her, and went out into the courtyard behind the other, broken kitchen, to relieve himself, and wash his hands and face in the cleaner pockets of the rain.

These procedures did little for him. He felt like death. He had a fever, he thought. But never mind that, today he must get on. If he could buy a handful more food, some drinkable water, he could continue on his journey to the eastern borders. This was his only method now he had become an outcast. Or, he supposed, he could go back and give himself up to the army, let them strip him of all honour and shoot or hang him amid the trees.

He found Teda had brought him a cracked china cup of coffee, and his eyes filled with sentimental tears. Through them he glimpsed the crooked distortion of her hands. What was it? Old age and rheumatism, no doubt. He thanked her and drank and said, "There's a wolf sleeps in this house."

"Yes," she said, softly. "That is Hris."

"Hris—a wolf. A choice pet."

"Not a pet. Always about. In former days."

He downed the coffee like medicine. "You mean, do you, when your master was—alive." If ever he *was* alive, Corlan added to himself. But deep within his body or his brain, the horror twitched, nearly lazily now, comfortable with him. *Shake it off.* "Who was this *master?*"

"We don't speak of him."

"Why not?"

"It is—" she left a long gap. She said, "There are partings, sir. Severences."

True, he thought. Death severs people. But *The Master* was *not* people—he did not *die*. He *remained*, and drank *his* coffee—blood—or else dined on the flesh and skeletons—of human things.

Corlan got up again and staggered, must hold on to the table to keep himself upright. A fever. Damnation—to be ill when it was so urgent to travel far away—

"You've been generous," he said, "but I'll be off in an hour. Is there any food I might buy from you—"

She had gone. He had not seen her go.

Swaying, he allowed himself to sit down again. She had refilled his cup, and he had not seen that, either. He drank it. It did not taste as if poisoned. From somewhere he must wrestle back his strength.

During the day, the castle was no better. Wan light interruptedly yet perpetually splintered through its narrow window-spaces and cracks, littering the stony floors.

Every so often a gushing sigh, or whisper, indicated the stone-dust which poured out of ceilings and walls. In certain spots it ran like water from a tap.

He had meant to leave within the hour, but had felt so weak and sick he had not yet attempted it. An appalling nervousness of going outside again into the forest began to assail him. He had resorted to biting his nails. He had not done this since he was a young boy in his father's cruel presence.

Corlan did return to the hall. It was as he recalled, though more bleak and empty in daylight. Scattered all over lay the shreddings and grains of the bones of rodents, while in all the spider-nets, dead spiders and their unconsumed prey became dabs of sticky tar. The hearth contained burned logs and the blackened glass of the destroyed lamp. He had done that, then. Crazy. God knew what might have happened—the filth-clotted chimney catching alight—he seemed to hear it crash . . . The armorial motto was less evident by day. We do not altogether die.

What about the wolf—Hris? Corlan forced himself up the stair and went along the passage, both of which seemed shorter, in height and length, than during the night. Yet he took an age to walk up and along them.

The bowl was still there. Most of the pink disgusting blood-milk was gone now.

He reached the door under the arch. In the chamber beyond dusty webs hung down like draperies. There was a gaunt bed, with four upright carved posts. The wolf lay there; it was real. As he stared at it, it opened one sluggish eye, which by day was a smoky amber. It watched him, not moving, as he, leaning on the door-frame, did not move either.

"Is *he* real too, Hris?" Corlan asked the wolf. "Your master? The undead lord. Risen like Christ out of some tomb. *Devouring* me. *Eating* me alive. And you, poor bloody animal. Draining you dry, and everything here. So many little corpses, bones—drained, sucked inside out."

The wolf's eye shut. It was clearly too tired to bother with him.

Corlan turned and went away.

Partly down the stair, every step seemed suddenly to spring upward at his face. Almost fainting he clung to the bannister.

Outside, within the dark deep of the forest, silence spread its towering wings like an unseen, unheard, non-existent wind.

In the larder, when he unearthed it, he discovered some pieces of unidentifiable meat, kept cold enough, but unmistakably nibbled by something: just conceivably the band of dead rats lying about. A beggar had no choice. The loaf was the same, somewhat mouthed. And he was stealing too, from the old couple, who had in their way been helpful. For God's sake, he must shoot something in the forest. Although, in the vicinity of the schloss he had seen nothing animate, nor made out even the call of birds.

He found it difficult to think, let alone plan. Inertia, depletion. But he must get out, now, instantly. He sat down on a stool, and rested his head on the wall.

Corlan was in this position when Teda and Tils came creeping back into the room. They looked at him, he believed, with a kind of bemused contempt.

But the old woman was polishing some glasses, and Tils put a black, webbed bottle on the table. Uncorking this, he exhumed a blood-black wine.

Tils beckoned Corlan to the table, where the old woman now placed the nibbled loaf and a grey slab of curious cheese she unwrapped from a cloth.

Her hands. They appeared as if they had been broken, every bone, then set awry.

"It is pleasant," said Tils, "for us to have a little company."

Teda too sat down, though at a slight distance, ready to wait on them. But "Like the days that are gone," she murmmured.

"But surely," said Corlan, "those days are still here."

"No, no, done for ever," said Tils, drinking deeply.

It was a fine wine, metallic and strong. Corlan was cautious with it, but beginning to feel it made him rather better. His hands steadied, some focus had come back to his vision and brain.

"But this is your joke," he said coldly. "Your nameless master never died."

Tils' head went up. A flash of what—anger? hurt?—for a second ignited in the dullness behind his eyes.

"Not so. He died."

Corlan flung off any restraint with the wine. He too drank deeply. He said, "Perhaps once, long ago. He died *then*, whoever he was, and is, your master of Veltenlak. After which—once again he was—animate, shall I say."

"Ah," said Teda softly. "Ah."

Tils put down his glass and gazed into the wine's thick residue. "The gentleman means that after death, we rise in spirit."

"No, I don't mean that. I mean your master—I'll call him for his house, shall I, since you won't say his name—Herr Veltenlak—is undead. A vampire or some other sort of thing. A ghost even, that preys on humankind without any respect or care, dishonourably, uncleanly, and seldom without unneeded pain. He *likes* to cause pain. He likes to play, like a cat. Hunting is a *sport* to him. And men are his quarry. Which must mean that I am, now, I suppose."

He waited. What would happen? Tils did nothing. But Teda rose and brought the wine and refilled both their glasses, and then sat down again at a distance.

Dust rushed from the ceiling. A minute scatter of stones dropped with it, clicketing across the table like thrown dice.

"Veltenlak even devours his own castle," said Corlan. "He's eating it up."

They did not reply.

In God's name, they were not old, but *ancient*. Tils two hundred, she not far short.

Well, finish the glass, *then* get up. Take them, and myself, by surprise. Leave the ruin. God—surely I can?

By day the undead creature should not be able to follow him. Corlan visualized the resumption of his grueling trek into exile. The desolation that there awaited him. A cloud of weakness unfurled. His eyes darkened.

As he surfaced from the lapse, he heard Tils begin to speak again, as if from another room.

"I must tell you, sir, he is gone. I will tell you how and when, and why. You should be told. For some it is no matter. But you—"

"Because I resist—" Corlan inadvertantly broke in.

"You must hear me out. It was just over one year back, a few months more. When she lost our child—"

Corlan again interrupted, unable not to.

"Who lost a child?"

"I," said Teda, in her soft, dead-leaf voice. "My first. Tils' child, it was. We were only seventeen. It was a terrible thing."

"Wait." Corlan stood. The chair screaked along the stone floor. The wine kept him upright. *Say to me again the age at which you lost your child—last year.*

"Why, at seventeen, he and I both. We were very young."

"Christ," said Corlan. "Oh, Christ on his cross. Why are you lying to me? You're lunatics. Or I am."

"She says the truth," said Tils. "Be calm, sir. I'll tell you. There is nothing else to do."

Tils at no point named the Lord of Veltenlak. At no juncture, even by letting a few words slip, did Tils describe the physical appearance, the age, the manner or personality of his master. Tils did not protest or imply that his master had been noble, or kind, or even wronged.

Tils outlined only what, according to Tils, had gone on one year and two months in the past.

However, he started his narrative with these sentences:

"We were not unhappy. The schloss was mighty, built many centuries. Everything of the best. And the woods full of game. There was a lake with fish, and swans, and wild duck would come. Five wells there were in the yards, each with pure sweet water. And the cellar of the most wonderful. This wine I brought from there. It was laid down in the time of the last true king. It tastes of steel and gold. There are others that taste like rubies and blackcurrants, and white wines like apples and honey and silver."

"We belonged to the estate, you will understand. Our parents had worked the fields, or with the livestock or vines . . . "

They were thought fit, Tils and Teda, to serve in the house. And then they were married. He married them, their master, as was usual. It was a nighttime wedding. A great many other servants, of course, worked in the house. There was a lot to do. But the tasks of Tils and Teda were not menial and always there was good food and drink, shelter and luxury. They felt themselves inexorably secure. The power and might, worldy (and otherwise) of their master, hovered over them always, the pinions of a giant eagle.

And then. Ah, then.

One evening late in autumn there was a strange, thick, greenish sunset, and out of this ominous twilight a column of riders advanced with, walking before them, iron figures in the black robes of priests.

Not many ever came to the castle. The stronghold lay in a wild region, and had, too, a dark reputation that for a great while had safeguarded it. It must seem the master, freely and supernaturally, could range where he wished after prey. (Though Tils did not specify this, it was inherently indicated. For how else did the predatory being nourish himself. Corlan had inferred the servants themselves were never troubled. Probably the vampire assumed some animal shapeshift or semblance. Or grew invisible. Of such talents the undead were capable, in legend. And Corlan himself was now preyed on by an element irresistible and unseen, detectible only by the hideous results it produced of witless lassitude and an almost self-satisfied despair.)

When the procession of priests and horsemen pressed up from the forest, the castle grew alert and uneasy.

Night was imminent, and although Tils did not stress that his master was most active between sunfall and rise, Corlan had concluded it would be so. And therefore the visitors, whatever their nature or intention, must wish to meet with him.

Were the humans in the house really afraid? Despite their serfdom and inbred loyalty, their faith in their lord's powers, they were.

They had some cause.

In an era of monsters, the arm of the Church that rallied to deter them was militant, obdurate. Sadistic. Fire to fight with fire.

"We are, you see, like infants before them. The aristocracy and the priests, equally," said Tils. "Both hold a sword above our heads. We cannot deny, must not withhold. Yet he—was like our father. And these ones were—" Tils paused. It was Teda, his ancient young wife, who whispered the single phrase. "Like the Devil," she said. "Like the Devil."

The priestly crusaders thrashed their way into the master's chamber, high up in the König Ragen, a tower which, a month after these events, collapsed and crashed through into the body of the house, just missing the great hall—as if it had tried, yet failed, to crush the heart out of the place.

"Above us we heard them at work. Something was done. Even he could not evade them—"

Corlan thought, How not? He was the bloody Devil, not they. But he did not now interrupt.

It appeared the soldiers and the priests got hold of the Master of Veltenlak. Held down with and by some form of alternate sorcery, in this case named Godfulness, they stripped and flayed him. Undead, yet he was alive enough to feel.

"We heard his cries, terrible shrieking. It was not fear," said Tils in sorrowful pride. "He feared nothing. It was only agony."

At length they smashed the master's jaw, poured boiling mercury into his throat and guts, struck all his bones to shards, and at last, in the hour before dawn, smote off his head with a consecrated sword. After which, there in the upper room, they burned his body.

"There was no smell of flesh," said Tils. He waited, courteously. Teda spoke; this was her cue? "Only the odour of fire."

Then she got up and tottered out of the kitchen, away into the house.

Tils said, "We lost our baby seven hours later. All the other women in child here lost the fruit of their wombs, through that day, and the next night."

Nevertheless, the priests examined everyone yet living. Every servant must parade before them, and even the part-dead aborted women were carried roughly in. Each was stripped bare, as *he* had been, perused for blighted marks, given a crucifix to kiss. A few had *signs*, abnormal birthmarks or warts, or else were too shocked and frightened to embrace Christ on his cross. All of these were shot, slung together in a heap by the lake, and also burned.

Tils and Teda, along with twenty others judged clean, merely simpletons, were allowed to exist. When at last the invaders went away, the castle was left much as it had been.

As autumn waned to winter, and after the König Ragen fell down, a huge lethargy replaced the terror and confusion. When winter commenced, all the house began, in slight or dramatic, always persistent ways, to disintegrate. Birds died and spun from the sky. The swans perished, and the fish, and the lake turned foul, and in another summer's heat dried up. Just as did all the courtyard wells. Trees nearby began to fail. In the farther forest things died, plants, beasts. The very light grew sickly. Of the castle retainers many determined to leave. None succeeded in getting far. They would sink down, often less than thirty metres from the walls, and never again climb to their feet.

"But I stayed where I was, and she, my Teda, with me. Each day was, and is, to us like a year, so long, so reasonless, so barren, so sad. We have aged, I think? Yes, I think so. In fourteen months she and I, we have aged more than five decades. But we do not go away, you see. Do you see, young gentleman? Nothing does go. Even the wolf that he tamed, the wolf our master called Hris for the pagan god of sunset, even he remains. How strong he must be, the wolf. But he can no longer hunt. We feed him milk and a little blood. But the last cow is dead, since yesterweek. And there is so little in a rat."

Corlan closed his eyes. He saw images of fire and heard a sort of thunder, miles off. An earthquake followed.

Tils was shaking him.

"What?" said Corlan vaguely.

"Did you hear me, sir? Did you hear what I must say?"

Corlan came back. "You're more than fifteen years my junior," said Corlan spitefully, "and a slave. Don't put your damned hands on me. I heard all you said. And now I'll depart this cursed and stinking hole."

"You will never depart," said Tils. "Only through death, perhaps not even then. Some nights," said Tils, "I hear them weeping still, in the walls, the others."

"And what about *him*, your Herren—" snarled Corlan, grabbing the ancient man—seventeen, eighteen?—by his corded throat, "does *he* weep? or does he visit in his doubly undead state, and sink in his teeth?"

"He is done, sir," said Tils, as if the fingers that gripped his windpipe were straws—perhaps they were. "He is over."

Letting go, Corlan said quietly, "He's eating everything up. You, your aged wife, the wolf, the rats, the plaster and the stone. How can such a carnivorous force be *dead*?"

"Oh sir," said Tils. And now tears ran out of his eyes that seemed themselves mostly fashioned of water, "sir—sir—it is not him. He was the strength of this house, its vitality—its soul. No, no, it is—" Tils stared beyond Corlan, beyond the castle, the forest, stared and stared, seeing in horror and anguished acceptance what was not there at all. "It is," Tils concluded, "his absence. All that is left—the emptiness—without him. The hollow. The *nothingness*. The vacant pit. *That* is the vampire. That is the thing which feeds."

### Three: The Night

An eagle swept out from the König Ragen, as the masonry cascaded downwards. Its wings filled heaven, darkness, without a spark of light. The captain jumped to his feet. Beyond the door the occluded sky was swarming, not into black but white. Snow, not stonework, fell.

How long now had he slept here, the fool? (The old man was gone. The fire was out.)

Corlan lurched about the kitchen. He felt drunk, as if he had been drinking for days, as once in youth he had, ill with drink yet needing it more. The bottle though was used up. No doubt he had finished it.

He knew he must go up through the House of Veltenlak, and take himself to the small door in the larger one. He must undo it, or beat it down. It was straightforward. One proviso: he must not, at any time, sit, must not even lean on a wall or against any upright thing—post, pillar—

Staggering along the corridors, the snow hitting his head like omissions of life. The passages were longer now. Miles of them. They were catacombs. It was a library shelved and paved with the dead. Bones and tiny corpses stacked everywhere, shrivelled remains of beetles, spiders, mice, a slender lizard like a lady's fan, close-folded . . . there had been a dance, the music drifted in his ears, a gorgeous girl in a white lace gown—no, forget the girl, and the music. A dead rat lay on its back—step over. Look, the vast pillar was ahead—Christ help me—wake me up—

Abruptly he was stumbling into the colossal hall.

*Absence, not presence.*

It is the *Void* that is the vampire.

It is the *Void* which feeds—

Corlan cried out, a crazed battle-scream he had heard other men give when hit by blade or shot, crumpling over, ending—

*I won't end here.*

Nothing is worse than this, whatever it is. I can survive the winter earth, the heartless forest. Or if not, I can die *out there.*

They were seventeen, eighteen, the man, the woman. He believed it, and how they had decayed.

The great tower crashing down. The house giving way when the central support of supernatural life was extracted.

The black eagle of Nothingness filling up the sky.

The Night.

Too much of the bloody night—

But the Night was there with him. Finally it showed, unmasked its faceless face.

It must be exactly *here*, just beyond the hall and the passages, just where—somehow—now he found himself. Instead of debris, for a moment he had the impression of the ghosts of walls that had once risen solid as mountains, but they were gone and a crater replaced them, as if the full moon had been thrown down and struck the spot. But what fell was the king Tower. And now, it was Nothingness. Corlan stood on nothing and nothing surrounded him, and all things faded from him. He was blind and deaf and dumb. Even his mind lost its voices and its pictures. All erased. And yet—he *felt*, without sensation, the painless fangs fasten on him, eating him up. The void had hunted him for sport and now the void was feeding, and he was its feast. It had been much simpler with him, obviously, in his human misery, having lost everything. Easy prey—he had believed his life was over already. And here he was in life, in the midst of death, beyond which lay only total annihilation. Let go. Give in. Softly merge with Nothing, and be nothing.

Perhaps no man can strive against a demon, the vampire or the ghoul. But mankind its very self enters the dangerous world already under orders, each a warrior, to resist the Enormous *Nihil* of the abyss. How else would any of us live five minutes?

Years and continents away a crazed voice was bellowing. No denial, for the abyss was *all* Denial. Instead an *assent. Yes!* bellowed the voice. *YES*.

In the centre of the hall, while he was flailing and bellowing unintelligibly, Corlan's foot slithered over some mess on the floor—bones, stones—And as he careered and swerved to save himself, he found he had come about to confront the staircase that rose up to the wreckage of floors above.

At the staircase top something stood. It was the ancient ruined wolf.

How heavy was its head. The ruff of fur seemed to weigh it down like a collar of lead. One golden eye, filmed to stagnant treacle, staring. The other stayed shut.

Damn the wolf. It was the monster's familiar. Like the moronic servants, Tils and Teda, stuck here like dying flies in grey jam—No—it was fodder, as they were, of Nothingness—

The wolf put down one paw toward a lower step. Then drew it back, as if afraid of treading in freezing water.

Corlan swayed with fatigue. He flung his arms about his own body in a ludicrous attempt to keep himself upright. *If you fall down you will lie here till Judgement Day.* Longer. You will be *nothing.*

"Hris," he called out to the wolf. Why? But the wolf had remained alive, if only barely, and maybe, just as he did not, it did not want to be consumed, but had not itself been able to fathom a route of escape. It did not grasp what it must fight . . . was Corlan the only one who could? None of the others had wanted to . . . even he—even *he*—

"But I can," Corlan said stubbornly aloud, "I can get free. Hris," he called, his voice strengthening suddenly again, "Hris— come on, my boy—come on."

The wolf dropped its heavy head right down, and turned away. It padded off into the dark above the stair.

A blazing rage filled Corlan Von Antal.

He found he ran forward up the stairs, leaping from shallow stone to stone, all his body, his skeleton, protesting, but never missing a step.

When he reached the very top Hris had vanished.

Corlan stood panting. Then he drew the sabre, and deftly sliced a thin line along his left arm, ignoring vital veins but letting out the blood. Its colour astonished him, as if never had he seen a drop till now. Vermilion beads dripping from a thread of air—What in God's name had he done?

"Well, Hris," Corlan said, leaning only his right elbow next on the upright of the door. "Well, wolf. What do you say?"

Outside in the corridor the bowl of blood-milk was dry.

Here the wolf was, fully leaning his side on the four-poster bed, but his head back to look at Corlan through the cobweb draperies. Both the wolf's eyes were open now, if one rather wider than the other.

"Come on."

The long nose of the wolf wrinkled.

Without further preface it shoved itself off from the bed, turned right round, and slunk across the floor. Its claws ticked on the stone. It halted about a metre from him.

"All you've had is blood with this muck in it. And I'm poisoned too, but only yesterday, and I'm still fighting, still *alive*. Let me share the life with you, wolf. *No*, not that way—" for Hris had thrust his head down to the floor to lap up one of the glowing drops. Corlan held out his bleeding arm. (Oh, how the vampire would have exalted. Fresh young blood, offered up. Insanity on insanity. He'll tear my arm off—)

The wolf's tongue slipped along Corlan's wounded skin. It felt like silk. The man reached out and dug his fingers into the coarse rich fur of the ruff. The wolf drank, stopped, politely lifted his head, both eyes wide and gleaming. They were like the eyes of a young man, a comrade. *Human*. Brother.

"Now we go out, Hris."

The wolf watched him.

Corlan covered up his arm with the torn coat, and swung out of the room. He felt like a dry husk inside which pain and flame and courage were writhing in a wild knot: the desperate agonies of a living thing.

He did not need to look back. Heard the measured tick of the claws padding after him, and the occasional sponge-like gourmet note as Hris licked his snout.

In the unlight everything had grown ghostly and insubstantial. The stairs, the floor, seemed spinning off in all directions. On the high cliffs of the walls banners and weapons nearly transparent.

Corlan reached the barrier of the outer door.

Its bolts—were all undone.

He pushed against it brutally, and the quarter door sighed and tumbled back.

Night was coming in after all behind the snow. The landscape seemed to Corlan like a shattered mosaic, white, black, the whole globe flying to pieces.

A voice without voice or words called behind him, silently, deafening as a trumpet note:

*Behold Emptiness. Behold Nothingness. Behold the Abysm of Unremitting Death.*

The hot nose of the wolf punched Corlan hard in the side.

"Behold," Corlan whispered, grasping the wolf's snow-glittered mane, "behold rebellious life. No surrender."

Swaggering, staggering, halting, faltering, they crossed the remains of the drawbridge above the cavity once a lake and white with swans, now patched white with snow. Down the steep hill they went, the man and the wolf. When they reached the first trees, those whose boughs were snapped, Corlan dropped headlong on the ground. He was laughing. Then he forgot to laugh.

He saw a ballroom, lit like topaz. The snow was warm and kind. He was barely aware when Hris came closer and his meat-breath steamed across Corlan's face. Oh he'll kill and eat me now. God bless him. "Welcome, my friend," murmured Corlan. And he sank into the depths of what must be the night. But *only* that.

Because of it he did not see, and could only afterwards surmise, how the wolf got hold of him, by coat and boot leather, probably, and hauled him on beneath the first impoverished pines, on and on into the thicker shadow of the forest. Forest-deep Hris dragged Corlan Von Antal, out of the Night of Nothingness and back into the night of the winter world. Behold the rebellion of the living. Pines tall as mountains posted up into the snow-starred ether; later a moon, ivory and aquamarine, rising to pierce and to engulf the dark with the bright.

And Hris lifted his platinum head and howled the lunar love-song of his kind, before the snow closed in again. Then the wolf sat down beside the fallen man. Then the wolf lay down beside him. The snow began to cover them both, as if caringly, with a long pale quilt.

## Afterword

Nacek was unable to sleep.

The untold story of Corlan Von Antal kept running through his head.

Of course, for Nacek, it was a compendium of rumour and gossip, which the old Commander—Ursus—had never confirmed or denied.

They said, back then, he had killed a fellow officer, some shameful scum the army was glad to be rid of, the murder therefore blamed on enemy action, and Von Antal exonerated. Yet by then he had gone missing. He was found some two weeks later, in deep snow—and protected by a huge hound at least part wolf, (evidently the progenitor of Von Antal's current companion.) The oddest thing about this tale was not the dog, let alone the murder and its hushing-up, but the fact—according to all versions—that Von Antal, then in his early thirties, appeared to have aged ten years: a man of barely thirty-four had become a man of forty-four. However, if anything he was soon proved stronger than he had been, courageous and cunning in the chess game of conflict. More than a score of secret missions (they said) had been successfully undertaken by him since. While his men loved and admired him, and for the many battles in which he and his troops shone, a whole galaxy of medals and concomitant wealth had been awarded. At last retiring from the field, he had found this remote place among the forests, some antique, ruined castle, and from its stones, its bones, had had rebuilt the colossal keep and lowering tower, a König Ragen more than seven storeys high. From miles off, as Nacek had seen, you could make out its crenellated skull looming up above the team of pines, and after dark always with a russet light burning like a beacon, or a vow.

No doubt Ursus was there now, in his rooms, sleeping, or reading—for old men did not sleep the way young ones did. Not that Nacek could sleep.

He swung himself off the narrow cot, pulled on his greatcoat, and went out into the passageway, where a single candle offered light.

Confound the old boy. He must know how they all fretted to hear the truth. Like some coquette, flirtatiously hiding it from them.

Up above the last twist of the stone stair, something shouldered forward. It was the wolf-dog, Hris, caught like a phantom between glim and gloom. It had a ruff like a lion's. Two blue emeralds for eyes.

Nacek braced himself. Hris' Master was not here now, and wolves were wolves—

A voice said mildly from above, "Come up, why don't you?"

In God's name! Had the bloody wolf spoken to him? Then a man's shadow, long and lean, fell sword-like downward from a blur of copper lampshine: Von Antal. Laughing maybe at Nacek, who had thought a dog might talk.

"I couldn't sleep," Nacek said humbly.

"At your age? Well it happens. Come and take a glass of Italian wine. You'll sleep after that. Even I do."

His own rooms were spacious, Nacek presently saw. Some swords, an old flintlock, hung on the walls, and two oil paintings, one a landscape, the other the portrait of a stern and upright old man, not so unlike Ursus himself. "My Grandfather," the Bear said, handing Nacek a silver cup of wine.

Afterwards Nacek was aware, given this rare chance with Ursus alone, he had meant to try to persuade from him some of the facts behind the stories. And so, as he sipped the full and fragrant wine, Nacek asked, "Is it true, what they say about your cloak, Sir? The bearskin."

"What *do* they say?" inquired Ursus, almost lazily.

In this lower, older firelight, despite the goblet-silver of his hair, Von Antal gave a definite illusion of youth. He had the effortless physical grace of a young man, while the clearness of his black eyes was remarkable; it always had been.

Nacek told him the consensus was that the dog—that was the first dog (wolf) all those thirty or forty years back—had killed the bear.

Von Antal smiled. He lowered his eyes for a second. Yes, he was a flirt where the truth of this was concerned.

He did not explain to Nacek that the wolf now was the same wolf, Hris, that he had redeemed from Veltenlak, the very wolf too that grappled and pulled him through the forest, and warmed him in the snow. The wolf he had given his blood, as perhaps Hris' original master, the vampire, had given it. As for the bear, they had killed it between them. Hris by leading it to the clearing, Corlan Von Antal by looking into its eyes, then touching it. It had died swiftly, quick and clean, but even in that moment he had learned that he need never kill his prey. As the Herr Veltenlak had done, Corlan required only very little to sustain him, and by a transfer—less will than desire—in return he could give back an incredible enduring energy and vigour to any who served him.

He wore the skin of the bear afterwards not as a boast, but to honour it for the lesson.

Corlan had been hesitant initially, concerned at what he had become. But subsequently, that way, he never harmed another. And soon his doubts were done. When at length he returned to the ruin, as he had surmised, the *Absence* was gone. Hunger had destroyed it. The pines grew close and thick. And so he had the tower rebuilt from its own stones. He did not take on the name of Veltenlak. For it was not the vampire lord of the castle who had remade Corlan Von Antal. It was his own duel with that infinitely more terrible demon, Absence, Nothingness, the *Void*. In such a pass the vampire and its power represented the vitality of Life itself. As Corlan's violent and frantic war with the void had also done. The vessel had been drained—but given that influx of courage and rage, vitality rushed back like a river breaking through a riven dam. This world lives, and, always, Absence must give way to Presence. While the transposition from decay to renewal aged Corlan, thereafter it made him *slow* to age. Just as the same force did with the wolf. They might not now be set to live for ever, but they would live longer and more hale than most. The phoenix rises from the ashes because the surrender to the personality of the Abyss must never be. Poor Tils, poor Teda, crumbled away by the hour Corlan reclaimed the Schloss, had not known to fight, had missed the basic principle of survival. But Corlan and Hris knew all along inside their warrior souls.

"Oh," said Ursus, to Nacek, "*that* tale isn't true. I won the cloak in a card game." And next Ursus, looking into the young man's eyes, fixed him in the gentle trance, then touched and took, respectful and with care, leaving him in exchange fitter and more sturdy, handsomer even—as Nacek's fiancée would observe, when again he met her.

But Nacek himself (knowing not a jot of any of that) would always count himself a perfect idiot. He had sat in the Bear's own study, with every possibility to wring from him the whole story. And Nacek had sipped Italian wine and fallen asleep like a child. When he woke in the morning, someone had carried him back to his bed—one of the tower servants, he concluded. And he had slept wonderfully well. They all had, it seemed. And really, if he had not uncovered the truth, none of his fellow officers had either.

As, if it came to it, none of them, ever, would.

*Natura Vacuum Abhorret* (Nature Abhors a Vacuum)
François Rabelais
(1494(?)–1553)
After the Latin of Plutarch

# I COME FROM THE DARK UNIVERSE

## *Cat Rambo*

I'd made it through an interminable day of scraping up cash to pay unanticipated back taxes—the government had changed again, this time to Alliance, and revised its finances accordingly. When the sour and steamy wafts from the soup cart in Tenney Corridor caught me, I figured I deserved a treat.

Three coins for hai-paji, spiced the way it was on my homeworld, pricey and time-consuming to merge the three ingredients. I'm patient. The vendor stirred a sludge of metallic particles before serving it to an Anoogah, who clicked away on its tripartite legs, clutching the plastic cone and sucking the liquid through its trunk tentacle. Finally the fragrant soup was ladeled into a cone for me; unlike the Anoogah, I merited a spoon.

Turning, I saw a woman crouched under the wall collage of tattered food advertisements, watching the passersby and holding out a hand. Whenever a rare moment of sympathy moved a tourist to give her money, she tucked the chit away and held out her palm again, ignoring the giver as though they no longer existed.

She was cartoonish beautiful: midnight hair artfully tangled around pen stroke eyebrows and dark eyes, a smudge of violet shadowing them; wide and generous mouth; pallid skin mottled with old bruises and older dirt. She wore the blue rags of a faded

**157**

uniform whose insignia, an eye atop a black triangle, I did not recognize.

I could not figure out what it was about her that tugged at my groin. She looked wrong, sounded wrong, was the wrong height and weight and gender. I told my body that it was mistaken. It ignored me, which was a bad sign. I continued to watch her.

It had been years since I sexed—ironic for a person in my profession, brothel manager. My needs are particular, and no others of my species live on this station. A few pay rare visits, years between. In other Houses I've worked at, the employees took this fact as a challenge, trying to stir my interest, but at this House, The Little Teacup of the Soul, they take no for an answer and understand there is nothing personal about it.

Sex would be nice, I admit, but you get used to the ache, the loneliness. If you pretend hard enough, you can make it vanish.

For a while.

Anyhow.

I squatted beside her, not speaking. She paid me no attention, only muttered to herself in low gutturals. A language I didn't know. That surprised me. Two hundred years in a spaceport and a good ear has taught me most of them.

After the lights had flickered twice to indicate the passing of a quarter hour, I said, "Are you hungry?"

She looked at me, but didn't answer. I couldn't read her expressionless face, couldn't figure out whether or not this was the result of incomprehension.

"I can offer you a meal and a place to sleep for now," I said. "Maybe some kind of work, depending on what you're suited for."

She still did not answer. But when I rose to my feet and walked away, she followed. We moved through the court, which smelled of fried dough, rotting fruit, the tang of metallic green blocks, motor oil and walnuts, meats of every shape and size prepared a dozen different ways. I stopped at a bakery nook to buy day-old pastries sprinkled with sweet sap and tiny purple seeds. Both I and the human whores liked them, and they were cheap.

We came up through the Midnight Stair, past the incense sellers, each cart surrounded by a scent-cloud passing from floral to musk, to fruit, to sex, to pine and citrus, to dung. Other vendors, selling perfumed body ornaments, called to us as we passed.

"Buy a pretty for your pretty, Bo," one coaxed me, but I shook my head.

She said something to the others and they exploded into laughter.

We moved on.

The Teacup sits atop the Midnight Stair, its doorway marked in stripes of indigo and aubergine neon. Passing inside, we went past the security bot sitting in the vestibule clicking to itself and into the main room. About a third of the handlers were in their rooms; a few joes were there socializing, either waiting until someone caught their desire or else lingering post-coitus.

Silver paper covered the walls, overlaid with flocked purple scallops, reflecting a dim vision of the inhabitants. KayKay noodled out some repetitive caterwaul on the music board, ignoring the joe who sat watching him. Linor must have been on break.

The kitchen's staff-only. I took her in there for the quiet. Net sat at the table that dominates the center of the room, shuffling tiles and dealing himself hands of solitaire.

Net's a whore like the rest, but he takes the types who want their grandfather to tell them stories or offer them wisdom and only occasionally fucks them. Prime human stock, wide-shouldered and white bearded, wrinkles around his eyes like a maze of attentiveness. He nodded as we came in, eying the girl but said nothing.

I doled her out a bowl of soup and she sat hunched over it, sopping it up with chunks of bread, thrusting each into her mouth, although they were almost too big to fit.

Pouring two mugs of chai, I sat to watch her eat while I nibbled one of the pastries I'd bought.

Her eyes were enormous, dark, long-lashed. I regarded them with a connoisseur's delight, mentally applying shades of make-up and calculating the look produced.

It wasn't an otherworldly beauty; I've seen a thousand races now, maybe more. But it was something indefinable, something more alien than alien, as though she came from someplace with different physical laws, where even the atoms dance differently, or perhaps don't exist at all.

"This is a brothel," I said. "Do you know what that is?"

Net snorted and dealt another hand.

She eyed me, then nodded.

"Can you speak Common?" I said.

"I can," she said. Her voice was harsh and low, like a rusty hinge. It held a peculiar buzz, as though coming from a transmission from incalculable distances away.

"Good," I said. "Are you human?"

She shook her head.

"Compatible with humans?"

"Compatible?"

I illustrated with my fingers. "Sexually compatible."

"Yes," she said.

"You can stay here tonight in any case. We've plenty of beds. Think about whether or not you'd like to work here. If you pass the meddie tests, that is. Are you clean?"

She rubbed at a grubby forearm with a wry expression, but understood what I meant. "Yes."

The fey look about her bothered me.

"Where are you from?"

"I come from the Dark Universe," she said.

"There's only one Universe. Hence the name," Net said, his tone edged with combativeness.

"There is space, there is time," she said. She relinquished her soup long enough to gesture, reaching a hand out as far as it would go. "There is this, which spreads out in all directions—reach high, reach low, and you are moving outward like this universe. There is time as well. But there are other universes, lying across this one like piles of crumpled cloth. Like internal organs. Like clocks. Reach inside, reach outside, reach anywhere but in the directions that describe this universe, and you will find another one."

She drank from her mug and wiped her lips, leaving a streak of dirt across her pale, almost green skin. "I came from one of the other ones. This is how I came to this here and now, where everything is enclosed and you cannot see the stars."

Net gave me a look that said as clearly as words, *she's crazy*, but I listened.

She said, "In the other universe, which we will call the Dark Universe, although like this one it has no name because it is all that there is, there is the Immaculate Shadow, which spreads outward taking new worlds. Its armies are infinite, because each fallen foe becomes a new soldier."

I nodded at her uniform. "And you're one of these soldiers."

Beside me, the clinking of tiles as Net laid out another hand said to me: *Play out this folly if you will, but don't expect it to come to anything.*

She said, "The day I first awoke, I did not know who I was, other than a soldier. I had the language, the concepts, and the skills, but of the person who occupied this flesh before me, there was no trace. I was clumsy at first, learning patterns of movement. There are whispers among Its soldiers that sometimes there are memories in the body: a way of holding an object, a familiar sensation when encountering a new thing, even preferences of taste and color, but I had nothing like that. It's only me in here; the ghost is gone."

Her voice was hypnotic in its cadence, a drone like I'd never heard, her soft, sweet purplish lips speaking each word as though chewing it.

"I don't know any technology that can animate the dead and make a corpse think it lives again," Net said.

She shrugged. "I do not know the science. I suspect it would not work here. Every day I look at my body and wonder when this universe will notice me, and flick me away, or make me crumble into dust, or however else it wishes to express itself."

She set down the mug and gave us a tired look. "Sometimes I think I live by force of imagination alone. Or lack of it. I cannot imagine not being alive, even though I am dead."

There was a commotion outside: a client gone awry or drunk. I told Net, "Find her a room to sleep in for the night."

And to her, "We'll talk again in the morning."

Out in the room a drunken soldier wearing Alliance colors was grappling with KayKay.

"But you love me," he bawled, tears gusting down his face. "You love ME."

They circled the room in a clumsy dance. KayKay's tail swished in angry arcs and his claws were starting to show. The security bot was stuck in the doorway, two of the soldier's fellows holding it back.

I shouldered the first soldier and the object of his affection apart. Two of the whores went over to the soldiers holding the bot and coaxed them into corners, whispering quiet solicitations. The freed bot behind me, I walked the soldier out, counting myself lucky that it's illegal to wear weapons on Twicefar. Some port stations don't enforce that rule.

"Don't come around any more," I said to the soldier. "Alliance are welcome, you're not." I didn't want him filing a complaint against our place for discrimination; this port is a maze of petty alliances and power struggles and I try to keep out of the way of the major players.

Tears coursed across his face, outlining a ragged red scar that marked his jaw.

"But he loves me," he said. "He loves me."

I shook my head. "You don't pay for love here," I said. "You pay for pleasure. You're buying the body, not the mind."

He went to his knees, holding himself with a desperate clutch as though keeping his guts from spilling out. "He loves me," he whispered. He looked up at me, his jaw jutting out and motioned to his face. "He's the only one who ever looked past this."

"Sober up, then try finding love elsewhere," I said. I swiped his ID across my record tablet and handed it back to him. "There's other Houses here, man. Some will say they love you. We don't."

I left him there by the mouth of the Stair.

Inside, the two soldiers were gone, as were the whores who'd been talking to them, presumably off adding to the Teacup's bottom line. I gestured KayKay over.

"I didn't do anything," he said, shoulder rising in a sullen shrug.

"Yeah," I said. "I know, I know. But you treat them nice when they're here, KayKay. Don't go cold on them just because they did something to piss you off."

"He was showing me trophies," he said. "Battle trophies. From little kids."

KayKay's culture, like my own, holds harming children taboo. Some species don't. I've lived long enough to watch taboos stronger than that one violated, but he was still young, had come to us only a year or two after becoming adult. I didn't want to inquire whether the trophies were ears, or eyes, or scalps. People collect all kinds.

"What am I supposed to do when that happens?" KayKay said, his voice challenging.

I leaned close to him. "Play it nice. You never let a joe know that you find them anything but appealing. Got it?"

In the kitchen, a pattern of tiles lay like a mandala in front of Net.

"You get the girl settled in?" I asked.

"I put her in the third hallway, one of the unused rooms," he said. "Says her name's Zoolie, or rather that's the name given her by the Immaculate Shadow." He rolled his eyes. "You sure know how to pick 'em, Bo. She's too crazy to work here, you do realize that?"

We've had crazies before; I had to agree that we didn't need any more. There were plenty of prima donnas and drama queens in the House if we wanted entertainment. But I still felt that itch.

"Yeah . . . " I said, drawing the word out like gum.

He eyed me. "What aren't you telling me?"

"It's complicated," I said.

He stared at me until I dropped my eyes, looking at the plastic swirls of the floor. "Well, I'll be," he said. "Bo, the creature of stone, wants to *fuck* her. I thought you couldn't do that outside your own race."

"I can't," I said. "But somehow—I don't know how—she's outside that rule."

"You're a loony moon. She does believe she came from another dimension, you know."

"We've got workers from all over," I said. "They end up here, because Twicefar's a way point between so many galaxies. And some crazy isn't too bad. Remember Dililo? It kept having false pregnancies, but all we had to do was humor it."

"Some crazy, yeah. Not 'I was a soldier in the zombie legions' crazy."

I rubbed the bridge of my nose between thumb and forefinger. "Maybe."

That night, before sleeping, I stripped and looked at myself in the wide mirror. To most, I look like a human male when clothed, despite my white, waxy skin. Pudge has settled around my midsection from too many pastries, but I am still strong enough to hold two humans at arm's length above the floor.

Unlike most humans, I have no body hair, except for colorless eyelashes, and the turquoise blue of my eyes would be unusual on a human—even though that race is now so widespread and divergent that it's hard to find any trait not held on one planet or another. My hands, four fingered, are supple and well-manicured.

Unclothed, though, it would be hard to consider me male; my cloaca rests behind a star of pale flesh that is not unattractive.

A long-dead lover once wrote a poem to that star: called it a flower, a meteor, the center of its universe. It recited the poem while coaxing the star open, a sexual preliminary I have always enjoyed. A long slow shiver worked its way down my arms and legs at the thought.

It would be years before another of my kind came to this station, and even then, there was no guarantee they'd be of the right sex. I sighed and passed my hand over the swell of my belly, and tried to pretend.

I n the morning, Zoolie was sitting in the kitchen, eating again. We take turns cooking—KayKay was at the stove, flipping pancakes for anyone who wandered in.

"Come with me when you're done," I told her. "I've got errands to run, and we can talk."

Pushing her chair back, she rose. She'd taken advantage of the facilities to clean up; the grime was gone, and her hair was combed. Someone had lent her a clean black shirt, which she wore over the uniform trousers and boots.

She fell into step, matching my stride.

"How long have you been a soldier with the Immaculate Shadow?" I asked.

"Four years."

"How do you measure time?" I didn't know if she meant a lifetime or a flicker.

"I don't know how long my race lives," she said. "I trained, and then I saw four battles."

"Training doing what?"

We descended the Midnight Stair and headed inward towards the Admin offices. I meant to feed the soldier's ID into Records and write up a formal complaint. I had no desire to punish him, but if he came back and there were problems, I wanted it on record. I've learned caution and patience over the years.

She glanced around her as she walked, not looking at me. "They wanted to get us used to killing. So we practiced. First on animals, then on people. If we didn't do it . . . " She shrugged and kept on walking.

"What happened if you didn't do it?"

"First they cut your ears and nose off, or whatever you had that served you that way. Balk a second time, and you were an example for someone else to kill."

"How many people did you kill?" I asked.

Her face was hard. "Counting battles? Hundreds."

"But how did you come here?"

She paused in the corridor, under the flickering lights, looking at me.

"There was a battle," she said. "The ship—I'd gotten to be friends with it; it called itself Morning—was damaged and couldn't fix itself. It couldn't move against gravity any more."

"Then what?"

Her eyes were distant, looking at the memories. "It was all confused, so I tried to find out what was going on. I grabbed at the sleeve of a soldier crawling past me in the tube. We hung there for a moment, ignoring the protests of those behind us. What's going on? I said. He told me that the guidance mechanism was out. The ship was falling into the sun."

She swallowed and went on. "The other soldier made to move on. I reversed my direction and followed him. He was moving with some purpose in mind, at least. We emerged into one of the bubbles that watch the outside, filled with people running back and forth in confusion. He said we could die with the ship, boiling away in heat, the air scorched in our lungs, burning from the inside. Or choose our moment, here and now. And as he spoke, I saw that many were choosing to die now, moving to the airlocks in order to jump out into the darkness, the vacuum. Some had joined hands, as though wanting to comfort and be comforted; they leaped in pairs, outward, falling into the stars in aberrant trajectories. One cluster of five or six flew out in a ring, as though parachuting, the circle of clasped hands tumbling in space and falling apart as they died and lost their grip on each other to float away, alone despite their efforts, visible only as they eclipsed the faint stars. I was so horrified I could not breathe. My guide moved away in the crowd, and I didn't see him again."

I watched her face and the flickers of emotion playing over it. People jostled past us in the corridor, but she stood as still as though she was a fixture. Finally, I spoke.

"But here, how did you get here?"

Her eyes rose to mine. "I don't know. I stayed on the ship while everyone else left. By the time I decided I wanted to jump, I was alone. I didn't want to jump alone. The ship screamed as something crashed into it, and I must have hit my head and fallen. When I woke up, I was here, in another ship."

Moving closer, she rested her fingertips on my arm. "I don't want to go back."

I took her to the meddie offices, signed her in to get tested. While I was waiting, I headed over to the closest bars, the bars spacers are likely to hit. At the third one, I got results.

"Sure, I remember her," the pilot said. He was a gnarled chimp, a gray wool cap covering the bulge of his modified brain. "You wouldn't believe where we found her. We were mining near the Planck twin suns, where the black holes are thick, and found her floating in space."

"What kind of suit was she in?"

He shook his head, his face creasing in a bemused, curled lip smile. "That was the really hyperbolic thing. No suit. We thought she was dead, took her in to see if there was any salvage. And she sits up, looks around at us. I nearly shit my pants. She couldn't speak Common at first—wild huh? Must have been from some backwater. But she picked it up soon enough."

I bought his next drink and thanked him.

Back at the offices, she was surrounded by medics. She moved through the crowd towards me, her face relieved, brushing them aside with ruthless ease to hand me the file.

"They want to buy me," she said, panic in her voice. "I don't want to be owned. I want to come work for you, and have my own room."

The medics dispersed at the sight of my scowl. I looked the file over and finally took it over to the nurse station. "Can you explain some of these results to me?"

It boiled down to this: they couldn't explain her. She shouldn't exist, really, they said, and offered a lot of money for her contract. I lied and said she was already locked down to me.

As we walked back, she kept moving close, touching me with little brushes and pats. I felt desire aching in me like a deep, hollow bruise every time I moved away, every time she looked at me, puzzled.

Training and four battles. That's all she experienced of life before she came here. That's all she knew.

At the House, I started assembling a kit with what she'd need, keycard for her room and the outside, voucher book, list of necessaries.

"You're going to hire her?" Net said in disbelief.

"Her story checks out," I said. "Or close enough. She wants a place to stay. Security. The Teacup can provide it."

"We don't usually hire lovers."

"Trust me," I said.

"You're the boss."

"Yeah. I am."

I went out into the main room, where she was waiting.

"All right," I said. "Here's the deal. We give you a room. If you want to help out with cooking, food's free, otherwise there's a cost of 40 solars a cycle. You get 50% of profits from every trick. Costumes, specialty items, and supplies come out of your pay, but we only charge you cost. The House pays your license, and splits the cost of meddie treatments with you. Clients can give you gifts, but if you're extorting or skimming, you're fired first time it happens."

I tossed her the kit. "And the other part is this: you don't fuck any member of the house. No one, no whores for sure. And not me, not Net, not Linor. Got that?"

She gave me a slow nod, her eyes full of questions.

I didn't pause, just said "Good" and went into the kitchen where Net was shuffling out tiles, pretending like he hadn't been watching.

He gave me a questioning look. "How long can you wait?" he said, nodding at the doorway.

I slumped into a chair and picked up the hand he'd dealt me. "Long enough," I said. "Long as it takes for her to grow up."

He laid his first tile down, and I matched it, but nothing more was said. My needs are particular, but I'm a patient soul.

# HAPPY HOUR AT THE TOOTH AND CLAW

## *Shira Lipkin*

### The Vampire
Agony Jones walks into the bar.

### The Werewolf
Mary Magdalene Kendall walks into the bar.

### The Witch
I'm already in the bar; I'm in all the bars. I am at a table facing
the door, back to the wall, and I am drinking a sweet tea and
not a rum & Coke because bending reality and alcohol don't
mix well. Things get tangled or severed. This is where someone
else might say "and then there's all the paperwork!" but I don't
do paperwork; I do, however, like to keep the bar tidy.

### The Bar
The bar is every bar. The bar has always been here. It's the tavern
where you meet your party, it's the saloon where all the action
goes down, it's the only place on the space station worth hanging
out in. I sit at a fixed point and the bars shoot off in all directions
like spokes on a rimless wheel, infinitely small slices of reality all
stacked up against each other, with minimal bleedthrough.

This one has karaoke.

### The Witch

I can work this little bit of bleedthrough because the vampire and werewolf bars are so similar—so similar, even, that my wardrobe is the same. I'm female in both bars, wearing tight leather pants that show off a tribal lower back tattoo where my slightly-ragged black tank top rides up in back. My stomach is perfectly flat here, and my hair is long and dark. My spine feels more malleable than usual, even. It's very precise, the wardrobe in this sort of bar, very cookie-cutter. I'm designed not to stand out too much in a crowd, but this sort of bar is more homogenous than most.

I doodle on my napkin in a language no one in this bar knows.

Well. Almost no one.

### The Angel

The angel who tends bar goes by the name of Jack. He won't tell me his real name, which is, I suppose, perfectly reasonable. I don't do name magic, but for all he knows, I know someone who does.

Jack is a cherub. Not a little Renaissance putto, a for-real cherub. Here we only see his man head, but he tends four bars simultaneously, and in the others I've seen his other heads—ox, lion, eagle. He hides his wings in this bar, too, but sometimes he sheds through the veil between realities, and I've found silvery feathers trodden under peanut shells.

Jack does not like it when I fuck around in here. He doesn't get bored—he has four separate places to be at any given time, and that keeps him more than occupied enough. I can *see* everything from here, but that's so passive.

### The Witch

I have siblings who've turned to stone from being so damn passive, from doing nothing but observing. I have siblings who've turned into stars or free-floating ideals or trees. But I'm restless. So I reach out and I apply a little friction to two realities. I wear the veil just a little thin.

**The Vampire**
Agony Jones is less than five feet tall. She compensates with screaming red hair cut short and choppy, tall boots, and an aggressive stomp. She cases the joint as she walks in; she notes all of the exits. She's freshly fed and looks nearly human, if a bit out of date. She claims a table in the corner and watches the crowd; she winces when the beginning of karaoke night is announced.

**The Werewolf**

Mary Magdalene Kendall, all worn denim and soft black tee and long black hair, goes by Maggie or Mags. Too many Marys in her family. She walks in with a few women from her pack, laughing; she nods at Jack when she passes him, and he nods back. Mags and her pack aren't trouble. Or, well, they are, but they keep the trouble outside. Here they are model citizens whose only crime is that they hog the pool table sometimes.

**The Angel**
Jack notices that Agony and Mags are in the same bar. He is not happy. I don't think I'm getting a refill on my sweet tea.

**The Witch**
Fuck it. I lean forward, shake some salt in my hand, and sing. Very quietly, and if even Jack knows this language, I will be very surprised. And pissed off at the family lorekeepers.

**The Vampire and the Werewolf**
They notice each other from across the room.

Agony straightens from her perpetual slouch as she watches Mags flip her long dark hair over one shoulder to make her shot—something ball in the corner pocket, I don't care, I don't shoot pool. Mags feels her eyes on her and looks up after the ball goes in, reflexively smiling—Agony's a solo predator but Mags is all pack, so she feels safe enough to smile. Agony doesn't get to show anyone more than that spiky fuck-you persona most days. Not many people smile at Agony Jones. They're usually running and screaming.

But Mags smiles. And then she smells what Agony is. She nods thoughtfully. But doesn't stop smiling.

Mags turns to talk to her packmates, and Agony notices that Mags has a truly superb ass. Also, that she is a werewolf. Agony thinks about whether that matters. She decides that it doesn't matter a damn to her, but she doesn't know what Mags's position on that would be.

And then the damn werewolves get into the karaoke.

Agony would leave right now if it wasn't for Mags. Because fuck karaoke. Very few people are good at karaoke, and the bar is full of people who are not those people. It's ear-assaulting shite, and Agony wishes she could still get drunk, because that would help. But the pretty wolfgirl in her supple leather vest keeps looking over shyly, and no one's looked at Agony like that in a damn long time, so she waits. Her skin itches, almost. She doesn't know what this is.

And then Mags gets up on stage, and Agony braces herself for her little crush to be over—

And Mags busts out a perfect Johnette Napolitano. Concrete Blonde. "Bloodletting." The wolfgirl is singing a vampire song. She is working the stage, and her hips are almost as mesmerizing as her eyes. Which are on Agony. Shy little wolfgirl needed a musical excuse. It's a hell of a way to say hi. She's got the ways and means indeed.

She finishes to great applause; she laughs, blushing, her eye contact with Agony a little less direct—and Agony meets her at the edge of the stage, hands jammed in her back pockets, trying to be casual.

"You wanna get out of here?" Agony says, fake-cool. "Karaoke sucks. Present company excepted."

"You don't want to sing?"

"You don't want to hear me sing."

"Fair enough." She laughs, her voice a little rough in the most interesting ways. "I'm Mags."

"I'm Agony. Long story."

"Wanna tell me about it?"

Agony grins, not bothering to hide her fangs. "If you want."

They leave the bar. It's drizzling just a little, more a mist than anything else. Miniature droplets gather like dew on Mags's long hair.

### The Witch

I bring my glass back to the bar. Jack gives me a look too dirty to come from an angel. "What?" I say. "They were lonely."

"You were lonely. They're not your toys, Zee."

"If they wouldn't have liked each other anyway, the charm wouldn't have worked. You know that. It doesn't create love out of nothing. It just jump-starts the process."

"Zee—a vampire and a werewolf?"

"Why not?"

"Different worlds?"

"Not *too* different. Some boundaries are arbitrary. This is one of them."

"And how long will this thinning between worlds last?"

I shrug. "A while. Would forever be bad? You wouldn't want to tear the new sweethearts apart, would you?"

Jack sighs. A small, downy feather spirals down from the empty space over his shoulder. It lands in the remains of a draft beer. "You need a hobby that doesn't involve violating laws of physics."

I pluck the feather from the beer and blow it back at him; he winces as it splats on his forearm. Angels don't like to be less than pristine. I touch his wrist, and with the slightest twist of two strands of reality, I am in another bar, grinning at his lion head. He grumps at me when he realizes what I've done, a little huff and a snort, and I slide off the barstool to track down Allemande Left.

### The Alien Stripper
"I'm not a stripper," Allemande Left says, her voice syrup-slow as she concentrates on sliding the strip of ridged silicone into one of the sliverthin pockets above her natural cheekbones. "I'm a courtesan."

### The Alien Courtesan
"And I'm not an alien; I just cater to them."

### The Courtesan
"Better."

Allemande Left studies herself in the mirror and shifts the ridge upwards a bit, then dusts the skin over it with opalescent powder to draw the eye. She looks over her shoulder critically, ensuring that her back ridges are aligned. Allemande Left is a perfectionist. I watch myself watch her, and I stretch, relieved to be out of the body I'm locked into at the vamp/were bars. Here I am preternaturally slender and genderless, ever so slightly silver, large-eyed, with a 1950s-atom halo of tiny processors orbiting my bare head. My clothes drape soft with a muted shimmer like a knife in a dirty mirror. Here I scan as a technomancer more than a witch. Allemande Left believes in science like Agony Jones believes in blood.

"Zee," she says. "Where did you come from this time?"

"Leather and beer and animal urges. Allemande Left, where are you going?"

"Dancing."

"You're always dancing."

"Breathing is dancing. Contract negotiation is dancing.
Sleeping is dancing."

Allemande Left comes from a dance background, she says.
Really, she comes from centuries of dance background,
ancestors and ancestresses at the Joffrey and ABT, Ballet
Russes and Alvin Ailey. She keeps them all in a slimline chip
embedded in the inside of her delicate wrist. All of them who've
been uploaded at least. Every Tuesday, Allemande Left takes
tea with them. It's all very formal. Allemande Left, who took
her name from a great-great-aunt with a secret love of folk and
square dance, loves ritual more than she loves anything but
dance.

She arranges her costume. The wearable parts—she was nearly
done with the insertable parts before I got here. She almost
always is. "Allemande Left, I have never seen your real face."

"They're all my real face."

I know that, too.

I would describe her, but next time she'll be different. She is
Allemande Left, and she is whoever you need, for an evening
and a morning. She kisses my cheek; she smells of sandalwood
and metal. The ribbons of her costume brush over me, and the
bells on her belt chime as she stands. Her smile is dreamy,
as if she's half-gone already, already well on her way to being
whoever she is tonight. Her eyes flash silverbright. "Come see
me soon, Zee. I miss you."

And she is gone.

### The Angel
"You know better."

Even Jack's voice seems furry somehow. Here at the Mercy
Seat, right at the tip of the sleekest space station I've ever
seen. It's been a damn long time since humans built it and
moved on; it crumbled only slightly into disrepair before the
Conglomerate moved in and made it better than new. The

Mercy Seat was gutted and revamped, with booths that cater to specific species.

No one here knows Jack's origin. No one here believes in angels, not like Mary Magdalene Kendall believes in angels, not like humans in general regard them as a nice story. Jack says he usually passes for some exotic bodymod addict. They can do lion heads and wings here, if you pay enough.

"Better than what?"

I am watching Allemande Left. She is graceful and sinuous and I swear the bells at her waist only chime exactly when she wants them to. I have no idea how she does that.

"Better than to hang around while she's working."

If Allemande Left turned around right now, she would not recognize me. I take another drink. "Do I have anything better to do? You don't like it when I quantum tunnel."

Jack growls softly. I know he doesn't like this place as much, because it's so perfect that he doesn't need to do anything—in any other bar, he'd be wiping things down to seem busy, but these are all self-cleaning surfaces. Instead, he folds his arms across his broad, bare chest. "You're not going to start anything tonight, are you?"

"You gonna kick me out if I do?" I smile and stretch. He can't kick me out. Things like him have no authority over things like me.

"I wouldn't mind so much if you finished what you started." He flicks the strictly-for-display towel at me.

"Oh yeah, huh? Agony and Mags."

"Among any other of your little experiments. And . . . " he looks over at Allemande Left meaningfully.

I dip my fingers into my drink and flick liquid at him; his feathers ruffle reflexively. "Don't even."

"I'm just saying. You might want to do something about that."

"This isn't my story, Jack."

## The Werewolf

Mary Magdalene Kendall is sprawled on a mattress on the floor of Agony Jones's studio apartment, nude and overly warm. Agony is propped up against the wall, looking like she's really wishing for the cigarette Mags denied her, also nude. She is painfully thin and always will be.

"How old were you?" Mags asks, and loops back with "If that's not a rude question."

Agony tousles her spiky hair. "Eighteen," she says. "Generally it is, but considering . . . "

Mags laughs and stretches, very happy in her skin. "Mmmm. Considering."

"1983. Dammit I want a smoke, but I don't wanna get dressed."

Mags taps her nose. "Super-sensitive, darling. Bad enough that the whole bed smells like smoke—"

"And sex—"

"That I don't mind. Especially considering." Another wicked wolfgirl smile. "We could find another way to occupy your mouth."

## The Witch

"See? They're doing fine."

I'm speaking to Jack's ox head now, which is probably my favorite. His human head is too pretty. Inhuman in its perfect humanity. I prefer him straight-up inhuman. He snorts and wipes down the bar, and I try not to grin. "So how long?"

"Until . . . I don't know." I shift in my seat, restless. I'm wearing jeans and an Oxford shirt on a male body here, taller than the body I wore at the Mercy Seat. My head itches a little from suddenly having hair. I don't scratch. I look around the bar and notice a bit of resonance in the corner. Finally, something interesting. I leave Jack a tip for nothing in particular and bring my drink over to the corner table, sit down with my back to the door. "Olly olly oxen free," I singsong, looking at Jack, who rolls his eyes in disgust.

"Zzzzzzeeeeeeee," the air shivers out, like thousands of gnats.

"Come on. I wouldn't have seen you if you weren't here to work."

### The Oracle

The oracle in the corner—I call it the oracle in the corner pocket because I'm a goofball, but also because the corner is a pocket universe of its own—shimmers into view. Zie cycles through a persona every eyeblink, headscarf and hoop earrings, punk-rock tatters, a tuxedo, and I kick back in my chair and wait until zie settles, flickers only occasionally. This persona I've seen before, a low-voiced man who seems more solid than the table and chair, with a deck of cards. "What do you want, Zee?" he asks, his voice rough music, callused fingers tapping the deck.

"People always ask me that. No one says 'How are you, Zee? Wanna get a drink, Zee?'"

"Then how are you, Zee?" He arches an eyebrow. I never could do that, just the one eyebrow.

"Apocalyptically bored."

He nods. "That's truer than you think."

"What do you mean?"

"Bad things happen when beings who can smash together universes get bored."

"Hey. I have a pretty good track record."

"But you want something more now?"

"Well. Yeah."

"What do you want?"

I stop. I think.

I deflect.

"Why aren't you using the cards?"

"You know they're just a prop."

"Yeah, but it's nice to pretend sometimes."

He shakes his head. Shuffles. Flips a card out of the middle and flicks it at me; before I snatch it out of the air, he says, "And how long has it been?"

It's a valentine, the kind kids give each other in school. Red construction paper heart taped onto a popsicle stick. "Since I hid my heart?"

"If that's what the card is asking you."

"Why should that matter?"

"How long, Zee?"

I think. "I don't tell time like you do. A while."

"How many hundreds of years is a while?"

"I'm not suicidal."

"Never said you were. But I asked you what you wanted, and the card's telling you you want your heart."

**The Witch's Heart**
is cold
is safe
is hidden

(is broken)
is hiding
is floating
is waiting

### The Oracle
"Do you even remember where you put it?"

"It's safe."

"Yes. It's hidden, and it's safe, and you'll live forever without it. But is that even what you want anymore?"

### The Vampire
Agony Jones will live forever and never grow up and she is tired. She masks it with fresh hair dye on the regular and boot-stomping music and brief torrid affairs that end in bloodshed (not hers).

Agony Jones is pretty sure that she's not built for a long-term relationship. Especially with someone who doesn't approve of her diet and, oh yeah, does not have a lifespan the equal of her own.

### The Werewolf
Mary Magdalene Kendall stalks the night, fists balled in the pockets of a leather jacket, fresh from another fight about fucking Agony bringing home what she likes to call "takeout." Mags cannot deal with walking in to find Agony face down in some random person, even if it's only food, not sex. She knows Agony needs the blood, she knew the first night what Agony was, but it wears on her. It just wears on her.

When she gets home, Agony's dinner will have wandered off with a dazed grin, and Agony will
a) be sullen and resentful
b) be pretending nothing happened
c) be quiet and withdrawn, which is her version of an apology.

Mary Magdalene Kendall is not sure she's built for this.

### The Vampire and the Werewolf

When Mags walks through the door, Agony is sitting on the mattress, miserable, and she says "It was a Duran Duran concert."

"What?" This was not a sentence Mags was prepared for, and she has difficulty parsing it.

"When I was turned. I was at a goddamn Duran Duran concert."

Mags can't help it—despite Agony's I-dare-you glare, she collapses into giggles and onto the mattress. "You? Punk-ass you? At a—"

Agony buries her face in her hands. "Right in the middle of 'Rio.'"

Mags can't breathe, she's laughing so hard, and it even forces a chuckle or two out of Agony. "At—at least—at least it wasn't 'Hungry Like the Wolf'!"

Agony whacks her with a pillow and she laughs even harder, until Agony is laughing just as hard. "Don't *tell* anyone!"

"I'm gonna tell *everyone!*"

"Don't you *dare!*"

Mags calms herself and looks at Agony. Little Agony, who went to a New Wave concert as a goofy teenager and got turned. Agony, who knows that she has to be a hardass or she'll be seen as prey.

Mags knows a little about that. She has a shy kid sister. She worries.

"I won't tell," she says.

Agony shifts on the mattress. "Are we okay? Ish?"

"Ish. I still—"

"I know."

"Can you not bring them *home*?" Mags's voice comes out higher than anticipated, plaintive, surprising them both.

Agony squeezes her hand, cold on warm. "I can do that."

### The Witch

Hiding your heart is standard operating procedure for witches. If there was a manual, heart-hiding would be in it. If we had soap operas, one would be called *The Hidden Heart*. It's a thing. If you hide your heart, no one can destroy you. You are untouchable, inviolate, immortal.

I don't see why I'd want mine back. It's messy.

### The Courtesan

Allemande Left is leaning on the bar, all grace and elegance. His extension is flawless, the line of his body impeccable. He has more instinct for this than I ever will, immortality or no. "Interesting reading," he says with a very small smile, sipping something blue.

"Should I look for it?"

"You don't know where it is?"

I wave a hand dismissively, disturbing one of the tiny processors orbiting my again-bare head. "I remember *most* of it, I think. It's been a long time."

"You have lost a piece of your heart," Allemande Left says thoughtfully, smile curving broader. "How almost mortal of you, Zee."

I suppress a flare of petulance. Mostly. "I don't *need* it."

"I believe that you might."

"I don't see why anyone would."

"You forget, Zee." Allemande Left brushes a small, dry kiss onto my cheek, his silver-threaded hair swinging over one shoulder. "You forget things when you don't have a heart."

### The Witch
Do not think I'm being literal.

The heart that I have hidden is not a lump of striated muscle. There are no veins flopping out of it. The heart I have hidden is an abstraction, a Platonic ideal of a heart. It's a rite of passage, being able to encompass one's heart. To remove it, to examine it.

Different traditions have different ways of safeguarding their hearts. One tradition swears by the hackneyed old methods: the heart should be kept in an egg on a mountain in the wilderness and so forth. Some traditions keep all of the hearts in one central location, which I find efficient yet foolhardy.

Mine is a heart divided.

### The Bar
I close my eyes.

I close my eyes.

I close my eyes.

I close my eyes and flick through realities like I'm skimming a just-read book for a remembered piece of dialogue, somewhere back there on page whatever, but these pages are universes. It's delicate work. I flash through world after world after bar after bar, keeping my Self contained in a tiny sphere at the center of me, about where my heart would go—my body changes too quickly when I do this. Too much cognitive dissonance. I am not a body, I'm a witch. And this is silly anyway, but witches are curious beasts.

I open my eyes.

The bar is enormous. The bar may, itself, be an entire world. I remember this one, and I smile. I nod at the bartender, Luminiferous Aether. It jiggles slightly in a way that indicates a raised eyebrow—I haven't been here in a while, maybe a few hundred years, but it remembers me.

The humors are playing bridge at the table by the door. As always, the biles are partnered, opposing blood and phlegm, who appear to be winning. The Odic Force and Elan Vital are twining at the bar as if they're attempting to fuse in search of scientific validity. Or maybe they're just tipsy. I don't know what they're drinking. I don't know what anyone else drinks here; they'e all too damn esoteric.

Phlogiston moves sullenly out of my way, allowing me a seat at the bar. Some beings never get over being discredited. Some of us just shrug it off and go about our business, enjoying the lack of attention. I've tried pep-talking Phlogiston before, though, and it never works.

Luminiferous Aether dims and brightens; a question. "Nothing to drink," I say. "But you were holding something for me."

It shimmers into view on the bar—a small leather book that emits a low but noticeable hum. I nod to Aether and place my hand on it.

### The Witch's Heart
sings home and home and home again
floods in
establishes its borders
waits

### The Witch
I close my eyes.

### The Vampire
Agony Jones is in too deep.

She is in love, heart wild and untrammelled, singing into the night! She is reckless and heedless and helpless and hopeless.

Because
a) Mary Magdalene Kendall is a werewolf from a proper werewolf family, and she has not introduced her to her parents yet, and
b) Mary Magdalene Kendall is mortal.

Agony Jones stomps down the streets, hair and aura spiked—
Mags is beautiful! and mortal. Mags is wickedly silly! and mortal. Mags is kind and funny and clever! and mortal.

And mortal. And mortal. And mortal. Like the heartbeat Agony doesn't have.

### The Werewolf
blood and scent of fear-on-prey and streaks of shades of grey
and
running running running
jaws snapping shut
the tearing, rending, flesh from flesh from bone
rich coppersweetsalt thick on muzzle

and

Mary Magdalene Kendall flows back, gasping, nude, streaks of gore on coppertan limbs. Shivering a little from cold, a little from the change.

She draws a hot bath, eases in, gasping as heat suffuses sore muscles, watching the water pink. She sighs, and she thinks,
*Agony*.

Her first thought after every change. *Agony, Agony, Agony*, a song in her head every time she emerges; *Agony*.

*Agony*.

### The Witch
I sit at a corner table, watching the vampire and the werewolf play footsie. This one seems to be sticking. Not just the couple: the worlds. The membrane seems to have become permanently permeable. Which is the sort of thing that might get me in trouble if anyone was watching, which no one ever is.

Belying that thought, Jack sets a highball glass in front of me. I look up and up at him, eyebrow raised; he sighs and sits. "And how's your quest?" he asks.

I scrunch up my face and take a sip of whatever. Boozycherrysomething. "What *is* this?"

"I am calling it The Witch's Heart," he grins.

I snort, equal parts due to the joke and to the fact that Jack made a joke and is smiling. "What's in it?"

"I'd tell you, but you'd forget instantly and you don't actually care. So." He flicks the towel at me. "Quest."

"I thought you didn't like it when I bend the laws of physics?"

"Well, it's been keeping you out of my hair—and I find that when you're out of my hair, I start to get worried. At least when you're causing trouble in my bars, I know what you're up to."

I take another sip of The Witch's Heart. "No shit, this is really good."

"Zee."

"*Okay.*" I spread my hand out on the scarred wooden table. Black nail polish in this bar, and no jewelry. "I found seven pieces. They're all knitted back together and humming in counterpoint to each other and it is highly weird."

"Seven? How many pieces are there total?"

"Nine? I think? It feels like nine." I turn inward, trace the borders of my incomplete heart. "It feels like two missing."

"So where are you off to next?"

I shrug.

"Don't you want to see what happens when the gang's all back together?"

"Well, I don't know. Is the thing. Where the other two pieces are."

Jack tilts his head skeptically. "Zee. Really."

My almost-heart stutters oddly, feels swollen. I watch a tiny fluff of a feather swirl down, and I catch it. It weighs nothing. "I lost them, I think. A while ago. I remembered where I stashed the first few pieces, and once I had those, they led me to the others, but I'm blocked now. I'm not being led anywhere. I'm just . . . *here*. And they ache, all along the edges where pieces are missing. Not a sharp pain, nothing acute, just this constant pull but I don't know to where or to what." I drink again. "This was a stupid idea. The Oracle's a jerk." I poke savagely at the cherry with the stirrer, stabbing it a dozen times, more. Cherry juice infuses the liquor, bleeding from the raggedly torn center of the fruit. I impale it and scowl.

When I look up, Jack is gone.

### The Vampire and the Werewolf

Agony Jones can deal with anything expect being without Mary Magdalene Kendall and
Mary Magdalene Kendall can deal with anything except being without Agony Jones.

It's okay that she's mortal; they'll figure it out.
It's okay that she drinks blood, they'll figure it out.

They are both killers in their own way, anyway. They both love 80s music and broken-in leather and each other, and you'd be surprised how far that'll get you. You really would.

### The Witch's Heart
aches

### The Courtesan
"It's not about being perfect," says Allemande Left.

I am perched on my stool in her corner again, watching her apply her prosthetics. She is effortlessly perfect, with an economy of movement that is truly impeccable. "I don't believe you."

She laughs, black eyes catching mine in her mirror. "It's not. Perfect looks artificial. Like old-Earth beauty pageants, where all the girls looked exactly the same. The same teeth, the same makeup job, the same dress, the same updo. Perfect is Teflon. It leaves nothing to catch the eye." She smiles and runs a hand along her arm, currently studded with small triangular implants. "I'm slightly asymmetrical. My coloring is uneven. I have scars."

"We all have scars." I realize that my hand is over my almost-heart.

Allemande Left realizes it as well. She kneels before me. Black eyes, tapered skull—I don't even know what species she's emulating today. It doesn't matter. When Allemande Left is with me, Allemande Left is with me; I would know Allemande Left anywhere. "What is it, Zee?"

"My heart hurts."

I hadn't planned to say it, but it's true. The ache has deepened, and my heart has begun to move. It is a wild thing in my chest. It thrashes to its own music.

Allemande Left takes my hands in hers, in her slender blue multi-jointed hands, and she kisses them gently. She places one back against my chest, keeping her hand over it, and she places the other on her own narrow chest, holds it in place.

And my heart *pulls* from two directions at once.

### The Witch's Heart
is desperate
is tearing
is almost almost almost

### The Witch
"Allemande Left! What..?"

She laughs. "You gave it to me for safekeeping, Zee. So long ago. I've kept it with my own."

I draw it from her chest, and she sighs as it emerges—a tiny flame. I press it into my own chest, and I am overwhelmed—

everything at once, and the singing, and the force of it all, I am unmoored, I am in my heart's riptide, feet torn from beneath me, out of control—

and I stop, close my eyes, *gather myself*, all the bits of me everywhere, and I breathe.

Until I am steady.

There is a hole in my heart, small and burning-cold and insistent. I look into Allemande Left's dark eyes and remember everything, remember how afraid I was of how strong my love was—my fear that it would distract me, preoccupy me, consume me. I remember dividing myself to keep from falling.

But I was fallen all along.

"There's a hole," I say, my voice unsteady.

"Do you know why now?"

**The Angel**

Jack is behind the bar, pulling pints, but he looks up the instant I enter the room, Allemande Left's hand in mine. The expression on his lion face is hard to read, but I think I read resignation in his posture—and then a stray shot of hope, like sun through clouds. It's in the way he straightens, and the formality of his pose as we approach, hand in hand. "Zee," he rumbles.

"Jack."

"Your quest?"

I slide onto a barstool. "I found my heart at the Mercy Seat," I say. A passphrase from who knows how many years ago.

He opens the cash register and hands me a red construction paper heart. It's tattered, feathered at the edges from age and rough handling, but it's mine and I'd know it anywhere.

I press it in.

I see all of Jack at once: human, lion, ox, and eagle. I see all of Allemande Left at once, all of the faces and bodies I have no name for. I see all of me at once, echoes down the worlds, hall of mirrors.

Jack takes my hand and Allemande Left's.

I am not afraid.

### The Vampire and the Werewolf

Both of the brides wear white lace; Mary Magdalene Kendall's dress is long and formal, with tapered sleeves, and Agony Jones's echoes 1984 Madonna. We sit in the back row, me and Jack and Allemande Left, silent through a lovely service. Allemande Left and I wear matching suits, grey pinstripe; Jack has eschewed matching as too silly, but he's deigned to appear human so's not to frighten the crowd. This is an all-humanoid world, after all. We must do our best.

The brides dance, and everyone is out on the floor before long; Allemande Left and Jack and I hang back by the door.

"What's next?" Jack asks. "Now that your heart is whole. Now that we're whole."

I smile. I see worlds around me, shimmering like heat mirages . . . places my loves have never been, never seen, never imagined. I take their hands. "Let's find out."

# LILO IS

## *Corinne Duyvis*

I've slept with plenty of men, and I can safely say that in our one night together, Ramon the spider-demon upstaged them all. The extra arms make for good multi-tasking. And then there were those mouth appendages—cheli-something—and as long as he was careful about keeping the fangs tucked away—

Let's avoid the details.

Here's what matters: Ramon the spider-demon was unique in a lot of ways, and the utter failure of my birth control pill was just one of them.

But it was definitely the one I least expected.

"And here's her little foot," the sonographer says. Her finger traces the screen by her side.

I follow the blurry monochrome lines of my daughter's foot up to her body, her arms, the curve of her head. I point towards the screen. "And this?"

"Oh." The sonographer leans in, moving the transducer across my belly without looking. I try not to squirm at the cold. "I think—that might be—yes. Probably just her other arm."

She already counted two of those earlier. She doesn't seem to remember. I stare at the screen.

Single motherhood will be interesting.

\* \* \*

A couple of months later I'm huffing and puffing in La Paz hospital, then focus on the midwife's reaction to three spindly arms on each side of my still-red daughter's body—but all they do is look her over and clean her up, noticing nothing.

My frown fades. Ramon could hide his arms, too. Maybe she'll be okay.

They wrap her and hand her to me.

"Hi there, Lilo," I whisper. My thumb brushes over the wisp of dark curls on the top of her head. "Do you know you have my hair?"

The middle hand on her right side balls into a tiny, perfect fist that reaches up at me.

I lean in. Press my lips to her ear. "And you have your daddy's everything else."

Lilo is magic.

Lilo is: Paper towels full of fingernail clippings. Sticky webbing in her sheets. Scratches on my tits from her fangs until I finally, regretfully, switch to bottles.

Lilo is: Learning to sew. Buying shirts and cutting them up before I even pull off the tag. Making brand-new, oddly-formed sleeves.

Lilo is: Wrapping two teeny hands around her sippy cup while she draws and scratches her neck and waves to get my attention. Arms fluttering by her side. Pressing her fingers onto all the keys to her red, plastic piano at the same time.

Lilo is: Hypnotic when she dances to preschool music I can barely tolerate, when her feet shuffle flatly over the floor and she sticks out her round belly and her arms spin and spin and spin. Fingers stretch and curl, align and flow through the air, and she smiles so wide the fangs in the corners of her mouth poke into sight. I don't tell her to be careful; no one but me sees. She belongs to just her and me.

Lilo is: Leaning over breakfast, her chelicerae dangling from her mouth to just outside of her yoghurt bowl. Thirty fingertips align along the rim of the table. Shiny black eyes look up at me.

She grins with yoghurt-smeared teeth too fragile to use.

\* \* \*

"*M*om-ma!" Lilo is five, and she puts the emphasis on the first syllable, always. "*Mom*-ma, we played soccer in gym class and my team *won*, and then we *climbed*, and I reached the top the fastest out of everyone."

While she talks she clasps her lower arms in front of her belly, but the top four, they wave and gesture in the corner of my eyes. They mimic climbing.

"I'm not surprised. You used to climb from your cot all the time."

She giggles. Hands flap excitedly. "Everyone else was slow."

And then I hesitate, like I always do. "Maybe you shouldn't go as fast next time. Okay, Lee? Give others a chance to win."

"But." Her hands slow down. "Why?"

I crouch and let my fingers run along her middle arms. I promised myself—and her, though she doesn't know it—to be honest, always. "You know how you shouldn't talk about your arms? Because people get confused?"

Lilo nods.

"This is . . . like that. People might wonder why you climb so fast."

And then, when they look closer? Right now no one but me sees her arms. Ramon could hide and show his at will. Lilo doesn't have that choice—she's not *all* him, never *all* him—but that might change. She might trigger it without meaning to.

Lilo jerks away one arm when I reach a tickly spot in the inside of her elbow. She suppresses a giggle, but then her face is all serious again. "When did you lose *your* arms?"

I stop mid-tickle.

Then I explain it doesn't work that way, and she asks further and I answer that, too, and we end up, finally, with that one dreaded question: "So . . . where do *mine* come from?"

Her school calls one day. They think the food I pack Lilo for lunch isn't enough.

"She's just," her teacher says, so very carefully, not wanting to imply anything at all because I've given him hell in the past and he doesn't want a repeat, "she's very skinny. Does she eat enough solids?"

I make up a story.

\* \* \*

"**C**an we have a kitty? Please?"

Lilo's on her haunches in the backyard, wild grass and weeds burying her feet and ankles. She pets the neighbor's cat, Momo; he looks like he doesn't know what to do with himself, what to make of stereo cuddles and big eyes hovering right overhead. He keeps his head low under Lilo's arms, his body tense. Just as I want to warn her away, Momo rubs his head against her knee.

Lilo spends her time on video games, on a hundred different K'Nex constructions. She has few friends. I wish I could give her this one.

"I'm so sorry, Lilo. My allergies . . . "

She's not sure what the word means so I explain it to her, and her face falls, breaking me in half.

**L**ilo is seven. I find her in the kitchen with her mouth wide open, her chelicerae extended inches from her lips. The fangs at the end grip a chunk of bread, mash it between them, shove it into her mouth and grab another chunk, until Lilo notices me and startles away from the counter. The bread drops to the kitchen tiles.

Her face looks—torn open. I try to look past the fangs. I rarely see them. She keeps them inside. She doesn't need them for the food I give her, mashed and blended to avoid damaging her too-fragile teeth.

Lilo tries to talk, but her lips can't even close; the chelicerae stretch open the corners of her mouth. She folds them back inside. One fang slips past her lip, slices it open. A drop of blood wells up.

"I just wanted to—I didn't mean to—" she blubbers. "I just wanted to try—"

"Lee," I say, "Lee-lee, baby. Don't worry."

I wrap her in my arms, press her face to my chest, wipe the blood from her lip. She's shuddering. Like she's scared. Like *she* did something wrong, and not *me*, for making her think this *wasn't* okay.

I have more reading to do.

I screwed up.

\* \* \*

I show her pictures, diagrams. We study spiders. I try to make it into a game.

But she's hesitant to even show her chelicerae anymore, let alone use them in front of me, and sometimes when she's cold, or when it's evening and she plays a last video game before bed, she likes to wrap herself in my robe so only two of her arms will stick out through the sleeves.

"*M*om-ma? Are you working?"

I peer over the computer screen. "Yes. Why?"

Lilo lingers in the doorway. Her fingers toy with some webbing, spreading it out, folding it back up. "You said *Dad*-dy is somewhere else. Can you make him come over?"

I'm thinking that the last time I did, with my belly ready to pop, Ramon still smelled of sulphur. He'd smiled, ever-so-pleased at the sight of me, then said, "Do I seem like a father to you?"

"You didn't do much to prevent becoming one. You could've warned me my pill wouldn't work."

"That only occasionally happens. Avoid screwing demons in the future."

I could've pushed, asked for support, for advice; there are some things the Internet doesn't cover. But then I saw his hands, two of them stained with blood I refused to ask about—and I didn't want him near my daughter. Didn't want him near me.

I don't need him, anyway.

"Why do you ask, Lee?"

"'Cause I need to ask him questions. For school."

"You can ask me." I push the laptop aside. My hand doesn't leave the plastic cover, though.

"But I want to . . . " Lilo frowns. "I want to talk to him."

"Aren't you a little young?" Now I just sound desperate. But she doesn't need him. Shouldn't need him. I screwed up but I'm doing better now, I'm reading, I'm learning. I'm letting her be the way she is.

"Everyone in my class knows about their *dad*-dies."

"Later," I promise. "Maybe later."

I take Lilo's sheets to the laundry room, pluck out bits of accidental webbing and dump them in the washer. When I return to make her bed anew, I open the window wide to air out her room. A glint under her desk catches my eye and makes me pause.

There's webs there, reflecting the sunlight. They stretch from the desk's underside to her chair and the side of the drawers, huge and clumsy and unevenly spaced, with big gaps and knots and threads that clump together. They look abandoned midway through.

I crouch. My finger traces the nearest web from millimeters away. Then I notice the garbage bin next to Lilo's desk; there's an empty juice bottle and plastic candy wrappers and wadded-up printer paper with bright scribbles. Some of the paper balls are blank. I reach in and unfold one. It's sticky with silk.

I bite my lip. I know Lilo. She's been trying and failing and cleaning up, then trying again.

My dad searched my room when I was young. I'm not sure what for, because at five or six there wasn't a lot for me to want to hide. All that came later: boyfriends—or simply boys—and alcohol and all those things I've sworn off for Lilo's sake. My dad said I could talk to him, but by then, the unease and distrust had trickled in and settled, because who knew if he was still going through my stuff? Who knew if he was just hiding it better?

I don't want to do that.

I don't.

But two minutes later, I find a photo in the inch of space between Lilo's carpet and the drawers, a space that was empty when I vacuumed just last week. It's a print-out from one of the websites Lilo and I studied.

The photo shows a spiderweb, the kind with dew drops that seem carefully placed for maximum effect and minimum damage. The sun highlights ruler-straight patterns that burn soft yellow.

It's a work of art. And when I compare it to Lilo's own webs, I see the frustration that laces every last, uneven thread.

I ask Lilo about the webs. I have to push a little, and I try to take it slowly, try not to make her feel any worse than she already seems to—she's shuffling and bowing her head and fiddling with all her hands at once.

"I didn't like making the webs, anyway." Tears well up. "I'm sorry, Momma."

"You need to talk to me. Okay? We can hang this photo up on the wall if you like. I can help you practice somehow. You have nothing to apologize for."

"But it's not normal."

And we talk and a minute later she says, quietly, almost like she's hoping for me not to hear, "I *wanted* to like it."

When did she stop dancing? I remember that suddenly, as I'm scanning in photos my parents took with their old camera. Lilo no longer dances.

Is that normal? Is that just growing up?

I miss her spinning arms.

Something is wrong.

Lilo wraps all six arms around herself like she used to do when cold. I can barely see her summery spaghetti top, hidden under rows and rows of tan arms. There's nothing but fuzzy dark hair, the outlines of bones under skin.

Yesterday, she turned nine.

"I didn't mean to." She stretches out her upper left arm, revealing the paler inside. Two irregular red scratches stretch across it. She looks up, pleading. Her lip is swollen, split open, like she retreated her fangs too quickly. "*Mom*-ma"—like she's a toddler again—"I didn't *mean* to. I thought Momo liked it when I petted him—he was purring—and then I—I—I couldn't—"

She's shaking as she leads me into the backyard, to a tiny, silken ball. She's hidden Momo behind the trashcan. The cocoon seems smaller than it ought to.

And that evening Lilo doesn't eat much and I am hoping praying begging that she just feels guilty over Momo, that she just lost her appetite and that is all.

When she changes the channel every time she sees a cat on TV, it can still be guilt, right?

But then it's *any* animal, any small animal. It's puppies on the street and peacock chicks in Retiro Park, and on the TV, it's hamsters and birds and anthropomorphized cartoon mice and, one time, a wolverine. After changing the channel, she always waits a bit, shooting furtive glances at the clock and at me while I do my translating or talk to clients on the phone. Her mouth distorts. Things press into her cheek. There's the faint click of— of something. Like chittering fangs.

And it's usually twenty minutes, thirty if she really stretches it, before she opens the candy drawer or asks when dinner is.

It never satisfies.

\* \* \*

L ilo asks, "Why doesn't anyone else see my arms?"
She knows I can't answer that, so I flick the tip of her nose
and say what I always say: "Because you're magic, Lee-lee."

"I told Conchita about my arms and she said I was crazy."

And my next words, my next joking, loving, apologetic words,
they freeze on my tongue. Inside my shoes, my toes curl and
press against the leather. "Why. Why did you tell Conchita?"

"'Cause I wanted to know." Lilo won't meet my eyes. "What
she'd think of me if she did see."

I promised her honesty. I tell her what Conchita might think.

Sometimes I wish I'd never made that promise.

L ilo sometimes pulls one hand away from her video game
controller to pop some candy into her mouth, to rub
something from her eye, to yank curls away from her face and
push them behind her ear. Then she returns the hand to the
controller and continues to play.

Other times, she stretches out my arms, pokes my sides
where my ribs are. She stares in fascination as I chew my dinner.

I try to make sure Lilo eats well. I let her choose the kind of
meat she wants and how she wants it: raw, for *her* to mash and
not me. I give her bugs I order online.

I tell her it's okay to use her arms, that she shouldn't hide
them, that she's beautiful the way she is. I tell her all of that.

But.

But I wonder if it matters what I *tell* her if I can never *show*
her.

H alf a year after Lilo's ninth birthday, I dig up a long-ago
phone number. Ramon and I meet up at the Sexta Avenida
mall, where it's safe. Where I can stand to be near him.

"Still not a father," Ramon says. He's changed over the years,
with blacker eyes, his mouth protruding even more.

"She doesn't need a father." Talking to him is easier than
I expected. I know he's dangerous, but it's all theoretical. He
doesn't have blood on his hands this time, so that *keeps* it
theoretical. "She needs someone like her."

\* \* \*

When Lilo meets Ramon's cousin, she backs away. She keeps her mouth shut, staring at the woman's arms. Just two of them. My brain won't see what I know is there, even as I scan the woman's shirt and focus on the sides. The stitching looks neat, the pinstripe pattern uninterrupted.

Lilo, though—she keeps staring at those arms. Her ears twitch as though she hears something. She inches to my side and presses her face into my shirt like she's terrified.

And I think: I screwed up. Again. Still. Because I know what Lilo hears, what Lilo sees: *Fingernails clicking in the air. Arms bending and twisting.*

And she should never be terrified of that.

The woman just smiles—a genuine smile. She's not like Ramon. I can tell already. She'll be good for Lilo to talk to. But I still wrap my arm around Lilo's shoulder and press her close, for both our sakes. I'm still relieved when the woman reveals her arms so I can see them too, even though it shouldn't matter and this isn't about me.

We sit down in my kitchen. I offer drinks, snacks. The woman accepts. Lilo just shakes her head fast, sending black curls whirling.

I try not to comment or stare, but find myself joining Lilo in watching the woman as she eats. Watching hands placed on the table and gesturing while she talks and grabs her drink, all at the same time, almost too many hands, moving too fast to keep track of.

"She was . . . " Lilo says afterwards. She pauses, pursing her lips as she thinks.

"She was magic," I say, dreaming of long-ago dances.

Lilo says nothing.

So I add, "She was pretty."

"I dunno. Maybe." Lilo shifts her weight to her other foot.

She takes a long time before asking—casually, quietly hopeful—if the woman will be back.

# SELECTED PROGRAM NOTES FROM THE RETROSPECTIVE EXHIBITION OF THERESA ROSENBERG LATIMER

## Kenneth Schneyer

1. **Three Women** (1978)
   OIL ON CANVAS, 30 x 40"
   DETROIT INSTITUTE OF ART, DETROIT, MICHIGAN

   Latimer painted *Three Women* while still a student at the Rhode Island School of Design. It is the earliest completed painting that displays the hyperrealism characterizing the first period of her work.

   Three young women sit close together on a park bench in autumn. Two hold hands, while the third has her hand on the knee of the center figure. Their expressions are serious, almost stern, as if they resent the artist's presumption in portraying them.

   At this stage of her career, Latimer was still experimenting with issues of compositional balance. The brightness of the orange trees offsets the dour colors of the models' clothes; the tilt of the models' heads and the orientation of their legs impel the viewer to look at the trees rather than at them. It as if the viewer is being pushed away from people and towards nature.

   None of these models appears in any of Latimer's later work. Presumably they were fellow RISD students. Latimer herself appears in early works of others who were at RISD at the time, including A. C. Stahl and J. J. Kramer.

*Discussion questions:*

a. Use the magnifying lens provided to examine the hairs on the models' arms, the loose fibers in their sweaters, and the veins in the leaves. Many details in a Latimer painting are not visible to those who view the work at ordinary distances. Why do you think she inserted such typically invisible minutiae? What effect do they have on your experience of the painting?

## 19. *Self-Portrait with Surrogates* (1984)

OIL ON CANVAS, 51 x 77¼"
RHODE ISLAND SCHOOL OF DESIGN MUSEUM
PROVIDENCE, RHODE ISLAND

The first of Latimer's paintings to draw critical attention, *Self-Portrait with Surrogates* portrays the notorious child abuse and murder case of the Wilson family, which dominated the Rhode Island news media at the time. Seven-year-old Lisa Wilson, clad only in underwear and displaying both old scars and fresh cuts, is being beaten with an electrical extension cord wielded by her father, while her mother holds her in place. None of the figures displays any emotion; it is as if they are spectators at the event.

The details, again in the hyperrealist style, closely match those of the Wilson case. The family home is accurately depicted, and the scars on Lisa Wilson's body correspond with photographs in the court file.

*Discussion questions:*

a. The composition and live-action flavor of this work resemble 18th- and 19th-century patriotic or polemical depictions of battles and famous events; David's *The Death of Socrates* (1787) (Fig. 5) is a clear influence. Why does Latimer employ such devices in a portrayal of domestic violence? Does it alter your perception of what you are "really" seeing?

b. Some biographers associate the painting's title with the emotional and physical abuse Latimer herself experienced as a child. Is there anything in the picture itself to show that this is really a "self portrait?"

c. Does the fact that Latimer's parents were living when she painted this work alter the way you perceive it?

### 34. *Magda #4* (1989)

OIL ON POPLAR WOOD, **30 x 21"**
PRIVATE COLLECTION

Sometimes called "Devotion" by critics, this nude the earliest extant work featuring Magda Ridley Meszaros (1963-2023), Latimer's favorite model and later her wife. The lushness of the flesh and the rosiness of the skin are reminiscent of Renoir's paintings of Aline Charigot (*see, e.g., The Large Bathers* (1887) (Fig. 8)). Latimer maintains microscopic hyperrealism even as she employs radiating brushstrokes which emanate from the model, as if Meszaros is the source of reality itself.

*Discussion questions:*

a.  The materials and dimensions of this painting duplicate those of Da Vinci's *La Gioconda* (c. 1503-1519) (Fig. 17). Is this merely a compositional joke or homage by Latimer? How does it change the way you see the painting?

b.  Most biographers agree that Latimer and Meszaros were already lovers by the time this work was completed. Is this apparent from the composition or technique? From the pose of the model? As you proceed through the exhibit, note similarities and differences between this and other portrayals of Meszaros over the next 34 years.

### 48. *Conjuring* (1993)

ACRYLIC ON MASONITE, **48 x 96"**
PRIVATE COLLECTION

Her largest composition and only known landscape, *Conjuring* appeared during a fallow period in Latimer's work. In 1992 and 1993 she completed only three paintings.

The scene is an overcast day in a valley in northern New Hampshire. Although it is summer, the foliage on the hills contains much grey and purple, conveying a wintery feel. While Latimer renders exacting details in rocks, trees, even blades of grass, in this work she also employs a forced monotony in the brushwork; the shape of every stroke is practically identical to every other.

In the precise center of the composition, wearing baggy khaki clothing, Magda Ridley Meszaros walks along an empty dirt road, recognizable only under a magnifying lens. She does not appear to be aware of the artist.

*Discussion questions:*

a. The aforementioned slack period in Latimer's work coincided with several crises in her life: her only interval of estrangement from Magda Meszaros, precipitated by parental opposition to their relationship; the death by drug overdose of her close friend, the singer Pamela Enoch (1965-1993); and Latimer's own life-threatening illness. Her hyperrealist period ends with this painting. Can we see these life crises in this composition? Is there any hint of Latimer's coming change in style?

## 49. *Performance* (1994)

ACRYLIC ON CANVAS, 32 x 41"

NATIONAL PORTRAIT GALLERY, WASHINGTON, DC

Generally regarded as one of the outstanding memorial portraits of the 20th century, *Performance* is also the first painting of Latimer's "highlight" period, which occupied the rest of her career.

Latimer was fascinated by the restoration of the Sistine Chapel ceiling (1980-1994), which sharply enhanced the clarity and brightness of Michelangelo's colors. Although some still doubt whether the restoration reflected the artist's intentions, Latimer was most interested in the side-by-side contrast between the pre- and post-restoration appearance of the frescoes (*see* "before" and "after" pictures of *The Creation of Adam* (figs. 11 and 12)). In one of her diaries, she wrote:

> *They stripped away the hurts and filth of five centuries and released the purity within. It's like looking at one of the Platonic forms—beneath the battered, mundane person, the person we see in everyday life, is the true person—the soul, maybe, or the heart. Of course it looks less "real" to us—we're so used to the violence and degradation imposed on us by the world that we're unprepared for ourselves without it.*
>
> *How did I miss this before? Maybe I wasn't ready, til now, to understand it. But after what happened, what's still happening, this is the perfect tool, maybe the only tool.*

After 1994, nearly all of Latimer's paintings feature one or more "highlight figures," people in a painting whose coloration has the clarity and brightness of the restored Sistine Chapel frescoes, as contrasted with the duller, more commonplace tones of everything else in the composition. They seem out-of-place and fantastical, even cartoonish, and yet Latimer employed the same level of microscopic detail in her "highlight figures" as in their surroundings.

The first critics who saw *Performance* misunderstood Latimer's introduction of "highlight" figures, because the painting is set on the stage of the Providence Performing Arts Center, and the central figure is the artist's recently deceased friend, the singer Pamela Enoch. Because she appears on the stage as if she were performing a concert, Enoch's heightened colors were taken at the time to represent the effect of theatrical spotlights. Arthur Mallory's review called the lighting "sentimental in an otherwise naturalistic work," noting that true spotlights would have enhanced the colors of the surrounding stage as well.

Magda Meszaros is visible in the front row, the only member of the audience. She has turned in her seat to face the artist. Meszaros is not portrayed as a "highlight" figure, but in the same comparatively muted tones as the theatre.

*Discussion questions:*

a. As you view the many "highlight" figures in the remaining paintings in this exhibit, consider whether these figures seem more or less "real" to you than those painted in ordinary colors. Why?

b. Critics and biographers have puzzled over Latimer's words, *"what happened, what's still happening,"* which seem to refer to the event or events that inspired or impelled her to adopt the "highlight" style. But what events were they, and how did they lead to this change?

c. Not until 2025 did Latimer paint Magda Ridley Meszaros as a "highlight" figure. Usually she appears in ordinary tones, as here. Why is this so?

d. Why does Meszaros wear a puzzled expression?

## 59. *Critique* (1997)

ACRYLIC ON CANVAS, 44 x 67"

DAVISON ART CENTER

WESLEYAN UNIVERSITY, MIDDLETOWN, CONNECTICUT

Latimer painted this piece to commemorate the addition of her *Self-Portrait with Surrogates* (#19) to the permanent collection of the RISD Museum. The setting is the Contemporary Artists gallery of the Museum; *Self-Portrait with Surrogates* hangs at the center of the composition, with adjacent works also visible, notably *Intelligentsia* (1986) by her friend and classmate J. J. Kramer.

In the foreground is the child Lisa Wilson (the subject of *Self-Portrait with Surrogates*) painted as a "highlight" figure. The young girl is presented as if she were a critical viewer of *Self-Portrait with Surrogates*; she is turned three-quarters toward the artist, but her left hand is raised toward the painting in a dismissive gesture. Her face is wry and full of humor; she appears to like the artist, even if she does not think much of the painting.

*Discussion questions:*

a. How do you interpret Lisa Wilson's apparent attitude towards Latimer's earlier painting? Is Latimer ridiculing her own work?

b. Why is Lisa Wilson portrayed as younger than she was in *Self-Portrait with Surrogates*? Why without visible evidence of abuse? What is the significance of the party dress she wears?

## 60. Excerpt from *The Silent Voices* (1997)

VIDEO RECORDING, 23 MIN.

BY PERMISSION OF WGBH TELEVISION

AND THE PUBLIC BROADCASTING SERVICE.

While working on *Critique*, Latimer was one of the subjects of Elijah Baptista's video documentary concerning contemporary artists, *The Silent Voices*. In the excerpt shown here, she stands in the Contemporary Artists Gallery, making preliminary drawings. Oddly, she is not sketching the gallery or the paintings on the wall, but detailing the face of Lisa Wilson herself. Although there are no photographs or prior sketches evident (apart from *Self Portrait with Surrogates*), the drawing is precise, showing the same wry expression that will appear in the finished work.

*Discussion questions:*

a. Now that you see Latimer's manner of speaking and moving, are you surprised? Does she seem like the sort of person who would produce this sort of work?

b. At the end of the excerpt, Baptista asks Latimer why she needed to come to the Museum in order to sketch a study of Wilson's face. Latimer's answer is, "You have to paint what you see, not what you think you're supposed to see." This admonition is a commonplace among visual artists. What does it mean when uttered by someone who paints with such obvious imagination?

## 72. *Grace* (2001)

ACRYLIC ON CANVAS, 20 x 60"
MASSACHUSETTS MUSEUM OF CONTEMPORARY ART
NORTH ADAMS, MASSACHUSETTS

One of several pieces recounting Latimer's difficult relationship with her parents, *Grace* portrays a Thanksgiving dinner in their home. Her father, Mason Latimer (1930-2008), poses as if saying grace before the meal, but both he and his wife Sheila Rosenberg (1935-2014) are staring scornfully at Theresa Rosenberg Latimer and Magda Ridley Meszaros, who sit at the opposite end of the table, looking down at their plates.

Standing behind the artist and Meszaros, apparently observed by no one, is Pamela Enoch (the subject of *Performance*, #49), the only "highlight" figure in the composition. Smiling, she holds her palms above the heads of her two friends as if in benediction.

*Discussion questions:*

a. Critics have noted references in this painting to both Rockwell's *Freedom From Want* (1943) (Fig. 18) and Dali's *Sacrament of the Last Supper* (1955) (Fig. 19). What is the point of quoting two such wildly disparate pieces together? Is this a parody?

b. Pamela Enoch appears in many of Latimer's works after 1994, always as a "highlight" figure in her mid-twenties, dressed for a performance. Why repeat the same person so often, and why always in the same clothes? Is Enoch a symbolic figure?

## 91. The Mourners (2008)

ACRYLIC ON CANVAS, 20 x 30"

AMERICAN LABOR MUSEUM, HALEDON, NEW JERSEY

The setting is a parking lot in Pawtucket, Rhode Island, that stands on the location of the 1908 Alger's Mill fire, in which 34 workers were killed. Two distinct groups of "highlight" figures appear. Near the center stand the Alger brothers, the Mill owners whose negligence was generally blamed for the deaths, although none were ever prosecuted. They bow their heads and clasp their hands before them. Standing in a circle around them are 25 victims of the fire, their own sorrowful gazes fixed on the Alger brothers. All are dressed as they would have been in the late 19th or early 20th centuries.

Here, as elsewhere, Latimer has been praised for the quality of her research. Although historians have authenticated the faces of most of the fire victims, many of the relevant photographs have taken years or even decades to find.

*Discussion questions:*

a.  Most of the figures in this painting are younger than they were at the time of the 1908 fire. Tara Aquino, in her assiduous tally of Latimer's subjects (2038), has calculated that 84% of the "highlight" figures are in their 20s and 30s, and the rest are mostly children. By contrast, Latimer's non-highlighted figures show an ordinary spread of ages. Why does Latimer make this age distinction between "highlight" and "ordinary" figures? Why not portray people as they were at the time of the relevant events?

b.  One of the striking things about this painting is that the victims appear to be mourning for those who were responsible for their deaths. What is Latimer's message here?

c.  Young Lisa Wilson, a recurring figure in Latimer's work, is visible at the far right of the composition, gesturing towards the group of mourning figures. Why include a contemporary figure in an otherwise period group? Is there a connection between this painting and the others in which she appears?

## 117. *Self-Portrait with Family* (2015)

ACRYLIC ON CANVAS, 36 x 45"

PRIVATE COLLECTION

The setting is Latimer's own bedroom, recognizable from the furniture and memorabilia. Latimer at her then-current age of

56 crouches in the bed in a nightgown, her face hidden in her hands as if in fear, sorrow, or pain. Standing by the side of the bed, glowering down at their daughter in reproach or rage, are her parents Mason Latimer and Sheila Rosenberg. They are "highlight" figures.

Kneeling on the bed with Latimer is Magda Meszaros. Both are painted in muted colors, as contrasted with the highlighted parents. Meszaros is in a protective posture, one hand on Latimer's curved back and the other gesturing as to repel an invader.

*Discussion questions:*

a.  Why does the artist paint her parents as they appeared in their twenties, before her own birth?

b.  Why are neither Meszaros's fierce gaze nor her guardian hand directed at the figures of the parents (the only other people in the composition), but at a point beyond the right border of the picture?

c.  This work was composed in the year following Sheila Rosenberg's death from brain cancer, which was also the year in which Latimer and Meszaros finally married. How many uses of the word "family" are implied by the title?

## 131. *To Interfere, for Good, in Human Matters* (2018)
ACRYLIC ON CANVAS, 30 x 60"
F. COOLEY MEMORIAL ART GALLERY,
REED COLLEGE, PORTLAND, OREGON

The scene is a crowded street in downtown Providence. A homeless woman with a young child sits on the doorstep of what may be a church; they are malnourished, shabbily dressed, and the woman holds out her hand as if asking for alms. The dozens of others on the street around her are a mix of both "highlight" figures and characters painted in muted colors (as are the beggar woman and her child). The composition pushes the eye of the viewer back and forth between the different groups in a sort of tennis match: from a "highlight" figure one is drawn to a muted figure, then to another "highlight" figure, then to another muted figure, back and forth until one has scrutinized every figure in the picture.

This oscillation forces the viewer to see the contrast between these two groups. Superficially, the muted figures wear everyday clothes contemporary to 2018, while the "highlight" figures are clad in varying styles from the previous 150 years. More significant, however, are their differing reactions to the homeless pair. The muted figures bypass the seated beggars, or approach them while looking elsewhere; a few are watching them from the corners of their eyes. The "highlight" figures, on the other hand, all stand motionless, each facing the mother and child, each with a look of pity or compassion on her or his face. Some reach out their hands as if to touch the pair, but none actually reach them.

*Discussion questions:*

a. As in other Latimer paintings, critics have observed references to other works, notably Courbet's *Real Allegory of the Artist's Studio* (1855) (Fig. 40) and Bosch's *Garden of Earthly Delights* (c. 1504) (Fig. 41). Again, why does Latimer quote from two such different pieces?

b. Athena Ptolemaios (2025) has suggested that there is a racial or cultural message here. The muted figures are turning away from one of their own, while the "highlight" figures reach out to the stranger. Are we being shown than it is easier to feel compassion for those who are far away, or different?

c. While her technique here earned much praise, Latimer has been criticized for the blatantness of the message. Thomas Taney (2030) was particularly scornful of Latimer's unexplained use of a passage from Dickens's *A Christmas Carol* (1843) as the title of the piece. Do you agree with Taney?


**146. *Almost* (2022)**

Oil on poplar wood, 30 x 21"

Private collection

*Almost* is the last portrait Latimer made of Magda Ridley Meszaros during the latter's lifetime. It is an unsentimental portrayal, detailing the damage done by both breast cancer and chemotherapy with all the hyperrealist accuracy at Latimer's command. From her favorite chair, Meszaros gazes quietly at the artist. One detects neither fear, defiance, nor even acceptance, only the affection of one life partner for another.

Standing on either side of Meszaros are four "highlight" figures: Pamela Enoch and three other women who have not been identified. They are looking not at Meszaros but at the artist, their arms held wide.

*Discussion questions:*

a.  The subject, size and materials of *Almost* are identical to those of *Magda #4* (#34), so that it is natural to compare them. Whereas the brushwork in *Magda #4* pointed to Meszaros herself, in *Almost* the strokes radiate from the "highlight" figures; even the strokes with which Meszaros is painted come from them. What other differences do you see between the two works? What similarities?

b.  Why are the "highlight" figures smiling?


**155. *Comfort* (2025)**
ACRYLIC ON CANVAS, 11 x 8½"
PRIVATE COLLECTION

The last known completed work of Theresa Rosenberg Latimer is *Comfort*, found among her personal effects after her death by medication overdose at the age of 66.

It is a quadruple portrait, somewhat reminiscent of her *Three Women* (#1). The setting is the exterior of Latimer's home, although the focus is so tight that only certain abnormalities in the brickwork allow us to identify it. The four figures are Pamela Enoch dressed for a performance, Lisa Wilson in her party dress, Magda Meszaros as a young model, and Latimer herself at 30, the beginning of her most productive period. Latimer stands slightly in the foreground, one step ahead of the others; Enoch and Wilson are to her left, Meszaros to her right, as if they are ready to catch her if she falls.

All four women are "highlight" figures, bright and clear with strong definitions and confident lines. They are more radiant than the "highlight" figures of Latimer's earlier works; light pours from them, and they drown out the color of the bricks behind them. Enoch's, Wilson's and Meszaros's faces are fixed on Latimer, who is smiling broadly, with flushed cheeks and eyes full of hope.

*Discussion questions:*

a.  The title *Comfort* was suggested by Paula Tarso, executrix of Latimer's artistic estate; we do not know what Latimer herself planned to call it. Do you think the name fits?

# THREE TIMES

## *Camille Alexa*

### 3.

Soon, for the third and, Zhee knows, final time, his body will slip beneath the surface of the river and that will be the end of this particular story. Deep wounds under his arms, between his ribs, across the backs of his legs fill with water and begin to feel almost pleasant as the fire of them is doused and starts to cool. He didn't know death would be like this, but is not surprised; instead of surprise he feels wonder. Even now, even with this, he feels wonder, and joy, and sorrow, and the lingering memory of her soft cool lips against his.

Her brothers disturb the jungle leaves as they move away, their rustlings growing fainter as the undergrowth along the riverbank swallows them into the swelling darkness. Or perhaps it is Zhee who moves away from them, his body buoyed by the warm sluggish currents of the wide muddy river of his birth and death. He feels himself turning slightly as he drifts, slowly rotating. His arms and legs have spread naturally outward from head and body, so he floats like a reflection of the five-pointed star rising bright and white in the purpling sky. When the moon rises also, rippling its reflected length across the water and across Zhee's glassy open eyes, it makes him smile, reminds him it is the same moonlight which also bathes her. His last conscious thought resembling anything human is that though they have been parted for now, she and he, washed with the light of the same moon, are as close this way as though they hold hands still, or touch lips, or press bodies one to the other.

If he'd lived more than just one day he might've understood she would be grieving. It's a blessing he didn't live long enough to understand tears.

## 2.

Her brothers are silent when they emerge from the trees. They don't bicker among themselves, or taunt Zhee. They don't berate their sister, or treat her particularly roughly as they drag her away still wet and glistening in afternoon sunlight, water from the river in which she's been floating with Zhee running smooth across her skin in rivulets to mimic the waves of her hair. Dry, her hair springs into tug-resistant coils, sometimes on humid days puffing up around her shoulders in a soft black nimbus. Wet, her hair reaches halfway down her back, its coils lengthening, water mimicking its undulating pattern in trails down her spine, her thighs.

Zhee loves her hair. He's spent the day thinking of her hair, touching it, sucking wetness from its ends where it trickles and runs. Too, he loves her skin. That's the thing that has surprised him most about the human form: skin. When someone who's never known the slide of skin against skin observes a human being, it's with no way to fully understand the electricity of the intersection of motion and intention, the communication of sensation through anticipation. When she looked at Zhee and he had human skin, it was as though her gaze alone stirred all the tiny endings of nerves and cells and atoms of his new-made surface; and when she touched him with the tips of her fingers—just the tips—he shivered from all the million zillion points at once, and when she tasted that same skin with her tongue, traced a wavy rivulet of moisture across it the way the riverwater runs down her back, he thought he'd melted again into that formless lifestuff from which he'd come.

So that morning, before he'd touched and been touched— skin to skin, breath to breath, electricity to electricity—humans had seemed to him to be loose-shaped sacks. He certainly hadn't thought of it as *morning*, nor had he viewed humans through human eyes and so saw only the configuration of their energies. To him, skin had seemed a mere knitted bag to hold together the countless zipping particles of the stuff he thought of as life. He knew, as a sentient being, that life was not the same as *living*, even to a creature whose spirit was capable of expanding to fill the voids between stars or of shrinking to the size a human might've said was able to dance on the head of a pin.

Zhee didn't know anything about pins, of course. Or dancing. Or even of the specific ways in which being a life did, in fact, differ from *being alive*.

And before he'd seen her it had never occurred to him to care.

## 1.

Zhee is born as human in a moment of glory. His birth is a silent backward explosion, a coalescing of billions of particles borrowed from the humming, buzzing, slithering, flitting, rotting, shining multitudes of living and unliving things which make up the sluggish muck at the bottom of the river, the wings of the dragonfly skimming its surface, the disintegrating bones of a fish long dead, the nameless motes dancing in the rays of morning sun and very light of the sun itself as it glances off the water. All these things donate a tiny gazillionth of themselves to Zhee, and he borrows them with what a human would call gratitude.

Zhee, brown and naked and perfect with all the glorious imperfections of the human form, floats out into the center of the river. He marvels already at the sensations skittering across this covering, this *skin*, which is stitched together over an impossibly complex and delicate network of bone and sinew and cartilage and capillary. It's inconceivable that such a fragile and fleeting construction should feel so . . . present. Everything feels so *here*, so *now*. A human body should feel like a brittle cage, easily bruised and quickly used up. But it doesn't. What it feels, Zhee decides, is *alive*.

He hears her before he sees her. He'd somehow not anticipated ears. They, like skin, like the sensation of touch, are astounding.

On his back, floating spread-limbed, spinning a lazy circle as slow eddies push him toward the nearer shore, Zhee's ears are half submerged. Some of what he hears is the glug glug of the river as it speaks its lapping lullaby into his soft cartilage shells. Some of what he hears is the world, the twitter and caw and shush and whine of living things droning and flitting and hooting between trees and shore and sun and water. Some of what he hears is his own body, the beat of heart and the rustle of blood flowing through brain, echoing in the hallways of the skull. Zhee had certainly not expected that; of all the things which surprise him about hearing, it's hearing his own body, hearing his stomach rumble and his lungs expand, that astonishes him most.

But as soon as he hears her, he knows her already. Before that day he'd merely sensed her in the aether, had ached to mingle his spirit with hers in the form her destiny prescribed for her. Now he hears her and knows her, even without seeing her, because all her human parts—her form, her sound, her smell, her motions where she disturbs the particles of the air—are merely expressions of her spirit, and *that* he'd know anywhere.

Splashing and gasping. More splashing. And then she touches him. The water even this close to shore is deeper than she is high, and so she must hook one arm around his slippery naked body and beat aside the river with her other hand as she kicks them both toward the bank. Zhee lies still in her grasp, patient and inert. It's enough that she's so close. His spirit is practically blinded by the brightness of hers.

She slogs heavily ashore, brownish river mud sucking at shins and ankles. Zhee feels but doesn't see the trough his body leaves in the soft bank, a human-width gulley which quickly fills with swirling water after they pass. She stops, kneels above him. He looks up into her face, sees her for the first time with human eyes. . . .

And then she does a funny thing, a thing he hadn't expected: she takes a deep breath, bends down, and releases that breath into him, fills him with mint and air and light.

Zhee is amazed, delighted to feel his lungs respond to hers. He'd been breathing before, but had he forgotten for a time, there, in the water? He's now unsure. His body, this body, is an amalgamation of its trillion trillion parts. It's a creation born of his longing and need to touch her. His own spirit is so long-lived and her life so brief, he was afraid a moment of inattention on his part would lose him his opportunity forever. He feels like one of the winged insects fluttering under the trees along the river's edge, as though he's drawn to the bonfire of her many-suns-bright core.

His lungs stutter to motion with her breath. She helps him sit as he coughs up river, crooning softly in a human language with her human tongue and lips and teeth. She smiles and nods, and he with a natural mimic's grace returns the gesture.

## 0.

Though Zhee has made up his mind to go to her, he doesn't know it.

He does not think with human linearity. No human agenda colors his desire for closeness with the bright burning flame he's crossed galaxies and bored through nebulae to be near. It doesn't occur to him that he has been alone for an eternity, nor that he'll be alone for another after her eyeblink's eyeblink time is spent. His consciousness simply isn't equipped for the concept of *alone*.

He only dimly grasps the concept of death. He does know that things are fleeting. All things: even himself in his vast eternity, everything being simply a matter of scale.

What he most certainly does not have is any sense of why her brothers will come seeking her after she's been at the river all day without them. Even had Zhee been capable of understanding their outrage and their intricate balance of honor and ownership and pettiness and tradition and survival and cruelty and fear and all the other trillion parts that make up human society the way the trillions of borrowed parts make up Zhee's temporary human form, it would've made no difference. Zhee would still have been unable to resist flitting into her flame; she would still have pulled him from the river, and breathed her life into his chest, and felt something in his gaze and touch she hadn't realized she'd ached for until he crossed the stars to bring it to her. The brothers would still have killed the man they found entangled with their sister, and she still would've been dragged away from him while he was bound and kicked and beaten with sticks by the silent human men who loved her most.

But Zhee won't mind. He will be grateful, having learned gratitude, for every second he floats in the moonlight, in the river, spread to five points like a reflected star. He will not have enough human understanding to feel pained by her pain, which will continue long after his first and only day and last the entirety of her brief brilliant flash of a human lifetime. And as his body begins to dissolve back into its gazillion particles, begins to sift back into mud and water and light and dead fish and live reeds and molding tree roots and stultifying heat, he'll have enough understanding to hope this: that after her spirit is done, after it slips loose its gentle sack of bone and blood and ivory, it will be free to bore through nebulae and cross galaxies to find him, and that together, they can be incandescent.

# THE BEES HER HEART, THE HIVE HER BELLY

## *Benjanun Sriduangkaew*

Under Sennyi's feet the mud is hissing a mantra for health and prosperity.

The path is a burial ground for seven hundred and seventy-seven monks, sealed behind yellow-paper firewalls. In death their vestments were stripped and torn to little talisman shreds, wards against illness and accident. Their prayer beads went too, spread out on merchants' mats on- and off-world, touted for their sanctity and bringing terrible misfortune to all buyers: virulent malware that scrambles networks in seconds, infects medical equipment in hospitals, upsets commute at rush hour.

She puts one of those beads, bought for this pilgrimage as offering, into the mulch and buries it deep. Within her the next batch of bees is fruiting, and each of their small hearts flutters in time to the monkly chants. At night they buzz for a queen that will never come. She can hear them between her ears, in her stomach, secret communication through the hive that is her torso.

When Sennyi was thirty, her closest crèche-sibling disappeared. She—or they, though Sennyi is fairly certain it was a sister—did this by erasing all records of her birth, childhood, and research. One moment Sennyi knew her name;

**216**

the next, after a routine network sync, she didn't. If they met now in the streets of their birth city or at the port, Sennyi would think her sibling a stranger. All she had to mind was the idea of a girl who giggled like a horse and who taught her to whistle.

It was the first time a deletion so drastic happened to her. Such things weren't unheard of, and she should have been able to take it with equanimity. Instead, when she first realized what had happened, she flung a paperweight against her window. The latter cracked; the former shattered. As she gathered and tidied up the shards, she became near-certain that this was a gift from her sister and spent the next hour forgetting that she was too old to cry.

By then, she had thirteen years left to live. Bio-theurges and physics-shamans had already attempted to solve her genetic timebomb, using nanomachines to restitch her soul and laser scalpels to slice at her dreams. They accomplished nothing, and she concluded that she would not die with the mystery of her sibling lodged behind her sternum; she would not die with nothing to show for having lived.

For six years she saved up to have her heart replaced.

She meant to have a hunting bird installed—an osprey, a hawk—and chose the best implant seed she could afford, one created by Esithu. It carried an implicit contract to become one of the cyberneticist's subjects, a solidarity spanning some two million across the stars. There were studies done to analyze why anyone would willingly accept a modification so unpredictable and occasionally fatal. A disease, some said, and madness to want it. Conspiracy theorists insisted it masked one's net-presence, turned one into a ghost, and let criminals escape justice. It might well, Sennyi thought, allow the bearer to erase themselves and evaporate.

She prepared to leave a life laid out for her in cradle-city Thirteen O'Clock: a career in virtuality, an engagement to a xenologist.

"You must understand, my dear," she told her betrothed, "I'll literally have no heart. That'll make me difficult to love. You could invest all the emotion but get nothing in return. Terrible business decision."

The fiancé was first puzzled, then pensive. "Is it that I'm the wrong gender? I could become a woman. I'm willing to compromise."

"No, no. Really without a heart it is impossible to love anyone. That is a fact." She did not say that she had never loved him.

"What about your condition?"

"It's more dignified," she said cheerfully, "to die alone, don't you think?"

She didn't tell him it was not dignity she sought, and she didn't kiss him goodbye. She'd never liked kissing.

The implant would function as her central processing organ. She imagined the bird a hungry, seeking thing that would help her dig a Sennyi-shaped hole, to spare her crèche-parents and friends unnecessary sorrow. It wasn't their fault they could do nothing to keep the clock of her body from winding down, and she thought it senseless they should be punished with the unrelenting weight of grief.

She went into the operating tank thinking of the sister-shaped absence.

She woke up with a chest full of bees.

Cradle-cities are numbered rather than named, designed to be identical: from above, a concave clock's face. From the ground, a labyrinth of low walls, low buildings. There used to be endless towers, compressed residential units, but that was before Samutthewi changed. A primitive time, when fetuses gestated in flesh-and-blood uteruses.

A citizen does not leave their cradle-city on foot; traveling is by paper ships, in the safety of the clouds. Between cities the ground runs on chaos intelligences. Between cities the ground belongs to Esithu.

Bearing the bees grants Sennyi some protection, but even so she keeps close to the monks' road, a precisely demarcated ribbon that runs parallel to the river Prayapithak. It is dense with carp AIs in search of the river's source, a machine-gate that—once leaped—will transform them from lowly intelligences to full-fledged cortices, incandescent overnight.

On the monks' path anything can happen.

Within the first day she is chased by an ambush of tigers which are only quarter-real: infused with a minimum of substance and a texture that suggests rather than manifests fur. Echoes of lashing tails, thump-churn against the humid wet. The one leading the hunt is more dimensional, with paws that leave deep imprints in the mud. Sennyi registers the mind behind the avatar, a woman on far-away Thotsakan, a planet whose chief exports are fabric made of leopard shadows cast at sundown and perfume distilled from the death of temporally non-linear eels.

Sennyi creates copies of herself and grafts them onto the blank replicants wandering this road, putting a bee in each. It is rough, hasty work and the decoys will expire in forty hours, but it will give her time to plan.

For the rest of the night she wades through the Prayapithak's shallows with an ear out for every hiss of water, every susurrus of carps, every ripple of network activity. Panic exerts a pull on her, gravitational.

Before the bees she never experienced danger; before the bees her life was mapped out in front and behind, precisely plotted like a replicant's verse. Each minute an update blip in public data streams, optimized for happiness.

The first year Sennyi coughed up dead workers and orange phlegm, saccharine fuzziness in the back of her throat, legs and wings spasming against the roof of her mouth in final rites.

She went to have her chest cut open and a small metal lattice installed between her breasts. When the bees became too much, she would open that little gate and let them out in a cascade of corpses and restless workers. The living ones always returned to Sennyi-as-hive, for they were creatures of habit. They drove her to eat voraciously and she developed a private memory. It jolted her to have a cerebral partition that could not be edited by anyone but herself. Still, what had already been forgotten couldn't be brought back. There was no epiphany that returned her sibling's face.

Months on, she was approached with offers to pose nude; she rejected them out of hand. Shortly after, portraits of her appeared in galleries on Samutthewi, Yodsana, and Laithirat, where Esithu's cult flourished. In the images, sculptures, and collages, Sennyi was always more waspish of waist than in reality, with mouth and tongue like invitations. Sometimes she was blindfolded; just as often she was suspended by the wrists, pendulating from the underbelly of spiders as though arachnids and insects are interchangeable. There was pornography featuring facsimiles of her coupling with any number of bugs, anthromorphic and not, on a bed of writhing leaves or pressed—Sennyi facedown—into dry, cracked chrysalises.

Around this time she discovered the bees did more than obscure her presence. They scrambled it. On the net she was a chameleon, able to borrow and discard identities as though they were shoes.

Sennyi tracked down the artists, and each was delighted to receive her. She entered their homes with coquetry in the tilt of her head and the angle of her throat. She left stepping over a body that had become a collection of swelling punctures. When she could, she deleted their works. When that was impossible— their works having spread too far, distributed too many times— she defaced them. A virus that latched onto each copy, spreading in that proven monk-bead method. Before long such pieces came to have the faces and genitalia of their artists instead of hers. It was possible, this way, to erase any recall that Sennyi had ever been spread open for public perusal. Who didn't synchronize? Who didn't want to stay up to date with everything?

Samutthewi being lawless justice must be seized in a clenched fist, or meted out with apidae venom.

She almost fell in love with one of those artists, who digitized her not as naked meat defined by open legs and wings emerging from vagina, but who reimagined Sennyi with faceted eyes and arms coated in gold.

It didn't last. Sennyi-as-bee, in retrospect, missed the point. She is habitat, not inhabitant. The sentiments of romance didn't in any case ignite a spark in her. A matter far more important awaited.

On the sixth day Sennyi reaches Twenty-Five. A city beyond clocks; a city that is no cradle, but a nexus of high towers bridged by reinforced resin. An amber skyline—look up and there are jaundiced clouds, brown skies, and paper ships that look as though they have been roasted over a slow fire.

Behind her, just outside Twenty-Five's perimeter, there are remains of tigers. Flecks of paint, cracked plastic, and machine hearts bleating sparks.

Sennyi's torn, bruised feet leave prints between puddles of orange shadows. Drops of her blood mingle with those, nearly the same exact shade, and her cranium fills with rapidly beating wings. Reacting to adrenaline they are wild, tickling her lungs with their feet. The ragged shreds of her hair scratches her face.

Rain begins, patter then thud against the bridges, the roofs. She hears owls.

Beneath a defunct banner advertising berserk firearms, a silhouette waits for her. An androgyne, she sees when she comes closer, with a youth's face and a spareness of body hardly obscured by saffron cloth. Gold at an ankle, gold at a wrist. Filigree snaking right into the veins to shine beneath epidermis.

"The rain will lap the flesh off your bones."

"Lucky that I'm in the shade." Sennyi tugs her clothes around herself even so, a gesture consciously useless. It was a decision she made to go forward without a carapace, and no fabric can withstand Samutthewi's precipitation. "Are you the welcome committee?"

"No." They have perfectly symmetrical dimples. "I am Esithu."

"Oh," she says, for want of any more appropriate thing.

"I'll give you a bed for some nights, food, necessities. Armoring, since you appear without. Enough to last you on the road back to Thirteen."

"You track everyone with your implants."

Esithu shrugs. "It's hard not to. And you're famous."

"Infamous," she murmurs, following them into an empty hall whose ceiling rears so high it is only a skeleton of iron and shadow. Old cobwebs, robot-spun, glitter with amber beads and brass bells.

"A serial murderer."

"Everyone on Samutthewi is a murderer, or a murder about to happen."

They give a short nod. There is no telling how old they are, but if they are Esithu the trail of deaths they've left across the planet's history is longer than most people have been alive. She tries to believe in the idea, that this is the cyberneticist who rules Samutthewi's interstitial ground, that all it took to meet Esithu was to step into Twenty-Five on a rainy day.

A bronze cage on hydraulics—quaint—brings them past floors full of broken prostheses, furniture suspended upside down, and tableaus of replicant animals in combat. Tortoise against crustaceans, rhinoceros against stags, broken anthills. They share the lift with owls, who hoot and hoot to no appreciable rhythm.

The cage slows to a stop, swinging against its tethers. A thrum of conversations comes to a halt. Sennyi looks at each face, but it is little use. There's no telltale sign or portent, no sudden flash of familiarity. Her searching gaze purchases no twitch of acknowledgment.

Esithu nods to a young woman, who without requiring instructions takes Sennyi's arm and steers her away from the tense, silent crowd. Esithu is joined by a pair of androgynes who look very much like them. Heads bent close together they converse in low voices.

"They're all Esithu," the young woman says as she shows Sennyi to a room of mosaic and throw rugs.

"Clones?"

A reverent sigh. "Esithu has three bodies. They always say one isn't enough to contain their mind, and it's true, you know."

Groupies, she thinks, with enough self-awareness to recognize she is one too. She experiments with thinking of herself as a headline—inexplicable citizen ran away from qualified fiancé to join a cult at thirty-eight.

The young woman, Ipnoa, treats the cut in her scalp as though it is normal to secrete honey from a wound, and wipes at Sennyi's face with delicate care. Sennyi lies down on her stomach, and does not object when Ipnoa peels away the rags of her clothes to clean the crusted lacerations. Tiger teeth, tiger claws. A Thotsakan woman whose brother, at the peak of his career, made an obscene sculpture of Sennyi.

"How long have you had your implant?"

"A couple years."

"Took you a while to come looking for Esithu."

"It wasn't an easy decision." The mess with the artists slowed her down, but taught her new skills as well. "I was told to go back, anyway."

"Esithu doesn't mean it. You can stay as long as you want."

Before Ipnoa leaves, Sennyi murmurs, "What do you have?"

"A small porpoise." Ipnoa taps her chest. "I'll be seeing you around."

Sennyi does not see Esithu much; she is told they seclude themselves high up the tower, to cultivate new seeds, to oversee—and this is said casually—the secession of Samutthewi.

"Are the rumors true then?" she asks Ipnoa.

"It depends on which rumors."

Ipnoa, a little shyly, shows Sennyi an upper body that is glass, translucent and green, brimming with brine and water. Between collarbones and hips there is no skin. Curious Sennyi touches it, her thumb drawing circles on the sheer smoothness of Ipnoa. The porpoise's eyes follow her fingers. "You can feel?"

"Embedded sensory receptors. Can I see the bees?"

Sennyi lets a few out. They alight on Ipnoa, rubbing their legs against a hard, rounded stomach. Sennyi peers closely at a plastic ribcage and pockets of organs. There's almost no give to Ipnoa, a peculiar soft-hard texture, cold to warm at junctures where flesh meets glass.

Ipnoa touches her in turn, fingers grazing Sennyi's hair. "Why did you come?"

"To see the person who gave me bees when I wanted something else, I suppose."

"Esithu told me you've compartmentalized a private memory. What is that like?"

"Very odd. Why?"

Ipnoa puts on her clothes and looks away. "Just curious. Let's walk together."

Morning in Twenty-Five comes down in slashes of sun and screaming birds pelting the skylight. It is near impossible to escape either the light or the sound, and when Sennyi does locate a shadow or some quiet she always finds it already occupied by another of Esithu's subjects. Consulting the building's life support, she learns that there are fifty-six of them in and out of the tower. A considerable percentage comprises androgynes, nearly half of which changed their gender after receiving Esithu's implant. Not because the budding seed compelled them, but so that they would feel closer to the cyberneticist.

Ipnoa does not make introductions. "Most of them are lovers. The idea is that since each of us bears an implant, to touch each other is to touch Esithu."

Sennyi's stomach twitches. "You don't participate?"

"It can be exhilarating. But it's not for me." Ipnoa takes her arm.

They walk bridges built as thoroughfares for trains and mass vehicles, still marked with traffic overlays that no longer function. A city of hundred-millions in a dim and distant era. Each cradle now contains some fifty thousand, a population level carefully maintained in a straight line. Closing her eyes

Sennyi can access a cartography of Twenty-Five as of formerly, a metropolis that covered much of this continent. Not so much interstitial ground back then. Not so much realm for Esithu to claim and redo.

Ipnoa brings her to the basin where carp AIs come once they've passed the machine-gate. An empty depression choked with weeds and specters of whiskered heads cycling through light spectrums. Carps-become-dragons monitoring and powering the city. "I wish they were a bit real," Ipnoa says. "I'd like to pet them."

She has endless questions for Sennyi: where she is from, what she used to do, what she left behind. Sennyi answers circuitously, and when she asks Ipnoa which cradle-city gave her birth the other woman looks away. "That's not important, is it?"

"Mostly not."

No one bothers her about having rapturous piety-sex that will purify them in Esithu's eye, for which she is relieved. But not even Ipnoa explains the nature of their work. Sennyi takes the liberty to probe and finds that they are refining and deploying deletion algorithms.

She explores her hive's capabilities to interface with Twenty-Five. Translating them into code, she uses one bee to snoop on data packets and another to attach to the dragon AIs—compatibility a matter of course, since Esithu made both. Everyone here synchronizes only partially; everyone has a discrete memory all their own.

The cyberneticist summons her after she's taken control of a dragon and found their fourth body.

Esithu's floor is a series of bone arches, each heavy with dozing owls. Feathers are not shed; pellets are not dropped. Replicants.

Sennyi's shoes strike no footfalls. They sink, disconcertingly far, into the alabaster sand that shifts and shudders as though deep underneath a great beast-machine hibernates. The chameleon mesh-gown Ipnoa lent her reflects the sand, starkly pale against her skin. Several workers cluster around her neck, eyes and antennae brighter than jewels.

Esithu sits in a circle of flight. Primitive flyers fueled by combustible batteries. Leather stretched on chrome frames. Paper, in all the permutations that paper is capable of.

She expects the three bodies to act in unison, but only one turns to regard her. "You needn't have dressed up."

"Ipnoa insisted. She believes in being presentable." Words come too quickly; her cardiac rate elevates. The cyberneticist unnerves more than she thought. "Is it true that you were around when this was a live city, with a real name?"

Esithu blinks at her. The other bodies are separately sketching a hologram of some chimeral beast and unpacking a data polyhedron. Neither has anything to do with each other in subject matter or medium. It's hard to decide which would be more unsettling—three bodies that function in tandem, or a single mind that can make them appear independent. "Everyone asks that. You can look it up."

"Most of the information about you is falsified."

"I'm a private person."

"I've also heard that Esithu is more title than name, passed from the original to a series of meticulously selected successors."

"People will believe anything," Esithu says, inflectionless. "You're dying, yes? You must realize that my implant won't help."

When she sits the sand coheres into clay, contouring to the jut and curve of her calves. "I didn't expect it to."

"Nor can I cure the disease or prolong what remains of your life."

"I came here," Sennyi says, smiling, "to die among strangers, so that I won't break my crèche-parents' hearts. I came here to become a ghost, and your implant lets me do that."

Eyes whiteless with augmens fix on her. "Five years are very brief," they say, then thumb the arch, bringing up a display. "Let's discuss the bees."

It was never an accident, of course. An experiment incompatible with extant subjects, for those already implanted cannot receive another. Sennyi's genetic timebomb, a glitch in Thirteen's birth-web, makes her a suitable candidate. Esithu's screen ripples and stretches to show a visual of where the hive has bonded to her, symbiotic filaments as ubiquitous through her system as lymph nodes.

"It self-propagates using your nutrients. You might've noticed needing more food."

Sennyi watches the other two bodies. They have moved on to assemble an exoskeleton out of detritus. Bar into joints, a welder wielded with deft speed. At least they are working together now. "They're hacking tools."

"Not so basic. I've always wanted to make Samutthewi a shadow planet. Our population is low, our cities few. A perfect condition for us to secede from the collective consciousness."

Two years in Twenty-Five slip by almost without Sennyi's notice. She receives messages from the ex-fiancé, which she deletes unread. The ones from her crèche-parents are urgent. Where is she? Why won't she see them? She sends light-hearted, mostly truthful answers about gainful employment.

"Why don't you talk to them properly?" Ipnoa asks Sennyi once. "They sound sick with worry."

She finishes off another brief note. "Says someone who's scrubbed off her cradle watermark. Even I didn't do that."

Ipnoa's cheeks color. It is a novel sight; Sennyi has never seen her lose temper, or even evidence that she might have a temper. "I have my reasons."

"So do I." Sennyi doesn't ask the question that burns in her mouth like venom at a stinger's tip. It is not ready; she is not ready. "Do you like your work here? Believe in Esithu's cause?"

"The work's what it is." Ipnoa untangles then obliterates ties between a Samutthewi factory and a weapons conglomerate based in Yodsana. She is effortless. "Their cause is specific and I don't think too many will agree with it, but it's necessary. Your memory should be your own, not something for the net to revise at collective whim."

"In that case," Sennyi says, "we are both hypocrites. And so is Esithu, unless they believe only the implanted deserve a private memory."

"There are limits to their influence. It's not as if the implants could be distributed to everyone in want of them. But, maybe, in time. It is possible."

Her parents' messages stop after Sennyi has expunged the final sliver of her existence. There will be no bereavement, she knows, only a nagging doubt and the outline of a solemn girl who grew to be the tallest in her class. In the last year her deterioration will be alarming, she's been told. A simultaneous malfunction of digestive and respiratory organs. The hive will fail too. But until then it is asymptomatic; until then she is full of health and courage.

Samutthewi is methodically rubbed out from awareness. Outside of Twenty-Five there's no such thing as truly offline, and to alter data is to alter memory. Her bees are adapted for this purpose, and under that aegis of anonymity Twenty-Five's deletion algorithms spread and contaminate with breathtaking speed.

When the moth ship lands she is asking Ipnoa, "Did you have family?"

The other woman begins to answer, then stops. Her expression pinches and Sennyi can hear the sloshing of water as the porpoise moves inside her, agitated. "Someone's here to see Esithu."

A moment later she understands why Ipnoa is shaking: a broadcast that tells them to head for the roof. At the top everyone has turned out, some having rushed up the stairs and panting into AI-serrated air.

Esithu is already there, serene and singular. The ship's hostellum unreels and parts, disgorging a pair of foreigners.

Sennyi shades her eyes. From their coloring—"Hegemony?"

Ipnoa draws close to her. "Yes." Her mouth is tight and her neck corded. Some of her tendons gleam more sculpture than skin.

Giving no regard to their subjects Esithu greets the dignitaries and leads them into the tower. There's a childlike quality to Ipnoa's and the others' distress, as though they are unsure their parent—and monarch, and perhaps deity—is so omnipotent after all.

She goes to see Esithu unsolicited. Two of the bodies, which she's irrationally come to think of as secondary, barely glance at her when she enters the hall of arches and owls. "This isn't a good time," one of them says.

"We aren't deleting Samutthewi quick enough."

"They are Hegemony. Different system. I would have dealt with them eventually, but they're moving faster than I predicted. Look up the Masaal-Yijun dispute."

A conflict over energy wells, one of many such that have kept the Costeya Hegemony at perpetual war with the Sovereignty of Suoqua. "None of that has anything to do with us." Samutthewi won free of the Hegemony three hundred years ago.

"Don't be a child. Every edge they can conceive of they will seize. Your hive would be useful to them, and they're always fascinated by the thought of feral implants. They think that if I put a tiger in a soldier it'll turn them into an unstoppable murderer, all aggression and no humanity."

"Are you," Sennyi asks, "speaking to them right now?"

"*You* know how to multitask. Talking and breathing simultaneously for one." Esithu jerks their head. "What is it about warring states? Always so convinced a single unconventional scientist will break a stalemate and decide their victory."

"You can't turn them down."

"Or what? They'll hardly rain fire and bioweapons on this planet. Even for them that would be heavy-handed—it's tricky to conjure up a pretext in which Samutthewi is a threat to anyone." An owl falls, an impact of plastic and metal on disquiet sand. The other body rises, picks up the bird, and gazes at it in thought.

"Where is your fourth body?"

Both sets of eyes turn to her, a lapse she thinks, a break in the illusion of multiplicity. "Difficult to impress, I see. Three are too mundane for you?"

"I've been scraping your access logs for two years. The bees do penetrate nearly anything." Sennyi nods, offering a data pulse, as though this is merely academic to her when in truth it means everything. "My evidence for your perusal, if you like."

"I profess an abiding disinterest."

Her hands tighten around the impulse to shake the cyberneticist by the shoulder or throttle them bare-handed, one neck at a time. "I insist on your interest. You need me for your project, and I may leave at will."

"This," Esithu snaps, "is a very bad time."

"You can multi-task. I want two answers. Is Ipnoa my sister? I can't tell from her DNA since crèche-siblings are genetically unrelated. Second, why did she know about the moth ship entire seconds before everyone else?"

"She is your sister." The cyberneticist shrugs. "Likely she expects you to respect her choice and not confront her with the fact, but who am I to arbitrate in family affairs. She's been an assistant to me on and off, and has channel privileges."

"There's no record of her working with you."

Esithu's laughter issues from two tracheas, two mouths. "I hope you aren't going to suggest that we are lovers or some such sordid thing. I've given you my answers, and frankly they're more than you deserve. Excuse yourself, please. The Hegemonic representatives are leaving, and I have evacuation contingencies to activate."

The next day a woman who wears her cobra outside, around her waist, is sent to Yodsana. Twins, who each have a stoat peering out between their vertebrae, are selected for Laithirat. The paper ships bearing them leave with two boxes of bees. Their passage will be obscured by a set of monk beads, strategically planted a generation previous.

Sennyi spends the day unwell, her chest hollowed out, her lungs alone for the first time in half a decade. The hive's absence makes her alien to herself. It takes a week to bud and birth, replenishing in twos and threes. When she is half-full, Sennyi forges the workers into a unit, and connects.

In the virtuality of Twenty-Five the monk's path is without end, winding high around the old towers, penetrating windows with assassin precision. It is alive, signposted with shrines and icons of old spirits. Monks in sedate progress move along the vertical riverbanks, clear-eyed and clean-shaven, black lacquer bowls in hand.

She's never seen them embodied before, only heard their voices.

A feather grazes the corner of her eye. She catches it—finds it soft, tactile. Dimensional. The scent of coconuts flavors the air. That too is new; before the virtuality has always been flattened, odorless.

The bees orbit her, humming apidae music. In her palms frangipanis have blossomed, yellow-fringed white, pale peach, orange. Funeral flowers, their roots moving slowly under her skin. She twists one off and tucks it behind her ear, inhaling its dessert smell.

Other tower residents pass through her, ghosts that do not mark their collision or her presence.

She climbs as a matter of course, in recognition of metaphor. By the time she has covered the height of two floors her calves begin to throb. After four sweat pours from her, honeyed salt in the crooks of her elbows, honeyed salt on petals and leaves.

When she mounts the last step, her feet are raw and red.

The chanting is loud here, skin-close, and Esithu could have been one of the monks in dress if in little else. "They were massacred, the seven-hundred seventy-seven, when Costeya conquered us," Esithu says, stepping away from the edge. "The atrocities an expansionist empire will commit to break a nation's spirit. No one remembers that now."

"Neither do you. It's data you inherited."

"Nothing wrong with inheriting data, as long as it is truthful. The trouble is when someone falsifies history and that history becomes truth in the collective conscious." Esithu flexes mud-stained fingers. "For the original Esithu to be standing here they would have to be five, six hundred. Not even a cyborg lasts that long."

"The successor would be someone who no longer exists. Someone who's removed every thread and trace of their identity."

"Like you," Esithu says amiably. "Do you aspire to the post?"

"I did what I did to spare people some tears. You, I wouldn't know."

"Back in the day when everyone was entirely offline it was the norm to die among loved ones." The cyberneticist kneels and opens their cupped hands. Water splashes on grass; a sapling springs, and in a moment they have shade over them, banyan leaves of mica and beaten gold.

Sennyi fingers the frangipani in her hair and discovers that it has become chiseled bone, sharp-edged, without smell. Those in her arms remain floral, continue to waft sweetness. "It strikes me as selfish."

"It is human."

The banyan grows roots with the strength of continents, trunks with the age of centuries. Sennyi cranes her neck after the tree until she can't anymore, until it has become the sky. Boughs in place of sunlight, heart-shapes in place of stars. "The bees unlock a total sensory load."

"You might have tried with a full hive—but here you are, and perceiving most of what you're supposed to. Fine, don't you think, a virtuality that engages all the senses and encompasses all the self?"

"Is uploading minds your ultimate goal?" The fantasy, once, of a certain kind of laypeople. "I didn't realize you would indulge in that."

"I wasn't always a scientist." Esithu chuckles as though the concept of ever having had a past amuses them. "People should have a choice to exist on their own terms, to forget if they want, to remember if they don't. To have a history which may not be rewritten. That was Esithu's wish."

Sennyi presses her nails deep into the grass. Soft-wet, the smell of mulch. "What happens if everyone connects to Twenty-Five through the hive? Through me."

"It is possible. It's inadvisable. Originally I intended for your hive to become Twenty-Five, but we haven't the time. For now we'll try again elsewhere."

"What happens," she repeats, "if everyone connects to Twenty-Five through me?"

Esithu motions at the sky. A slash of horizon opens. "You'll be providing the protocols for everyone else's implants. In essence you will *be* Twenty-Five. A mind separated from the frailty of your skin."

She laughs, surprising herself with its loudness. "I thought so. It's lovely being right."

"You've an abrupt imagination."

"Three years," she says, "are so very brief."

She has prepared a long time for death. It is jarring to think that there is an alternative now, one that has gestated in her two years and which tastes like delirium.

Once the idea has taken hold Esithu does not allow her time to second-guess. Her hive is monitored more closely. How many bees generated over a given period of time. Do the particulars of what she eats affect their temperament and lifespan. The candidates on Yodsana and Laithirat proved incompatible. Two are dead, four comatose, and Esithu does not try any more after that. The lethal genetic combination that Sennyi bears is both rare and exacting.

Esithu creates back-ups of Twenty-Five and sends them to Thotsakan. "A Hegemony armada came looking for us," they say. "They went to the wrong system. Tricky to find a planet that doesn't exist on charts anymore and which doesn't present coordinates on standard axes. Bless their AI pilots. Such stupid, straightforward things. I prefer to be careful, even so."

On the day of transition Ipnoa holds her tight, and clutches her hand as long as she may while Esithu runs Sennyi through diagnostics one final time. During the initial stage, Esithu has warned her, she will be a closed loop. All interactive channels will be shut to her. She won't be able to reach Ipnoa or anyone else.

The casket that would house her body is featureless, hostile. As she slips into it claustrophobia clots her gullet and for a precipice moment her reflexes howl *no*. Nutrient feeds latch onto her, and she lies there with the bees' thunder in her ears.

Then she goes in, and becomes Twenty-Five.

Detached from the net at large and walled into herself, she does not perceive time. She hears from no one and sees little that is not raw data. Even Esithu is spectral and mute to her, their face a paper mask, their torso a convex lens through which the substance of Twenty-Five may be examined. Sennyi exercises her will like a muscle newly discovered. The city gains flocks of ospreys and hawks nesting under each eave, in the crooks of amber bridges. A dilapidated theater finds its lost plays brought back onstage, to an applause of phantoms.

There are caches of history Esithu left behind, and from those she reconstructs the city as it once was. She fills the streets with vehicles like sleek sharks, and ignites the walls with commercial overlays pulsing directions to secret nooks where shoppers will find curios they've seen in dreams. She gives the mausoleum bone jars rattling in ancestral voices and a frangipani forest that buds in every color of that species, thick with butterflies the size of her head.

Her hunger for solitude ebbs; the need for company aches. A month might have passed, or more. Her physical body might have met its expiry date, or not. Network activity tells her no Costeya moth has yet descended to destroy them.

The next phase comes in an earthquake.

The edges of her city, her world, fall away. When she looks across tectonic cracks she sees low walls and low buildings.

She crosses to stand before the crèche in which she was raised.

"What do you think?"

"What's been happening?" she says to Esithu's reflection.

"Success. I've converted Thirteen's system to ours. You'll be able to contact your parents. If you wish to."

"I don't." There's no physicality here unless she permits it. But there is a simulation of pain for all that, of a heart clenched between terror and want. "Am I dead?"

"Functioning brain, functioning hive. The important parts. For what it's worth I offer my condolences."

"I've made my peace."

"You make peace too easily."

"Wrong," Sennyi says. "Is Ipnoa your fourth body?"

Esithu's image flickers. "How long have you suspected?"

"A while. Circumstantially. How evasive you were when I pressed about Ipnoa; how well she understands your cause, when everyone else is going along out of sheer sycophantry. How she is the only person in this city who's erased herself so completely. A price, I'm guessing, she—you—paid to become Esithu."

"Was it not instinctual then? A reflex, some buried recall."

"You were thorough. I had only my reason and deduction."

"I am not," Esithu says, "your sister. It is more appropriate for you to interface with Ipnoa in that capacity. The convergence protocols that merged me into Esithu have been thirteen years running. There's no going back, no turning it off."

Sennyi presses her palm to the glass. It is impermeable; it will not allow her to reach and touch. Esithu—Ipnoa—does not want it, and the long tooth of that knowledge pierces deep. "Why did you do this? Take up Esithu's goals."

"To keep you alive, what else." Esithu's expression has not changed. A stranger's. "Successfully, I should like to think."

It takes five years for Samutthewi to fall under the shadow of Sennyi's hive. City by city, ruin by ruin, one patch of interstitial ground after another. Her control over Twenty-Five grows finer-grained even as the limits of her space expand. Well past the death of her original flesh she lives; she imagines her gums shedding molars, her face caving in and peeling away to bare cranium.

In the virtuality the dragons' basin brims cool and clear, shot through with the ruby of scales, the ivory of antlers. By its shores a young woman sits, whistling a plaintive tune, knees tucked to her chest. Grass sways in a wind that brings the rich truth of honey. The weather is never imperfect. The hour is never too early or too late.

They sit side by side, sometimes, two young women who don't speak. One has created this; the other has become its god. In the face of such facts words can only be rare, are of limited use. One laughs into the other's hand, over a shared joke that requires no voicing. She sounds slightly equine. The edge of her pitch has been blunted by adulthood and time, and a cyberneticist's legacy. They lean against each other even so, cheek to cheek, shoulder to shoulder.

In the virtuality they can still be family.

The sky lightens and banyan leaves patter down, green-gold rain. In the distance their parents wade through shallows, slowly as though waking from a dream. Their names are called through cupped hands.

Fingers laced, the sisters turn away from the basin. Arm in arm they raise their heads, and stand to answer.

# THE OLD WOMAN WITH NO TEETH

### *Patricia Russo*

When The Old Woman With No Teeth decided to have children, she didn't go about it in the usual way. Well, really, what else could you expect from The Old Woman With No Teeth? If she ever did anything the usual way, even boiling a pot of water, the world might start spinning widdershins on its axis.

"Now you just stop that. I can read perfectly well, you impudent ragger. Set down what I told you, and don't believe all the stories you've heard about me."

There are many stories about The Old Woman With No Teeth, but people should not believe all of them. The most popular one is that she wore away her teeth by chewing a tunnel to the six-sided world. Nobody knows if this story is true. Many people have looked for the passageway she is supposed to have gnawed through reality, but none of the venturers have managed to pinpoint it.

"None of the ones who've come back, you mean. Silly bastards."

Another common story about The Old Woman With No Teeth is that she once drank the river on a bet, and then spewed it out again after she caught a cold, which is why all the fish in the river taste of phlegm, no matter how one prepares them—fried, baked, boiled, poached, in hundred-herb sauce—

"You ragged little ragger, stop wittering about fish recipes. Besides, the fish always tasted like that. I had nothing to do with it. People always blame me for everything."

People always blamed The Old Woman With No Teeth for everything, which was not fair. Most of the time she kept herself to herself, in her cavern in the mountains, where she made thunderstorms and sweaters and silver jewelry and high tides, magic whips that could seek out all the thieves in a crowd and give each one a good hiding, sandals for three-legged dogs, and sourbark lozenges that would cure a cough inside of a year. She lived in this simple way for ages and ever, not bothering anybody and wishing that people would stop bothering her, until one afternoon of soft rain and citron skies, the notion came into her head that she would like to have children.

Children, of course, are a comfort and support in one's old age, but The Old Woman With No Teeth had reached, in fact surpassed, old age eons ago. The only person in the known world older than The Old Woman With No Teeth was Aunt Far Away, and Aunt Far Away had retired to a rented room in a sketchy part of the city, where she sat in an armchair and drank tea all day.

"Stop it this instant. I don't want that person in my story."

The Old Woman With No Teeth had many stories. This one is strictly about children. She wanted some because she was lonely, and bored, and desired to pass on her vast and unique knowledge to others who would continue making sweaters and thunderstorms and sourbark lozenges after she had wriggled through the passage to the six-sided world for the last time.

"Nonsense. Don't you remember what I told you?"

You didn't really go into specifics on this part. And, you know, Aunt Far Away does come into the account.

"All she did was wave from her window. Big deal."

When The Old Woman With No Teeth made her decision to have children, she went to the city, for children, indeed any living beings other than blind snakes and naked rats, are difficult to come across in caverns. I don't understand why you just didn't get yourself a cat, or something.

"Cats can take care of themselves."

The Old Woman With No Teeth wanted something she could take care of. Naturally children need to be taken care of; in fact, one might say that that is the primary characteristic of children. Hence, when the concept of caretaking first came into the mind of The Old Woman With No Teeth, the image that accompanied it was that of younglings and kiddies, little bundles of energy and giggles, nightmares and quick-drying tears, hugs and kisses and lisped words of love.

"This fancy stuff is getting on my nerves. I just wanted a little company."

The Old Woman With No Teeth found that she longed for company in her mountain lair, and so came to the city. She had a look at a couple of orphanages and a school or two, and quickly came to the realization that children were more trouble than they were worth.

"That's better. But I wouldn't say I longed for anything."

The Old Woman With No Teeth did not long for company. She merely thought it would be nice to have some. Children would not suit her, but there were plenty of other people in the city who needed to be taken care of. The Old Woman With No Teeth walked about for a while. If folks recognized her, they had the sense to keep their mouths shut. She was not stopped by any municipal authorities, or bothered by autograph hunters. Her wanderings took her past the rundown building in the rundown part of the city where a previously mentioned individual had a room. This individual waved from her window. She waved in a particular direction. The Old Woman With No Teeth thought it over for a moment, and then decided to go that way.

"I was headed there anyway."

The Old Woman With No Teeth was headed toward Adams Park anyway, so she continued on her already chosen path. In the park, she saw a sign she had never noticed before, not in the park, nor anywhere else. The sign read: Be Alert for Elderly People.

Be Alert for Elderly People? she thought. What an odd sign. She imagined hordes of ravening white-haired half-deads shambling through the bushes and lurking behind the heaps of trash on the walking paths. She pictured gangs of knife-wielding seniors, slitting the throats of the middle-aged. She—

"I pictured nothing of the sort! I imagined nothing of the kind! If you keep on with this claptrap, I will go back to the Underpass Settlement and find another starveling scrivener, do you hear me?"

The Old Woman With No Teeth made no hasty assumptions or judgments. She took great care as she walked through the park, and applied her vast intelligence to come to an understanding of the meaning of the sign.

There were many elderly people in the park. Some of them were sitting on benches. Some of them were simply standing. Some of them seemed to know each other, as they were chatting. Some were clearly strangers to the rest, as they kept silent and bore expressions of discomfort, as when one finds oneself at a party at which one does not recognize a single other guest.

The Old Woman With No Teeth cautiously, but with kindness, asked several of the elderly people what they were doing in the park. She heard the same tale from each: a law had been passed at the end of the most recent legislative session. Elderly people unaccompanied by family members or attendants were now required to restrict themselves to certain areas of the city. Adams Park was in bounds, so those who lived in the vicinity took themselves there on pleasant days, as it was better than staying at home and staring at the walls.

The Old Woman With No Teeth thought this was a dreadful law. The elderly people in the park agreed, but explained that it had been passed in order to make the city more attractive to tourists. The Old Woman With No Teeth did not think this was a very good reason to do such a thing.

"What are you stopping for?"

Just to see if I got that bit right.

"Everything except for that part about kindness."

The Old Woman With No Teeth thought logically and dispassionately, and then made the elderly people in the park an offer. Would they come with her, she asked, and be her children?

The elderly ladies and gentlemen in the park were rather surprised by the proposal, and several of them refused outright, and others asked for time to think it over, but a good hundred or so accepted. They all recognized her, of course. And a life in a mountain cavern with The Old Woman With No Teeth, who could make sandals for three-legged dogs and extremely useful whips, was a more appealing proposition than exile in one's own native city.

"I should think so, too."

Thus it came about that The Old Woman With No Teeth led her flock of children out of the park, and if a municipal warder gave them a glance—and more than one did—then The Old Woman With No Teeth had a repertoire of glances much more intimidating than any in a security man or woman's arsenal. No one interfered with their progress.

They passed the rundown building when a certain previously mentioned individual lived. She was still at the window. She waved again, and smiled.

"Humpf."

The Old Woman With No Teeth called up a wind of cushions, a wind of pillows, and the hundred children she had gathered were wafted in comfort to their new home. They have settled in quite well, despite a few squabbles here and there, now and then. The Old Woman With No Teeth runs a tight ship. Or cavern.

"I hold no one against their will."

The Old Woman With No Teeth holds no one against his or her will. Her children are content with their new accommodations and their new lives. She has even began to teach some of them a few of the simpler workings for which she is so renowned. The Old Woman With No Teeth is content as well, for she has plenty of company, and more than enough people to take care of.

And so everybody will live happily ever after, until they die.

"Why did you put that last word in?"

To be truthful.

"All right. Leave it. Here's your payment. You can go now."

Much obliged. There's one more thing. I have a message from that previously mentioned individual.

"I don't want to hear that woman's name."

But would you care to know the message?

"Damned busybody. Always poking her nose in. How did she get this message to you?"

She whispered it in my dreams.

"Ah. She could never leave well enough alone, that one. Very well. What does she want to tell me? That she's going to climb up here and make my life a misery—again?"

No. She said to tell you, "Well done." And that the next time she sees you, if there is a next time, she will kiss your hand if you will allow it. She will kiss your lips, if you would allow that.

"She's got a nerve. But then, she always did. Go, you ragger, you tattered scribe. But take this warning with you. Do not go around telling people I have been kind. I will find out if you do. And I will make you very sorry for telling such a monstrous lie."

You have my word.

"Go. The children are hungry. I must get their dinner prepared."

If you should ever require my services again . . .

"Don't hold your breath."

Then I shall take my leave.

"Wait."

Yes?

"Thank you."

It has been a great pleasure.

"Right. I'll believe that when birds fly upside down and the shadows of the sourbark trees blaze red."

Have you not heard? Those things have already happened in the county to the north.

"Get out of here before I lose my temper."

Of course. But I hear the old children crying.

"I told you, they are hungry."

I can cook, as well as set down words in a noter. Old Woman With No Teeth, I would rather not go back to the city. I am close to being old myself. Do you not have room for one more child?

The Old Woman With No Teeth thought for a long time.

"Stop writing."

The Old Woman With No Teeth weighed the advantages and disadvantages. She didn't trust the ragged scribe she'd hired from the jostling liars in the Underpass Settlement.

"Stop writing this second. And give me that noter."

Very well.

"Now go."

"As you wish. But I would like to come back some day."

"People don't always get what they want. In fact, they usually don't."

"You did. That gives a person a certain degree of hope."

"Only children believe that hope is a good thing."

"Fair enough. I will think of you each time there is a thunderstorm, and every time I cough."

"Just for that, you're going to walk the whole way back to the city."

"I expected no less."

"Wait. It is too dark to start down the mountain now. You will leave in the morning."

"Whatever you say."

"The first thing in the morning."

"Absolutely."

"Don't get any ideas."

"Absolutely not."

"All right. Get inside. And if you call this kindness, I will plant you head-down in a bog of blistering mud."

"I'd never dream of saying such a thing."

"Move, before I change my mind."

"Wait."

"Yes?"

"Thank you."

"Move your legs, not your mouth. Hah. Got you now. Oh, a nod. Well, nod if you like, shake your head if you like. I am The Old Woman With No Teeth, and tomorrow I might just decide to send you all back where you came from. Did I hurt you when I grabbed your arm? Do not expect an apology. We cannot ever truly change what we are. You'll find that out, if you live long enough."

"I think though that sometimes, we can—Ouch!"

"Told you."

# THE HISTORY OF SOUL 2065

## *Barbara Krasnoff*

It all started at Rachel's first real seder.

Until then, the only Passover seders she had attended had been at her Grandma Isabeau's house, where she and several of her cousins—all of whom were older than she, and not very nice—sat at the end of the table while her grandfather droned through incomprehensible Hebrew verses. The children were then conducted to their own table in the living room, where they threw pieces of matzoh at each other until one of the grownups came in and yelled at them.

This year, however, Rachel was also going to the second-night seder that Aunt Susan—who lived with Uncle Mark, Rachel's mother's brother—held every year.

She was a little frightened. Since, at age seven, she was going to be youngest person there—her best friend Annie, who came with them so Rachel wouldn't be the only child, was four months older—Rachel was going to have to ask the ceremonial four questions.

"She's a little nervous," her mother told her Aunt Susan as they took off their coats. "I told her that she didn't have to say them if she doesn't want to."

"Of course she'll say them, Eileen," Aunt Susan said, and she grinned at Rachel as though they were sharing a secret. "I've heard her recite. She has the makings of a damned good actress. She'll do a fantastic job."

Despite her nervousness, Rachel grinned back. Rachel liked her aunt and uncle, especially because they never talked down to her.

It was hard to move around in the living room, which was largely taken up with a long, rather unsteady metal folding table decorated with a bright blue paper tablecloth and white paper plates and cups. There were real knives and forks, and wine glasses, and two white-and-blue ceramic candleholders with tall blue candles in them.

A bright purple paperback book sat at each place setting; Rachel picked one up and paged through it. It was a Hagaddah, the book that was used for the ceremonies before and after the meal. But unlike the one at her grandparents' house, which was only in Hebrew and had nothing of interest in it, this one had a lot of English in it, and had lots of pictures and photographs of foreign-looking people celebrating the holiday.

Because the living room was so crowded, everyone had to sidle around the table in order to get to the dining room, which, because it was actually used as a sort of library, was nearly empty of furniture, and so had space for people to stand and chat. Rachel took the Hagaddah and she and Annie made their way to a corner and started to page through the book. But they lost interest quickly, and Rachel started describing the adults in the room to Annie in a careful whisper.

"The man over there, the one with the beard? That's Abram, an old friend of Uncle Mark's. They were both in high school together."

"He's bossy," Annie observed. "And he interrupts all the time."

Rachel shrugged. "I don't like him," she said. "But Mom says it's not polite to say so."

She pointed surreptitiously at a stout, smiling young woman who was talking to Abram. "That's Yolanda, Aunt Susan's best friend. She brought a pineapple for dessert. She's studying to be a minister and used to live in Namibia."

Uncle Mark came into the kitchen with a quick stride, holding a thin brown bottle, and thrust it at Abram. "Here," he said irritably. "Kosher enough for you? Oh, hi, Eileen. Glad you brought Rachel and—Annie, is it?—with you this year." He kissed his sister on the cheek and ruffled Rachel's hair.

"Hi, Uncle Mark," said Rachel. "It's raining."

"Really hard," Annie added, unwilling to be left out of the conversation.

"Of course it is," said Uncle Mark. "God forbid we should have good weather on a holiday."

Abram, who appeared not to mind Uncle Mark's tone, was examining the bottle carefully. "I don't see anything problematic," he said. "The reason I had a problem with the glaze you used last year was the corn syrup. Things need to be kosher for Passover."

"This from a man who has milk in his coffee with his hamburger," said Uncle Mark, addressing the room at large. He grabbed the bottle back and returned to the kitchen.

"Time to start," Aunt Susan said loudly, and everyone wandered slowly into the living room and began to sit at the table.

"So I was looking for something to watch the other day," Abram said, as he started opening a bottle of wine, "and I stopped at a channel where a writer, a rabbi I think, was talking about a legend that there were originally only 600,000 souls in the universe. At some point after the creation, each soul broke into many pieces. Which means we are all actually made up of a piece of a soul, and when all the pieces of that soul find each other, part of the universe is healed and made whole."

Yolanda looked thoughtful. "How many pieces were in each soul, originally?"

Abram shrugged. "I missed that part of it," he said, handing her the bottle. "Some say that each soul was made up of two parts, and when a man and a woman find each other and marry, that is the entire soul. There is also some argument as to whether the souls truly blend during life or after death. But as with everything, it's all a matter of interpretation."

Yolanda handed the bottle to Aunt Susan, who poured some for herself and Uncle Mark, and then passed it to Rachel's mother. "Here," she said, reaching across the table to another bottle, "we bought some grape juice for the girls." She poured generous helpings into their wine cups.

"Suppose that we're all part of an original soul," Yolanda said, leaning across the table, "is it possible that by coming together tonight, we're helping to heal the universe? Would that include all of us?"

"I don't see why not," Susan said. "After all, in this presumably enlightened age, we can assume that whatever fractured soul is involved, all the pieces aren't necessarily Jewish. Here, it's going to be a while before we eat," and she broke a large flat matzoh into two pieces and handed them to the girls.

Abram's finger came up, a sure indication that he was going into lecture mode. "Actually," he said. "Most rabbis would probably argue that the legends only refer to Jewish souls—not that they are saying that other souls aren't valuable," with a nod toward Yolanda, "but they aren't part of the Jewish mythos."

"I'm not Jewish," said Annie, distressed. "Can't I be part?"

"Of course you can, Annie," said Yolanda, frowning at Abram. "There is enough room for everyone."

"How many?" asked Rachel, carefully biting her matzoh into a circular pattern.

"How many what?" Yolanda asked, puzzled.

"Rooms in heaven?" said Rachel, and the two girls giggled.

"Six hundred fifty two and a half," said Uncle Mark, sitting down. "The half is a bathroom. Which everyone has to line up for each morning."

The girls broke up and Susan blew a kiss at her husband.

"You know, maybe it's more like a union," Uncle Mark continued. "That would make us all official members of, say, Soul 2065."

"Does our union have a good health plan?" asked Yolanda.

Rachel's mom smiled. "Maybe we should have tee shirts. 'Member of Soul 2065.' Or hats."

"Can I have one?" asked Rachel, immediately perking up at the idea of a present. Then she suddenly remembered. "Even if I get the four questions wrong?"

"Of course," Aunt Susan said. "And you won't get them wrong. I promise. Even if you make a mistake, just pretend you did it on purpose, and everybody will believe you did it right. That's what actresses do."

"Really?" Rachel brightened.

"Really." Aunt Susan grinned. She stood and tapped her wineglass with her knife. "I hereby declare that this meeting of Soul 2065 is called to order." She sat down. "Now, let's start the seder."

\* \* \*

Ten years later.

Passover had come practically at the same time as Easter this year, which meant that Yolanda, who had pastoral duties in Minneapolis, wouldn't be present. To make up for the loss, Rachel's mom invited her friend Edward, who was getting a name for himself writing horror novels.

"You wrote *Bite Me, Darling?*" asked Annie, awestruck, as they took their places at the table. "That is just so incredible!" At age seventeen, both Rachel and Annie were heavily into vampires, and Edward's latest, in which a Jamaican lesbian vampire works the late-night shift at a NYC cable station, was right up their alley.

"That's me!" Edward beamed, delighted to have found a cheering section.

Rachel's mom leaned over and whispered, "I'm sure he has a copy of the book with him. If you want, I'll ask if he'll sign one for you."

Annie grinned and hugged Rachel's mom. "Oh, thank you so much!"

"Hey, I'm the famous author with the book and the autograph," Edward objected. "Don't I get hugged?"

"She's seventeen," said Aunt Susan, staring at him with mock sternness. "So you get bupkis."

Uncle Mark came back from the kitchen, having taken the turkey out of the oven. "That's what we're having with the turkey," he said. "Baked bupkis. With an olive sauce."

"Should we start?" asked Abram. "It's getting late."

"You're right." Aunt Susan tapped her fork against her wineglass to get everyone's attention. "This meeting of Soul 2065 is hereby called to order."

Edward leaned over to Rachel. "Okay, what's going on?" he whispered.

"It started ten years ago," Rachel whispered back. "We decided we were all part of a single soul, and so every year, everybody tells everyone else about the most significant thing that happened to them the past year, because it affects us all."

"Cool," said Edward. He looked intrigued.

Aunt Susan continued. "One of our members couldn't be here in body, but is here in spirit—and email," and she waved a tablet. "Okay, Mark, you start."

"I had a bit of a scare when I woke with chest pains a couple of months ago," said Uncle Mark. "I went to the emergency room, but it turned out to be a bad case of acid reflux. Which isn't good, but is a lot better than a heart attack."

"Damn right," said Rachel's mother. "You gave us all a hell of scare, you know that?"

"No comments allowed," Mark reminded his sister.

"I reconnected with my sister after five years," said Abram. "She called me out of the blue right after Yom Kippur. We talked for about a half hour, and I got her email address, so maybe we'll stay in touch."

"I tried out for a part in a Broadway show," Rachel said. "They wanted a bunch of teenagers who could sing and move, and I tried out for that. I was so nervous that I went into the bathroom and threw up and had to make my face up all over again, and then I got eliminated in the first round. I was really upset at first, but then I thought about how much fun it was just to be there. Which was important."

"You were wonderful," said Annie. "She showed me what she was going to sing before she went. She was great."

"Isn't she a bit young to be running around to auditions?" asked Abram, looking as if he disapproved of the whole idea.

"It's fine," said Aunt Susan. "She's very responsible. Annie, it's your turn now."

Annie brightened. "I've been looking into my family's history," she said enthusiastically, "and found out that they were really interesting people. Very politically involved, in a number of causes in Italy and then in America. I want to find out more."

Rachel's mom looked down at the table. "There's somebody I, well, sort of like," she said. "I haven't had the chance to ask him out yet. I need to do that." She bit her lip as though she was going to say something more, but had decided not to.

"Yolanda writes," Aunt Susan said, reading from the tablet, "I am slowly learning about how difficult and wonderful it is to be a minister, although I have to deal with red tape and bureaucratic idiocy, and some of these people really test my patience. But it's all worthwhile."

Aunt Susan put down the tablet and sighed. "Okay," she said. "My turn. As most of you know, I lost my job, which isn't something we need right now. But I'm getting some freelance gigs, and this gives me a chance to work on some of my knitting techniques."

"You knit?" asked Annie. "Hey, I just started learning."

"You know," Edward said, "this one soul thing doesn't sound bad. Can I join as well?"

"Don't know," Aunt Susan said, grinning. "Rachel, what do you think?"

Rachel propped her chin on her fist and looked at Edward thoughtfully. "You have to do something to qualify."

"Like what?" Edward said, amused.

"Rachel . . . " said her mother, a warning note in her voice.

Rachel ignored her mother and continued to study Edward carefully. "I know," she finally decided. "You have to write me and Annie into your next book."

"Cool!" said Annie.

"Done!" Edward said.

Twenty years later.

The new apartment was in a rather inconvenient part of Brooklyn, but they were all there—all except, of course, Abram.

Even though Mark insisted on cooking the meal, Susan had asked several of the guests to bring side dishes to make things a bit easier. "I don't want him to overexert himself," she told Rachel's mom.

"Of course," Eileen said, and then smiled as Rachel, who had appointed herself and Annie the unofficial serving staffers, brought in some of the silverware. "And just think," she added, "you have a famous actress shlepping for you."

"So I understand," said Yolanda, who was sitting at the table. "Congratulations."

Rachel wrinkled her nose at Susan. "It's so Off-Broadway that even a GPS could hardly find it," she said.

"What Rachel isn't telling you," Annie said, "is that live theatre is what everyone is into these days. They don't want fake 3D—they want real 3D."

"And they want twenty-year-olds," said Rachel. "I'm already too old for a lot of producers."

"Modesty isn't a virtue in an actress. I saw your notices," Edward said. "Good ones, from major sites."

"And she got interviewed," said Eileen proudly. "It's on at least sixteen different streams."

Rachel smiled tolerantly at her mother and leaned over to Susan. "It really doesn't mean anything. You have to be on at least thirty to be noticed."

"Give it time," said Annie. "I think you're starting to create a splash."

"Could it go viral?" asked Yolanda. "Is that still a used term?"

"Occasionally," said Edward. "And even if it isn't, the general idea is the same. It's what happened to my latest book. Especially after I did this," and he waved his hand at the top of his head— he had shaved off most of his hair except a small white round patch at top.

"It looks like a monk's tonsure, reversed," Yolanda said.

"Makes good video, though," Edward said. "Especially the 3D version. It looks like a weird sort of halo."

Susan tapped her glass. "This meeting of Soul 2065 is hereby called to order," she said. Everyone quieted.

"I . . . I was thinking how to handle . . ." She paused, and cleared her throat. "We greet Abram and ask him to remember us," she said. Mark looked down at the table. Nobody said anything for a minute.

Susan looked at Yolanda. "Things are going well with my new assignment," Yolanda said, "although I still think that Minneapolis is too cold for humans. As you know, there has been a new movement among some of the more radical members of my faith to disallow female ministers; sometimes it feels as if we're running backwards at a fast clip. But with any luck, this too shall pass."

"I'm thinking of moving to Los Angeles," said Edward. "My new series is doing well, but I can't afford to be a one-shot wonder. Out west, I can diversify more. And—well, I think it's better for me and for others." He glanced at Eileen, who stared back coldly. There was a moment of silence.

"With Rachel no longer around, and my job being only part time, I find myself sitting in my apartment watching too many movies," Eileen finally said in a careful tone. "I don't think that's healthy. I'm going to have to find something else to do. Somebody else to be with." She looked away.

"I'm having a great time doing live theater," said Rachel, quickly, "but it isn't enough, even with the feeds. The pressures are just too great—if we charge as much as we need to in order to keep it going, nobody comes, and if we charge less, we won't be able to keep it open. And only the big studios can afford to do a 3D feed. So I was actually also thinking of going out to the West Coast—maybe even next month."

"And I'm coming with her," said Annie. "Oops—sorry, did I interrupt?"

Rachel smiled, and touched Annie's cheek. "It's okay. I was done."

"Well, actually," Annie said cheerfully, "so was I. Except that if Edward is going west, I think we should wait a few months, so he can get settled and then help Rachel out a bit." She grinned at him.

Edward reached over and tugged a lock of her hair gently. "Honey, I'm too old to move quickly," he said. "You go when you want to, and as soon as I get there, I'll make sure Rachel gets in to see the right people. Promise."

Annie smiled. "Okay," she said.

"I'm tired of doctors," said Mark. "I go, and I go, and they give me tests, and feed me pills, and nothing changes. I'm just . . . I've had it with doctors."

"I want Mark to take better care of himself," said Susan. "That's all."

"Oh, for Christ's sake," said Mark. "Can't you give it a rest?"

He stood and limped back to the kitchen.

"He'll be fine in two minutes," Susan finally said. "He just gets angry at not being healthy. He doesn't think it's fair, because he stopped smoking and has been taking good care of himself, and now this."

Rachel reached over and took her hand. "He'll be fine, Aunt Susan," she said.

Susan smiled, and kissed her gently on the cheek. "Of course, he will," she said, and then looked around the table. "Well, as soon as Mark gets back, we'll start."

Thirty years later.
  There was no seder, because there was no longer a New York City.

Forty years later.
  Susan kept saying that she would find someplace else to live. After all, she wasn't all that badly off. She rather liked California, and Congress had finally come through with at least a small amount of compensation for former residents of NYC. She was sure she had enough to invest in a condo somewhere.

Rachel, who knew exactly how much income her aunt really had, and who also knew how much medication Susan needed to sleep at night, told her that she wasn't going anywhere. Rachel and Annie had more than enough room in their house, and anyway, Edward depended on Susan to help him with his latest series.

"Don't be ridiculous," Susan said, while she watched Rachel put the spinach kugel in a warmer. "You girls don't need to have an old lady tottering around in your way, and Edward doesn't need my help. He's just trying to make me feel useful. Which is very sweet of him, but there is no way in hell . . . "

"Oh, for the sweet love of Shiva," Annie cried, throwing down the towel she was using as a potholder. Annie had taken on quite a bit of weight over the last few years; she insisted on blaming genetics, since, she said, she and Rachel ate the same foods and Rachel was still absurdly svelte. "Do you have any idea how ridiculous you sound? Edward has a writer's block so big that you could run a truck into him and he wouldn't feel it. He is driving us completely insane. You are the only one who can save us."

"Besides," Rachel added, "he said that once you and he come up with a new series, he could sell it as a dramatic stream, and I could star in it. So please, don't do the oh-poor-me thing. Please, Aunt Susan."

Susan shrugged. "Well . . . "

"Edward is asking for admittance," the house said. It had an Italian accent this week, which Annie said was in honor of her great-grandmother.

"House, yes," said Annie loudly, and then turned back to Susan. "We're agreed?"

"So," Edward said, having just come through the security door, "have you told her that resistance is futile?"

Susan didn't laugh, but one side of her mouth quirked. "Edward, stop quoting old TV series that Rachel won't recognize," she said. "It's a symptom of senility."

"Hey," Rachel protested. "I'm an actress. I've studied the classics."

Edward kissed Susan loudly on the cheek and gave both Annie and Rachel a hug. "Hey, baby doll," he said to Rachel. "Were you able to get Yolanda to come?"

"She wanted to," Rachel said, "but there was another transportation lock-down yesterday, and her tickets were cancelled. So she'll just have to vid in."

The house was sparsely furnished—simplicity was the fashion these days—and much of the furniture was foldaway, so it took only a few minutes to put away the couch and replace it with a dining room table and chairs. Annie fiddled with the display while the others set the table.

"I wasn't able to find the Haggadah that we used to use," said Rachel, putting a sheet of epaper next to each place. "It was probably never digitized. But I did find a 'roll your own' Haggadah, and put together something as close as I could get it."

"I'm sure you did a great job," Edward said, settling himself into one of the chairs.

"Okay, we're all ready," said Annie. "Going to external visuals." The display, which she had set up at one end of the table, brightened to show Yolanda sitting in an old-fashioned armchair in what looked like a living room. She grinned.

"Hi, there," she said. "Sorry about missing the seder, but I've only got a third-tier priority in the airline's lists, and got bumped at the last minute."

"Of course," Susan said. "Don't even think about it."

"Should we begin?" asked Rachel. "Susan, you start."

Susan shook her head. "It's your house," she said. "You or Annie head the seder."

Rachel was going to protest but Edward put a hand on her arm. "Go ahead," he said.

Rachel took a breath. "This meeting of Soul 2065 is hereby called to order," she said, a little huskily. "We greet Abram, my mother Eileen and Uncle Mark, and ask them to remember us." She glanced over at Susan, but the woman was dry-eyed. "Yolanda?"

On the display, Yolanda nodded. "I'm doing well, although I still have moments where I become very sad at the loss of our friends, and of all those who died, even ten years later. As you know, I've been part of an organization that represents many of those who were forgotten in the compensation agreements. I'm also concerned at reports that the environmental damage may be worse than we were led to believe." She stopped, and shook her head. "Sorry. I'm so involved in this stuff that I can get boringly didactic. Forgive me."

Edward drew on the tablecloth with the tip of his finger. "On a more selfish level," he said, "I haven't been able to produce a lot that was worth anything for the last year or so. It could be just a temporary setback, but I'm a little nervous about it. I'm hoping that certain people will help," and here he paused, and directed a long look at Susan, "and that next year I'll be able to report several well-paid sales."

Annie sat back in her chair. "I don't have much to say about myself," she said. "I've been helping Yolanda with fundraising. And I want to add that we're doing well enough that certain members of this household should shut up about money and just remember how devastated we'd be if they left." She took a deep breath.

Rachel reached out and smoothed Annie's hair. "What Annie said. Especially the last."

Susan looked down for a moment, and then said, "Thank you. I'm not going to talk about how much I miss Mark, and your mother," looking at Rachel, "and everyone else who is gone now. I'm trying not to feel guilty that I happened to be visiting here when . . . when it happened. I'm trying not to feel that I should have been with Mark."

She paused. The rest waited. "I remember my mother talking about how hard it was to outlive all the people she grew up with, and now I know what she meant." Susan looked around. "But still, I'm luckier than many—I have you all now, and perhaps the rest of Soul 2065 to take care of me later. Who knows? Stranger things have happened."

Fifty years later.
　　Although the seder had to be cancelled when Susan had a sudden crisis, after three days she had recovered enough that Annie and Rachel decided to hold what Annie dubbed a Late Seder. They called Yolanda and Edward, and two evenings later they all sat together in the bedroom and nibbled on matzoh.

"We greet Abram, my mother Eileen and Uncle Mark, and ask them to remember us," said Rachel a bit too brightly; despite the help of the mechanized bed and the nursing aid who came once a day, she insisted on tending to Susan herself, and hadn't been sleeping well at night.

She looked at the others and said, "I called my agent and told him that I was taking a vacation. I just don't have the personal bandwidth to handle any jobs right now."

"I disagree. I think Rachel needs to go back to work," Annie said. "I'm perfectly capable of looking after things here, and the knitting shop practically looks after itself."

"No," said Rachel. "Just . . . no."

"If somebody is offering you a part," said Susan, "I don't see why . . . " She started to cough.

"It's not up for discussion," Rachel said. She put a hand behind Susan's back and supported her until the coughing fit subsided, and then settled her again.

"Actually, it is," said Edward, and put up a finger when Rachel started to speak. "It's my turn. I'm tired of the rat race. I've decided that I'm going to hang out here instead and visit one of the few people around who still remembers when I was young and good-looking."

He smiled gently at Susan, who smiled back. "Thank you," she mouthed.

Rachel stared at him. "Edward!" she said. "I can't ask you to . . . "

"It's okay," he said. "It's a purely selfish act. I'm expecting you to mention my name to your public at least twice a week until somebody re-options one of my series."

He grinned, and Rachel threw a pillow at him. "Ouch!" he protested.

Yolanda smiled slightly and simply said, "Susan's asleep."

They quietly stood and left the room.

Sixty years later.

Yolanda called Rachel and said that one of the members of her congregation—a former child survivor from New York—was giving a seder and would be delighted if she and Annie came. Rachel said she'd think about it. Annie glared at Rachel, then said that of course, they'd be happy to come.

"I can't do that to your friend," Rachel said impatiently. "Ever since I mentioned I attend an annual seder in that interview a couple of years ago, our systems are deluged every year by cards and gifts from fans. It's a pain in the ass. We have to farm out part of our feed to avoid bringing the whole thing crashing down."

"His wife works in communications," said Yolanda calmly. "We've got it covered. Reserve your flight."

Yolanda and her congregants lived a few miles outside of Minneapolis in a suburban community that was protected from airborne toxins by a large bubble of forced air and chemicals that surrounded a couple of miles of territory. By the time Rachel and

Annie had arrived, preparations were well under way. While the adults bustled around in the kitchen and dining room, the family's children put on a play for their guests, who laughed and applauded.

"Kids," came the cry, "Come set the table!" The children dashed away, leaving a sudden silence, broken only occasionally by the voices at the other end of the house.

"They're great kids," said Rachel. "But isn't it strange for them, growing up in such an artificial environment? I mean, they never get outside. Really outside."

"It's healthier for them," Yolanda said. "Better that than having to reach for an airsock every time the particle levels get too high. And we take them on trips in the cooler weather, when things are safer."

They sat quietly for a moment. Suddenly, without speaking, Yolanda reached out to Ann and Rachel, and took their hands. Rachel took Ann's other hand, completing the small circle.

"Go ahead," Yolanda said to Rachel.

"We greet Abram and Edward and . . . " Rachel started, and then pressed her lips together. "I can't," she whispered. They just sat, heads bowed, remembering, while an errant breeze stirred the window curtains.

S eventy years later.
   Rachel sat and stared at the ocean. These days, she liked to come to the shore as often as possible to watch the birds dip and soar, scuttle along the shore hunting for small shellfish and insects, or dig through the sand for leftover food from human visitors.

It was getting harder, though. Oh, Rachel could get herself to the boardwalk easily enough; her chair moved her around with only the twitch of a finger. But the discomfort—hell with that, the pain—was getting worse. At some point, even these days, medications could only do so much.

So a few days ago, she had filled out all the necessary forms and had all the required interviews. They then fitted the small ampoule in a special section of the chair.

Now, Rachel sat for a few more minutes, watching the birds and listening to their distant calls. After about half an hour, she lifted her head and said, as clearly and loudly as she could, "Annie."

The small holographic portrait appeared on the tray that extended from the left arm of her chair. Annie, gray-haired but still mischievous, blew a kiss and grinned at her.

"I'll just be a few more minutes," Rachel told her lover, dead these three years now. She tried to smile at the holo, failed, and shut it down.

It was a nice sunset. A few passersby walked along the boardwalk, and from a small building just behind her, there was a sudden spurt of sound: The raucous but pleasant noise of people singing badly but enthusiastically. Rachel had chosen this day and this spot purposefully—the small building was a shared religious center, and tonight was the second night of Passover.

She listened for a moment. Had it really been that long since . . . ? A sharp twinge bit at her stomach like a small arrow.

"Okay," Rachel said out loud. "Enough of this shit."

She reached down into the bag that hung from one arm of the chair and pulled out a glass of wine. She peeled off the top and then tapped the glass lightly with the ring that she still wore on her left ring finger. It rang faintly but satisfactorily.

"This meeting of Soul 2065 is hereby called to order," she told the seagulls. "I greet Abram, Yolanda, Edward, my mother Eileen, Uncle Mark and Aunt Susan, and my loving Annie, and ask them to remember me." She paused. "No. I am the last living member, and so I ask them not simply to remember me, but to allow me to join them."

Rachel placed her hand flat on her chair's arm, and carefully recited the series of numbers and letters she had memorized. She felt an almost imperceptible vibration against her palm. Then she smiled, and raised her face to the ocean. A breeze caressed her cheek.

"You were right, Aunt Susan," she said. "If you just pretend you got it right, nobody will notice the mistakes."

She sighed.

And part of the universe was made whole.

# PINIONS

## *The Authors*

**Yves Meynard** was born in 1964 in Québec City. Active in Québec SF circles since 1986, he served as literary editor for the magazine *Solaris* from 1994 to 2001. In addition to over forty short stories, he has published eighteen books, alone or in collaboration. Sixteen of them are in French, his native language, and two in English, the most recent being *Chrysanthe* (Tor Books, 2012). Yves holds a Ph.D. in computer science from the Université de Montréal and earns a living as a software developer.

"There's no set routine for me to get story ideas," he writes. "I usually note them down in a text file, which is more convenient than my old spiral-bound notebook but even less romantic. Since I put down the date and the source of the idea, I can see that I've been inspired by watching *Roman Holiday*, by visiting the Titanic exhibition, and very often by listening to a panel at Readercon. In all cases, the idea tends to go at right angles to the source material. I also note down some of my most vivid dreams, but those I mostly fear would be stillborn if I tried to shape them into stories. Still, many of the ideas have only a date attached, which presumably means they came to me while I was taking a shower or walking to work. 'Our Lady of the Thylacines' did not come from any particular source. I recall I found myself imagining a child mistaking a Tasmanian tiger for a real tiger. My Apollonian self wondered how this mistake could ever be made, given that thylacines are extinct. Then my Dionysiac self supplied an answer—a cruel, cruel answer—and the seed of the story was born. It lay dormant for four years until I finally got around to planting it."

**Ian McHugh**'s first success as a fiction writer was winning a short story contest at the 2004 Australian national SF convention. Since then, he has graduated from the Clarion West writers' workshop (in 2006) and sold stories to professional and semi-pro magazines, webzines and anthologies in Australia and internationally. His stories have won grand prize in the Writers of the Future contest and been shortlisted four times at Australia's Aurealis Awards, winning Best Fantasy Short Story in 2010. His first short story collection will be published by Ticonderoga Publications in 2014.

He lives in Canberra, Australia and is a member of the Canberra Speculative Fiction Guild.

Of "The Canal Barge Magician's Number Nine Daughter," he says, "This story started with the title, which elves slipped into my brain one night. Or something. One day it was just there, and there's no way a title like that could go storyless. If it had come to me to write its story, well, I had to oblige. My dad's a geek for transport history, so I borrowed a couple of his books on canals, and man, Industrial Revolution Britain really was totally steampunk. Only a little bit of that incredible infrastructure made it into the finished story (like the barge lift), but it gave me the the first flavour of the world and, from there, the rest just kind of fell together."

**Nicole Kornher-Stace** was born in Philadelphia in 1983, moved from the East Coast to the West Coast and back again by the time she was five, and currently lives in New Paltz, NY, with one husband, two ferrets, one Changeling, and many many books. She is the author of *Desideria*, *Demon Lovers and Other Difficulties*, and *The Winter Triptych*. Her newest novel, *Archivist Wasp*, is forthcoming from Big Mouth House, Small Beer Press's YA imprint, in Spring 2014. She can be found online at www. nicolekornherstace.com or wirewalking.livejournal.com.

She says that "On the Leitmotif of the Trickster Constellation in Northern Hemispheric Star Charts, Post-Apocalypse" was "an initial swipe at some of the worldbuilding and characters that went on to be featured in my latest novel, *Archivist Wasp*. Wasp and her ghost pal end their story-to-novel journey virtually unrecognizable, but the constellations remain."

**Richard Parks** has been writing and publishing fantasy and science fiction longer than he cares to remember . . . or probably can remember. His work has appeared in *Asimov's Science Fiction*, *Realms of Fantasy*, *Lady Churchill's Rosebud Wristlet*, and several "Year's Best" anthologies and has been nominated for both the World Fantasy Award and the Mythopoeic Award for Adult Literature. He blogs at "Den of Ego and Iniquity Annex #3," also known as www.richard-parks.com.

He writes, "The genesis of 'Beach Bum and the Drowned Girl' is the easy part to explain. Not too long ago I was in a writer's group. We met once a week, partly for social reasons but every now and then we'd try to get something done. The 'something' this time was an assignment to write a story around the theme of a modern myth. So what's a modern myth? Odds are it's an urban legend. Only urban legends have been done to death, so I decided to make up my own. Something plausible, but one I'd never actually heard of. And there, waiting, was The Drowned Girl. So where did she come from? I wish I knew. Or maybe I don't. It's probably better that way."

Born in England and raised in Toronto, Canada, **Gemma Files** has been a film critic, teacher, and screenwriter and is currently a wife and mother. She won the 1999 International Horror Guild Award for her story "The Emperor's Old Bones." Her fiction has been published in two collections: *Kissing Carrion* and *The Worm in Every Heart*, and five of her stories were adapted into episodes of *The Hunger*, an anthology TV show produced by Ridley and Tony Scott. She has also published two chapbooks of poetry. In 2010, her first novel—*A Book of Tongues*, Part One of the Hexslinger Series—was published, followed in 2011 by *A Rope of Thorns*, the second novel in the series. The third and final installment, *A Tree of Bones*, was published in May 2012, just in time for the Mayan Apocalypse. She is currently at work on a novel with no gay outlaws or Aztec gods in it whatsoever.

She says, "I think it will probably surprise no one at all to be told that my mind is a mulch-heap, dark, deep and foetid, fed by many different obsessional streams. In the case of 'Trap-Weed,' I had a few introductory paragraphs told from the point of view of a selkie, a mythical creature I have a genetic predisposition to find interesting yet have very seldom come across in fantasy (almost never male ones, in particular), and some vague notes about how later he might find himself trapped aboard a pirate ship with a shark-were (not a were-shark, because that would just be boring).

"This percolated at the back of my mind for maybe five years, not catching fire, until mid-2012, when I suddenly rediscovered my love for British actor Peter Cushing through revisiting his work with Hammer Horror: *The Curse of Frankenstein*, *The Horror of Dracula*, then down into a bunch of lesser-known titles, including a loose adaptation of *The Scarecrow of Romney Marsh* called *Night Creatures*, in which Cushing's character is a former pirate turned small-town Cornish parson with a sideline in smuggling. A few tweaks, some juggling and a little alchemy later, Captain Jerusalem Parry emerged, glancing haughtily around; he was soon joined by the little-seen former Captain Solomon Rusk, whose relationship with my Five-Family Coven stories provided a couple of neat plot twists. Fun fact: This story was so much fun to write that it now has both a prequel and a sequel. The first, 'Two Captains,' will appear in *Beneath Ceaseless Skies*; the second is massive, so I may have trouble finding a venue. But my Hammer Pirates trilogy is complete, and I'm happy."

**Yukimi Ogawa** lives in a small town in Tokyo, where she writes in English but never speaks the language. She still wonders why it works that way. Her fiction has appeared in *Expanded Horizons*, *Jabberwocky,* and *Strange Horizons*.

About "Icicle," she explains, "There is no English word which conveys the meaning of 'Yohkai' correctly, so I'm going to call them spirit-monsters, just here.

"Our folk tale about the spirit-monster snow-woman—who kills a man who loses his way traveling back home in a snowstorm—never scared me much. It's probably because I grew up in a relatively dry area, and somehow as a child I knew the snow-woman would never come down out of the snowy mountain to harm me. I very recently learned that this was really the case: spirit-monsters rarely move away from their usual habitat.

"Tsurara was half snow-woman, half human, and that was how she managed to find her way out of the mountain and see the world for herself; only I didn't know she was such a special girl while I was writing this story."

**A.C. Wise** was born and raised in Montreal and currently lives in the Philadelphia area. Her work can be found in publications such as *Clarkesworld, Apex, Lightspeed,* and *The Best Horror of the Year Volume 4,* among others. In addition to her writing, she co-edits *The Journal of Unlikely Entomology,* an online publication devoted to fiction and art about bugs. You can find the author online at www.acwise.net.

About "Lesser Creek: A Love Story, A Ghost Story," she writes, "With most stories, I have a very clear and specific genesis, something I can point to as an origin. This story is much more fluid. I had a vague idea of wanting to play with folk stories and urban legends and the concept of hungry ghosts and devils. I also wanted to play with the idea of gender roles—a female ghost vs. male devil. Beyond that, the story grew out of a particular creek that I know, and wanting to mess around with language. What else can I say?"

**Marie Brennan** is the author of the Onyx Court series of London-based historical faerie fantasies: *Midnight Never Come, In Ashes Lie, A Star Shall Fall,* and *With Fate Conspire,* and the urban fantasy *Lies and Prophecy.* Her most recent novel, the adventure fantasy *A Natural History of Dragons,* came out in February 2013 from Tor Books. She has published more than forty short stories in venues such as *On Spec* and *Beneath Ceaseless Skies.*

She describes the origins of "What Still Abides" this way: "True story: one day I'm driving along listening to a new CD, and suddenly I notice the singer (Heather Alexander) cheerfully belting out 'and we shall drink his blood!' Utterly confused, I restart the track, and realize what I'm listening to is an English folksong called 'John Barleycorn,' which is basically an extended metaphor about turning barley into beer (the 'blood' of the final line). Okay, it all makes sense.

"A few years later, I'm walking around London doing research for one of the Onyx Court books, and the song comes up again on my iPod. And out of nowhere, I think, 'what if it weren't a metaphor?'

"This story took a long time to get written because my subconscious latched onto the notion of doing it entirely in Anglish, aka English sans all non-Germanic-derived words. I owe a great debt of thanks to Sara Bryan, my Old English language consultant, who not only caught places where I'd slipped up, but made many useful suggestions regarding sentence structure and more."

**Alisa Alering** was born and raised in the Appalachian mountains of Pennsylvania and now lives in the somewhat flatter environs of southern Indiana. She is a 2011 graduate of Clarion West and a 2012 winner of the Writers of the Future contest. Her fiction is forthcoming from *Flash Fiction Online* and Aqueduct Press. She contributes the "Writer's Room" column to *Waylines* magazine. For more, visit http://www.alering.com, or follow her on Twitter @alering.

About "The Wanderer King," she writes, "I wrote this story in my final week at Clarion West. I was bruised and abused, wrung dry of every story idea I had ever had, and wondering how on earth I was going to come up with *another* idea—and write it—in just five more days. I was sleeping in 35-minute snatches during the day and writing through the night. I walked miles around Seattle's U district, caffienating heavily and listening to music on headphones, hoping that I'd figure things out.

"In my delirium, I got stuck on a couple of lines from the Iron and Wine song 'Woman King': *One day we may see / a woman king / sword in hand / swing at some evil.* Those lines gave me the feeling that became the story: mythical, majestic, foretold—yet somehow off-kilter. And, of course, a similar image does appear in the story. The song led me to a mood and a landscape, but the engine for bringing it all together was Chool's voice. Once she started talking, it became her story, and the rest fell into place."

**Tanith Lee** was born in 1947, in London, England. After non-education at a couple of schools, followed by actual good education at another, she received wonderful education at the Prendergast Grammar School until the age of seventeen. She then worked (inefficiently) at many jobs, including library assistant, shop assistant, waitress, and clerk, also taking a year off to attend art school at age twenty-five. In 1974 (curious reversal of her birthdate) DAW Books of America accepted three of her fantasy/ SF novels (published in 1975-6), and thereafter twenty-three of her books, so breaking her chains and allowing her to be the only thing she effectively could: a full-time writer.

Since then she has written seventy-seven novels, fourteen collections, and almost three hundred short stories, plus four radio plays (broadcast by the BBC) and two scripts for the British TV cult SF series *Blake's 7*. Her work, which has been translated into over seventeen languages, ranges through fantasy, horror, SF, gothic, YA, and children's books, and contemporary, historical, and detective novels. In 2009 she was awarded the prestigious title of Grand Master of Horror. She has also won major awards for several of her books/stories, including the August Derleth Award for *Death's Master*, the second book in the Flat Earth series.

Speaking of Flat Earth, Norilana Books has been reprinting the entire Flat Earth opus plus two new volumes in the series, as well as the *Birthgrave* series and the *Vis* trilogy—with one new novel that links both these stories together. Lee also has several contemporary (though very bizarre) novels either out, or about to be out, from Immanion Press, UK.

She lives near the southeast coast of England with her husband, writer-photographer-artist John Kaiine, and two tuxedo cats of many charms, whose main creative occupations involve eating, revamping the carpets, and meowperatics.

About "A Little of the Night" she writes, "The basic principle of this tale—the strength within the void—came from my husband, John Kaiine (my work is by now star-littered with such acknowledgements to this so-helpful gentleman.) The dark forest—like a cupboard stuffed with eerie challenges and horrors—is of course a planet-wide obsession in one form or another, and certainly a constant entity in my own mind-library."

**Cat Rambo** lives, writes, and teaches in the Pacific Northwest. Her 100+ story publications include *Asimov's*, Tor.com, and *Clarkesworld Magazine*. Her work with *Fantasy Magazine* earned her a spot on the 2011 WFC award ballot, while her first solo collection, *Eyes Like Sky and Coal and Moonlight*, was shortlisted for the Endeavour Award. Her most recent book is the SF collection *Near + Far*, from Hydra House Books.

Asked about "I Come from the Dark Universe," she says, "I wrote this story in 2005, for Gordon Van Gelder's week teaching my Clarion West class. Notable things about it: it was my first (but certainly not my last) space opera piece; it's my 9-11 piece, in response to something Gordon had said in class about drawing on emotion; and its setting, TwiceFar Station, is one I've used in several other stories, including 'Kallakak's Cousins' (*Asimov's*) and 'Amid the Words of War' (*Lightspeed*), and shares some characters and mercantile establishments with the other stories."

**Shira Lipkin** has managed to convince *Apex Magazine*, *Stone Telling*, *Chizine*, *Interfictions 2*, *Mythic Delirium*, and other otherwise-sensible magazines and anthologies to publish her work; two of her stories have been recognized as Million Writers Award Notable Stories, and she has won the Rhysling Award for best short poem. She credits glitter eyeliner, and tenacity. She lives in Boston with her family and the requisite cats, most of whom also write. She also fights crime with the Boston Area Rape Crisis Center, does six impossible things before breakfast, and would like a nap now.

About "Happy Hour at the Tooth and Claw" she has this tale to share: "When the Kickstarter for this anthology crossed the $10,000 mark, thereby obligating Mike Allen to start a new magazine, I took the opportunity to happily needle him on Twitter. I asked him when he'd be opening submissions for the new magazine, 'because I have a thing about a werewolf and a vampire who fall in love.' Rose Lemberg suggested that they fall in love with a demon and a witch, that it's a poly love story. I jumped in with angels and selkies. Obviously we were all joking.

"And then Mike replied, 'I'm curious if someone could write a story like that I'd actually buy.'

"Challenge accepted.

"I intended to write something completely different for *Clockwork Phoenix 4*, but this ridiculous unwieldy preposterous thing wouldn't get out of my way. So I wrote it, with everything but the selkie, but also with a scifi courtesan, several discredited scientific theories, an oracle, and karaoke. And Mike *did* buy it. And I hope you liked it."

**Corinne Duyvis** lives in Amsterdam, where she writes speculative YA novels, indulges in the occasional short story, and gets her geek on whenever possible. She also sleeps an inordinate amount.

Her debut YA fantasy novel *Otherbound* is forthcoming in 2014 from Amulet Books, an imprint of Abrams Books. For more about her and her work, find her at www.corinneduyvis.net and @corinneduyvis.

She writes that "Lilo Is" was "the first full story I wrote during my time at Clarion West in the summer of 2011. I arrived armed with a dozen story ideas. When the time came to start writing, I promptly ignored all of them. Something new had started to take form in my mind, something fragile and lovely and slightly freaky. I had an image of a child on a swing: laughter and too many spinning arms and wriggling fingers. 'Lilo Is' grew from there."

She adds, "I am, it should be noted, an arachnophobe."

At one time or another, **Kenneth Schneyer** has joined the Science Fiction and Fantasy Writers of America, the Academy of Legal Studies in Business, the Project Management Institute, the American Association of Variable Star Observers, the American Indoor Archery Association, the Society for Humanistic Judaism, the American Bar Association, the Cambridge Science Fiction Workshop, the Alpha Delta Phi Society, Phi Beta Kappa, Ergasterion, Codex Writers, the International Technology Education Association, the American Association of Individual Investors, the Planetary Society, The Heinlein Society, the Working Group on Law, Culture and the Humanities, the Democratic Party, and Mensa. He still belongs to some of these, but can't remember which ones. A graduate of the Clarion Writers Workshop, he has sold stories to *Analog, Strange Horizons, Beneath Ceaseless Skies, Abyss & Apex, Daily Science Fiction, Bull Spec, Escape Pod, GUD, The Drabblecast,* and elsewhere. His story "Lineage" appeared in *Clockwork Phoenix 3.* Born in Detroit, he now lives in Rhode Island with one singer, one dancer, one actor, and something with fangs that he sometimes glimpses out of the corner of his eye. You can find him on Facebook, on Twitter, and at ken-schneyer.livejournal.com.

About "Selected Program Notes from the Retrospective Exhibition of Theresa Rosenberg Latimer," he writes, "The voice came first. I love unreliable narrators, indirect voicing, and looking at paintings, so I knew I wanted to write a story in which the only voice was the curator of an art exhibition, and that the narrator would entirely misunderstand the story that was being told by the paintings. The first scene I wrote, which didn't appear in the final draft, was a painting of the 'war presidents' at sunset, looking up mournfully at the White House. Another such painting was a crowd scene at Auschwitz. Ultimately I needed to delete the more overtly political scenes in order to have a coherent character arc, because I although knew very early that this would be a ghost story, I didn't understand until late in the first (or possibly the second) draft that I was telling a love story too.

"The writing of the first draft was funded by my Kickstarter project, 'Are You the Agent or the Controller?' and I had help on later drafts from artists and museum workers who gave me pointers on what such program notes should look like. Particularly the suggestion to add discussion questions at the end of each section significantly increased my narrative efficiency."

**Camille Alexa** is an American and Canadian author whose stories have appeared in *Alfred Hitchcock's* and *Ellery McQueen's* mystery magazines, *Machine of Death,* and *Imaginarium 2012: The Best Canadian Speculative Writing.* Her book *Push of the Sky* received a starred review in *Publishers Weekly* and was an Endeavour Award finalist and an official reading selection of Powell's Books Portland SF Book Club. Her short fiction and poems have sold to nearly a hundred magazines and anthologies and been translated into eight languages, and she co-edited the superhero/supervillain superanthology *MASKED MOSAIC: Canadian Super Stories.* She currently resides in the Pacific Northwest, making frequent sojourns to such exotic distant lands as Denmark, Grenada, and Texas.

She says, "I wanted to tell 'Three Times' backward in a way that didn't *read* as if it were backward: the narrative flow revealing what has already happened, what is currently happening, and what might yet happen without any backward tug from past events, only the forward momentum of the unfolding tale. The result makes perfect sense to me; it's one of the most straightforward pieces I've ever written."

**Benjanun Sriduangkaew** spends her free time on words, amateur photography, and the pursuit of colorful, unusual makeup. She loves cities and wishes landlords would let her keep bees for pets. Her fiction has appeared in *GigaNotoSaurus, Beneath Ceaseless Skies, Clarkesworld*, and several anthologies.

About "The Bees Her Heart, the Hive Her Belly," she shared this: "The story let me write out some of my long-term obsessions: technology intertwined with flesh, ideas about what we might do with our bodies if given almost-unlimited options. But I also wanted to ground it in the fierce, complicated love between siblings because my sisters are some of the most important people in my life. Why bees? I wanted to be an apiarist growing up. Sometimes you write not so much what you know but what you'd like to have, like bees and porpoises. Probably wouldn't keep them in my chest, though."

**Patricia Russo**'s first collection of short stories, *Shiny Thing*, has been published by Papaveria Press. It even has its own website: www.shiny-thing.com. But not the collection's author, who asserts, "I don't have a website and never will."

Discussing "The Old Woman With No Teeth," she adds, "I don't drive, so if I'm ever in a car, it is as a passenger. I tend to look out the window and notice things, especially if the driver keeps exclaiming, 'Where are we?' or 'I don't know this street,' or 'I think I took a wrong turn.'

"So this one time, I was driving with a friend who has a bad sense of direction. (She also has two cockatoos, one of which has tried to kill me several times—but that is another story.) I was looking out the passenger window, and noticed a sign. The sign read: 'Watch out for elderly people.'

"Watch out for elderly people? I had never seen such a sign before. (Perhaps I lead a sheltered life.) Obviously the intent was to convey something along the lines of 'Be alert/be aware of elderly people crossing the street'—a warning to drivers that the neighborhood had many elderly residents and therefore the roads shouldn't be treated as racetracks. But WATCH OUT can have a different meaning, and that was the first meaning that popped into my head—watch out, the elderly people are dangerous. In 'The Old Woman With No Teeth,' the elderly people are not dangerous. They are merely unwanted. But that sign was the kernel from which the story grew."

**Barbara Krasnoff**'s short fiction has appeared in a variety of online and print magazines, including *Cosmos, Crossed Genres, Space and Time, Electric Velocipede, Doorways, Sybil's Garage, Behind the Wainscot, Escape Velocity, Weird Tales, Descant, Lady Churchill's Rosebud Wristlet*, and *Amazing Stories*. Her work can also be found in a number of anthologies, many with very long names, including *Menial: Skilled Labor in Science Fiction, Fat Girls in a Strange Land, Subversion: Science Fiction & Fantasy Tales of Challenging the Norm, Broken Time Blues: Fantastic Tales in the Roaring '20s, Clockwork Phoenix 2: More Tales of Beauty and Strangeness, Such A Pretty Face: Tales of Power & Abundance*, and *Memories and Visions: Women's Fantasy & Science Fiction*.

Barbara is also the author of a non-fiction book for young adults, *Robots: Reel to Real*, and is currently features and reviews editor for the tech publication *Computerworld*. She lives in Brooklyn, NY, with her partner Jim Freund and lots of toy penguins. Her website can be found at brooklynwriter.com.

Here's how she says "The History of Soul 2065" came to be written: "While doing some research into Jewish culture and mythology (using the wonderful reference book *Tree of Souls: The Mythology of Judaism* by Howard Schwartz), I came across the legend that, because there were just 600,000 souls present at Mount Sinai when the Torah was given, most people today contain the spark of a soul. (This is only a tiny part of the mythos, of course; there are probably whole volumes of commentary out there dealing with the creation of souls.)

"For many years now, Jim and I have held a seder on the second night of Passover. Soon after I read about the 600,000 souls, the idea for this story came to me as I was sitting around the table and listening to the conversation of friends and family members I've known for many years—and hope to know for many more."

**Mike Allen**'s biographical notes need not be nearly so lengthy for this volume as they were for *Clockwork Phoenixes* past, as this time around he shared all the raisons d'être for the book up front in his introduction.

He lives in Roanoke, VA, with his wife and frequent editing assistant Anita, their dog Loki, and felines Pandora and Persephone. By day he works as the arts columnist for the *Roanoke Times*.

His first novel, *The Black Fire Concerto,* a dark fantasy of music, magic, and the undead, is being published as a trade paperback and as an e-book by Haunted Stars Publishing. Furthering the experiment, three of his short works, *She Who Runs, Stolen Souls,* and *Sleepless, Burning Life,* are also available as e-books.

Other short stories have appeared in *Weird Tales* (during the Ann VanderMeer years), *Beneath Ceaseless Skies, Not One of Us, Cabinet des Fées, Interzone,* the podcast sites *Pseudopod, PodCastle,* and *StarShipSofa,* the anthologies *Cthulhu's Reign, Steam Powered: Lesbian Steampunk Stories,* and *Solaris Rising 2: The New Solaris Book of Science Fiction,* and other places. His horror tale "The Button Bin" was a finalist for the Nebula Award for Best Short Story. Dagan Books is bringing out his first collection of short fiction, *The Button Bin and Other Stories.*

He's also written five collections of poetry, one of which, *Strange Wisdoms of the Dead,* was a *Philadelphia Inquirer* Editor's Choice selection. His poems have turned up in *Asimov's Science Fiction, Strange Horizons, Goblin Fruit, The Best Horror of the Year One, Nebula Awards Showcase 2005, Nebula Awards Showcase 2008, Nebula Awards Showcase 2009, Stone Telling,* and over a hundred other publications.

He's employed his voice talents, such as they are, recording podcasts for *Clarkesworld Magazine, StarShipSofa* and *Stone Telling,* and with periodic help from his fellow scary movie fan Shalon Hurlbert, he records a mostly monthly column, "Tour of the Abattoir," for the horror podcast *Tales to Terrify.*

In addition to the *Clockwork Phoenix* series, he's edited and published a long running do-it-yourself poetry journal, *Mythic Delirium,* which is about to transform into a possibly long-running webzine that will showcase both fiction and poetry. You can find it and other Mythic Delirium Books productions at mythicdelirium.com.

You can find Mike, by the way, at descentintolight.com, and he also sometimes pops up on LiveJournal, Facebook and even on Twitter, as @mythicdelirium, of course.

# ACKNOWLEDGMENTS

So many people to thank: the creation of this book was a community effort.

Thanks, first, to Anita, who in addition to helping me select the stories, drafted the order they follow in the book and gave me the support and strength to see this through.

To Sally Brackett Robertson and Sabrina West, my assistant editors, who helped me cope with more than 1,400 story submissions. To Elizabeth Campbell, who tackled formatting the e-book edition, and who helped Anita and I copyedit, and to Francesca Forrest, who took on the daunting task of proofreading.

To Michael M. Jones, who gave me the idea to try Kickstarter in the first place. To Rose Lemberg, who was an indispensible sounding board and generator of ideas both before and during the Kickstarter campaign, to Liz Campbell again for the same, and to Ken Schneyer for his insights as a Kickstarter veteran. To the others who made suggestions and offered critiques, including but not limited to Mike Jones, Leah Bobet, Samantha Henderson, Michael DeLuca, Scott Andrews, Alexandra Seidel, Matt Kressel, and Nicole Kornher-Stace. To Eric Van, who threw every ounce of showmanship into promoting the campaign launch at Readercon 23.

To Anita again, and Liz, and to Cherie Priest and Paula Friedlander, who selflessly donated their talents to the Kickstarter reward prizes and kept the campaign energized. To Neil Gaiman, Jeff VanderMeer, John DeNardo, Charles Tan, Marshall Payne, John O'Neill, the Interstitial Arts Foundation, the members of the Secret Poetry Cabal (you know who you are), and the dozens and dozens of others who helped signal boost the campaign to all corners of the virtual world.

An extra special thank you to the following, who because of their generosity are from now on designated as supporters of Mythic Delirium Books: Saira Ali, Cora Anderson, Anonymous, Patricia M. Cryan, Steve Dempsey, Oz Drummond, Patrick Dugan, Matthew Farrer, C. R. Fowler, Mary J. Lewis, Paul T. Muse, Jr., Shyam Nunley, Finny Pendragon, Kenneth Schneyer, and Delia Sherman.

And last but not at all least, thanks to the more than 270 people who contributed to our Kickstarter campaign. The list below is not complete, but contains all the names of those who have granted their permission to have their pledge publicly acknowledged.

Our gratitude goes out to the following:

Danny Adams

Djibril al-Ayad

Saira Ali

Erik Amundsen

Cora Anderson

Julie Andrews

Scott H. Andrews

Anonymous

Anonymous Fan

Liz Argall

Daniel Ausema

Kate Baker

Dominic Balasuriya

Michele Bannister

Helena Bell

Martin Bernstein

Deborah Biancotti

Chris Bissette

Ellen Blackburn

David Blakeley

David Burkett

Deborah J. Brannon

Rosemarie Brizak

Samantha Brock

Dean Browell

Dana Bubulj

Dan Campbell

Lisa Cantara

Leilani Cantu

Loki Carbis

Niki Carlson

John Chu

Neal Chuang
Blase Ciabaton
Alicia Cole
Judith Collard
Cathy Cordes
Linden Couteret
Patricia M. Cryan
Carrie Cuinn
Matthew J. Davis
Christian Decomain
Rhel ná DecVandé
Pablo Defendini
Vincent Degrez
Michael J. DeLuca
Arinn Dembo
Steve Dempsey
John Devenny
Evans Donnell
Oz Drummond
Patrick Dugan
David Eggerschwiler
Caroline Elliott
Amal El-Mohtar
ElectricStory.com
Patricia Engel
Elizabeth Fallon
Matthew Farrer
Fabio Fernandes
Gemma Files & Stephen J. Barringer
Sam Fleming (ravenbait)
Deanne Fountaine
C. R. Fowler
Stephanie Franklin
Deby and Daron Fredericks

Fran Friel
Joanna Galbraith
Peter and Hilary Galbraith
Gwynne Garfinkle
Zvi Gilbert
Jenny Graver
Arthur C. Green
Cathy Green
Sandra L. Green
William Groenendijk
Stephanie Gunn
Alex Haist
Amanda Halperin
Jessica Hammer
Dr. MJ Hardman
Andrew Hatchell
Paul Hattrem
Michael Haynes
Kate Heartfield
Kevin Hemingway
Samantha Henderson
Woodrow "asim" Hill
Erin Hoffman
Jeremy Holmes
Rich Horton
Andrew Hovanec
Claire Humphrey
Shawna Jacques
Chandra Jenkins
Keffy R. M. Kehrli
Brian Kitchell
Steven Klotz
Brent Knowles
Yoshio Kobayashi
Jay Kominek

Jeanne Kramer-Smyth

Matthew Kressel

Stefan Krzywicki

kytyn

Jamie Lackey

Ai Lake

Eric Landes

Lauowolf

Corky LaVallee

Lucas K. Law

Richard Leaver

Michael Lee

Sandi Leibowitz

Rose Lemberg

Kirsty Lewis

Mary J. Lewis

Shira Lipkin

Geoffrey Long

Joanna Lowenstein

C.S. MacCath

Alex Dally MacFarlane

Kate MacLeod

Stefanie R. Maclin

Kris Marchu

Duffi McDermott

Mo McFarlane

Ian McHugh

Kate McKinley & Melissa Kennedy

Corey McKinnon

Ieva Melgalve

Frederick Melhuish III

Merry Blacksmith Press

Andrew Mike

Adam Mills

mobile247

Virginia M Mohlere

Ian Mond

Nayad Monroe

Brendan N. Moody

Sunny Moraine

Lisa Nohealani Morton

Brooks Moses

Andreas Mügge

Simo Muinonen

Cathy (Nolly) Mullican

Deirdre M. Murphy

Paul T. Muse, Jr.

Next Friday

Larry Nolen

Shyam Nunley

Michael O'Brien

John Osmond

Nancy E. O'Toole

An Owomoyela

Sarah Page

Dominik Parisien

Chuck.Parker

Caitlyn Paxson

Hélène Pedot

Finny Pendragon

Lisa Poh

Rrain Prior

Professor Raven

TJ Radcliffe

Cat Rambo

Suzanne Reynolds-Alpert

Julia Rios

Sally Brackett Robertson

Marsheila (Marcy) Rockwell

Helen Rodriguez
Eric Rosenfield
Gessika Rovario-Cole
Anastasia Rudman
A. Merc Rustad
Sofia Samatar
Shirl Sazynski
Ken Schneyer
Scorcha
Alexandra Seidel
Diane Severson
Wendy A. Shaffer
Delia Sherman
Alex Shvartsman
Silvernis
J. Simmons
Jason Sizemore
Michael Skolnik
Sabrina Sloyan
Cislyn Smith
Janice Smith
Tara Smith
Bennett Snyder
Mary Spila
Jeff Spock
Jasmine Stairs
Ferrett Steinmetz
John Stevenson @jr0cket
Tad Stewart
(milliondollarloser)
Rabbit Stoddard
Bryce Stoddart
Jason Sturner
Robert E. Stutts
summervillain

Julia Svaganovic
Rachel Swirsky
Tamathy
Cecilia Tan
Dave Thompson
Kendra Tornheim
Tori Truslow
Twelfth
TwistedSciFi.com
UncommonGrace
Dave Versace
Vnend
Zoe Wadsworth
Emily Wagner
Ann Walker (just_ann_now)
Rachael Walker
LaShawn M. Wanak
Brittany Warman
Jen Warren
James Weber
Anke Wehner
Sabrina West
Lindsey Wicks
Betty Widerski
C. Glen Williams
Cai Wingfield
Beth Wodzinski
Missy Woford
Sandra Woodbury
Amanda Wright
Micah Ian Wright
Wyrdwright, Inc.
Alan Yee
Kaila Yee

# Copyright Notices

www.ingramcontent.com/pod-product-compliance
Lightning Source LLC
Chambersburg PA
CBHW020612260626
47157CB00003B/984